I0666193

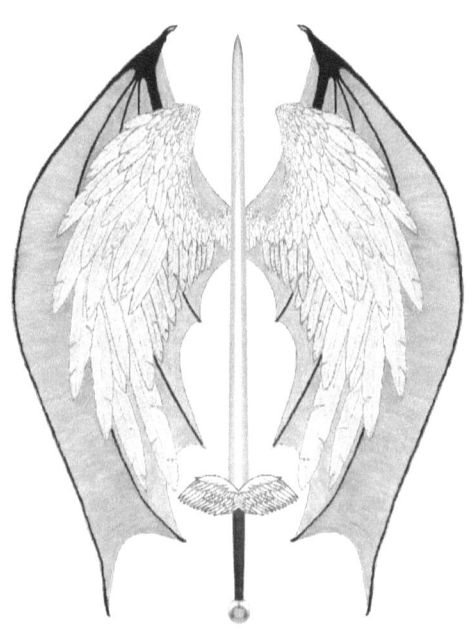

Destiny's Wings

(A Land of Destiny Novel)

By D.S. Schmeckpeper

Printed in the United States of America

First Printing: September 2014

Published by Seraph Wing Publishing

ISBN-13 978-0-9907111-0-0 (ebook)
ISBN-13 978-0-9907111-1-7 (print)

Acknowledgements:

A huge thank you to my wonderful husband, Steve. Your love, support and encouragement means so much to me. Most of this story would not have been possible without your ideas. You really stepped up and did anything and everything I could have possibly needed to allow me to write. I am honored to be able to list you as my co-author. Another special thank you for the world map and other art you contributed.

I'd like to thank my editor, Ella Medler, for your extreme patience with me. You'll never know how much I appreciate all of your advice and encouragement. I have so much respect for you, and am so glad to call you my friend.

A special thanks to the very talented Megan J. Parker of EmCat Designs for the wonderful job you did on the cover.

Katie Harder-Schauer, you are the best "Pretend PA" ever. Your unfailing support has meant the world to me. You've been with me every step of the way, and I know it is safe to say I never would have made it through this process without you there.

Colleen Treep, you're the most awesome boss in the world! Thanks for listening to me go on and on about anything and everything to do with this book. I appreciate you more than you'll ever know. Thank you for being so understanding, and for helping me with my last minute problems.

Kristie Haigwood and Nathan Squiers, the two of you encouraged me to start writing, and I am forever grateful. Without you, I would have never taken that first step.

Thank you so much for taking so much time to answer my many questions during this process.

To my Beta Readers – Laura Ice, Katie Harder-Schauer, Jeannie Holbrook, Victoria Clemente, Colleen Treep, Laurie Bianchi, Sally A. Peckham, Jacinta Brown, Heather Heslip Alexander, Jessica Tarrats, Lacia Carabas, Don Martin, Sam Pearce, Sheila Ryals, Toni Michelle and Kelly Clevinger – thank you for everything you have done. Each of you has touched this book in some way, and helped to make it better.

Last, but not least, a huge thanks to you, the reader. Without readers, there would be no reason for writers to write. I hope you enjoy Destiny's Wings.

This book is dedicated to Charlie and Robbie.
Always follow your dreams.
I love you both.

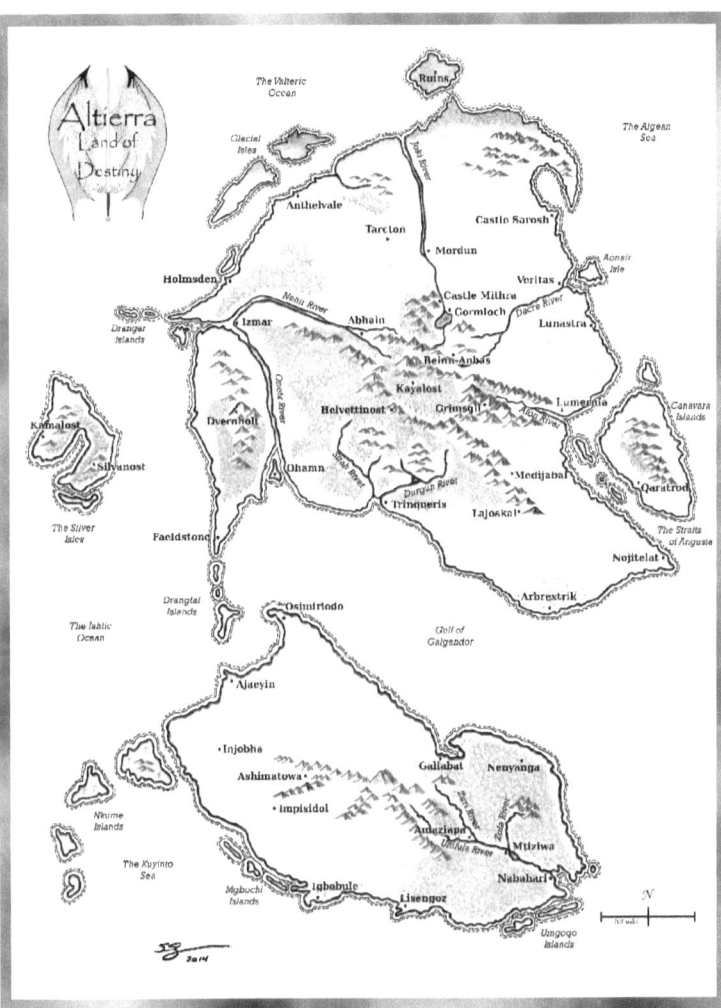

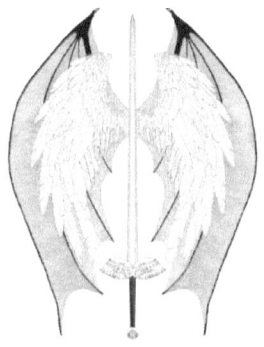

Chapter One
A Dragon's Request

"You have been summoned," said the disembodied voice. Celeste looked up in surprise.

"I? Where?" she questioned.

"To Axistra's chambers," came the reply.

Celeste sighed. This couldn't be good. She had been hidden away in self-imposed isolation for many years, and the fact that the great silver dragon had made the effort to locate her was not a good sign at all. Few were ever summoned to Axistra's castle in the clouds, and when they were, it was always because she'd had some sort of vision of great importance. Just for a moment, she stopped to consider the implications. Then she transformed into a small red-tailed hawk, and took to the skies.

She didn't need to transform to fly to Axistra's home. In fact, it would have been faster if she hadn't. However, it was the middle of the day, and she was too near the human lands. There were no cities in the immediate area of her forest, but she never knew when there would be travelers passing through. Humans who caught a glimpse of her tended to believe she was some sort of sign or omen, and all she needed was for one of them to see her massive, ivory wings as she took off above the tree line. Then, the rumors would really start to flow. If anyone ever found out she was there, the pilgrims would come to find "The Sacred Herald" and would seek her council for every little thing. The curious onlookers would come to ogle her and stare; her solitude would be destroyed. She couldn't honestly say which group would be worse. She had been careful to make sure she could not be located by magic, but the effort involved in hiding herself from people searching inside her forest seemed exhausting. Too exhausting for her to risk it, especially because she had been so tired lately. As a result, she had been spending more and more time communing with nature as one of its servants.

Strictly speaking, she wasn't a full herald. Her father was a seraph, herald to a dead and almost forgotten god, and the wings were from him. Her mother was an elf, a nurturer of the balance. As a product of their love, she was caught between both worlds, unable to blend into either. She had chosen to walk the path of the druid like her mother, as it was what she was raised knowing. However, she had abandoned her mother's druidic village in favor of solitude centuries ago, choosing to be alone with nature.

Things have been so quiet, she thought to herself. *What could Axistra possibly want from me?*

Celeste glided on the air thermals for many hours. Finally, a tingle ran through her, which told her that she had almost reached the dragon's realm. She began to climb higher and higher into the sky. The air began to feel thin, but Celeste knew the castle wasn't much farther. Over six hundred years had passed since she had last seen it, but she still remembered everything about Axistra's castle as if it were yesterday. Soon, she saw the telltale clouds that were ever-present, and flew faster, enjoying the feel of their soft caress whispering against her wings. Once she had broken through the other side, in front of the castle, she changed back into her elven form as she landed. She took a deep breath and closed her luminescent green eyes as she ran her fingers through her raven black hair and tried to calm her nerves. Axistra's castle was a beautiful, shimmering, silvery blue color that almost looked reflective, like ice. The spires rising from the turrets reached for the heavens, and were almost lost to even her keen elven sight. The castle foreground was full of massive oak and sequoia trees, which were always in full glory, like it was perpetual spring. Wildflowers in every imaginable color filled the space between the trees. The castle was beautiful, but Celeste felt very small when she looked upon it. She continued to stand outside, trying to work up the nerve to approach. After several minutes, the massive door opened soundlessly and someone Celeste never expected approached her.

The newcomer was obviously a kedistam, a cat person. She resembled a leopard – in that she had soft tan-colored fur with black spots and a long tail that swayed when she moved – but she walked upright and was dressed in a red form-fitting tunic. Her yellow eyes glowed with intelligence. She extended her hand to Celeste, and gave her a toothy grin, exposing her sharp fangs.

"Welcome to the party. Celeste, is it? I expected someone a little more... feathery. The name's Therinsalla, but my friends call me Theri," said the kedistam in a throaty voice.

Celeste ignored the offered hand. "Party? I'm not here for any kind of party, Therinsalla. I'm here to see Axistra, and nothing more."

Theri's grin drooped a little and she lowered her hand.

"How did you get up here anyway? Last time I checked, cats couldn't fly," taunted Celeste. She watched the grin drop off the kedistam's face entirely; her kind hated to be called cats. Celeste had never spoken to one long enough to inquire why. Celeste paused for a moment, wondering why she felt the need to be so hostile toward this stranger, but shook it off. It didn't matter; she just wanted to get back to her forest and be left alone. Without waiting for an answer, she began walking toward the door Theri had left open.

"I was sent by my village shaman. He said I would be needed, so I came," Theri answered while jogging after Celeste.

"That explains why. Well, sort of. It still doesn't explain how."

Theri smirked. "Pterodactyl. He's around here somewhere."

Celeste stopped, and looked at her more curiously. "Seriously? I've never even seen one."

"Yes. In fact I think he is Axistra's great-grandson or something like that. You'd have to ask her. There are many of them in the far south. Can I see your wings? I've heard all about you, and I've been dying to see them."

"From whom have you been hearing all about me?"

Theri looked embarrassed and stared at her feet. "Uh, well, okay. Maybe not all about you, but Axistra told me that we were waiting for you, and she told me you are a half-seraph."

Celeste sighed. "Fine." She summoned her wings and stretched them, spreading their twelve foot wingspan out fully, allowing the ivory feather tips to skim the floor. "Now I need to find Axistra."

Just as Celeste remembered, all the doors inside Axistra's castle were unlocked. Theri moved ahead, down several hallways. They passed the great room and kitchens, which seemed almost eerie in their emptiness. She told Celeste that she would be staying in the room across the hall from her. Theri threw open a door and gestured for her to go inside. The kedistam played the part of the gracious hostess well, as she pretended that this was her castle that she presented. Celeste frowned. "I'm not staying here. I am here because I was summoned. After I determine why, I will be leaving. That's it. I see no reason to linger here."

Theri shrugged. "Whatever you say, but that voice told me you would stay in this room."

Celeste continued to walk deeper into the castle, and approached Axistra's audience chamber. That door wouldn't budge. Celeste pushed on it in surprise, but without luck. The disembodied voice rang out from very near, sounding the same as in Celeste's forest. "Axistra requests that you make yourself at home. She will see you soon, but is detained at present."

Celeste growled in frustration, then turned on her heel and stomped toward the room Theri had indicated. She sat down hard on the fluffy bed, crossed her arms in frustration and stared out the window at the trees and flowers. She sighed as she heard Theri enter the room behind her.

"You know, you're nothing like I expected," Theri began. "Maybe I just don't understand, but from what I have heard, you spend your days alone in a forest. You have no friends or family that you speak to anymore, and you have nowhere you have to be. Why are you acting like a child? Yes, I'm sure it was inconvenient to be called all this way, but you're here now. You might as well make the best of it."

"You're right, you don't understand," Celeste retorted. "I'm tired. I've lived for more than eight hundred years, and, as of late, I have felt every one of them weighing heavily on me.

I've seen the gods themselves die. I've seen my father die because he blindly followed his master's ill-fated cause, all in the name of 'good'. I watched as my mother and her people turned a blind eye to the evils of this world in the name of 'balance' and 'neutrality'. I've been stared at, poked at, and talked about for more years than you, in your short lifespan, can fathom. I prefer the silence. I prefer the solitude. I don't like it here, and I just want to go home. I can't even begin to guess why I was even called. I've been so far removed from everyone and everything, that I'm practically not even part of this world anymore. So you will just have to forgive that I'm such a disappointment to you."

"You're eight hundred years old?" Theri exclaimed. "I had no idea."

"*That* was the part of my speech you focused on?" Celeste sighed. "Yes, give or take a few decades. I think I am closer to eight hundred fifty, but who's counting after that long anyway? Certainly not me. Look, I want to rest for a while. In silence. Can you just leave me alone?"

"Not a chance. You're the only one here to talk to, besides the voices that speak or bring me things on occasion. They are really creepy. How long has this place been haunted?"

"It's not. Axistra uses her magic to create invisible servants. Much quieter, and less bother, than having real servants about. She wouldn't tolerate a ghost here," said Celeste.

"Well, that's a relief. I thought there were spirits following me around and spying on me. So tell me more about what you were saying. You've seen gods die? Really? I've never seen a god at all. Tell me about it. I can't take the silence anymore. Please?"

Celeste sighed, resigned to her fate. "Very well, if only to pass the time until Axistra will see me. What exactly do you want to hear? I don't know what you already know."

"Anything, everything, I want to hear anything you want to tell me," said Theri.

Celeste leaned back against the pillows and stared at the ceiling. Her eyes became unfocused as she thought back. "Long, long ago, there were the Three. They created all life here as we know it. According to the druids, the god of good, Aurinko, created the humans and the kedistam. The goddess of balance, Kamara, created the dwarves and the elves. The evil god, Kuunkierto, created the orcs and the tumasi. Together, the Three created the dragons and the demigods. Then, according to many, they left. Some, like the druids, believe they simply became part of their creation, themselves. Aurinko became the sun. Kamara merged with the very earth beneath our feet. Kuunkierto became the moon, which used to shine a brilliant white, like a huge star. Millennia passed, and eventually, Kuunkierto decided his siblings had far greater power than he did. Jealous, he returned to Altierra with the intent to take control of the entire world. Thus began the Great Deity War. Many of the good and neutral demigods rose up to fight against him and his evil demigod lackeys. It was a bloodbath, with many deaths of both sides. My father, who was a herald of Melek, the god of protection, was one of many that died. Ultimately, they triumphed, and Kuunkierto was entombed in the northern wastes. That's why the moon is that dark grayish red hue; it's dead. I remember the night the moon changed color, dimming from the sparkling brilliance it once was to the ghastly shade it is today. I was a mere forty years old then – a child among the elves. I remained with them in the druidic village of Kayalost until the year I turned two hundred."

"What happened to the remaining gods? Also, what happened to Aurinko and Kamara? If Kuunkierto could come back, why couldn't they? I've never heard this story. My people never speak of any old gods... I wonder why."

"I don't have any idea why the other two didn't return to fight Kuunkierto. Remember, a lot of the old legends are just that: legend. I know the Three are real because I remember the day Kuunkierto returned, but I don't have any real, solid facts about what happened to his siblings. As for the demigods, they left too, after the Deity War. They all agreed to a pact to no longer interfere in the lives of mortals, and withdrew from Altierra. I have no idea where they went. I have no idea if they are still here watching us all make fools of ourselves, or if they left this plane of existence to try again to make another world somewhere else. I know the heralds are still here and show up on occasion. As for the fact that you haven't heard the stories, I've found that other races tend to have short memories. It stems from having such short lifespans, and from societies who do not care about what happened eight generations back. My people, after all, are burdened with eternity, while yours get but a few short decades."

"That must be really hard, but it can't be all bad – living forever?"

"It is neither hard nor easy. It's simply the way things are."

"Why did you leave the elves?" Theri asked.

Celeste bit her lip. "That is a long and uninteresting story, I assure you. Suffice it to say that I prefer the solitude. Now tell me, Therinsalla, do you have any idea why we are here?"

Theri shrugged. "Nope. Like I said earlier, my village shaman believed I would be needed, so I came. Axistra seemed to be expecting me. We've spoken a little, but she seemed to be waiting for you. I will do whatever is needed of me; I promised my shaman."

"Tell me about this shaman and your people. I've never made it that far south."

Celeste and Theri continued to talk, which filled up several hours. The sun began to set beyond the tree line. As Theri told her stories about growing up in the south, among the kedistam, and their troubles with their canid neighbors, the tumasi, Celeste began to consider all she had missed during her isolation. The pair wandered to the dining room to find food.

"Somehow, the kitchen, or I suppose these 'invisible servants,' always knows when I am hungry, and what it is I want," said Theri.

"That's part of the magic here. The dragons have unimaginable control over their magic."

"Dragons? I only just found out about Axistra when the shaman sent me. How many are there?"

"Six in total. They were the original heralds of the Three. Like the angels, demons and other spirits are to the demigods, but much more powerful. They are almost demigods themselves. They are loners and are spread all over Altierra. One of the others, Khellendriox, lives near the dwarven capital. I'm not exactly sure where, because he keeps his lair cloaked in magic. You can only find it if he wants you to, even if you've been there before. I have no idea where any of the others live."

The pair, indeed, found plates already set out for them. Celeste moved to a plate of wild berries and vegetables, smiling at them before lifting her wine glass filled with jambuticaba wine in a toast. "She remembered how much I enjoyed the dragon fruit last time I was here. I think it was her version of a joke. Cheers." Theri sat down next to her and lifted her goblet of sparkling water in response before digging into a delicious roast pheasant.

The two fell into a companionable silence while they ate. Finally, the sound of a bell rang out through the halls. The all-too-familiar voice spoke from very near, "Axistra is ready to see you, Madame Celeste."

Celeste rose to her feet and looked to Theri. "Perhaps I shall see you later, Therinsalla, if you are near after I speak to Axistra. It was nice talking to you."

Theri grinned her toothy grin. "I suspect we will, and call me Theri."

Celeste took Theri's hand and shook it firmly, as she offered her own smile. Then she turned and swept from the table.

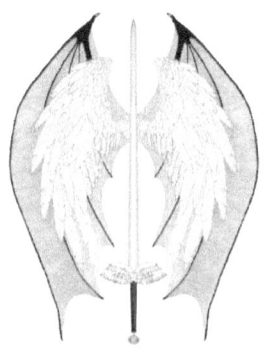

Chapter Two
The Perils of Pursuing

"How do you always get yourself into these messes?" Arcus demanded.

Joseph shrugged. "Just a skill of mine, I suppose."

"You know Victoria isn't interested, so why do you keep bothering her? Last time she set your clothes on fire, and this time she covered you in these sticky tentacle things. Leave her alone. Try learning from your mistakes, man." Arcus growled. His brow furrowed as he tried to think of what kind of healing spell he could possibly use to cure whatever this disease curse was. "It's not like I'm always going to be here to patch you up, and there are not healers on every corner. Not real ones anyway."

"You're not going anywhere, so stop it. You'd miss all the fun."

"Whatever. I'm only here to learn to master this magic inside me, before it rips me apart. Once I have that worked out, I can reconcile what I was born to with what I chose to be. Then maybe I can figure out what my destiny is supposed to be." He sighed. "Whatever it is, I know it isn't to be here, in this mundane existence." Arcus' hands glowed blue for a moment. "Ah, there you go. Now your face is just normal-ugly instead of tentacle-ugly."

"Thanks. They had at least been flesh colored tentacles when she hit me with that spell. It wasn't until I tried to come up with the counter-spell that they turned green." Joseph looked at his reflection, happy to see his normal brown eyes and hair, and his normal smooth complexion, which were no longer covered in green tentacles. "Maybe *you* should try your luck with Victoria, at least you –"

"Not interested," Arcus bit out.

"You didn't even let me finish. You'd at least –"

"I said, not interested." Arcus stood up and stomped away from his friend. He shook his head. Joseph meant well, but Arcus couldn't care less about most of these people. He certainly didn't want some chatterbox female bothering him all the time. He had better things to do.

His parents had been killed by orc raiders near the elven woods when he was a small child. The elven druids saved him. They took him in to their village and taught him the ways of healing, balance, and nature. Arcus was comfortable there and he felt at home. On his fifteenth birthday, however, everything changed. Suddenly, strange magic seemed to jump from him as if it were overflowing. The druids told him not to worry, and they urged him to just remain calm and commune with nature, as he always had. Sadly, he couldn't concentrate. He felt like there were small bolts of electricity shooting through him at random intervals, destroying his focus. Then, one day, Arcus accidentally set a tree on fire. An important tree. He fled the grove, and left his surrogate family behind, to find out what this strange magic that tainted him was. He arrived in the city of Izmar, west of the elven woods.

Izmar was a large trading port located at the point where the Nehir and Onetz rivers merged together to flow out to sea. It was a jumbled, disorganized mess that had started small, and grown too big to be controllable. The streets were a confusing puzzle, the homes and businesses placed haphazardly. The city itself had kind of a seedy feel, and all types arrived and departed every day by ship.

A sorcerer, Damon, found Arcus in one of the Izmarian bars, looking at the beer mug he was holding in alarm as ice formed all over the outside. Damon approached Arcus, and the two struck up a friendship of sorts. Damon offered to teach Arcus to master his magic in his school of sorcery. In return, Arcus offered to try to teach Damon healing magic, but the pair soon discovered Damon did not have an aptitude for it. Damon was fond of Arcus, however, and agreed to continue teaching him. It was in Damon's school that Arcus met Joseph, and the two sorcerers had been close friends ever since.

"Arcus, wait up!" Joseph jolted Arcus from his musings, as he ran to catch up. Arcus slowed his steps, but did not stop. Joseph soon caught up, and they walked along in silence. When they reached the eastern edge of town, Arcus gazed sadly in the direction of the forest he had once called home.

"What?" Joseph asked. When Arcus didn't answer, Joseph stared at him with sympathy. "Is there someone from the forest you're thinking of? Someone special?"

"No. Yes. I swear, Joseph, you do nothing but think with your hormones." He dragged his hand through his unruly black hair. "I miss them all. It was my home, but I know I don't fit in there anymore. I don't fit in anywhere. I don't know what I'm even doing anymore. I just wish something would happen that showed me the way."

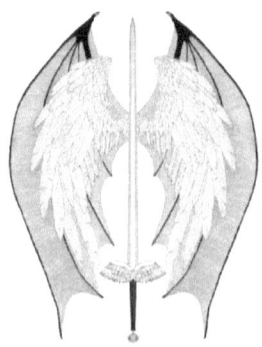

Chapter Three
The Truth about Elves and Dragons

Celeste once again approached the doors to the audience chamber. This time, they were already open and awaiting her. She paused just outside and waited, suddenly hesitant.

"Come in, child," came a voice from inside. It was warm and comforting, like a summer breeze, but it also held an air of authority and warning. None that heard it would ever think that this was someone to be crossed.

Celeste entered and dropped to her knees. She bowed her head and made a fist over her heart, as the elven traditions demanded. After a moment, the voice came again with a hint of amusement. "Rise, Celeste. I trust you've found everything within my home to your liking since your arrival? My apologies for not being prepared to receive you, I was indisposed."

Celeste rose to her feet, looking upon the dragon for the first time in six hundred years. Gazing up into Axistra's glowing blue eyes, Celeste felt a familiar tug of fear pull at her spine. She swallowed nervously and held her gaze. She knew it to be the effects of the dragonfear that radiated from all of her kind. The sensation would be much worse if the dragon were actually *trying* to intimidate Celeste. The majestic beast's scales were shining silver, and the wings that sprouted from her back were enormous. Two long, slender horns lifted from her forehead and curved backward in a graceful arc over her long reptilian head. She was crouched down on all fours like a sphinx; her long neck curved in a graceful arc and her tail wrapped around her body.

Celeste never felt prepared for the sheer size of Axistra. She licked her dry lips and shifted her weight from one foot to the other. "Yes, everything has been perfect, as usual. Though I can't help but wonder why you brought me here."

Axistra nodded her great head in approval. "Do you know what I've always admired about you, Celeste? Your ability to be so direct. Most of the elves are content to bandy pleasantries about all day, no matter the circumstances. Your directness will serve you well in the future, with what is to come."

Celeste said nothing, continuing to look into those hypnotic eyes. After a few moments, Axistra continued. "I have brought you here because Altierra is in danger." She paused. "From Kuunkierto."

Celeste blinked in shock. "Wha – what? That's not possible. He's dead."

The dragon shook her massive head. "No, child, he isn't. He's merely locked away in the holy tombs in the northern wastes, waiting to be released. I never thought this day would come, but I have had a vision of the humans releasing him."

Celeste swayed on her feet. A chair appeared behind her and she sat down with a nod of thanks. "Why would they do this?"

Axistra looked sad. "I heard what you said to young Therinsalla, and it was very true. The humans, like the kedistam, have short memories. It is my belief that they do not remember the full story of what happened there. King Liam has decided to send an excavation team to open the seal."

Celeste's eyes widened in horror. "What of the other gods? The heralds? My father? Are they still alive and trapped in there with him?"

"No. They are gone, well and truly. It's a shame, too, because we could use their help if the humans succeed. You can't kill the moon, Celeste. I know I don't have to tell you what could happen if Kuunkierto escapes. He would be unchallenged on this plane with all of the others gone. It must not happen."

"What would you have *me* do? The humans will not listen to me; they'll think I'm a freak."

"No, they'll think you are a herald, unless you hide your wings. You are one of the last elves still alive who remembers that day. In addition, your ties to the late god, Melek, will also be an asset."

Celeste stared up at Axistra, puzzled. "What do you mean I am one of the last? What happened to the others?"

Axistra replied, "Elves are only immortal if they have something to live for. Otherwise, the exhaustion takes over and they eventually withdraw into themselves and die. You have been away a long time, and I was surprised that you've held on all this time and kept the exhaustion at bay. I can only assume you have yet to reach your destiny. The village is still there and flourishing. You'll just find that many of the faces have changed."

Celeste was stunned, but Axistra continued. "Celeste, Claudestellassa succumbed almost three hundred years ago."

Celeste inhaled sharply. "My mother? Why did none of the others send for me? How could they do this to me?"

"They, or specifically one in particular, tried to. You were missing. Look inside yourself. Three hundred years ago, did you or did you not have several magical blocks in place just to avoid being found? Even now, those wards are in place; I can feel the magic pulsing around you."

Celeste's face darkened with shame and grief. "I never would have done so if I'd thought, for even a moment, that this could happen! None of the elder elves died in the way you describe in the two hundred years I lived with them. Not one!"

"You were raised in a time of war, and a time of rebuilding. One or two did, when you were a baby, but you were too young to understand."

"Well, why did *you* never find me? It couldn't have been any more difficult for you than it was now." Celeste was angry in her grief, and she struggled to maintain her composure.

"Stop being petulant, child. First of all, the elves never approached me to find one missing member. Second, you, yourself, were the one that came to *me*, to learn the magic that cloaked you from *them*! Why would I have disclosed your location? That wasn't part of our deal. Third, why would the loss of one elf who was well over one thousand years old concern me more than others? The world does not revolve around you." She rose up on her haunches and spread her wings in annoyance, then shook her head. "Now, it's time to focus on the task at hand. I understand this is a lot to process right now, but she has been gone for many years. What is to come is more important now."

"Well, why can't *you* go stop King Liam? Or someone – anyone – else? I'm not a hero, and I never wanted to be one," pouted Celeste.

"Enough!" The great dragon roared in a tone of finality, and the very air seemed to vibrate. Dust from the ceiling tiles, far above, rained down.

Celeste trembled, and leaned back against the cushions of her chair. The dragonfear was stronger when Axistra was unhappy. She nodded her head in acquiescence.

"That's better. Suffice it to say that it needs to be you, because I have foreseen it. Furthermore, you will need to find allies to help, but you must lead them. I have no reason to believe King Liam will not listen to reason, although the kedistam shaman tells me he suspects one of the lesser heralds, a demon, may be whispering in the king's ear. Plan to reason with him, but be prepared to use force if necessary. Do not go alone, or I fear all will be lost."

Celeste rose to her feet and turned to walk out. "Oh, and Celeste?" She turned back around and saw Axistra make the chair vanish. "You know as well as I that the pact applies to dragons as well. We are not to get involved in the affairs of mortals. You would do well to remember that. Farewell, and stay safe."

Celeste walked from the audience chamber in a bit of a daze. She tried to collect her thoughts, but they spun out of control. *"Gather allies? What allies? Raccoons? I don't know anybody. This is insane, I'm no hero; I'm just a hermit."* Briefly, she considered requesting a meeting with the Paladin King while surrounded by raccoons. *"Right. He'd think I was a crazy raccoon lady. That won't work. Crazy raccoon lady, like a crazy cat lady, but with raccoons. Cats? Cats! Theri!"*

She took off at a jog, searching the castle for Theri. She checked the guest rooms, the kitchens, dining room, great room, library, everywhere and anywhere she thought Theri might be. *It's almost midnight. Where could she have gone?* Celeste wondered. Finally, she opened the front door and went to check outside. She paused in the entryway, and listened to the silence of the night. She gazed up at the moon with fresh eyes, and contemplated its muted red color. To her, it appeared dead and scab-like. Suddenly, she heard a scurrying sound approaching. Theri was dashing between the trees, back toward the castle.

She panted heavily as she ran straight to Celeste. "Thank goodness you're here. I went to check on Talon, the pterodactyl that brought me here, but he's gone! I have no idea why or where he could have gone, or if he's even coming back. What will I do if he doesn't come back? We train them to stay in one area, so there's no reason he should have flown away."

Celeste turned to look back at the castle, arching her eyebrow in suspicion. "I suspect he won't come back; I think he has been sent home."

"What? By whom? What will I do?"

"By Axistra, but listen, did you mean it when you said you would help out however you could?" Celeste asked.

"Of course I did, but what does that have to do with anything? What is going on, Celeste?"

Celeste smiled. "I was hoping you'd say that. I had been looking everywhere for you. Come with me." Celeste led Theri toward the edge of the forest in the clouds, straight away from the castle door, to the very last tree before the ground dropped off into clouds. The tree was a massive baobab in full bloom, the only one like it on the castle grounds. Like the others in Axistra's realm, it would never lose its leaves and was always laden with fruit. Celeste stopped and gazed at it. She chewed her lower lip in contemplation. Then she walked up and whispered to the tree, running her hands up and down its trunk. As she did, intricate patterns on the trunk began to glow gold until a shining door appeared. Celeste slid the door open and grabbed Theri's wrist, pulling her inside.

They felt an odd falling sensation, and then the inside of the tree lit up, bathed in golden light. Celeste slid the door open and they stepped out of another large baobab, this one without leaves, surrounded by a grove full of cypresses.

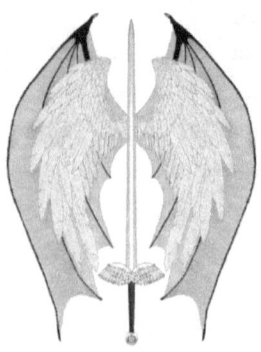

Chapter Four
Heart-Stopper

"Come on, let's head to the bar," said Joseph. "Maybe I'll find a pretty traveler."

"You really don't ever learn your lesson, do you? Fine, let's go."

Arcus turned and started walking the familiar path to the local tavern. The Dragonfire Tavern was a rundown bar near the docks. Many travelers frequented the place due to its convenient location and cheap swill. Joseph used it as a hunting ground. There was a time when Arcus had, too, just to fit in, but he no longer saw the point. They walked in the front door and were greeted with the familiar sight of the bartender cleaning a greasy mug with a greasier rag. Joseph immediately took off toward two females he'd never seen before, while Arcus approached the bar and ordered four mugs of the tavern brew. He carried the mugs over to the group, and mentally shook his head. He handed three of the mugs to Joseph and then focused on the last mug. His hands flashed green for a second. Joseph glanced over and laughed. One of the girls, a redhead, looked over curiously and asked, "Who's your friend? What did he just do with his hands?"

Joseph waved his hand dismissively. "He's no one of consequence. You're much more important, and better looking, than he is. As for his hands, he thinks he's too good to drink what the rest of us do."

Arcus scoffed. "It's the same stuff, I just refuse to drink it without purifying it a little first. I'm over hurling without even having the benefit of being drunk." With that, he drained the mug and slammed it down on the table.

"Whatever. You're the one always bragging that your magic protects you from poison."

"Poison, yes. Horrible, unknown diseases, not so much."

The blonde walked over to Arcus; her hips swayed provocatively. "Hi there. Can you show me anything else? I think magic users are sexy."

Arcus glared down at her. "Too easy." Then he turned and started back for the bar. Before he could reach it, however, the door flew open and in walked three of the strongest looking men Arcus had ever seen. They shoved roughly past Arcus and marched straight for the table with the two girls and Joseph. Arcus stepped out of the way and waited.

"Hey, you!" The man in front had brown hair and a full beard, and a ship tattoo on his upper arm. He pointed angrily at Joseph. "Yeah, I know it's you. Joshua or Joseph or something like that. I know what you did – Sam told me! Now you're gonna die!"

"Excuse me, gentlemen." Arcus had snuck up behind them and was standing with his hands behind his back. "What seems to be the trouble here?"

"This doesn't concern you, boy," one of the other two men snarled.

"Oh, but it does," answered Arcus. "You see, this man may be an idiot, but he's my friend, and I'm not going to stand idly by while you kill him. If anyone will kill him one of these days, it will be me."

"Thanks, Arc."

"No problem, idiot. Now, what did you do this time? Shall I guess that Sam is a girl?"

"Umm…that would probably be a safe bet. Though, honestly, I don't remember anyone named Sam," said Joseph.

"Why does that not surprise me?" quipped Arcus.

"What do you mean, you don't know who Sam is?" shouted the leader. "Sam is my girl, and you... you..."

"Rocked her world?" Joseph grinned mischievously, and winked at the blonde and redhead, who had already backed away to another table, and were observing the proceedings with curiosity.

"Was that really necessary, Joseph?" Arcus questioned, as the leader roared in fury.

The leader lunged for Joseph, who ducked under the man's arms, laughing. Arcus whipped his hands out from behind his back, and fire blazed up and down his forearms. He reached for the other two goons and slammed their heads together, scorching their hair. They bellowed in pain. The two girls and most of the other patrons all got up and rushed to the opposite side of the room, to avoid getting caught in the crossfire. The bartender cursed and demanded they break it up. The bystanders shouted taunts and cheers at the group, though to Arcus, the sounds all merged and then vanished altogether as he focused his magic. The man on the left pulled out a dagger, while the one on the right swung at Arcus. He absorbed the hit with his burning hands, which then flickered out. Then, he glared at the one with the knife. *"Stop moving,"* Arcus hissed in a hypnotic voice, and the spell immediately took effect as the man froze in place, still holding his knife awkwardly. He then turned to the other goon.

Joseph ducked another swing, and then another. He dodged a vicious kick by hopping toward the table. The leader was clearly becoming more and more enraged. Finally, he found purchase and punched Joseph square in the nose, which shattered. Blood sprayed everywhere. Joseph lost his rhythm, and fell hard onto the table. He raised his arms to block the assault, curling in on himself. The man hit him hard in the ribs with his elbow. Joseph held up a shaky hand to cast a small, glowing bolt of energy at his attacker, which struck him in the face, just under his left eye. The man grunted in pain, but didn't pause in his assault.

Arcus shoved both of his hands flat against his remaining attacker's chest. Lightning flashed from his palms and the man fell onto a chair without a sound. The chair crumbled to pieces under the onslaught as the smell of ozone filled the bar. Arcus turned to the leader. "Are you sure you don't want to rethink this plan while you still have a chance? Take a look at your men; you are clearly outmatched."

The leader paused in his assault. "What have you done to them?"

"Well, one of them will be just fine. The other has probably suffered a heart attack. I'd have to look closer to be sure, but that's what usually happens when you get hit in the chest by that spell. Would you like to find out what it feels like? If not, then I suggest you take your hands off my friend and step away. This is the last time I will warn you. Whoever she is, she isn't worth it, or she wouldn't have gone with Joseph in the first place."

Joseph gripped his nose to attempt to staunch the flow. He moaned as he tried to breathe, the pain excruciating due to his broken ribs. The crowd continued to jeer and shout, while the bartender shook his fist at them and glowered, clearly hopping mad.

"How dare you come into *my* bar and fight like this? Who will pay for the damages? Who will pay for the loss of business?"

Arcus silenced him with a glare before turning back to the leader. "What's it going to be?"

The man slumped in defeat as he stepped away from Joseph. "Good choice," Arcus said. "Joseph, come here. It's time to go."

"You're not going anywhere," shouted the barkeep. "Somebody has to pay for this."

Arcus' right hand lit on fire again. He glared at the bartender in warning as he pointed at him. "I said we are leaving. You will not stop us." With that, he grabbed Joseph with his left hand, and pulled him from the tavern.

Once outside, Arcus set a brisk pace in the direction of their dormitories, practically dragging Joseph along with him.

"Can we stop a minute? I feel a little light-headed," Joseph whined.

"No, we cannot. This is all your fault. If you had been able to keep it in your pants, we wouldn't be in this mess. Now, we have to leave," retorted Arcus.

"Leave? Why? Where are we going?"

"Don't be stupid. That bartender is alerting the town guard as we speak. I just killed a man! We are leaving. We are going back to the dorms and packing as fast as possible."

"Well, I just think it would be better if I didn't leave a bloody trail for them to follow then, but what do I know?" Joseph rolled his eyes.

"Fine, hold still." Arcus' hands began to glow a brilliant blue. He reached out and grabbed Joseph's broken nose with his left hand, gripping it hard and twisting, his right hand going to Joseph's side. Joseph yelled in shock and pain as his nose and ribs reset.

"Ow! Not your gentlest work, Arc," Joseph whined.

"Quit complaining and move."

They hurried along, taking side streets and trying to blend in as much as possible. Arcus pointed in the direction of Joseph's room. "Pack light and fast. Don't burden yourself down with useless crap." Then he turned and started banging on the door at the end of the hall. "Damon, open up, damn it!"

The door swung open and Damon stared at Arcus in consternation. "What's the problem?"

"Joseph and I are leaving. Right now. I wanted to let you know before they started looking for us."

Damon's eyes widened. "Before who starts looking for you?"

"The town guard. I had to defend that idiot *again* and things got out of hand. I had to end the fight faster than I ordinarily would have. Don't look for us. Don't get involved. Thank you for all your help; my time here is over, though." Arcus clasped Damon's forearm briefly, then hurried to his own room and packed his few belongings. After he was done, he turned and shoved the door to Joseph's room open and prepared to drag him out. Joseph was packing with a dazed look on his face, so Arcus took over, gathering the essentials. When he was done, he pulled Joseph out the door and down the street. They hadn't even made it a full block away when Arcus paused, his head cocked to the side.

"Do you really think they will be looking for us?" Joseph asked.

"Shhh!" Arcus clapped his hand over Joseph's mouth and yanked him back into the shadows, behind some crates. Joseph squirmed beneath his hand but Arcus held him tight. Then they both heard the sound of metal clanking against metal, and heavy footsteps on the pavement.

BANG! BANG! BANG! "Open up in the name of the law," came the singsong baritone. *BANG! BANG! BANG!*

A door farther down opened. Both Arcus and Joseph could tell from the sound that it was Damon's door. "Can I help you, gentlemen?" Damon asked. They heard more footsteps and clanking as the men walked over to Damon.

"We're looking for the one called Arcus and for Joseph Hale. They are registered as living here."

"They do live here. They are students of mine. What do you need with them?"

"They are wanted for murder and destruction of property," answered the guard.

"You have the wrong men. It's not possible," argued Damon.

"We have positive identification from five different eyewitnesses. Now, do you have the key to their rooms, or shall we kick down the door?"

"One moment, I'll get the keys. Though I'm warning you, you're making a huge mistake," snarled Damon.

There was silence for a moment, and then Damon came back out and unlocked both Arcus' and Joseph's doors. The guards clanked into each of the rooms.

"Now!" whispered Arcus. He released Joseph and they dashed out from their hiding place and out of town, racing toward the trees to the east.

After about an hour or so of forced running as best they could, they finally made it to the tree line. Once they were safely hidden by the forest, they stopped to catch their breath. Joseph slid down the trunk of a tree as he panted heavily. Arcus stood doubled over, his hands on his knees. Finally, after several long minutes, they caught their breath enough to speak.

"Man, am I out of shape. Can we have a do-over for today? I think we should definitely not go to the bar after all."

Arcus rolled his eyes. "Come on. We can't stay here, so close to the border. They'll look here, eventually." He began to walk into the darkened forest.

Joseph followed, his eyes wide. "Not to pry, but do you know where we are going? I know you used to live here, but it's been a while and it's dark. Plus, the elves could have moved on."

"You clearly don't know much about elves. Besides, do you have a better idea?"

Joseph sighed. "No, I suppose not. How did you know the guards were there right then? I didn't hear them until after you manhandled me into the corner."

"I was listening for them. How do you think I knew?"

"Is it my turn to ask how you get yourself into these messes?" asked Joseph.

"Don't start. I didn't have to save you."

"You didn't have to kill that guy, either! We could have worked out the destruction of property charge!"

"Yes, I did. Were you seeing your idiot life flash before your eyes yet? You should have been. That guy was going to kill you, and the only thing you could think of to defend yourself was an energy bolt?" Arcus spit out.

"I – I'm sorry, Arc. He broke my nose and my mind blanked. I don't have your instincts, and my magic has never been up to your standards. You know that I'm not as quick on my feet as you,"

"That's another thing. Don't toy with your enemies. All that darting around did was piss him off. Finish the fight or run away. Don't just dance around. What happened to you was inevitable. This is the real world, and from here on out, enemies are real. Knowing your affinity for trouble, you'd better learn to fight and do it now."

"I'm a lover, not a fighter, Arcus."

"You are a sorcerer. From now on, you are both. Listen, we aren't going to be able to make it all the way to the village tonight; it's much too far. We'll have to find somewhere to rest, but we need to get far enough in that the guards will not pursue us."

They continued to walk through the forest, which began a gradual rise up into the Kayalik Mountains. They arrived in front of a shallow cave that was basically just a large alcove. Arcus gestured they should enter.

"We should sleep in shifts, just in case," said Arcus.

"I'll take first watch," replied Joseph. "You know I'm not a morning person. I'll do better if I can stay up later and sleep until the sun is up."

"Fine. Wake me up immediately if there are any problems."

Arcus collected a bunch of leaves to place on the rocky ground of the cave to soften it. Then he pulled a thin blanket from his bag and covered himself with it. The bag, he used as a pillow. He lay down, falling asleep almost immediately.

Arcus looked around, but couldn't see anything. It was dark. Oh, so very dark. He strained his eyes, trying to make out any shapes, but could barely see his own hand in front of his face.

"Hello?" he called out, confused as to where he was and how he had ended up there. This must be a dream, *he thought.*

A pair of huge glowing blue eyes blinked open above him. Way above him. Arcus swallowed hard and licked his lips.

"Ah, the orphaned human. I've been watching you for years, you know," said the voice. It seemed to echo in the chamber and reverberate through his body.

"Y – you know me?" Arcus asked. "How? Who are you?"

"Good questions, child. Unfortunately, they are questions I do not have time to answer. I have but a moment. You must go to Lumernia. Your destiny awaits."

"How do you know what I need to do?"

"I must go. Lumernia... remember, Lumernia." The voice began to fade out. "If you remember nothing else when you wake, remember you must get to Lumernia; it is the only place you will be safe. Your destiny a..."

"Arcus! Arcus, wake up!" Joseph whispered urgently only a short time later.

Arcus jerked awake and sat up. "What's going on?" Then, he heard a growling sound from just outside the cave. "Stay here." As Arcus stood and walked out of the cave, he saw the massive bear stand up on her hind legs. Arcus made eye contact with the beast and glowered at her. The bear dropped back down to all fours and ambled up to Arcus.

"Arcus? Is that you?" Arcus heard the bear's voice inside his head.

Arcus nodded in recognition. *"Tarah, it's been a long time."*

"I'm glad I recognized you. I thought you were trying to steal my cave. You aren't, right?"

"No, Tarah, we're just passing through. We're in a bit of trouble and are heading to the druids. I didn't know this was your cave. May we share? I promise we'll be out of your way in the morning."

The bear nodded. *"Of course you can."*

"Let me just tell my companion what is going on first, okay?"

Arcus turned and walked back into the shallow cave. "The bear is Tarah. She is an old friend. Turns out, this is her cave. She has graciously decided to let us stay here with her tonight."

Joseph's eyes were huge. "With her? Is it safe?" he exclaimed.

"Of course. In fact, we will be safer with her here. The guards won't mess with a bear her size, and neither will any of the forest predators. Now we can both sleep." Tarah entered the cave and approached Joseph, lowering her head submissively as a sign that she meant him no harm.

Joseph didn't look convinced, but he didn't argue. He was clearly out of his element. He patted her on the head, then moved into the corner farthest away from Tarah, arranged his blankets from his bag, then he lay down and tried to get comfortable.

All three drifted off to sleep.

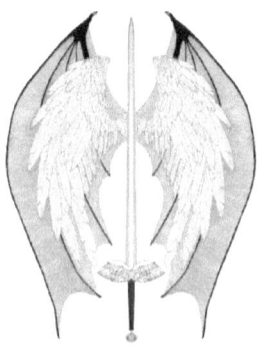

Chapter Five
Love Hurts

The cypress grove Celeste and Theri entered was silent and still. Theri shivered. "What did you do? Why do the trees look so different?"

"Hush, Theri. That tree, and its twin here, were set up long ago as portals, for those who know how to use them. I transported us away from Axistra's castle." Celeste gestured to the massive baobab, noticing then the old and faded scorch marks on the side of the tree. She frowned slightly.

"You what? What about my stuff? What about Talon? He may go back looking for me."

"Trust me, he won't go back. I'm relatively sure he was sent away. Though, even if I am wrong, Axistra will make sure he is taken care of. You were right, you were there because you were needed. Turns out, I'm the one that needs you. As for your stuff, it's all replaceable, assuming you actually had any stuff there, which I doubt you did."

Theri paused. "How do you know that?"

Celeste smiled. "You arrived via pterodactyl. I doubt he could carry much with you on his back. I've never seen one, but I do know a thing or two about flying."

"I suppose you would. So what's the plan?"

"Plan? Well, we need to work one of those out. The general plan is to go see King Liam and talk him out of doing something stupid."

"The Paladin King? But... but he's on the other side of the continent," Theri exclaimed.

"I know, and I don't know what kind of timetable we have," murmured Celeste.

"What happens if we don't make it in time?"

Celeste sighed. "Not much, just the end of the world."

"What?"

"Turns out, King Liam intends to excavate the holy tombs in the north," said Celeste.

"The ones you were telling me about, where Koonerto is buried?"

"Kuunkierto, and yes."

"Well, what will happen if the king succeeds?"

"Apparently Kuunkierto isn't dead. If the seal is broken, he will escape and take over the world. Trust me when I say having Kuunkierto as the one and only god on Altierra will be a terrible, terrible thing. Those that survive will be trapped in a living hell. I doubt any of the kedistam or humans will be allowed to live at all. Axistra's advice was to try to talk the king out of this madness, but to be prepared for anything, and to not go alone. That's where you come in."

"Great," Theri grumbled.

"There's more," said Celeste. "I don't think talking to him will be easy. Apparently your shaman has reported that he suspects a herald may be involved. Specifically, a demon."

"A demon? But I thought paladins were supposed to be all perfect. You know, the exact opposite of a demon."

"They are, but demons will lie and disguise themselves to fool even the most pious. It's kind of their job. The king may be corrupted."

"Okay, so we stop the king. I still don't understand why we are *here*," grumbled Theri.

"We're here now, at this moment, so they could hear the explanation. I knew you would bombard me with questions the second I brought you here."

"Wait, what? Who's they?"

Celeste smiled and gestured outward with her hands. "Them."

As if on cue, all around them, six of the cypress trees curled in on themselves and became smaller and smaller until they had taken the form of the elven druids.

The six elves that appeared before them all possessed an otherworldly beauty. All of them had luminescent green eyes, exactly like Celeste's. However, they had blond hair, ranging from platinum to dark ashy blond, as opposed to Celeste's deep black hair.

Celeste bowed low, her right hand making a fist over her heart. Then she rose and looked at each of them in turn. Her brows lifted in surprise and she became very pale as she made eye contact with the sixth, a male with long golden blond hair, wearing tan breeches and a loose fitting forest green shirt. He was tall and slender, as elves tend to be, without the added muscle of human men. When he approached her, he moved with the grace of a willow branch bending in the wind.

"Celeste," he breathed. "It's been a long time. You've grown even more beautiful than the last time I saw you."

"Tarnelius, it has been a while." She smiled, though it appeared forced.

Theri cleared her throat.

"Theri, this is Tarnelius, one of the druids. These men and women are tasked with guarding the Sacred Tree." She turned back to Tarnelius. "Though I don't remember that being your job."

Tarnelius smirked. "It's not, though I do enjoy it. Communing near the Sacred Tree is an honor. When I stand here as the cypress, I can feel my roots mingling with the roots of our people, I take strength from the soil, and from the magic coursing through me."

"You stand here and pretend to be a tree all day, when you don't even have to?" Theri asked. "Doesn't that get boring?"

"Not at all, young kedistam. Days or even years are but nothing to an elf," Tarnelius replied.

Suddenly, a red-tailed hawk flew down and landed on a low hanging branch of one of the remaining cypress trees. Tarnelius looked over at the bird for a moment, before the hawk took off again, flying west.

Celeste smiled, "I always was fond of that particular species."

"I know, he reminded me of you," Tarnelius said with a small, strained smile. "Firewing is flying ahead to tell the others you are coming. Come, I will take you to my father."

A female with long, flowing, platinum blond hair stepped forward. "My prince, should any of us accompany you, or would you prefer we remain here?"

"Stay here. Return to your posts, all of you. I do not require a guard."

With that, the other five druids all saluted Tarnelius and resumed their positions near the large baobab.

The three set off to the west, toward the druids' village. It was only a few miles, but every step was torture to Celeste, who was bombarded with memories. Memories of her mother, of growing up here and playing in these woods. Memories of Tarnelius, though she struggled to push those from her mind. They had grown up together as best friends, and he was her first and only love. The young prince, however, was promised to another. He had offered to reject the throne and his father's plan for him for Celeste, but she knew it was an empty offer. He had a duty to his people, and her duty had been to let him go. The prince and his bride had never met and began in a loveless relationship, but such was often the case with the arranged unions of elves. Celeste, for her part, had been heartbroken. She couldn't take the thought of having to see him with another, and couldn't help the way she felt. Their upcoming union had been the final straw that forced her to leave. She had never felt like she fit in anyway, but now she had lost everything. Seeing him again was like opening an old wound.

Together, they walked toward the elven village of Kayalost. Celeste and Tarnelius were each lost in contemplation. Theri kept breaking the silence with incessant questions, which went unanswered, until she eventually gave up and fell silent.

650 years earlier...

Tarnelius flew after Celeste, their feathers shimmering in the sunlight. She had shifted into a small red-tailed hawk, and he had turned into a handsome golden eagle. She screeched in mirth and attempted to evade him. She never would; he would always find her. He was sure of it. She was perfect, she completed him.

They finally touched down at the base of a massive waterfall high in the mountains. It was early summer, and all around them, the world was a lush green. Everything was beautiful, perfect. The way nature intended. They changed back into their normal forms, and Celeste stripped off her clingy hunter green gown and jumped into the river. He hurried to disrobe and jumped in as well. They splashed each other playfully in the water, laughing and screaming with mirth. Finally, he caught her in his arms and gazed into her beautiful eyes, staring into her very soul. Today was the day, he just felt it. Today he would ask Celeste to make the lifebond with him. Just as soon as he got back and told his father his intent. He was fortunate his father had never meddled in his life the way most parents meddled with their children. He leaned down slowly, still making eye contact as if he were soothing a wild animal, until his lips made contact with hers. Then they both closed their eyes and lost themselves in the moment, devouring each other. His pulse quickened as his body reacted to hers, as it had so many times in the past. The moment would be fleeting, as it always had. Elves almost never mated unless they were bonded, but those few moments before they had to stop were pure bliss. She was perfect, she completed him. She set his very soul on fire.

"I'm sorry, Son. That is not possible," King Audelthus stated.

Tarnelius stared at his father in surprise. He'd expected his father to be happy for them. They were so happy together. "I don't understand, Father."

"You were promised to Princess Velonessa, of the Silver Iles, on the day of your birth. I thought you knew that. On your two hundredth birthday you will be joined, and one day you will be king of both of our kingdoms. Velonessa will be much better suited to be queen than a mongrel half breed that you can't even be sure is capable of bonding."

"Don't talk about her that way. I love her and she loves me," roared Tarnelius.

"Remember your place, Tarnelius. Your duty is to your people, and you must keep the promise that was made. Tradition demands it. Etiquette demands it. Love has no place in our traditions. Besides, you will learn to love each other after you are bonded. That is my final answer, and you are dismissed."

Tarnelius hurried past his father down the stairs, trying to maintain as much dignity as he could. What would he do? What could he do? He had a duty to his people. He was their prince, but he could not make the bond with Velonessa. He didn't love her, he loved Celeste. She was perfect, she completed him. She was his.

"Celeste, I'm sorry. I didn't know it would turn out this way! I don't love her, I love you. I wanted forever with you. Say the word and we can run away together."

"No, Tarnel. I wish I could say this didn't surprise me, because I always should have expected it. I allowed myself to believe we could be happy, but we can't. You have responsibilities. You must stay here."

"I can't, don't you understand? How can I see you every day, and never touch you? It could never be like it was. We should leave, it's our only chance," he begged.

"I won't leave with you. I am sorry, Tarnel. Maybe I don't love you enough, maybe I love you too much. Either way, I cannot let you abandon your family or our people. We were foolish to believe your father would ever give a freak like me a place in his house. You are right, though; I cannot see you with her every day, either. It would be too much to bear." Celeste leaned backward into a tree, covered her face in her hand and wept. The other hand stroked the tree she leant upon. "T-tell my mother that I love her." With that, Celeste fell backward into the tree and vanished without a trace.

Tarnelius had tried many times to divine her location, but he never succeeded. He refused to make the bond with Velonessa, despite his father's wishes, demands, and even threats. Eventually, his father gave up and the princess returned to the kingdom to the far west. Centuries after, he continued to try to find Celeste. She was perfect, she completed him. She was gone.

Tarnelius shook himself a little to escape his reverie. He looked at Celeste and gave her another sad smile. "I've missed you, you have no idea how much."

Celeste glared back at him. "In fact, I do have some idea, but you mustn't say such things. Nothing has changed. Nothing will change."

"So I'm guessing you two have some kind of history?" quipped Theri.

"Ancient history," confirmed Celeste. Tarnelius clenched his jaw shut, a pained look on his face.

They continued into the forest, which was rapidly rising higher and higher into the mountains. After four torturous hours of walking and climbing, they finally climbed up on a flattened plateau. Theri caught her breath in surprise.

It was exactly as Celeste had remembered. Every emerald tree, every perfect home, all was the same. Elves rarely changed though, as they were nothing if not creatures of habit. Celeste almost expected to see her mother running toward her, arms outstretched. She frowned slightly, and reminded herself that would be impossible now. Her mother was gone.

"Oh no, Celeste, I should have told you sooner, but I just realized you don't know about –"

"My mother? I've already received the message, don't worry."

"I – Celeste, I'm so sorry. I tried to find you."

"Don't worry about it," Celeste bit out.

Tarnelius sighed. "Okay, well, would you prefer your friend to be given guest quarters, or to stay with you?" Tarnelius asked.

"With me? You mean my home is still mine?"

"I refused to let anyone else touch it, in case you ever came back. I hope you don't mind, but I sometimes go there to remember."

"Tarnelius, I do mind. You have to let me go. Really. You have Velonessa now. You made the bond, didn't you?" Celeste retorted.

"Celeste, you left me, and I –"

"It was the right thing to do," she interrupted.

"My feelings for you never –"

"Tarnelius, stop. This conversation is over. Don't say it. I'm here for a reason, as I know you overheard. Theri can stay with me," Celeste snapped, her face darkening in anger.

"Fine. I trust you remember the way, then. When my father is ready to receive you, I will send word." Tarnelius stormed off, clearly hurt. Celeste bit her lip.

Theri started to ask, "Celeste, is he –"

"Don't start, Theri."

Theri sighed. They walked in silence to the house Celeste used to share with her mother. Celeste opened the door and felt the memories and smells wash over her. Her eyes filled with tears; she chewed on her lower lip to keep herself under control. "I have to go make myself presentable enough to see the king. Make yourself at home. Don't break anything." She paused. "Theri?"

"Yes?"

"I'm sorry for the awkwardness of the last several hours. He is the reason that I left. A long time ago, I dared to love the elf prince, but it wasn't meant to be. We were not good for each other. It's an awkward situation and I never meant to return here. Actually, I took painful measures to ensure I never had to return here. On top of everything else, this house smells like my mother, and I recently learned of her death. I'm having a tough time coping and I am sorry you are caught in the middle. The sooner we are free of this place the better."

"Why are we seeing the king at all?"

"I have to at least ask for help. I doubt he'll give me any, but I have to ask. I'll be back in a few minutes." Celeste turned away and wandered into the washroom where she scrubbed herself meticulously. She went to her room and found her best gown still hanging in her closet, untouched. The white dress was made of shining satin, and it hugged her curves closely. When she finished dressing, she went into her mother's old room and picked up some of her jewelry, putting on a sparkling necklace and a couple of rings. The necklace was shaped like a ruby hawk, and her mother had often told her the pendant had been imbued with defensive magic. Just as she was finishing, she heard a knock on the door.

"Yes?" Theri answered.

"His Majesty, King Audelthus, is ready to see Madame Celeste," announced the messenger.

"On my way," said Celeste.

"Do you want me to come too?" asked Theri.

"Yes, but they won't let you. Just wait for me here. I'll be back soon."

"The king is waiting in the Chamber of the Sky," said the messenger.

Celeste nodded in thanks and started in that direction. She approached several gigantic trees, their limbs stretching far up toward the heavens. A spiral staircase circled the massive trunk of one of the trees, and Celeste began to ascend them. The Chamber of the Sky was an elegant auditorium with no ceiling and only tree branches for walls, designed to allow the king and his court the ability to view the beauty of the skies.

She climbed all the way to the top, where she was surprised to see the king waiting for her alone. Where were his advisers, his court, or the other various people that always surrounded him? She paused for a moment in confusion.

"Come closer, Celeste," he said in a quiet voice. "What brings you back here?"

"I come to humbly request assistance, Your Highness." Celeste bowed low to him.

"Tell me what is going on."

Celeste relayed her story to the king, then fell silent, waiting for him to ask her questions.

"I suppose you want me to send my son with you on your quest?" he asked.

"No, Your Highness. I would prefer that you didn't, actually."

"Oh? He told me once that you loved him. Was that not true?"

"I did, once, but I don't see how that has any bearing on the events currently in question," she answered cautiously.

"Tell me, Celeste, why did you leave?"

"I couldn't bear to stay."

The king stood up and circled her slowly. "I'm sorry about your mother. Tarnelius redoubled his efforts to find you after she passed."

"I haven't come to speak about my mother. Or Tarnelius. Please, your majesty, can you help us?" Celeste begged.

"I realized then that you did love him. You also loved your people and tried to do what you felt was right. When you first ran away, I thought you expected him to chase you. When I realized the effort you took to avoid detection, I understood that your intent was not to ensnare him at all, that you were trying to do your duty to your people."

Celeste clenched her jaw in anger. "This was a mistake. Axistra was right; all of you are content to do nothing but bandy words around all day, no matter what or whom they affect. I'm sorry to have wasted your time, Your Highness. I will be leaving soon."

King Audelthus could only stare at her in surprise. "I will not risk the lives of my people for your mission. Liam Callaghan is unreasonable and stubborn, and he will only be worse if there is, truly, an evil herald influencing him. Either way, he will not take kindly to interference from us, and you will be outnumbered. I will provide you and your companion any gear you would like. That is all." He waved his hand dismissively and returned to his throne.

Celeste bowed low to him. "Thank you, Your Highness." She hurried down the stairs and back to her home.

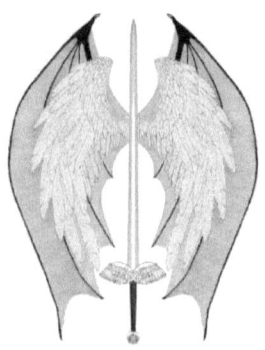

Chapter Six
Familiar but Foreign

Arcus and Joseph awoke with the sunrise the next morning and gathered their belongings. They said goodbye to Tarah, and then set off toward the west again.

"Hey, Arc, where exactly are we going?" Joseph asked.

"To the druid village in the center of the Kayalik Mountains."

"At the *center* of the…that will take *weeks* to walk to, maybe even months," Joseph exclaimed.

"Trust me on this one."

They walked on, passing several deer, raccoons and squirrels. Many of the animals seemed happy to see the pair of them, and made skittering sounds in greeting. Arcus acknowledged them all when this happened, at least with a small nod of his head. After several hours of walking, they heard the scream of an eagle overhead. Arcus stopped and looked up into the trees. "Wait right here," he said to Joseph. Then he spread his arms high in the air and shifted into a grackle. He made a strange sound that was reminiscent of a rusty gate being forced open and took off into the trees. After about five minutes, he fluttered back down and landed at Joseph's feet, shifting back into his normal, human, self.

"Wow! How long have you been able to do that?" Joseph asked, his eyes wide.

"Long time."

"Well, why am I just finding out about it now?" Joseph asked.

"What was I supposed to say? 'Hi, I'm Arcus and I can turn into a bird.' Come on, Joseph, that wasn't going to happen. It never came up. Let's take a break."

Joseph sat down on the ground while Arcus plucked some berries from a nearby bush. He brought them over and they ate them while Joseph contemplated what had just happened.

"So what kind of eagle was that?"

"That wasn't an eagle. That was a sentry. I had to show him I was one of them or he would not have allowed us to continue, since he doesn't know who I am. That species of eagle is not native here."

"Wait, I don't understand. The eagle is really an elf, but you don't know him. How is it you do not know him, but you do know most of the animals in this forest?" Joseph asked.

"I don't know most of the animals, but they can sense what I am and are respectful. I, in turn, respect them. Anyway, I knew almost all of the elves from the village, but the sentries stay separate most of the time. We may have met at some point, but I don't remember him."

Just then, two of the trees nearby lit up with golden light in the shape of a door. The "doors" opened and an elf stepped out of each of them. Joseph yelped in shock.

"Hail, humans. What business do you have in our forest?" asked the female with honey-colored hair. The other was a male with dark blond hair, who was significantly taller than the female.

"I am Arcus, here to see the druids. I was raised here."

"The human that was rescued from the fringes of our woods as a child? I have heard of you. Why have you returned?"

"We seek the safety of the woods as we may be being pursued. I hoped one of the druids may be familiar enough with the trees in Lumernia to help us get there. What about you two?"

They exchanged glances. "None will pursue you into these woods. Neither of us has been to Lumernia, so we cannot take you. In truth, I doubt they even have the same kind of trees as us and we never have anything to do with them, so we wouldn't have planted any. However, perhaps those in the village will have a different answer. We will take you there," said the female.

They each returned to the tree they had stepped out of, and ran their hands down the trunk, preparing the spell. Then they each held out a hand to one of the humans and pulled them inside.

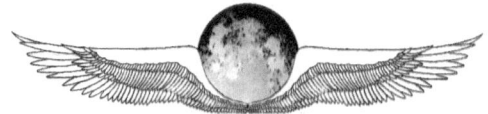

Celeste angrily flung open the door to her mother's house and stomped inside, slamming the door shut behind her. Theri looked up, startled. "Is everything okay?"

"No, everything is *not* okay. This was a waste of time, and I should have known better," snarled Celeste.

"What happened?"

"Well, shockingly, King Audelthus has not changed one bit in over half a millennium. He is content to interrogate me regarding my private life, but is so set in his assumption that nothing will ever change, he fails to recognize the gravity of our task. We cannot count on the elves for help. He offered us equipment, but that is it."

"Maybe we can ask around on our own? He may be the king, but he isn't in charge of every single decision from every single person," Theri said.

"True, and we can try. However, the only people I have recognized around here are Tarnelius and his father. I've noticed some people staring, but I suspect they have been hearing rumors. I doubt any of them will side with us over their king."

"Well, what about Tarnelius? I have the distinct impression that he would do whatever you asked," questioned Theri.

"That may be, but that ship has sailed and I don't want to be around him. I can't," she said the last part in a whisper.

"Well, I understand, but-"

"Shhh! Listen!" Celeste tilted her head, trying to hear. She dashed to the door and threw it open to look out.

Celeste looked out upon the crowd that had gathered nearby. There were two humans standing in the center of the group. One of them was an olive skinned man with piercing gray eyes, messy black hair, and the scraggly beginnings to a beard; he was short for a human male at only about five and a half feet, the same height as her. The other was a few inches taller, with fair skin, sandy brown hair and dark eyes. The elves all seemed excited to see them, and despite their usual formality, several of them were actually hugging the scruffier looking one and shaking the humans' hands. Scruffy, for his part, seemed rather embarrassed, from Celeste's perspective, and kept trying to keep to the elves' normal tradition of bowing to each of them with his fist over his heart.

"What's going on?" Theri asked from behind her.

"I'm not sure. Apparently some humans have arrived here. That's strange because humans are not normally welcome, or at least they weren't. I guess things have changed. Come on, let's find something to eat and get some rest. The garden may be overrun, but I should be able to work with it. We'll leave tomorrow morning."

"Now that you mention it, I am really tired. I haven't slept at all since before you arrived at the castle in the clouds."

"Neither of us has. Come on, the garden is out back," said Celeste.

"Garden? Hey, are there any markets around here that sell meat? I need real food," said Theri.

"Nope. There are shops around, but they mostly trade fruit, vegetables, various wines, breads, and other things of that nature. The animals around here are like family. We don't eat them any more than we would eat our own siblings."

"Great," said Theri.

"Don't worry, you'll be fine." Celeste smirked. "Plants are good for you."

To Celeste's surprise, the garden was exactly as she remembered. It seemed Tarnelius hadn't just stopped at visiting her house from time to time, he had also seen to it the garden was meticulously tended to. The pair picked several different types of fruits and vegetables, then went back inside. Celeste found some sweet apricot wine in the cupboards, and they sat down to eat.

"How are there so many different kinds of plant life here? I never thought that mangos would grow in the mountains," Theri remarked.

"We druids can grow just about anything. It's all about making a connection with the plant type and finding out what it needs to thrive. We can control the weather in small areas, so we can work out most anything."

Once the two had eaten, they went to rest for a while. Theri curled up on the couch, falling asleep immediately. Celeste, after hesitating for a moment, went to her mother's room rather than her own.

"Why did you ever leave here, Arcus? They all seem to really love you," wondered Joseph.

"It's not important. I just didn't fit in," said Arcus.

"Funny, it doesn't look that way."

"Let it go. Anyway, did you see that dark haired woman?"

"No, but this place sure is full of beautiful women; how would a man choose just one?"

"Knowing you, you wouldn't. I would advise you to leave them alone. They are capable of far greater damage than Victoria was. My point, though, is that she looked like an elf, but I've never seen her before. Actually, I've never seen an elf with dark hair at all."

"Wait, wait, wait, you noticed a female? *You?* You never look at women anymore. Let's go find her now," exclaimed Joseph.

"First of all, I look at women plenty. I'm just not interested in the type of women you chase. Secondly, I would never be interested in an elf, because they would never look twice at me. Elves are almost immortal, and I am most certainly not. I'm not sure what she is doing here or who she is, that's all."

"Whatever you say. What are we going to do now though, since none of the elves can apparently get us where you wanted to go? Should we pick somewhere new? Maybe they could send us south instead?"

"Bah, there's nothing for us among the kedistam or tumasi. What few humans we would find would not be worth the trip. We'll have to find another way. Maybe we can get some gear and walk to Lumernia," said Arcus.

"That's a long walk. Are you sure we can't pick one of the smaller human cities to the north of the woods? What's so great about Lumernia?"

"Maybe you're right. I was just thinking Lumernia would be the best place because it's the capital. There are so many mages we could learn from or apprentice to. We may have to keep trying, but eventually we'll find something like that in the north. Let's stay here for a day or two and we can decide where to go."

They had been given a guest house by Tarnelius when they arrived. Others had moved into Arcus' old home in the six years since he had left the village. The guest house was small, with only one actual bedroom, but it was cozy and would suit their needs for the short time they would be staying. They ate food that Tarnelius had sent over to them, and refreshed themselves, cleaning the forest dirt away.

When the sun was barely beginning to set, but before the red moon had risen, Arcus decided to take a walk. He left the small guest house, telling Joseph he'd be back later, and walked among the trees of the village. They were so beautiful, the trees near the Chamber of the Sky growing so huge, while others in the village proudly displayed their leaves from a somewhat shorter perspective. He had always admired the way the elves made their homes around the trees, always making them appear as extensions of the trees themselves. Or maybe the trees were extensions of the houses. He realized it was a tough call, and one that was perhaps best left to the philosophers. He approached an old willow tree which had always been his favorite, and stood before it. The greenery seemed to shimmer with the radiance of emeralds under the light of the setting sun. He was so entranced staring at the tree that he didn't notice the strange woman he saw before step out from behind the tree and pause, staring at him.

"Who are you?" Celeste asked.

She wore a dark green gown that hugged her thin frame in all the right places, and also wore a large ruby bird pendant on a chain around her neck. Maybe it was an eagle, but he couldn't be sure. Her almond shaped eyes glowed green – definitely elven eyes. Her hair was a peculiar shade for elves, inky black, like his. He knew right away she was a druid, from the magic that seemed to radiate off her in waves. She exuded power and control; he could almost taste it.

"Name's Arcus. Who are you?"

"Celeste," she answered.

A slight frown marred his forehead. "That's an unusual name for an elf. It doesn't have enough syllables. In fact, if it weren't for your eyes and where we are I would have never guessed you for an elf, as I've never seen one with black hair before."

"I'm pretty unusual, I suppose. My father named me, and I got my hair from him as well. Are you done assessing me now?" Celeste bit out.

"You started it. Now you have the nerve to act all high and mighty when I ask you questions?" Arcus wasn't even sure why he was wasting time talking to this female, though something about her did intrigue him. *She wasn't here a few years ago.*

Maybe she knows how to get to one of the other cities, away from Izmar, he thought.

"I…" Celeste frowned, seeming to consider his words. She began again, "What are you doing here? How do you know everyone here, when you are clearly a human?"

"The elves raised me after my parents were murdered by orc raiders outside these woods. I left here only a few years ago. My turn; who was your father, then? Was he human? You don't really look like a half-elf, except for your hair," Arcus asked her, looking her up and down.

Celeste blushed under his scrutiny. "No, he wasn't human," she whispered.

"Then who was he? If he was an elf, then I restate my question about your name, and you clearly don't have any other kind of blood in you."

Celeste sighed. "I'll make a deal with you. I'll tell you everything…eventually. The deal is, I'm here trying to get help on a mission given to me by –" She paused. "Since you were supposedly raised here, do you know who Axistra is?"

"Of course, though I've never had the honor of meeting her."

Celeste nodded. "Good. Anyway, I've got to get to King Liam and try to talk to him. King Audelthus won't help me, and I know very few others here. If you agree to come with me and help, I will tell you anything you want to know."

Arcus' eyes widened, as a jolt of shock coursed through his body. "You want me to go with you all the way to Lumernia?" *Well,* that *was unexpected,* he thought. "That's a long way from here, probably a month or more, depending on how you choose to travel. Do you have a plan?"

Celeste sighed. "Look, I'm sorry, you don't have to agree. I didn't mean to blurt that out so abruptly; I'm just kind of desperate for help. No, I don't have a plan. It's been many hundreds of years since I was there, or anywhere east of here really, so I can't use the trees. Who knows what the humans may have done to them? I could end up stuck inside a chair for all I know. I could travel quickly myself, if I had to, but I can't get an entire group there as quick. We may have to walk, but the task is important."

Arcus stood very still, regarding the strange female. Celeste fidgeted under his gaze, then finally said, "I can see that I shocked you. I'm sorry. This wasn't the right way to do this. I'll leave you alone now." She started to turn away.

"Wait, I didn't say no. I have to speak to my traveling companion before I could commit to anything, anyway. What did you mean by you could get there quickly if you had to?"

Celeste paused but didn't answer. As Arcus watched, smoke almost seemed to appear behind her and wavered for a moment before forming into gigantic angel wings. She spread them wide and then took off from the ground like a giant bird of prey, disappearing from sight behind the trees.

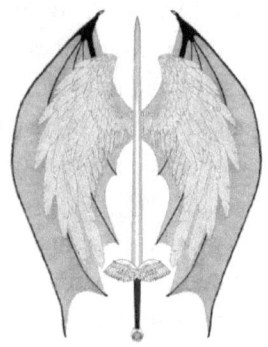

Chapter Seven
Another Door Opens

"Joseph! Wake up, Joseph!" Arcus shook Joseph by the shoulder.

"Unnnnng...what? I was having a nice nap. Victoria was in it."

"What you get up to in your dreams is none of my business. Please don't *ever* tell me. Anyway, I have news," Arcus said.

"What?"

"I found the woman, the brunette I saw earlier. She is going to Lumernia! I knew we'd find a way."

"How is she getting there?" Joseph asked.

"Walking probably, not sure. Either way, there's safety in numbers. Plus, this girl has power. I could almost taste it."

"Walking? Arcus...we talked about that. Lumernia is hundreds of miles from here. I thought you agreed we should go to one of the closer towns."

"I did. But she needs our help, Joseph. She has some idea she's on some all-important mission given to her by one of the dragons, and –"

"Dragon? Whoa, Arc. I'm not on board. I'm sorry, man. I don't want to go all the way to Lumernia on foot. I don't. Not even for a girl, especially not for a crazy girl involved with a dragon. Let's go settle in one of the closer towns, maybe even Gormloch or Abhainn. My folks are in Abhainn," argued Joseph.

"Which means there is no suitable sorcery school there, otherwise wouldn't you have been there instead of Izmar? Look, won't you at least consider it? I think she is part herald, and I feel almost as if we are meant to go. It just seems serendipitous that she would happen to be going to the same place I've felt drawn to."

"It's too far. The path is too dangerous. Besides, I miss Izmar. Maybe someday we can go back, and it will be better if we aren't so far away."

"I don't know; I have doubts it will ever be safe again. Someone always remembers stuff like that at the most inconvenient time," muttered Arcus. "All right, all right. You win. I will try to find someone who can take us to one of the other towns tomorrow. Let's stay the night; it's too late to get a good start today. Come, let's go visit the armory. I'm sure they won't mind if we take a look at their healing salves. The elves store tons of it, like bees with honey."

"Okay, so weapons are over here. Armor is there, various accessories and consumables are on the shelves," said Celeste. "Don't be shy; the king said we could have gear, so feel free."

Theri ran her hands over a set of beautiful, hand crafted, leather armor with a paw print stitched onto the chest piece. "Seriously? Well, that's at least something. I've never seen anything like this stuff."

Celeste looked up. "That's druid armor; they stamp the paw print to show that it's designed to shift with the wearer. It's like a second skin and reforms magically to fit over fur or feathers. Which reminds me. I don't mean to seem rude, and believe me, I appreciate your willingness to help, but we haven't talked about what kind of skills you have. Can you fight? I don't sense any magic in you."

"I can fight a little. My people don't often use weapons, choosing instead to use what the gods gave us." Theri flexed her hand, showing her sharp looking retractable claws. "Plus, I'm a pretty decent tracker, if I do say so myself."

"Hmm...try this one," Celeste led Theri to a set of leather armor with leaves imprinted up and down the sides. "This armor is meant to help you blend in. It looks like it's a perfect fit for you, and look at this." She held up some bracers. "These are for shifters. They are called 'bracers of the bear'. Basically, they are meant to give druids extra power when turned into an animal with claws, like a bear. I bet they will work for you even without being able to shift."

Celeste picked up a longbow and quiver full of arrows, examining each of them, before replacing them on the rack. She moved farther and grabbed another longbow, this one a pale blue color that appeared translucent. The quiver next to it held only three arrows. Celeste grabbed an arrow and nocked it, before releasing it toward a target on the other side of the room. As the arrow made impact, ice formed and spread around the target. Celeste looked back at the quiver, seeing there were still three arrows inside. "Perfect," she said. Celeste grabbed the druid armor, bow and quiver, then moved over to the shelves to examine the consumables. She picked up a few jars of salves and several bottles of a glowing blue substance, and then shoved them into a bag. Finally, she moved over to the jewelry and was examining the rings when she heard footsteps approaching. She quickly chose one and placed it on her finger, before turning to greet whoever was entering.

"It's no trouble, Arcus. Of course you may take whatever you like. We make this stuff, but rarely have need of it. I can have a couple of sentries take you to Abhainn in the morning. We trade with them regularly, as you know. From there, you'll have a much easier time traveling to Gormloch," Tarnelius stated.

"I appreciate everything you've done for me, Tarnelius. Now, as well as before," said Arcus.

"Yeah, thanks a lot," agreed Joseph.

"So, you're leaving for Abhainn in the morning?" Celeste interrupted.

Arcus blushed. "Celeste, I didn't expect to run into you again so soon. Yes, we are leaving for Abhainn. I am sorry but we will not be accompanying you."

"I see. Well, I suppose I understand," Celeste mumbled sadly.

"Celeste, I'm glad I found you; I wanted to give you something for your trip. Wait here, please. I'll be right back," Tarnelius said. He turned and left the way he came before Celeste could protest.

"Great. Well, Theri, come meet Arcus and, I'm sorry, I don't believe I know your friend's name," Celeste said.

"Joseph," said Arcus.

"Joseph," repeated Celeste, still staring at Arcus.

"Hi," Theri put her stuff down, trotted up to the others and stuck out her hand, with a huge toothy grin on her face.

Arcus and Joseph both shook her hand, and gazed at her with curiosity. "You're a kedistam!" Joseph exclaimed.

"Shhh, don't tell anyone," said Theri as she winked.

"What are you doing so far north?" Joseph asked. "I've only seen your kind once, in Izmar, on a trading ship."

"I'm doing what I can to help Celeste. My shaman sent me, so I know it must be important. We have to stop King Liam from destroying the world."

"Theri!" Celeste scolded.

"Well, it's not like it's a big secret. It's true. If he isn't stopped, he will release some big evil to control and destroy the world," argued Theri.

Arcus stared at Celeste and Theri with wide eyes for a moment. "How is this possible? King Liam rules the paladins; they don't have a single evil bone between them."

Celeste sighed. "We think he has been corrupted. I don't know; I haven't even spoken to him or done anything to assess the situation. All I know is he will be leaving to excavate the holy tombs in the north at some undisclosed time in the future. Axistra has seen it. Maybe it'll be tomorrow, maybe next year. Either way, we have to try to stop him. Axistra warned me to bring help, or I would fail. I hope I can pick up some others on the way."

"Excuse us for a moment, ladies. Joseph, I need to speak to you, privately." Arcus gestured out of the armory, back the way they had come.

They walked a fairly good distance away before Arcus spoke. "Elves have excellent hearing, so we needed some space. Even so, keep your voice down. Look, I still think we need to go. I've been feeling an inexplicable draw toward Lumernia ever since we arrived in the woods. I think it may be our destiny."

"Your destiny, Arcus. Not ours," said Joseph.

Arcus stared at Joseph, at a loss for words.

"I feel nothing toward Lumernia except apprehension. It's far. The way to get there is dangerous, and the destination now sounds dangerous as well. I never wanted to be a fighter. I may have magic in my blood, but I don't have your instincts. You should go. I see how you look at that woman."

"I'm not looking at her any way at all!" Arcus protested. "I just think she needs our help."

"Whatever you have to tell yourself, but all I know is she is the first female I've even seen you speak with, for more than two words, in a long time. Look, that Tarnelius guy said he could send us to Abhainn. He could send just me, alone, even more easily. My folks are there. I'll be fine."

Arcus continued to regard Joseph silently.

"As long as I've known you, you've wanted to find your place. It wasn't here, it wasn't in Izmar. Maybe it's in Lumernia. Go! I'll just have to learn to keep myself out of trouble," Joseph said with a wink.

Arcus chuckled. "But you never learn, Joseph."

"Well, I'll have to. Don't worry about me, seriously. Go save the world." Joseph reached out and clasped Arcus' forearm in a handshake, then turned and walked back toward their guesthouse without another word.

Arcus stared after him, torn in his decision on what to do. On the one hand, he did feel an instinctive draw toward Lumernia and Celeste's task; on the other hand, he was convinced Joseph would get himself killed on his own.

Tarnelius found Arcus like that several minutes later. He was carrying a rapier with intricate script on the scabbard and a beautiful leaf-patterned guard.

"Everything all right, Arcus?" he asked.

"Yeah, um, yes." Arcus cleared his throat. "Yes, everything is fine. Listen, there's been a slight change of plans. Can you arrange for Joseph to be taken to Abhainn tomorrow alone? I am going to help Celeste get to Lumernia."

Tarnelius smiled. "I'm glad to hear that. I'd go with her myself, but my father has forbidden it, and truth be told, I don't believe she would allow it. I'm glad to hear she will have someone watching her back. Please keep her safe for me."

"Who is she, Tarnelius? I've never seen her here before."

"No, you wouldn't have. She and I grew up here together, over eight hundred years ago. She left here when my father told me that she and I could never be together; but that was eons ago, back when he thought he still had some control over my decisions. Anyway, I've always loved her, and I think that, once, she felt the same. Does she know yet that you will go with her?" Tarnelius asked.

"No. I'd hoped Joseph would come too, but he refused. He's just left."

"Let's go tell her together," said Tarnelius. The two set off back toward the armory.

"So elves don't kill animals for food, but doing it to craft armor is okay?" Theri asked Celeste, as the two men approached.

Celeste chuckled. "The leather is actually made of flax fiber and palm oils. It's been magically enhanced and is stronger than traditional leather. Nice try."

Tarnelius cleared his throat, drawing the two women's attention back to them. He approached Celeste and held out the rapier to her. "I wanted you to have this. It's called *Yildurim*. It's from the royal vault, and used to belong to my mother."

Celeste took the sword and drew it, admiring the etching up and down the blade. She replaced it in its scabbard and caressed it. "It's beautiful, Tarnelius, but I can't accept it."

"Why not? You won't accept anything else from me, Celeste. Let me give you this. Let me make sure you are armed and ready to face anything you come across. If I ever meant anything to you, take this sword. For me."

Celeste swallowed hard. "All right, Tarnelius. You win. I'll take it, but only on the condition that you let me go, me *and* my memory. What is can never be changed, and you need to let go."

"I accepted that I lost you long ago. Seeing you here again has just been a shock," he whispered, a pained look on his face.

Celeste nodded and strapped the sword to her thin waist. She gathered up the rest of the gear she had chosen and started to walk past the men.

"Celeste, there's more," Tarnelius said. She stopped and looked back up in annoyance. "Arcus has news for you as well."

Arcus cleared his throat. "Celeste, I will come with you to Lumernia, if you still want my help."

Celeste froze, stunned. "What made you change your mind?"

"I have been trying to fight it, but I feel drawn to Lumernia. I think whatever my destiny is lies that way. Plus, you clearly need help," said Arcus.

"I don't 'clearly' need help! I only asked because Axistra told me to find help."

Theri ran up, dropping her stuff on the floor. "What Celeste means is, 'thank you, yes, we appreciate all the help we can get.'" She flung her arms around Arcus' neck, who patted her on her back stiffly, not sure how to respond to the furry woman that was hugging him.

Celeste sighed, chagrined. "She's right, I was out of line. Thank you so much for coming with us. We really can use all the help we can get. Help yourself to supplies. King Audelthus said he would provide us with whatever gear we needed. Come on, Theri, let's go. Get your stuff." She breezed past the others. "We'll leave at dawn. Meet us by the path to the sacred tree," she called out over her shoulder.

Theri scrambled to catch up, while Arcus watched Celeste walk off. "What have I gotten myself into?" he asked Tarnelius, who had no answer.

"Celeste, don't you think you could have been a little nicer to Arcus? He didn't have to come with us, you know?" Theri scolded.

"I know, I know. I already apologized. I kind of freaked when he said I needed his help. I've gone so long by myself I'm not used to needing anyone."

"Well, if you want to have any chance of making this work, you need to learn to accept help and do it graciously."

"I know. I'm sorry." Celeste moved around the house, looking for anything else she might need to take with her. She'd already decided to bring her mother's ruby pendant, as well as some other small jewelry with less sentimentality, in case they needed to sell them for equipment on the way. Never hurts to be prepared. She packed the druid armor and other magical items from the armory. She also gathered a few of her signature green dresses, as well as her beautiful white satin gown for her audience with King Liam. She grabbed a couple of blankets for herself, and brought some more out for Theri. She bundled the dried food and canteens she had picked up, as well as a few other odds and ends, and finally placed everything in the magical bag her father had left behind. The bag was special because it looked like a small nondescript satchel but, in reality, could hold an amazing amount of items. As a child, she had loved stuffing anything she could find into it, trying to fill it up. When she finished packing, she set the bag near her bed and bade Theri goodnight.

Celeste woke early and sat in the dark, thinking about their upcoming trip. Elves don't need much sleep, luckily. It was then she realized Joseph hadn't returned with Arcus, and there had been no mention of him. *What is going on?* She wondered. *Why would he leave his friend to help us?* About an hour before dawn, she woke up Theri, then began to get ready.

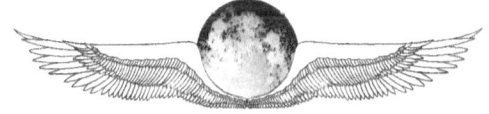

"Well, I guess that's everything," Joseph said, sealing his pack.

"You're sure you don't want to come with us?" Arcus asked.

"Yes, I'm positive. You may be destined for big things, but I'm destined for warm beds and beautiful women. You were right, by the way, none of the women here would look at me twice."

Arcus laughed. "Most elves live hundreds or thousands of years. They know you aren't in it for the long haul."

"I never offered commitment. I don't see why race should matter," complained Joseph.

"You might not, but they do. Listen, take care of yourself, man. Remember, don't toy with your enemies –"

"It just pisses them off," finished Joseph.

"Exactly." Arcus smiled and shook Joseph's hand. "Here, I brought you some healing salves from the armory. Save them for emergencies, and be careful out there. I hope we see each other again someday."

"Me too."

They were interrupted by a knock at the door. Joseph picked up his bag and answered, seeing the female sentry they had met on their trip in. "I've been told you want to go to Abhainn. I can take you there."

Joseph answered with a charming smile. "Sounds great. I'm all set. When we get there, you can let me buy you a drink at the local bar, maybe let me show you around."

Arcus chuckled. "You really aren't ever going to learn. See you around, my friend."

"Take care, Arcus." Joseph waved.

Arcus stood for a moment and stared at the door after it closed behind Joseph, then went and gathered his belongings to go meet Celeste and Theri.

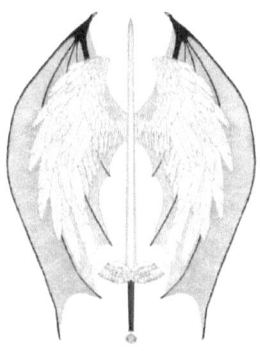

Chapter Eight
Revelations

"For the last time, I don't think he's coming, Theri. We should go."

"Five more minutes?" Theri asked.

"It's already been half an hour since dawn. He's clearly decided to go with his friend to Abhainn," said Celeste.

Theri sighed. "I guess you're right." The pair started walking down the path. They had travelled only a few minutes when Celeste suddenly stopped and whirled around.

"He's coming!" Celeste exclaimed.

"He is? That's great! How do you know it's him, though?"

"Humans have heavier footfalls than elves. Let's go back."

They hurried back to where they had been waiting, and found Arcus standing there.

"This wasn't the right spot?" Arcus asked.

"It's the right spot; we just thought you had changed your mind. I'm so glad you're here," Celeste exclaimed.

"Sorry, I was running late. I had to see Joseph off. Let's go."

They started back down the path leading to the grove, picking their way carefully along the rocky mountain path.

"Why didn't Joseph come along?" Theri asked.

"I'm not really sure. I think he doesn't have enough confidence in his abilities. He said he wanted to go home and see his parents," said Arcus.

"Why didn't you go with him?" wondered Celeste.

"I don't know. Just after arriving in these woods night before last I felt a pull toward Lumernia. To be honest, I was astonished to find out you were going there as well."

"Night before last?" Celeste stopped to look at him directly.

"Yes, we came in via plant walk. I found a sentry after we ran into the woods," said Arcus.

"Night before last was when Axistra told me to go to Lumernia. What are the chances?" Celeste murmured and started walking again.

"So, Celeste, you said you'd tell me everything, so spill. Now seems as good a time as any," urged Arcus.

"What do you want to know?" Celeste asked.

"Well, for starters, explain the angel wings."

"My father was a seraph, a herald of Melek. He died in the Deity War over eight hundred years ago. I was raised in the elven town of Kayalost until I left there at around the age of two hundred. That story is long and depressing, and you probably already heard it from Tarnelius." Celeste continued to talk, explaining about the history of the deities, leading to the Deity War. Arcus listened intently, asking few questions. After several hours, they arrived at the cypress grove and the Sacred Tree, where they stopped to rest for a bit and eat, fully aware they were under the scrutiny of the cypress guard.

"If we keep going at this pace, we should be able to reach the eastern edge of the forest in a little over a week. The tough part will be getting down out of the mountains. The ground past here is rocky and sometimes treacherous, as it isn't well maintained or even used often. Watch your footing," Celeste advised. "Theri, you may want to scout ahead a bit. Arcus and I don't exactly clank like paladins when we walk, but you'll still be quieter than we will."

"If you run into any trouble, be sure you come back to us, don't try to deal with it on your own, and don't get so far ahead we can't help you quickly," Arcus added.

"Right. Exactly what I was about to say," said Celeste. "Anyway, past this point, other than the odd sentry keeping an eye on things, the forest becomes wild and unclaimed. Anything could be hiding in the woods."

"I'll be like a shadow, don't worry about me," exclaimed Theri. She jumped to her feet. "Are we ready?" The other two stood up and Theri dashed off to get a head start.

Arcus and Celeste both knelt before the Sacred Tree, fists over their hearts, as was the custom. Then they stood and followed after Theri.

"Can you shift forms, Arcus?" Celeste asked after walking a mile or so.

"Only into bird form. I take the form of a grackle. I left before I ever attempted any other forms."

"Maybe on our journey I can teach you some more," said Celeste. "It won't be too hard to figure out now, since you've already mastered one form. It's just mind over matter. As a druid, our animal forms are just as much a part of us as the ones we were born with. I can turn into most of the animals I've seen in the forest – aah!" Celeste yelped as her foot slipped on some loose rocks and she skidded down a few feet before catching herself.

"Celeste, are you okay?" Arcus called, trying to get down to her without falling himself.

"Yes, fine, just a little shaken up. Looks like I should have taken my own advice," Celeste answered, chagrinned. "I hope Theri is being careful. I can't see or hear her at all anymore."

"I'm sure she'll be fine," said Arcus.

They continued walking for a short time in amiable silence. "So what is the deal with you and Tarnelius?" Arcus asked.

"We used to... um... we had –" Celeste sighed. "Didn't he tell you?"

"He told me that he has always loved you. He offered no details and I didn't pry. When I was a child, I never heard any mention of you. Although, now that I think about it, I thought the house I often met him in seemed a little feminine. I figured it was his mother's, but it was the same house I saw you standing in when I arrived."

"His mother died in childbirth. Neither of us has any memory of her. Anyway, I used to love him, but he was promised to the Princess of the Silver Iles and I stepped out of the way so they could be together."

"Who?"

"Princess Velonessa. His mate," Celeste spat out bitterly.

"His mate?" Arcus asked with a shocked look on his face. "Celeste, Tarnelius isn't bonded to anyone. Why would you think that?"

Celeste whirled around and slid down more loose rocks. "You're wrong. His father told him he was to be bonded with her. Perhaps she was with her people on the Silver Iles while you lived there."

"I'm telling you he isn't bonded with anyone. That is a fact. He and his father have a very strained relationship, and there are rumors it had something to do with a broken betrothal."

"If that were true, why wouldn't he tell me? I know I apparently was too hard to find over the last few centuries, but what about the last couple of days?" Celeste demanded.

"I don't know why he wouldn't tell you. I suspect he thinks you have moved on and don't love him anymore. Or perhaps he tried to tell you and you wouldn't hear it. Or maybe a mixture of the two, or an entirely different reason," said Arcus. "Either way, does it matter? You – we – have a mission in Lumernia to focus on."

"I – I mean, you're right." Celeste sighed, a tormented look on her face. "The mission is the most important thing right now. Anything else can come after, if it is meant to be."

They continued to walk toward the eastern border, their trip uneventful. Toward nightfall, Theri reappeared to tell them that she had found a defensible area where they could make camp for the night. Celeste cast a simple spell to create delicious berries that were perfectly ripened and sweet. Eating them made the group feel refreshed and revitalized. Theri chased a rabbit, and although Celeste tried to stop her, she was too late. Before long, Theri was smacking her lips happily, and licking the last of the rabbit juices off her fingers with a distinctly feline grin on her face. They set the watch for the night, which passed uneventfully.

The second day continued much the same as the first. Theri took to hunting small game alone while scouting ahead and eating it raw. During her watch that night, she caught and cooked a squirrel that came too near. Celeste and Arcus both continued to create the magical berries at regular intervals. So began a pattern that they all fell into as easily as if they had been traveling together for years.

Almost a week into their travels found Arcus and Celeste engrossed in a discussion about their druidic abilities, as well as Arcus' sorcery, when they came across an area of underbrush that had been trampled not long before. The ground was covered in patches of fresh blood, and the two stopped in concern. They had not heard from Theri for a couple of hours, which wasn't unusual, but she should have let them know something was up. They searched the clearing for any clues that could explain what had happened.

Celeste found a patch of fur that looked like it came off a leopard. "Oh no," she whispered. "Theri's fur. I haven't seen any signs of predatory cats out here, so it must be hers."

"Orcs!" Arcus snarled, with all the vehemence of a venomous snake. He grabbed a poorly made black tipped arrow with raven feather fletching from the ground. His hands, which had burst into flame as he struggled to maintain control, shook as the arrow incinerated into ash.

Celeste released her wings and looked around, her eyes wide. "We have to find her," she exclaimed. She closed her eyes, trying to concentrate on any sounds, but heard nothing but the wind.

A moment later, her eyes snapped open and she twisted to the left, deflecting another black arrow with a swoop of her wing. She and Arcus turned to face the oncoming threat as ten orcs ran into the clearing from between the trees. They were short and muscular with thick necks, large noses and small, close-set eyes. Their skin was a greenish-gray color, and they were dressed in crudely made armor. Seven of the orcs were brandishing swords or machetes. Celeste began to chant as they approached. The vines and grass under the orcs' feet came alive at her words, slithering toward the orcs and ensnaring two of them. Two more orcs made it through and swung their swords at her. She parried one by deflecting the attack with her right wing, but the other stabbed her in the side. She gasped in pain and drew her rapier.

Three of the orcs charged Arcus, whose hands and arms were now covered in flames. Their crudely made swords flashed in the sun. Arcus screamed out his fury as his body began to grow larger and hairier. Within seconds, he was the biggest black bear any of them had ever seen. Even more intimidating, his front paws and legs were still on fire. He swung at the nearest orc, cleaving his head clean off his body. Blood spurted in a pulsing rhythm, matching the still-beating heart of the dead orc. He roared again as the two other orcs slashed at him with their swords. The final three were all archers. They all shot their arrows at the massive bear, which embedded deep into his hide.

The two orcs who were entangled fought hard to struggle free. They hacked at the vines, but every time they cut through any of the entangling plants more would appear to take their place.

Celeste thrust her rapier at the orc that had stabbed her, plunging it deep into the creature's thick neck and twisting. Then she released the sword as she beat her wings and rose into the air, hovering about ten feet off the ground. The orc gurgled and squealed in agony as it tried to remove the sword from its throat, while the other swung in vain at Celeste as she lifted into the air. Her eyes rolled back into her head as she once again chanted. Storm clouds gathered above them and it began to rain. Thunder boomed in the air.

Arcus swung at the orcs with his fiery front paws, roaring in anger. He began to resemble a massive hairy pincushion as the archers relentlessly shot at him. He bit one of the orcs hard on the face, latching on and shaking his head as he lifted the creature into the air as easily as a rag doll.

Giving up on his prey, the unwounded orc that had been attacking Celeste rushed to dog pile on the bear with the rest of his brethren. Celeste's eyes snapped open abruptly, and she screamed and pointed at that orc. Lightning flashed. The orc was struck in the face and collapsed to the ground, dead, smoking slightly in the gathering storm. *Three down, seven to go,* she thought as she looked around.

Arcus finished ripping the face off his second victim, and tossed him aside like a broken toy. Then, he lunged onto his third, and final, sword-wielding attacker, crushed him to the ground and snapped his neck. More arrows made purchase in his thick hide and Arcus fell onto the body of his last victim, severely wounded.

Celeste cried out and pointed at one of the archers, lightning exploding from the sky to strike the orc. The air was heavy with the smell of ozone and cooked orc. *Make that four still left. I sure hope Arcus is okay. Looks like it's up to me.*

The remaining two archers returned fire at her, and one managed to strike her in the thigh with his black feathered arrow. Her concentration broken, the vines released the two orcs who were still entangled, and they quickly charged the one target they could reach – Arcus.

Suddenly, a lone warrior in a dark green hooded cloak jumped out of the trees behind the remaining two archers, slicing the head off one of them before spinning in place to deliver a fatal stab to the second with skillful use of his dual swords. Grateful for the help, Celeste pointed at one of the last two orcs that were rushing toward Arcus, and lightning struck him dead, mid-step. The unexpected stranger tumbled into the air, nimble as an acrobat, over the two bodies of the orcs he had slain. His swords flashed a dark purple color as he swung his weapons at the last orc, who parried one sword but squealed in pain as the smaller sword in the warrior's left hand was buried deep in his chest.

Celeste landed clumsily on her injured leg, which still had a black-tipped arrow sticking through it. Releasing the spell controlling the storm, she limped toward Arcus, who lay bleeding on top of the orc he had last killed. Her hands glowed bright blue as she began healing him. "Hold on, Arcus, it will be okay," she soothed, in a sing-song voice, as she cast healing spell after healing spell.

The stranger's head jerked up at the sound of an awful wet gasping sound. His sword ready, he prowled toward the orc that had Celeste's sword still protruding from its neck. The creature had fallen to the ground, and was writhing as he struggled to breathe. With a quick stab of his longsword, the stranger quickly ended the orc's suffering. Removing the delicate elven rapier from the body, he hurried back to Celeste and Arcus.

"Where is the kedistam?" Tarnelius asked, as he pulled his hood back.

Celeste was so shocked that she fell over, unceremoniously, onto the ground next to the great bear. Her wings stretched across the ground behind her. "You?" she gasped. "What are *you* doing here?"

Arcus began to stir and tried to rise to his feet, but Celeste was having none of it. "Don't change back," she said. "We have to get the arrows out first. I know shifting will heal you, but I want to make sure we don't rearrange those arrows into any important organs. Right now, none of them are sticking into anything vital; let's keep it that way." Arcus grunted in understanding.

"Well, Tarnel, your timing could not have been better. Since you are here now, could you help me with Arcus?" Celeste tried to stand, but her leg shook beneath her and she fell back to the ground.

"You haven't called me Tarnel in a long time," he said, his voice gruff. "Of course I will help, but let's get you patched up first."

Tarnelius knelt down next to her, and handed her a stick to bite on. "This is going to hurt a lot; brace yourself." Tarnelius examined the arrow, which had embedded all the way through her leg. He snapped the head off the arrow, causing her to cry out as the arrow pushed against her wounds. Then he yanked the arrow out and tossed it away. His hands turned blue under his bracers and he touched one to her leg and the other to her bloodied side, healing both. He stood and reached his hand out to her to help her up. The two turned toward Arcus, and went to examine the arrows.

"A lot of these are really deep," Celeste murmured. "Unfortunately, the heads are barbed. We'll have to make incisions to get them out. Do you have a dagger, Tarnel?" Tarnelius reached under his cloak, pulling out two daggers. "These will do. Arcus, I thought you said you couldn't shift into anything but a grackle."

Arcus growled, unable to answer her. His bear form didn't allow for human speech.

"Well, let's get started," she said to Tarnelius. "I count eighteen in all. We'll need to heal locally as we go; we don't want to send him back into shock." Tarnelius nodded in agreement and they set to work.

They made small incisions, so they could safely pull the arrowheads out of Arcus' thick hide. Brief flashes of blue punctuated each successful removal, until they were finally all free. Arcus shifted back into his human form, the last of his wounds closing as he transformed.

"Thanks," he said. "I've never changed into a bear before. I didn't know I could. All I know is, I saw the orcs run in, and I felt rage course through me. The next thing I knew I was all huge and hairy."

"Well, you didn't lose your burning hands when you changed. That was really something," Celeste said. "I was impressed. I bet, in time, you could learn to cast while shifted." The group began to take stock of the situation as they searched the dead orcs for anything useful, but they only found weapons that weren't worth the effort of carrying. Celeste cleaned off her rapier and replaced it in her scabbard.

"We need to find Theri. Other than 'that way'," she said, gesturing toward the trampled underbrush leading deeper into the trees, "I don't know where they might have taken her."

"Are we even sure she is still alive?" Arcus asked.

"No, but we need to try to find her, in case she is," said Celeste.

"They just tried to kill us. I can't see any reason they would have for keeping Theri alive," said Arcus. "It certainly wouldn't be to try to ransom her off; who would they ransom her to, with us dead?"

Tarnelius cleared his throat. "Celeste, I think Arcus is right. There is no way she is still alive. We should mourn her and move on. We have to finish your quest or we are all dead."

"First of all, Tarnelius, 'we' do not need to finish any quest. Your place is with your people and you need to go back to them. Second, I do not care what the likelihood is of her survival. Until I see proof that she is dead I will not give up. Third, the king may not have even thought of going to the tombs yet. That might not happen for ten years, or ten months, or maybe it already happened and we are too late. Axistra's visions never have a timetable attached to them. Last point, I refuse to give up on her. I know she wouldn't give up on me, if the roles were reversed. That's final! Are we clear?" Celeste glared at the two men.

Arcus stared at the female, shocked at her outburst.

Tarnelius looked a little chagrined. "Yes, we are very clear, except for one point – your first point. My place is here, by your side. This has always been my place, even when you took away my right to make my own decisions. You need me right now to help you complete your quest, so for once in your life will you stop being such a stubborn and intractable female? Now, let's go find your friend." With that, he pulled his hood back over his head and began walking in the direction the orcs had come from, leaving no room for argument.

"Tarnel, wait!" Celeste called.

He paused, turning back to glance at her. "What?"

"We should shift. All of us can shift, and we would move much faster with wings or on four legs. Plus, we can track her better with an animal's keen sense of smell."

Celeste shifted into a sleek Amur tiger, while Tarnelius nodded and shifted wordlessly into a bloodhound.

Celeste looked back at Arcus. "Go ahead, Arcus. Think of whatever animal you want to shift into. Picture it. Imagine what it would feel like to be that animal. Focus. You can do it."

Arcus' eyes went wide. "How are you talking to me like that?"

"Lots of practice," answered Celeste. "Now focus."

Tarnelius sniffed around the entrance to the clearing as he tried to pick up Theri's scent. After only a short search, he howled in success.

Arcus shimmered momentarily, then dropped down onto all fours as he became a sleek black panther.

"Nice job," said Celeste. "Now, let's go."

The three raced into the forest to the southwest, as fast as Tarnelius' nose would allow.

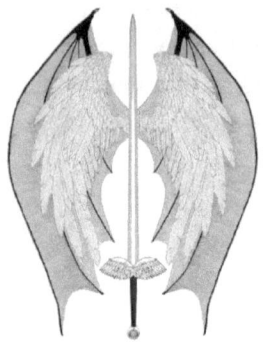

Chapter Nine
Full Disclosure

The trio raced through the woods and managed to catch up to the large band of orcs in only a little over an hour. They had Theri, her hands and feet bound to a long stick that two of the orcs carried between them. The three could not tell whether she was unconscious or dead. Her head hung unsupported at an uncomfortable looking angle. They scrutinized her as the orcs passed, and were finally able to make out shallow breathing. Two other orcs, wearing hooded cloaks, were walking either side of their prize and appeared unarmed. Five archers were recognizable from their bows and large quivers, while there were a dozen more armed with swords of various type. The two large cats and hound exchanged glances; this group was more than twice the size of the last one. They needed a plan.

The three crept away from the group without a sound. When they were a safe distance away, they transformed back into their normal forms.

"I have just the spell in mind. I'll hit them with the sun's radiance first, to blind them. Tarnel, think you are up to a minor earthquake spell?"

"I don't know, Celeste, it's been a long time since I've attempted that spell. Even if I manage it, it's tough to control," answered Tarnelius, his tone doubtful.

"Do you have a better idea to knock them off their feet?"

"No, I don't," Tarnelius sighed.

Arcus thought for a moment. "Celeste, can you cast the earthquake spell? I could probably do something to hamper their vision. Though it will also make it hard for us to see them, as it would be a thick fog."

"Hmm," said Celeste. "Possible, but problematic."

"It's too bad there is no fire. I could set off some pyrotechnics that would blind them," said Arcus.

Celeste smiled, as she exchanged a look with Tarnelius. He nodded and knelt down to pick up some berries from a nearby bush. "Not a problem, Arcus. We'll need to get ahead of the orcs, and Tarnel will enchant some berries to burst into flame when stepped on. Then, do your thing, and I will knock them over. With them blind and down, they should be easy pickings. Arcus, please try not to transform during the battle. I think your spells will be more useful, and we still need to work on controlling your magic while shifted. Be ready to take them out once they hit the ground. Other than our two opening attacks, try to avoid large area magic; we don't want to hurt Theri."

"She may end up blinded as well, though," pointed out Arcus.

"I know, but we can fix that afterward. Besides, she's unconscious. It may not have any effect on her at all," said Celeste.

"Well, it wouldn't need to be fixed; the blindness is only temporary. I just didn't know what your plans were for getting to her."

"We maintain focus and rescue her when her captors are dead," said Celeste. "Okay, are we all ready? We'll need to fly to get far enough ahead of them."

The two men agreed. Tarnelius cast his spell on the berries and placed them carefully in his bag before shifting into a golden eagle. Celeste transformed into a red-tailed hawk, and Arcus turned into a grackle. The three took off through the trees, dodging and weaving. They caught back up to the orcs in only a few minutes, as the large group was making slow progress through the dense trees with their heavy burden. They kept flying, stopping about a half a mile ahead of the group and shifting back.

Tarnelius pulled out the berries and began spreading them across the ground as strategically as possible. Then they all backed away from the path and hid behind the trees.

Before long, the orcs made their appearance, joking and laughing with each other, oblivious to the danger they were about to be in. Suddenly, the one in the lead stopped as a berry went up in flames with a minor explosion. Then, there was another one, and another, as more berries were stepped on. The orcs looked perplexed as they began to gather around the flaming berries. Arcus cast his spell, and the small fires lifted into the air and exploded in a spectacular rainbow of colors. The three, still hidden behind the trees, turned their backs as soon as the spell was cast. Once they heard the shouts of confusion, they spun back around and saw the orcs clutch their faces. Celeste rushed to the edges of the orc band and knelt down to cast her spell. As she concluded, she slapped the ground and backed up as fast as she could. Small tremors started from the place she had touched, and moved toward the group of orcs. The small vibrations escalated into a massive earthquake. Celeste stared at the mayhem in complete concentration, as she willed the quake to increase and decrease at her whim.

The two hooded orcs were the only ones that weren't in a full blown panic. They each put a hand on their prize – Theri – and simultaneously spoke a word of magic. All three vanished with a pop. Seeing this, Celeste shouted in rage. A fissure opened in the ground on which the mages had been standing. Three of the orc band and a tree all fell into the chasm. Tarnelius stepped forward and placed a hand on her shoulder, wordlessly trying to tell her to calm down. Then, he ran forward into the earthquake zone, drawing his swords as he went. Arcus chased after him, holding his hands outstretched in front, with his palms facing outward. A massive fireball shot out of his hands, hitting the line of archer orcs that were in the back of the group. Celeste fell to her knees in exhaustion and buried her face in her hands, feeling defeated by the loss of Theri. The ground stopped shaking the moment she released her focus on the spell.

Arcus and Tarnelius made short work of the blinded orcs, using swords and magic to kill them with ease. Tarnelius knelt near the fissure and cast a spell to cause the ground nearby to soften and fill in, burying those inside.

Finally, all that were left were the two that had been carrying Theri before the orc mages had whisked her away. Arcus zapped the nearest one with lightning to the chest, but as Tarnelius reached to slit the throat of the final one, Celeste's head snapped up.

"Wait, don't kill that one!" Celeste shouted. Tarnelius froze, the screaming orc held fast in his arms. Celeste stood up and ran toward him. "They took Theri. This orc is our only chance of finding her," she insisted.

Tarnelius nodded. "Find something to serve as rope."

Celeste grabbed some vines off a nearby tree, reinforcing them with magic before handing them to Tarnelius to tie the orc up with.

"How long will the blindness last?" Tarnelius asked Arcus.

"Not long, maybe only another minute or so."

"Good, then he can walk if need be," Tarnelius said.

Celeste circled the orc with a sneer on her face. "Where did they take her?"

"How should I know? Do I look like a mage?" The orc's voice was high-pitched, but scratchy. The sound grated on their nerves.

Celeste slapped him across the face. "Tell me now, or I will kill you where you stand. Where were you headed with her?"

The orc spat at her. Tarnelius shoved him face first onto the ground.

Arcus stepped forward. "I can make this scum talk. Leave me with him for a little bit."

Celeste looked uncertainly at Tarnelius. "Are you sure? What will you do with him?"

"Ask me no questions, and I'll tell you no lies," Arcus answered.

"Walk with me for a moment," said Celeste. "Tarnelius, you have our prisoner under control?"

Tarnelius nodded.

Arcus and Celeste disappeared into the trees. "What is your intent?" Celeste asked after they'd made it out of earshot.

"I'm going to torture and interrogate him. It's better if you delicate elves don't see it," said Arcus.

"We can take it," Celeste argued. "It was my idea to begin with."

"Trust me, you can't."

Celeste swallowed, nervous because of her friend's matter-of-fact tone. "You don't like orcs much, do you, Arcus?"

"Nope. They killed my parents in front of me. If it weren't for the elven sentries, I'd be dead now myself."

Celeste thought for a moment before answering. "You know what? You're probably right. I don't want to know."

Arcus nodded as he started to head back to the orc and Tarnelius. "You two come to this spot," he instructed Celeste. "I will come find you when I have answers."

They returned to the battle site to find Tarnelius exchanging insults with the orc, who had obviously regained his vision. Arcus took over holding the rope, and Celeste called Tarnelius over so they could walk back to the appointed location.

Once they arrived, Celeste plopped down onto the ground at the base of a tree. "Thank you for coming after us," she said. "I – I really do appreciate it."

Tarnelius knelt on the ground next to her. "I've been tracking you since you left. I will never let you get away from me again. You have no idea how hard I've tried looking for you over the last several centuries. Then, when you were finally back within my grasp, you wouldn't even hear me out. Though, I don't know why that should surprise me. You didn't listen back then either."

"I'm sorry, Tarnel," she said. Her eyes were shining as she looked up at him.

"I didn't take the bond with Velonessa. How could you ever think I would? You were supposed to be my soul mate, my *rakastan*. I never wanted anything more than to spend forever with you. I was even willing to run away with you. Instead, I spent six hundred years in utter misery because you wouldn't listen to me," he bit out.

She stared at him, fighting back a lump that had formed in her throat.

"My father is not in charge of my life. Even if that means I can never be king, there are more important things. Only I am in control of what I do with my life. Although you, like my father, seem to think that you are in control of my decisions. Unlike his, your decisions did have a direct impact on mine."

"Tarnel, I'm so sorry! I only wanted to do what was best for both you and our people!" Celeste cried, tears beginning to fall down her cheeks.

Tarnelius glared at her, a furious look on his face. "*You* were what was best for me! You! But you were so impetuous and so convinced that only you knew what was right that you wouldn't hear anything else. I would have done *anything* for you," he continued, his voice pained.

Celeste stared at him, seeing for the first time with absolute clarity what her decision had done to both of them, and to her mother as well. Her self-imposed isolation had ruined so much. She had never felt so lost, so stupid.

Tarnelius snarled in frustration and then he was on her, his lips pressed to hers with a passion she hadn't expected. To be honest, neither had he.

The kiss seemed to ignite them both, and he pulled her on top of him so she would be as close as possible, and even that didn't seem close enough. She moaned against his lips, awakening feelings in him he hadn't felt in centuries. He demanded entrance into her mouth with his tongue, and she was only too glad to give in to him. They explored each other's mouths; their tongues joined in an erotic dance that felt as familiar as if they had had no separation at all. She might not have been perfect, but she still felt perfect for him, and she still completed him. Their closeness wasn't close enough, not for him. Not for her either.

"Tell me where you were taking the kedistam girl," snarled Arcus.

"None of your business," was the answer from the orc. Arcus had tied him to the base of a tree in a sitting position.

Arcus gave the orc a cruel smile and pulled out a dagger. An orc dagger, or at least it used to be. "Do you know what this is?" Arcus asked. He flashed the dagger in front of the orc's eyes. "This is one of the daggers used to murder my parents. As you can see, I've taken the liberty of making some improvements to it. Your poorly made weapons would have never survived the last couple of decades without some work. The elves pulled it from my mother's body before they cremated her. I've repaired it, sharpened it and imbued it with magic. Now, tell me where you scum were taking the kedistam."

"Go to hell," spat the orc.

"That's where you're headed if you don't talk," snarled Arcus. He grabbed the orc's filthy left hand and sliced the thumb off. The orc howled and screamed in pain. Fire flashed as the dagger passed through it, cauterizing the wound as it was created, so that very little blood was spilled. The digit fell to the ground, landing with a slight thud.

"Where?" Arcus shouted.

The orc spat in his face.

Arcus grabbed the other hand and removed his right thumb with another fiery flash. "Pity, you'll have such a hard time gripping things in the future without thumbs. You might as well talk before I get bored with one finger at a time and remove your entire hand, or some other appendage that you might miss even more."

"You…you bastard!" the orc spat.

Arcus stabbed the knife between the orc's ribs, then he twisted it and separated them before removing the dagger. The orc screamed and wheezed; breathing was now painful. "I'm not hearing the answer to my question."

The orc tried to laugh, but it came out more like a cough. "She…she will make an excellent slave," he wheezed.

Arcus stomped on the orc's kneecap, feeling deep satisfaction as the bones shattered under his foot. "You're making this much more painful than it needs to be. Tell me where."

The orc wheezed again and glared in defiance. Arcus knelt down and scooped up a thin tree branch that had fallen to the ground. He examined it for a moment and jerked suddenly, jamming the branch hard between the two of the ribs on the orc's other side, continuing to press in until the orc coughed up blood. Then he knew he had pierced the lung and he smirked.

"I can stop the bleeding with this very dagger, you know. I can end the pain and kill you in the blink of an eye, or I can stop the bleeding and you might live. Doubtful, but possible. I could also simply let you bleed out now. I hear that drowning in your own body fluids is quite horrible. Decisions, decisions."

He stabbed the orc up near the branch and dragged the dagger down across his belly with agonizing slowness, watching the skin seal as he went. The orc gasped rapidly for air, blood dripping from the branch wound and his mouth.

"I'll make a deal with you. Tell me where you were taking her, and I will kill you quickly. Your pain will end mercifully.

Continue to refuse, and I will cauterize your lung and you will experience a new definition of the word 'pain', the likes of which we have only begun to scratch the surface. I wonder how many more parts of you I can remove before you die. Shall we find out together?"

The orc coughed up more blood, finally showing the fear in his small piggish eyes. He opened his mouth and spoke one word, "Medijabal." Then he choked some more and gripped his chest with his mutilated hands.

Arcus nodded once and moved the orc's hands out of the way before placing his own hand on the bloody chest. Electricity shot from his hand, stopping the orc's heart mid-beat. He cut the vines that had served as rope, and let him fall onto to the ground. Then, he turned and left the orc and his comrades to be eaten by the scavenger animals of the forest.

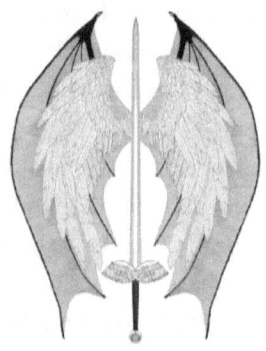

Chapter Ten
Out of the Frying Pan...

Tarnelius broke off the kiss and pushed her away. She stared at him, her large eyes shining. She reached up to touch her swollen lips, shock evident on her face.

"That didn't change anything," he snarled. "I'm still mad at you."

"What was that then?" Celeste asked.

"I just wanted to know if there was still a spark between us. It's been so long, and there you were, and I felt –" he sighed. "I felt like I needed to find out if there was anything still there. I needed to kiss you; to feel your lips on mine."

"Well, did you find out what you wanted to know?" Celeste asked, with a nervous quaver in her voice.

He groaned and buried his face in his hands. "Yes. Yes I did, Kamara help us both."

They continued to sit in awkward silence for several minutes.

"Arcus only just told me after we left Kayalost that you didn't take the bond with her."

"You should have found out from me, not him. It wasn't his place to tell you, but I'm glad he did, because you were, once again, unwilling to listen to *me*. You should have never left. We could have worked things out."

"I thought I was doing the right thing. Truly. I may have made mistakes, and believe me, I know that leaving you is the biggest mistake I have made in my entire life, but I was never trying to hurt anyone."

"Is that so? I believe your exact words were 'maybe I don't love you enough.'"

"I'm sorry, okay? I never meant that." Celeste wiped her nose on her sleeve.

"I never believed you did. Didn't change the pain every time I looked back on that last time I saw you. I wanted to hate you. Sometimes I almost managed it."

"Then why didn't you go ahead and bond with her? Why cause a huge rift with your father over someone you hated?" Celeste asked.

"Because I didn't love her. I felt I would never love her, and that wasn't fair to her or to me. Besides, I said 'almost', and even in the years I was angriest my love for *you* never wavered."

Celeste's heart swelled and she reached for his hand, which he immediately jerked away. "But I'm still angry with you," he said with a glare.

Just then, the pair looked up in surprise as a small fox ran straight toward them before shifting into one of the elven sentries. He was wearing dark green shifter armor and had strawberry blond hair. His large green eyes were angry and reproachful.

"Prince Tarnelius, your father has ordered that you must return to Kayalost."

"Is that so? Well, you may let my father know that I will return when I am good and ready to do so. Right now, Celeste and I have a job to do."

"You know as well as I do that he has decreed none may help her on this mission."

"And yet that was the wrong decision. Her mission holds the lives of us all in the balance. No matter what he says, I will not be returning at this time."

"Prince Tarnelius, I —"

"Did I stutter?"

"No, my Prince, but —"

"But?"

"Prince Tarnelius, he sent all of the sentries out after you. If I were to return without you and he found out that I had let you go, he would station me in Helvettinost."

Tarnelius sighed. Helvettinost was the underground dwelling place of their subterranean cousins, dark-skinned elves who avoided the sunlight. Tarnelius had been there and knew that being stationed in that underground hole might as well be a prison sentence. His people didn't do well underground.

"Come with us, Chathaniar. The king will not be able to reach you."

The sentry lowered his eyes in shame. "In truth, my Prince, I only wish to stay in my forest. Here, I know every tree, every animal. I am afraid to leave, and I do not wish to disobey the king's wishes. You must come back with me; the king's word is law."

"It's okay, Tarnel. I understand. Your duty is to your father, to our people," said Celeste, her voice almost a whisper.

"Do *not* start this with me again, Celeste. I make my own decisions, remember?"

"At the cost of one of your own?"

Tarnelius snarled in frustration as he jumped to his feet and began to pace.

"What is this?" Arcus asked as he approached. "Am I interrupting something?"

"He's here to take Tarnel back with him. King Audelthus has demanded it. Tarnel doesn't want to go, but the king will torture this poor man if he doesn't."

"Is that all? Leave this to me."

Arcus walked over to Chathaniar and snapped his fingers in front of his face before speaking in a hypnotic voice. *"Listen to the sound of my voice. My words are truth. Anything you knew that differs from my words is false."*

"I am listening."

"You have been searching for the prince all this time. You haven't found him." Arcus tipped his head to the side, trying to urge the two elves to get out of sight. To his relief, they caught on quickly and ducked out of sight. *"What you have found was an orc raiding party. They were capturing animals in your forest and you ambushed them just over there, through those trees. There have been many orcs in the woods of late, and they are becoming bolder. You are a hero. You are to return to the village to tell the others what you have done and to advise them to tighten their borders with more sentries."*

"I must return to Kayalost. There are orcs in the forest!"

"There are?" Arcus asked, after snapping his fingers again.

"Yes, I just ambushed a raiding party over there. We need more sentries patrolling our borders. We need to keep the animals safe."

"You should hurry to tell them. I know they will be as worried as you are, and want to do something about this threat."

Chathaniar turned back into a small red fox and spun around to rush back to Kayalost with his big news. Smiling, Arcus set off to find Celeste and Tarnelius.

"Thanks, Arcus. Looks like you've learned some new tricks since I last saw you," said Tarnelius, when Arcus caught up to them. "How did it go with our orc friend?"

"Predictably. In the end, he came around to seeing things from my point of view. Turns out they kept her alive because they intended to sell her into slavery in Medijabal."

"That must be where they teleported," Celeste exclaimed.

"Let's go," agreed Tarnelius.

"Did the orc tell you how to get there?" Celeste asked.

"Nope, he didn't survive long enough."

"We'll need to take to the skies then. A city large enough for an official name could be spotted from the air. Arcus, you'll need to try for a different bird. A grackle won't be able to keep up with us, and doesn't have the necessary eyesight."

Arcus wrinkled his forehead in thought as he focused. He began to rapidly shrink, transforming into a peregrine falcon, his black feathers glistening.

"I'm starting to notice a color theme with you," giggled Celeste. "Anyway, it's perfect." She and Tarnelius transformed into their hawk and eagle, respectively, and they all took off high into the skies.

They soared on the air thermals high in the air, keeping an eye beneath them for any large cities. A little more than three hours later they finally found something promising and began to descend. The city was large and, as they approached it, they could see that it appeared dirty and unkempt. There were many buildings and dwellings made from clay bricks, so the whole general impression was brown and boring. The group split apart and circled at differing heights and different directions so as to not attract attention. On the south side of town, they found an obvious looking market made up of tents of varying colors and stability. Orcs were selling whatever stolen goods they could get their hands on, as well as various food items, weapons, armor, articles of clothing, etc. There was a huge paddock full of grazing horses, cows, pigs and other livestock that was attached to a large barn. Not far from that was another barn without a paddock. This one was locked down tight with bars on the windows and doors, and guards standing outside. Celeste dropped down and landed gracefully on the roof of this building, then pecked at it, trying to listen inside. She heard the sound of various humanoid sounding creatures inside as they moved around and groaned. A few spoke in frightened voices, and chains rattled as they moved. Satisfied, Celeste took back to the skies and flew a short distance away from the city to shift back, safely hidden behind some large boulders. Before long she was joined by Tarnelius and finally Arcus, and they all shifted.

"That barn is clearly where they are housing the slaves. I couldn't tell for sure if Theri was in there, but she probably was," said Celeste. "Anyone have any ideas?"

"Are we only freeing Theri, or all of their slaves?" Arcus asked.

"I'd like to free them all, but my main concern is Theri. We'd never be able to sneak them all out of there, so freeing them all may endanger our escape. On the other hand, they could make a good distraction, but I worry about what cost would come of it." Celeste chewed her lip as she thought.

"This might be a dumb question, but exactly how are we even gaining access in the first place?" Tarnelius asked.

"Honestly, I'm not sure. The way I see it, we have two options; we can use stealth or we can use force," said Celeste.

"Either option is risky," said Tarnelius.

Celeste chewed on her lip, lost in thought. "Arcus, do you have any invisibility spells that would work on all of us?"

"I do, but I think we need to think bigger," countered Arcus. "Personally, I think we need to burn this place to the ground, taking every orc down with it. However, since there are only three of us and many hundreds – or maybe even thousands – of them, this is probably not the most feasible solution, especially considering our limited timetable. What I propose, though, is that Tarnelius and I go in after Theri while you do your level best to flatten some other, yet nearby, location. While the orcs are distracted, we'll rescue any that we can and meet back here." He paused. "However, yes, I do like your invisibility idea. I will cast it on myself and Tarnelius before we go in, as an added precaution."

Celeste stared at him in surprise. "I'm impressed. I – I think that just might work. Anyone have anything to add? Any questions?" Both men shook their heads. "Let's turn back into birds to get into position." With that, they all shifted and took off.

Celeste flew to an area around a mile north of the slave barn, then shifted back in mid-air, her angel wings glistening in the sun. She double-checked to make sure she was too high to be anywhere near arrow range, then decided to begin. Her eyes rolled back in her head as she chanted, and strange reddish storm clouds engulfed the city. Lightning and thunder crashed in the sky menacingly, while rain poured down onto all those below her. After the stage was set, Celeste cast her next spell and waited. East of her location, and well outside of town, some of the heavy clouds began to swirl and circle, forming a funnel which reached all the way down to the ground. Celeste began to fly slowly in large circles, almost dancing in mid-air with her creation, which she then directed into the city itself. South of her, the animals in the paddocks screamed and bolted away from the tornado, breaking the fencing in their terror as they ran for whatever safety they could find. The tornado struck the town, causing massive destruction. Entire buildings were picked up and tossed around like rag dolls, and what wasn't uprooted and thrown was destroyed. Celeste maintained complete single-minded focus as she circled the storm and directed it to start moving slowly and ominously south. The orcs in its path scattered, trying to escape the wrath of the cyclone, and all ran to the west as fast as their legs could carry them. The ones that were not fast enough were picked up and hurled to their doom.

Arcus stared in shock at the storm, which was creeping nearer. The orc guards watched what was happening and took off in fear. They abandoned all those in the slave barn without a second thought and just got out of there. Arcus looked back at Tarnelius. "I think that invisibility spell is unnecessary now. This is nothing like what I expected when I suggested this plan. Remind me to never piss her off."

Tarnelius nodded, and they ran to the door to the barn, trying to shield themselves from the whipping wind and rain as best they could. They tried the door, but it was locked tight, the key most likely with the fleeing guards. Tarnelius kicked at the door, but it was solid and did not budge.

Arcus reached forward, grasping the handle in his hands. It began to glow a bright silver. Ice began to form all over the handle and spread across the door. When it was coated in ice, Arcus stepped back and gestured for the elf to try again. Tarnelius kicked at the door once more. The hinges shattered and burst open.

They wrinkled their noses and gasped at the atrocious smell assaulting them as they entered. The building reeked of feces and death. The interior lighting was poor, though the roaring sound of the wind became muted. They paused for a moment just inside the door, allowing their eyes to adjust.

"What's going on out th – hey! Who the hell are you?" snarled the warden, who had risen from his desk to approach the door. His hand flew to his sheath, and he drew his sword.

Arcus strode toward him. *"Stop moving,"* he said in a hypnotic voice. The orc froze. "That's better," said Arcus. "Now, tell me, are there any more guards in here?"

The warden didn't answer or move in any way. He didn't even blink.

Arcus sighed. "You have to love the weak-willed; they always take things so literally." He approached the orc, and stopped mere inches away. He locked gazes with him and spoke again in that same hypnotic sing-song voice. *"You work for me now. You have always worked for me. I am a good master and you always show me complete loyalty. I release you from my hold spell."*

The orc slumped as he relaxed, dropping his sword on the floor with a clatter.

"Are there any more guards stationed inside this building?" Arcus asked again.

"N – no, master," the warden stammered. "Only myself and the guards outside."

"Excellent," said Arcus. "You have done well. There has been a change of plans for these slaves, and we are moving them to a new location in a different city. Grab your keys and release them immediately."

"Immediately, master," groveled the orc. He grabbed the keys and jogged along the main aisle, unlocking cells and running inside to unlatch leg chains along the way.

Arcus and Tarnelius looked in all the cells, where the slaves were being slow to get up and move. They didn't see Theri in any of the open cells. Arcus called out, "Guard, where is the kedistam that was brought in today?"

"She is in this last cell, master. She has already been purchased and will be picked up tomorrow."

"Release her at once," Arcus commanded.

"M – master, I was told to not open this door under any circumstances," whined the orc.

"I gave you a command, and you work for me, remember? Open that door!"

"Yes, master." The guard fumbled with his keys for a moment, then unlocked a panel next to the door lock and pushed the lock open. Then he swung the door open and gasped. "She's gone! Master, I have no idea where she could be!" He stepped further into the room and was yanked out of sight. There was the sound of a scuffle and the sickening sound of bones snapping. Arcus and Tarnelius ran over to see what was happening. Inside the cell the leg chains were unlatched and the guard was laying on the ground with his neck bent at an odd angle.

"Theri?" called out Arcus. "It's us, come out."

Theri strode out, her face breaking into a wide grin when she saw Arcus. "About time you showed up. I thought I was going to have to break myself out. They believed those chains would hold me; it's insulting, really." She looked at Tarnelius then and frowned. "What are you doing here? Does Celeste know? Actually, where *is* Celeste?"

Tarnelius gave a small smile. "Yes, she knows and we need to get back to her. Help us round up these slaves and get out of here."

Arcus turned around and shouted, "Listen up, everyone. I need you all to move in an orderly line out the door, and we will try to get you all to safety."

There was no response, other than some shuffling about in the cells. The slaves seemed to be confused.

"They are worried you are guards and they will be beaten if they come out. I've got this," said Theri. She ran down the main aisle and screamed, *"Hey everyone! Prison break! Move! Move! Move!"*

That did the trick as around twenty men, women, and even a few dirty children ran from the cells. Most of the slaves were human, but there was also a lone dwarf among them, running out. They ran out the door and saw the storm outside. Most froze in place, panicking. A few ran to the southeast, trying to get away from the storm and out of the city.

"The storm will not hurt you, keep moving, keep moving," Tarnelius shouted.

"How on Altierra could you know that the storm will not hurt us?" asked the dwarf.

"Because we are with the storm. Now move it! You need to be out of here before the orcs notice anything," bellowed Tarnelius. "Head southeast, away from the city!"

The group ran as directed, finally making it back to the same spot the would-be rescuers met to plan their attack. "That's far enough for the moment," Arcus panted. "What do we do about Celeste? We failed to work out how to recall her."

"Celeste is doing that?" screeched Theri in shock.

"I have no idea how to reach her," said Tarnelius. "Her storm winds are too severe for either of us to reach her. It's too risky. We have another problem, too; what do we do with all these people? There are way too many for us to move with any sort of speed, and I doubt many of them know how to fight."

"I could probably help there, lad," the dwarf jumped in. He spoke with an exotic accent that sounded almost musical. "My city is the closest non-orc settlement, though unfortunately we are still looking at a couple of weeks' walk to the north. My kin could help these people return to their homes. Ya?"

Tarnelius nodded. That sounded like the best option for everyone. "Thanks, um, what was your name?"

"Gunnarr," answered the dwarf.

"Thank you, Gunnarr."

Gunnarr bowed his head.

"Wow, just look at the destruction," Arcus mused. "How long can she keep that up?"

"I can't imagine it will be too much longer; a spell like that will drain her quickly. It takes an immense amount of control and focus," Tarnelius replied, chewing his lower lip.

"Help me find materials for a small fire," said Arcus.

Arcus, Theri and Tarnelius began searching the rocky ground for anything they could use for kindling, gathering some dry leaves and a few twigs and small branches. In almost no time at all, Tarnelius had a small campfire built.

"Everyone avert your eyes if you enjoy having your vision!" yelled Arcus. Then he cast his pyrotechnics spell again, sending a rainbow of colored flame exploding high into the sky. "I hope she saw that and the orcs didn't," Arcus said.

"I think she did!" Theri yelled. "She's looking this way!"

Celeste commanded the storm straight into the slave barn, sending debris flying everywhere. In mere moments, all that was left of the building was the foundation. Then, she dropped her arms and the storm began to dissipate. Once the funnel was gone, Celeste turned back into a hawk and began to fly up higher and higher in a northern direction.

"Where is she going?" Theri wondered.

"I'm not sure," Tarnelius answered. "The only thing I can think of is that she didn't want to come straight at us and betray our position in case she was seen."

"We'll wait for her," said Arcus. "She knew where to go, she saw my signal."

The large group settled down to wait behind the boulders. Some of the former slaves were anxious to go and kept fretting that they were going to be found. Arcus, Tarnelius and Theri kept telling them to remain calm and quiet, and promised that even if they were found, they would be safe. A little more than half an hour later, the red-tailed hawk flew around to them from the south, landing near Tarnelius and shifting back. Celeste stood unsteadily without her wings. She was noticeably trembling, and reached out an unsteady hand toward Tarnelius without saying a word. She didn't make it to him and collapsed to the ground, unconscious. Tarnelius gasped and scooped her up in his arms, cradling her to his chest. Arcus helped to pick up the belongings she had dropped when she fell.

"Is she okay?" Theri asked in concern. "What's wrong with her?"

"The spell took too much out of her. She's breathing, so she will be okay. I'm glad she at least made it to the ground before she lost it. Come on, let's get going before the orcs notice this lot is missing."

"I think, technically, they will assume the slaves are all dead, not missing," Arcus said. "She really did a number on that building."

"Okay, everyone, gather round," yelled Tarnelius. "Master Gunnarr has kindly offered to help us get you all home. We need to stay together, and get away from the orc city as quickly and quietly as possible. The distance is not insignificant, but it is necessary if you want to keep your freedom. Onward, Gunnarr! Please lead the way."

The group formed a line following Gunnarr and Theri, who were up at the front. Arcus and Tarnelius, carrying Celeste, brought up the rear behind all the former slaves. They began their steady march toward Gunnarr's homeland.

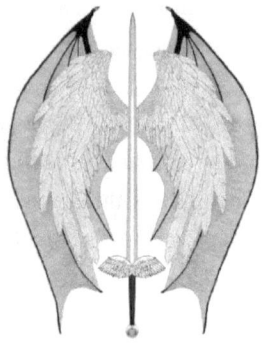

Chapter Eleven
... Into the Fire

The first several miles passed slowly, and everyone looked often over their shoulders to make sure no orc raiding parties were in pursuit. Nothing seemed amiss, however, and the day passed into night. Still, Celeste did not wake up, and Tarnelius began to feel concerned. When they set the watch that night, Tarnelius agreed to a double shift, since elves did not need as much sleep as humans. He and Arcus cast the spell to make the magic berries, and they created a small rain shower to capture the water to drink. Tarnelius made sure Celeste was near him all night, just in case she needed anything, but she seemed to have slipped into a deep coma. Having her so close at all times while he carried her everywhere with him was messing with his head. She seemed so helpless. She needed him. He knew that when she was awake she was anything but helpless, but for now it stirred something deep within him. He struggled to push those feelings away. He needed to hold on to his anger to protect himself. After all, *she* had been the one to leave *him*.

The next morning, the group got up and ate breakfast before preparing to continue their journey. Arcus noticed Tarnelius murmuring to Celeste in the old elven language as he picked her up to begin the march again.

"Do you want me to carry her for a little while?" Arcus offered.

"I've got her, don't worry. She's not heavy," Tarnelius answered.

"Why won't she wake up?"

"She must be too drained from yesterday," said Tarnelius, but the worry was obvious in his green eyes. "She'll wake when she is ready."

"Have you tried poking her with a sharp stick?" interjected one of the refugees.

"You watch your mouth and show respect. If it weren't for his woman, you'd still be chained up like an animal!" Tarnelius snarled.

"Whoa, just asking. I meant no offense," he said, holding his hands up in supplication.

The group walked on, farther and farther north. They stayed together instead of having anyone scout ahead, so that it would be easier to defend the former slaves if they were attacked. After a couple of hours, Theri held up her hand and cocked her head to the side, her ears twitching atop her head. The others strained to listen as well, and after a moment, Tarnelius' eyes widened and he set Celeste down behind some large rocks and placed his satchel on the ground next to her. He gestured to three of the refugees to come to him.

"You three guard her with your lives. Do not stray from her. If you have to run, take her with you. I'm holding you personally responsible for her," he murmured in a severe tone. The three men exchanged nervous glances and nodded.

Tarnelius glanced at the rest of the group. "On second thought, all of you are on guard duty. Stay out of sight over here and be quiet. Theri, Arcus and I will handle this." He wrinkled his nose as he caught a whiff of what was coming.

"I can fight too, if you have an extra sword or axe," Gunnarr offered.

"Ever fought an ogre before?" Tarnelius asked.

"No."

"Well, Celeste has a bow and a rapier. Arcus, give him whichever he wants. If he can't use either, send him back with the group. Theri, you and I need to keep them off Arcus so he is free to cast his spells."

"Them?" Theri asked, her eyes wide.

"That smell is too strong to be only one."

"Should we try to hide, let them pass us?" Arcus asked.

"We could, but the odds are they will notice us. There are an awful lot of us to try to hide. If they are allowed to get close enough, Celeste and the others could be more at risk. Better for us to take them out on our own terms. Come on." He and Theri crept through the rocks and boulders, trying to stay as silent as possible. The others ducked behind rocks and tried to disappear. Arcus handed the weapons to Gunnarr, who set the rapier down and examined the bow and three arrows, wondering what they expected him to do with just those. He decided to save them for emergencies since he only had three shots and had never used a flimsy rapier before. He hid himself behind the rocks with the rest of the group, ready to defend them if the need arose. Finally, Arcus cast an invisibility spell on himself, Celeste and the refugees to try to keep them all safe.

The group fell silent as they waited.

Before long, three of the ten foot tall monsters wandered into sight. Two of them led the way, their beady eyes dull. As they walked, they swung heavy looking clubs that looked like at one time they might have been small trees they had uprooted. The third one looked around as he walked, his sharp eyes taking in every detail. While the other two were almost indecent, clothed in nothing but shredded animal skins, this one was wearing ornate robes and carried no obvious weapons.

The third ogre spoke a sharp word, his guttural language impossible for the elves or humans to understand, and the other two stopped. They looked all around, their expressions suspicious, as Tarnelius and Theri leapt out from their hiding places and attacked.

"Keep the third distracted," shouted Tarnelius as he engaged both of the club wielding ogres at once. He was a blur as he spun around and slashed at the two with both his magical swords.

With a flash of purple light, he sliced an arm off the ogre on his right, causing him to drop his club. The ogre's sickly orange blood spurted out, spraying Tarnelius and the fallen club. Then, he spun around to thrust his shorter sword into the chest of the one to his left.

Theri tumbled past the two fighting Tarnelius and pounced onto the third one. Had she been fighting a normal sized creature, her lunge would have taken them both to the ground. However, the ogre was so large that her pounce merely caused her to latch onto it. She scratched into the ogre's thick skin with all four of her limbs, snarling.

The two on Tarnelius roared. The wounds from Tarnelius' opening attack healed and the one that was still armed swung his club, causing the elf to soar through the air. He crashed several feet away with a loud thud. The other picked up his club with his newly reformed arm and stomped after his prey.

Arcus, who had been awaiting his moment for Tarnelius to get out of the way, became visible as he cast his lightning spell. A long bolt of lightning flew from his hand into the ogre that was moving to Tarnelius. It struck him in the chest, and formed a blackened hole in the monster's flesh. Greasy looking orange blood poured from the wound and the ogre slumped to the ground, dead.

The ogre that had struck Tarnelius turned around to knock Theri from the third ogre's body. She dug in her claws and scratched hard. Unfortunately, the wounds continued to heal. The club wielding ogre smashed his club into them both. Theri lost her grip and was shoved to the ground, as the robed ogre was forced back by the strong hit.

Tarnelius saw stars for a moment, then pushed himself back to his feet. He was sure a couple of his ribs were cracked. "Fire, Arcus, not lightning," he yelled as best he could through the pain, as he retrieved his swords.

"Lightning seems to work just fine, thank you," responded Arcus. Then his eyes widened as the ogre he had killed stood up and grabbed his club. His chest was still blackened, but the hole had sealed. The ogre looked to Tarnelius, but then his head swung back toward Arcus and he grinned as he charged toward the caster who had struck him. His teeth were brown and rotten, with gaps where several had fallen out. Arcus quickly uttered a spell and a large ball of flame shot out and struck the ogre, causing him to writhe as his gray-green skin caught on fire. The ogre fell to the ground, bellowing out a horrible death cry.

The ogre in the back saw this and, responding by yelling out his own garbled spell, he shot an answering ball of fire. Arcus dodged, but the spell still caught him in the arms and shoulder as it hurtled into a boulder. His clothes caught on fire, and Arcus threw his arms into the air and cast again. A huge deluge of water appeared above him, from out of nowhere, and soaked him from head to foot.

Tarnelius charged the ogre mage, swinging both swords at him and cutting deep slashes into his torso. The ogre bit out a guttural command, and the other turned to swing his club at Tarnelius just as Theri pounced and pinned down his arm. The ogre switched the club to his other hand and clumsily smacked himself with it, trying to dislodge Theri.

"You need to get out of the way," yelled Arcus. With his friends in the way, he couldn't attack either of the ogres with his magic. He cast a spell and held out his burned arm, trying not to pay attention to the blackened skin and blisters. A small orb of fire formed in his hand, about the size of a cantaloupe. He threw it toward them and directed the ball of fire with his mind. It dodged and circled around the mage's head, moving ever closer, but to his other side, away from Tarnelius. The ogre pointed a gnarled finger at it and a small beam of ice shot out and extinguished the flame.

"Just do what you need to do," Tarnelius answered, bracing himself.

Theri was glued to the fighter ogre, who was injuring himself more than he was her. They needed to take down the caster. Tarnelius swung his offhand sword and removed the ogre's right hand, but delayed using his longsword in order to watch the ogre carefully. The mage howled in pain as blood spurted from his wounded arm and his torso healed. He raised his left hand to cast a spell and Tarnelius lunged, slicing that one off as well. It threw the ogre's aim off enough to make the lightning spell he'd cast veer off course and ricochet off another boulder, catching one of the refugees in the face. He had been standing much too close to the battle, invisibly watching the proceedings. The spell keeping him invisible was broken as he was struck. The man tried to scream, but was cut off as the lightning bolt struck him.

Ignoring the mayhem around him, Arcus cast the massive fireball spell once more, right at the mage's chest. Tarnelius ducked as it hurtled toward him. Though the full impact missed him, the fire caught him anyway. His clothes caught on fire and his skin blistered. He threw off his cloak and hood and tumbled around on the ground, trying to beat the fire off him that way. The mage cried out and dropped to his knees, fully engulfed in the flames as he died.

After rolling clear of the ogre, Tarnelius cast the water spell on himself to quench what fire remained, and he coughed and sputtered as the water poured over and off him. Theri had jumped free as the fire had rushed toward them, and had tumbled her way to safety. The remaining ogre had been hit in the arm and had cried out in agony, but he was still alive, though his left arm was charred and useless.

Seeing that his comrades were both dead, the remaining ogre dropped his club and turned to run. He had only made it a few feet before Arcus cast a final fireball at him, which struck him in the back. As the fire spread over his body, Tarnelius and Theri returned to Arcus to regroup.

Arcus and Tarnelius were both badly burned, plus Tarnelius was in serious pain from his ribs whenever he breathed. Theri's left arm was swollen from being hit with the club. She was having trouble squeezing her hand.

The final ogre died, and his last screams of agony echoed in their ears. The group breathed a huge sigh of relief as Arcus reversed the invisibility spell he had cast on them all.

Tarnelius rifled through his bag. After a short time, he grabbed an ointment jar with a bright blue salve inside. He opened it up and spread the blue concoction over the worst of his burns before he tossed the rest of the jar to Arcus. The blue ointment began to glow brightly on his skin, and he sighed in relief.

"Celeste picked up some jars that looked exactly like that," said Theri.

"She did? Praise Kamara." Tarnelius walked to Celeste and opened up her bag. He thrust his arm inside, and chuckled when he realized the bag was magical and contained far more space inside than it appeared it should. The jars of burn ointment that he was seeking were right on top, just within reach. He withdrew his hand and the ointment.

"These bags are so useful. They hold so much, but somehow the item you are looking for is always right on top. Too bad they are so rare. She got this one from her father, as I recall," said Tarnelius as he removed the top and finished covering his burns with the glowing ointment. Then he cast a healing spell on his chest, mending his ribs.

Arcus walked over to Theri after he finished coating himself in the blue ointment, and examined her arm. "Looks like a minor break, but at least the bone is still in position. That is good news; means I don't have to set it." His hands flashed blue as he gripped her arm.

"Thank you, Arcus, that feels much better," she said with a toothy smile. Arcus nodded to her, a small grin on his face.

"Anyone else hurt?" Tarnelius asked the group. They all shook their heads. A few stared at the dead man on the ground. He exchanged glances with Arcus, who cast one more fire spell, this one a small, short-range spell that shot from his finger, lighting the body of the dead man on fire.

"Poor man," said Theri, her voice sad.

"He should have been hiding, like the rest," Arcus remarked. "Does anyone know who he was?"

They all shook their heads. Many of them had been brought into the slave quarters alone, and did not know any of the rest. They had all been too wrapped up in their own misery and fear of the orcs to socialize. Not one of them knew who he was or where he had come from.

Tarnelius went to pick up his cloak so he could retrieve his daggers. Some of his long hair had scorched in the fire, so he took the dagger and handed it to Arcus. "Would you mind removing the burned parts?" Arcus took the dagger and made a single slice through Tarnelius' golden hair, chopping his hair down to a little longer than shoulder length. Tarnelius took his dagger back and cast a spell to mend his cloak and another to mend his clothing. He cast it one final time to repair Arcus' tunic. Then he replaced his dagger and checked on his burns. The blue ointment had soaked in, leaving his skin as flawless and unblistered as it had been before the fight.

He pulled his hood over his head and then grabbed Celeste's weapons from Gunnarr before shoving them in her bag. Finally ready, he bent down to pick Celeste up off the ground. "Shall we?"

"How did you know it had to be fire?" Arcus asked him as they all set off once more, Gunnarr and Theri in the lead.

"That particular breed of ogre sometimes blunders into our forest. We found out through trial and error. Nasty things, ogres. They completely heal within seconds. They don't usually have one with them that can cast spells, though. That was the first one of those I've ever seen. Had I realized, I would have stood back with you and maybe we could have both used fire spells. Or maybe not, because then Theri would have been on the front line alone. Plus, I haven't used any sort of offensive spell in years. I wasn't really prepared."

They stopped at midday to rest and eat what Tarnelius and Arcus could provide with their magic. It was then that Celeste finally began to stir. Her eyelids fluttered and she whimpered. Tarnelius stroked her cheek tenderly to encourage her to wake. After a few moments of this, she opened her eyes and looked up at him.

"W-water please," she croaked. Tarnelius grabbed his water skin which he had filled that morning with fresh water. Then he helped her to take a few small sips. "Where are we, Tarnel?"

"Probably about fifteen miles north of the orc city. You did it. You were great." He gazed deep into her eyes.

"How did we get here? How long was I out?" she asked.

"Almost a full day. I carried you while you slept. That was some serious magic," said Tarnelius. "Here, do you feel up to eating anything?" He passed her some of the magical berries he had created. "You need to regain your strength."

She took the berries he offered and ate them, the color slowly returning to her cheeks.

"Glad you're still with us, Celeste," said Arcus.

"Me too! Thanks for rescuing me!" Theri chimed in.

Celeste smiled. "I'm just glad to have you back, Theri."

"Back at you, Celeste."

"We need to keep moving," Gunnarr called out. "We do not want those orcs, or anyone else, catching up to us."

"The orcs?" Celeste questioned. "I had hoped they wouldn't look for the slaves after I destroyed the barn. I figured that after my big obvious avenging angel routine, they would assume I had come to destroy them all, and the slaves would all be taken for dead."

"I suspect they do think that," said Arcus. "You did an amazing job with that spell, and our dwarf friend is probably utilizing an excess of caution. I'm confident that the orcs will be spending the next several months just trying to rebuild."

Celeste rose to her feet on unsteady legs. Tarnelius held out his arm to her. "Lean on me. I'll help you."

"No, I've got it." She found her center of balance and started walking after Gunnarr and the rest of the group. "Where are we going? Are all these people coming to Lumernia?"

"No, we are taking them to the dwarves. Gunnarr says his people can help them find their homes. It's obvious none of these humans knows how to fight."

"What happened to your hair?"

"Fire fight while you were out. Some of it burned away and I had Arcus cut it."

Celeste nodded her head in acknowledgement and continued walking. After a few moments she heard Tarnelius fall into step just behind her. Arcus stepped into her line of sight and said, "I'm going to walk near the middle of the group, in case there are any attacks from the side. Theri is helping Gunnarr up at the front; why don't you help Tarnelius bring up the rear and aid any stragglers?"

"All right." Celeste slowed her steps to allow all the humans to pass in front of her, walking alongside Tarnelius, who gave her an encouraging smile. Truth be told, she felt exhausted from her ordeal, but she wasn't going to give the others – especially Tarnelius – the satisfaction of seeing her weak, if she could help it.

Tarnelius sighed. "You don't have to be so proud, you know? It's okay to need help once in a while."

"I don't need help. I'm fine." She continued in silence, choosing to conserve her energy for hiking on the rocky terrain.

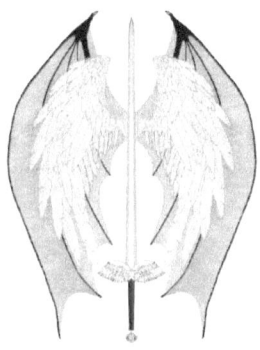

Chapter Twelve
Ageless Risks

The days seemed to be unending for the refugees. They pushed onward as much as possible to cover as much ground in a day as they could. When the few children became tired, the adults took turns carrying them. There were no attacks on the group, from orcs or anyone else. Other than complaints of being forced to eat the same magical berries and water day in and day out - unless Theri managed to catch something large enough to cook and share - as well as general complaints about tiredness, the group was in good spirits. Finally, on the twelfth day of marching, Gunnarr announced that they were almost there.

"The entrance to my home is barely a mile from here! We made it, everyone. Under your feet, even as we speak, is the dwarven city of Grimsgil."

The refugees all cheered and immediately perked up, and that last mile sped by. Before they knew it, Gunnarr walked up to a tall cliff face and started poking at the nondescript rock, brushing away small pebbles and dirt. In moments, he had uncovered an indented handle, which he grasped and pushed inward and to the side. The door gave way silently and easily, opening up to a smooth stairway lit by wall sconces with flames that gave off no heat. Gunnarr gestured to the others to wait a moment, then stepped inside and walked over to the edge of the stairs, peering down.

"Who is there?" A gravelly sing-song voice shouted from down below.

"Are your eyes so bad you do not even recognize me anymore? It is Gunnarr!" His voice seemed to echo in the stairway.

Another voice spoke up. "Gunnarr, you have come back! What on Altierra kept you?"

"Alrek! Roald! It sure is good to see you, lads," Gunnarr hollered. "I was on my way back here almost a month ago when I was set upon by those damnable orcs. They ambushed me and were going to sell me as a slave."

"Orcs? You let orcs catch you? So it took you this long to kill them all, ya?" Alrek asked.

"No, I was chained up and still working on my escape plan. Luckily for me, I was rescued by a couple of elves and a human. Actually, everyone come in here, ya? Everything is fine!" The group, led by Celeste, Arcus, Theri and Tarnelius, crept forward into the entryway.

"These are the ones that saved me, as well as the rest the orcs had captured. I have offered to help my fellow captives get to their homes. We need to prepare some guest quarters. Notify the others; I will need some help from the warriors and mages in helping these people get home. First things first: we could all use some cleaning up from the road and some food, *real* food! All we have had for days is magic rations, and you do not even want to know what the orcs were feeding us. Well, go on you two, quit staring and move! I will get this door sealed again," said Gunnarr. The other two dwarves took off at a run to follow his instructions, disappearing around a corner and out of sight. Gunnarr sealed the door, then turned and stomped down the long staircase. "This way everyone. Today you will experience the gratitude and generosity of the dwarves."

"I wonder how they made this," Theri murmured. "This staircase is huge, feels like close to a hundred stairs!"

Gunnarr led the group down the stairs. They turned the same corner Alrek and Roald had, to find a long hallway that seemed to glow from the walls themselves. The end of the hallway opened up into a large chamber. Many doors led out of it, and were all lit by the same glow. Numerous dwarves moved through this room, entering from one door only to leave again through another. A few stopped to stare at the newcomers as they followed Gunnarr, who continued on his path with single-minded purpose. They walked through a wide door on the far side of the room, which opened into another hall. Several rooms with open doors led off from this hall, including a bar and a few store rooms. They turned another corner and saw some dining areas. Then came another turn and some more stairs, followed by yet another hall. By now, the humans were looking confused by the maze, and the elves were feeling downright claustrophobic. Celeste gripped Tarnelius' hand until her knuckles were white. Still, they continued on.

Finally, Gunnarr flung open a door to an inn and led everyone inside. The main entry contained several tables and chairs made of shining marble. The bar was made of the same material, and everything was polished and gleaming. Gunnarr spoke a few hushed words to the innkeeper for a moment before addressing the group. "All of his rooms are available, as we do not get many visitors. Stay here. Eat, drink and rest. Everything is on me. I will go speak to the Lord of Grimsgil about upcoming arrangements and come back to you soon. Try not to wander around outside this inn; Grimsgil is huge and I worry you would get lost."

The other dwarf stepped forward, taking charge. "Right this way, everyone, to these tables. The name's Dagnar. I am Gunnarr's brother, and I will be taking care of you. I was not expecting a crowd anywhere near this large; just the normal stragglers who come in for ale. I will be a few minutes as I go prepare more of my famous stew and I will bring out my best ale and some fresh baked bread. Ya? Enjoy yourselves, everyone. When you have eaten your fill I will show you all to your rooms." With that, Dagnar rushed off, returning with several pitchers of dwarven ale and mugs for everyone, as well as water for the children.

"Joseph would love this," Arcus said, taking a deep chug of the ale and chuckling. "Well, maybe. The ale is great but I don't know if he would be interested in the dwarven females."

"Perhaps you will see him again someday, after all this is over," Theri said, also taking a long draft of hers.

"Maybe. Assuming he hasn't gotten himself killed."

Celeste sniffed hers, wrinkling her nose in disgust. Tarnelius took a sip and coughed, but tried to stifle it and look like nothing was amiss. They were both on edge, clearly out of their element this far underground.

Dagnar whisked back into the room, carrying a huge tray of steaming breads and some wooden plates. He dropped them onto the tables and rushed back to the kitchen.

"That man needs some help running this place," observed Theri.

"Well, he did say that he's unaccustomed to having this many people here," answered one of the refugees.

"Oh, right. I guess that's true," said Theri.

Everyone devoured the bread, laughing and really relaxing for the first time since they'd escaped the orcs. After what felt like ages to Celeste, Dagnar returned with steaming bowls of stew, which he passed around the table. Each bowl was filled with huge chunks of beef and several vegetables and potatoes, all smothered in a creamy broth. The stew was quite aromatic. Uninterested, Arcus and the two elves just pushed the food around. Theri, noticing this, asked Arcus, "Are you going to eat that?"

"No, all my time with the elves has kind of turned me off meat. I tend to avoid it."

"Can I have it?" Theri asked. "This stew is incredible!"

Arcus slid his bowl over to her without a word and chewed on some more bread. Celeste and Tarnelius also pushed their bowls over toward the others, and two of the humans grabbed them up and devoured them.

"I guess the dwarves aren't used to having elf visitors," said Theri.

"Likely we are the first in a long time. Elves don't like being trapped underground," Tarnelius answered.

Dagnar kept busy, refilling drinks and stew as often as requested. The group became loud and boisterous. They sang songs that were badly out of tune and told stories of the places they had come from. Arcus, Theri, Tarnelius and Celeste decided they would leave their new friends to their party and went to inquire about rooms. They were each shown to a separate room, all four near each other down a short hallway that started inside the tavern.

Theri settled down onto her straw mattress and curled up like a kitten on the linens that were provided. She immediately fell into a deep and peaceful sleep, full of good food and ale. Likewise, Arcus also fell asleep without trouble.

Celeste sat on her mattress and drew her knees up to her chin, her eyes darting around the room. Her heart rate quickened and it began to feel hard for her to breath. Those walls were definitely closer than they were before. She rocked back and forth on the mattress, with hot tears stinging her eyes. She could hear her pulse in her ears and began to panic, her breath coming in quick bursts that didn't seem to provide any oxygen. With a sob, she leapt from the bed and ran into Tarnelius' room, not even bothering to knock. He jumped up with a shout and grabbed his sword when the door flung open, but dropped it in a rush and hurried to her side when he realized it was her. Gently, he shut the door behind her and pulled her into his embrace, stroking her long black hair while she cried.

"Shh! Celeste, I'm here. I've got you." She continued to cry into his shoulder and he led her to his bed. He helped her to lie down, then climbed in next to her. He held her like that until she calmed down, rubbing her back in a soothing way. Eventually, she cried herself to sleep in his arms.

Tarnelius, for his part, didn't like the feeling of being buried alive any more than Celeste did. Before she came in, he had been well on his way to losing it himself. Now that she was here, in his bed, he was consumed by the need to protect and comfort her. Luckily, this had the added bonus of distracting him from his own discomfort. He fell asleep holding her, and they slept all night in his room. They clung to each other in their sleep, both seeking and offering solace. He felt hope and love flare up in his heart, pushing the pain and anger that had resided there for so many centuries aside.

The next morning, Arcus awoke and stepped out to the dining area of the tavern. To his amusement, he found several of the male refugees stretched on the floor near the tables or sleeping with their heads on their arms while sitting up. The smell of ale was pungent in the air. *Looks like the party stretched out longer than they intended*, he thought. He sat down quietly in the corner, nodding to Dagnar, who was bustling about, trying to clean around the men without waking them. Within minutes, Celeste and Tarnelius entered the room together and came and sat with him in silence. Dagnar brought out a new mug of ale for Arcus, and smiled at the two elves.

"Be right back with your drinks and breakfast," he whispered.

"Just water for us, please. It's too early for ale," Tarnelius interjected, also in a whisper.

"As you wish," Dagnar answered with a raised eyebrow.

"Oh, and do you have any more of that bread and maybe some fruit for breakfast?" Celeste murmured.

"Ya, I will get it. What about the rest of you?"

"Same for me, please," Arcus whispered. Tarnelius nodded in agreement. Dagnar tiptoed to the kitchen.

Theri skipped over to their table and plopped down. "Good morning, everyone," she said in a cheerful voice. "What's for breakfast? Think he has any more of the stew?"

A couple of the men on the floor groaned, and several squirmed uncomfortably. One sat up and gripped his head, placing it between his knees.

"Shh!" Arcus scolded her.

"Oh, sorry!" Theri said in an exaggerated stage whisper.

Dagnar brought their order back just as Gunnarr pushed the door open, then left to get breakfast for Theri. "Good news," Gunnarr exclaimed. "Nickolai, the Lord of Grimsgil, has agreed to assign the mages' guild and the warriors' guild to help locate these people's homes and get them sent there, so you lot have nothing to worry about." He grinned broadly, noticing the humans' discomfiture as they forced themselves into upright positions and regained their places at the tables. "What is the matter, lads? You could not handle the ale? We dwarves know how to do it right, ya?"

"That *is* great news," Celeste agreed in a weak voice. "Since our task here is done, we need to be leaving soon to complete what we started." They had filled Gunnarr in on what was going on while they travelled from Medijabal to Grimsgil.

"Any chance you would be willing to come with us?" Tarnelius asked. "We could use all the help we can get."

"Or anyone else from the guilds you mentioned?" Arcus interjected.

"No, lad. I have learned my lesson about travelling in the outside world. Everything I need is here, and besides, I doubt an evil god would be interested in taking over the underground cities anyway. I think you will find most dwarves do not like to leave their homes, and when we do, it is for a very short time with a very specific return time. The sun is too harsh, the night too dark. Better to be indoors and underground in the comfort of the earth. It is not that I am ungrateful for your help, it is just that I only got back and do not want to leave again."

"We understand, Gunnarr. Thank you for all you've done with helping us to get these people home."

"You can ask the others yourself if you would like, ya?" Gunnarr offered. "Nickolai has ordered that there be a great feast prepared tonight in your honor in gratitude for rescuing me and punishing the orcs."

Celeste's eyes widened. "Please tell this Nickolai that, while we very much appreciate the offer, we really must be going if we want to make it to Lumernia in time. We don't have time for celebrations, especially if you believe none of them would be willing to come with us anyway."

Gunnarr nodded his head in understanding. "I will tell him. Is there anything more we can do for you before you leave?"

"Just please send along our apologies and deep regrets," said Celeste.

"Actually, there *is* something," spoke up Theri.

Everyone turned to look at her expectantly. "Well," she began. "Is there any way you could replace the gear those orc mages took from me? I could use some new armor."

Gunnarr smiled broadly. "Of course! It will have to be magical armor. I doubt any of our standard armor will fit you, but the magical armor should adjust well. I will take you as soon as you finish your breakfast, ya?"

The rest of the refugees came out of their rooms and joined their hung-over friends at the table for breakfast. Dagnar busied himself tending to the large crowd, and after a few trips, Gunnarr took pity on him and got up to help him wait tables. While the group ate their breakfast, they explained to everyone what was happening and that they would soon be going home. The refugees thanked them for rescuing them and getting them to Grimsgil safely. Gunnarr spoke excitedly about the feast for that night, telling them they would be guests another day while they were each interviewed to find out where they needed to go and how to best get them there.

The four friends followed Gunnarr to the armory, where he managed to find some leather armor that magically adjusted to

Theri's size. He couldn't do anything about her lost bracers, but gave her a belt that was reputed to make her stronger, as strong as a giant. He offered the others any gear they would like as well, and Arcus accepted a diamond necklace that was promised to increase the potency of his sorcery. Celeste and Tarnelius declined his offer, stating they didn't need anything more.

Celeste started to pull out her old jewelry to offer them as payment, but Gunnarr stopped her. "No, I will take care of it. You keep your baubles. Helping you re-equip your friend makes me not feel so guilty about not coming with you," he said with a wink.

"Does that mean you would come with us if I didn't take this stuff?" Theri asked.

"No, it just means I would feel guilty about it," Gunnarr said with a loud chuckle. "Come on, I will take you to the east exit of the city, so you do not have to climb the outside of this mountain, ya?"

"Are you sure we shouldn't stay for the feast?" Theri asked. "I mean, *maybe* we would be able to talk someone into coming. You never know unless you try."

"I'm quite sure," said Celeste. "It's definitely time to be going."

"What's the rush? I thought you said we didn't even know the timetable. We could be arriving months before the king even thinks of going to the ruins," demanded Arcus. "I agree with Theri, we should stay for the feast."

"Why? Because you want to drink more ale?" hissed Celeste.

"Maybe I don't see the need to hurry up and do nothing!"

"Guys," Theri tried to interrupt.

"If you want to stay here, go ahead and stay here! No one is stopping you," Celeste snarled.

"Oh, because that's it, is it? Your way is final, and no one else's opinion matters," snapped Arcus.

"I don't think that's what she –" Tarnelius tried to interject.

"Oh? Then by all means tell me what she did mean," said Arcus.

"Will you guys *stop it*?" Theri yelled. "This is neither the time nor the place."

Gunnarr was staring at them all with wide eyes.

"I meant, I – I can't stay here," Celeste said in a small voice, her eyes downcast.

"What do you mean, you can't stay here?" Arcus asked.

"If anyone here should understand, it's you, Arcus," said Tarnelius. "We aren't used to being boxed in underground. Inside a building with windows is one thing, but she – we – are uncomfortable down here." He stepped forward to try to take Celeste's hand, but she pulled away, embarrassed. "I'm sorry, Gunnarr, we don't mean to be rude, and we really do appreciate everything you've done."

"It is all right, I actually understand that. I feel the same way when I am stuck outdoors too long, almost too – exposed, ya? Tell you what, how about if I take you all to the eastern exit now. There is a nice waterfall that feeds the river. You can acquaint yourself with the path down and take the day to rest. Then, this evening, I will lead you down with enough time for the feast, and you can decide then what you want to do for tonight, ya?"

"Thank you," Tarnelius said.

"You mentioned a mages' guild earlier," said Arcus, avoiding eye contact with Tarnelius. "Do you think it would be possible they would talk to me a little bit this afternoon? Maybe teach me a little, if they have time?"

"We can certainly ask. I will take you to them after we get these two outside, ya? How about you?" he asked Theri.

"Oh, I'm not picky. I don't think the mages would care about me, so I guess I'll go outside. Maybe I can explore a bit."

"Done! Let us go, then," said Gunnarr.

The group walked behind Gunnarr in silence, up several stairways and through twisty hallways. They had no idea how the dwarves didn't get lost here. Soon they found themselves in a hallway where the air felt damp, and as they approached the door they could hear the roar of rushing water outside. Gunnar slid the door open, and they all squinted in the harsh light that assaulted their senses. Just on the other side of the door, they could see a huge waterfall thundering down into the depths below.

Celeste stepped forward and reached her hand out until her fingertips skimmed the water. She turned around and smiled at the others, finally feeling the pressure of her anxiety begin to release its grip on her spine.

"If you turn to your left, you will find a path that leads down to the base of the waterfall. I will come back for you in the midafternoon, ya?" Gunnar said. "This river continues for miles and miles, widening after it gets out of the mountains. Eventually, it will lead you to Lumernia, as long as you stay on the north bank."

"How deep is the river here?" Celeste asked, dropping her bag near the doorway into the dwarven kingdom.

"Well, it gets down to about five or six feet deep over there," pointed Gunnarr, as he walked down the path a short way to get out from behind the waterfall. From where they were standing, there was a stunning view of a hidden pool of water about sixty or sixty-five feet down. The pool was surrounded by some moss-covered rocks along the shore, and beyond that, the edges of a lush forest. For Celeste, it truly seemed to be a magical oasis. "However, right here at the base of the waterfall, the pressure has eroded everything away, creating a natural pool. I am not sure how deep it is, but I have never found the bottom. I know it is hard to tell because of the foam from the waterfall, but if you look at the edge of the pool feeding into the river, you could get a feel for it from the darker shade of the water. Why do you ask?"

Celeste smiled at him. "I'll see you this afternoon," she said. Then she launched herself off the path, spreading her arms wide as she dove into the pool in a graceful swan dive. Theri gasped in shock as they all stared down at her, waiting for her to break the surface. She rose up and waved her arm to them in joy, beckoning them to join her. Tarnelius let out his breath in a rush.

"Um, if it's all the same to you, I'm going to take the path, okay?" Theri said.

Tarnelius laughed and leapt from the path, himself, and landed feet first in the pool. Arcus shook his head. "You'd think, with as long as they live, they wouldn't take such risks," he said.

"Perhaps that is why they take risks," added Gunnarr. "Come on, let us go to the mages. You will be okay here, ya?" He nodded to Theri.

"Yup, just going to walk down like a normal person," she said as she started down the path.

Theri walked to the base of the path, but rather than getting in the water with the two elves, she chose to climb one of the trees instead. She moved easily from tree to tree in the small grove, and looked around for anything interesting. Her people were as comfortable moving about in trees as squirrels were, and in fact, her tribe lived high in the trees. She prowled around the trees for a while, until she finally decided to rest on one of the central branches and watch the elves.

As soon as Tarnelius emerged from his jump, Celeste swam over to him and splashed him, shrieking with laughter. Treading water, he splashed her back, then shifted into a dusky dolphin and dove deep into the pool. She turned into a sleek bottle nosed dolphin and followed him. Together, they explored the hidden pool, and they danced and twirled around each other in the water. After they frolicked for several minutes, they rose back to the surface and shifted back before they clambered onto the rocky shore. They lay together at the water's edge and stared up at the sky. Both were breathing heavily from the exertion. Theri climbed down to join them when she was sure they weren't planning to get back into the water. They stood up and Tarnelius summoned the winds to dry their clothes. By this time, the sun was directly overhead, so they went for a short walk along the north riverbank, finding several more small waterfalls as the elevation dropped. The river, though small at this point – barely large enough for two canoes to pass each other – stretched on into the east, beyond what they could see. After about an hour of walking, the trio turned back to wait for Gunnarr at their appointed spot. As they made it back to the secluded pool, the clouds became heavy and it started to rain.

"Can't either of you two do something to make it stop raining?" Theri asked.

"Could we? Sure, but this beautiful waterfall depends on the rainfall. The trees need the rain. It would be wrong to stop it just because it is inconvenient," said Celeste.

"Says the woman that doesn't have to worry about damp fur."

"Are you so sure about that? Remember, I can change forms. I've had my share of wet fur too," teased Celeste.

"It doesn't count when you can send it away in seconds." Theri pouted.

Tarnelius chuckled at the two of them and they climbed the path back to the eastern door of Grimsgil, taking shelter in the alcove behind the waterfall. "What are we doing about tonight, Celeste?"

"Well, what do you think about staying out here?" Celeste asked.

"Out here? In the damp and noise?" Theri asked in horror.

"It's a soothing noise, and yes. Out here. It's a nice protected alcove open to the stars. I really feel comfortable and safe here," said Celeste.

"Out here is perfectly fine with me, though instead of up here in the damp, perhaps we should move into the trees," suggested Tarnelius.

"That's a good idea," agreed Celeste.

"So there's no way we can sleep in those nice warm and dry beds, huh?" Theri whined.

"Hmm. I kind of doubt Arcus will be interested in sleeping outside anyway, so why don't you make arrangements for the two of you to sleep inside and meet us out here tomorrow morning?" Celeste said.

"And leave you two all alone out here? Are you sure you don't mind?"

"Oh, I think we will be fine," Tarnelius affirmed with a smirk.

Theri gave him a wicked grin. "I see. Okay then, but maybe we should ask Arcus rather than telling him. I think he would appreciate that."

"Yeah, you're probably right," agreed Celeste.

Chapter Thirteen
Dragon's Gift

"This is the door to the mages' guild," said Gunnarr, gesturing. Arcus reached for the handle, only to be stopped by Gunnarr. "Do not *ever* barge in there without knocking first. I did that once, only once, and learned my lesson!"

"Um, okay then." Arcus tapped the door three times. A moment later it swung open and a dwarf in red robes that clashed with his red hair and beard opened the door and peered up at him.

"You must be one of those humans we are tasked with sending home. Ya? We will come to you when we are ready to begin the interviews. Do not worry," he said, his accent a little heavier than Gunnarr's, but no less musical sounding.

"Me? No, they are still waiting in the tavern. Name's Arcus. I had an entirely different type of favor to ask you."

The dwarf sniffed and looked him up and down. "Ya, I see you have dabbled in the arts. So much potential. Shame I see an elf magic taint on you." He continued to examine Arcus before continuing, casting an incantation under his breath. "On the other hand, I see you are teaching yourself to make the two sides of you work together. Come in, come in. Tell me what it is you seek. Ya?" He gestured into the room and Arcus started to enter.

"Listen, I am going to go help my brother prepare for tonight. Could you please get him back to the tavern when you are done here?" Gunnarr asked.

"Ya, I will guide him, or more likely I will simply escort him to the feast tonight. Do not worry." The mage turned and followed Arcus into the room, shutting the door behind him.

"Now, young Arcus, my name is Malaki. How may I be of assistance to you?" the mage asked.

"I was hoping you could train me today. Perhaps teach me some dwarven magic, please?" Arcus asked.

"Why do you want to learn dwarf magic? You have the dragon's gift coursing through your veins. You must have found favor among elves for them to teach you their ways, as well."

"Knowledge transcends race. I seek to learn from any willing to teach me. Ignoring any avenue of learning would be ignorant on my part," answered Arcus. "What do you mean by 'the dragon's gift'?"

"You are very wise, young Arcus. The dragons are the source of all arcana. They are the masters, and we, the students. No one can just learn this magic; it must be in your very blood. For those of us lucky enough to have their blessing, we are given the right to learn. Ya? Dragon magic, or arcana, is the same no matter what race casts it. Now, follow me into this training room and show me what you can do, then I will decide if there is anything I can teach you. Do not bother showing me any elf magic. It is not of the dragons and I cannot help you with it."

They entered the large room, which seemed to hum with its own magic. There was a large circle on the floor, which Malaki indicated the two of them should stand in, while the rest of the room was filled with various targets and dummies of different materials. "As long as you stand inside this circle while casting, you will not experience spell exhaustion and will be able to continue casting over and over."

Arcus focused for a moment, then reached his hand toward one of the targets, causing a massive ball of fire to shoot outward toward it. The target incinerated within seconds. Then he reached his other hand out and shot lightning at another target, blasting a massive hole through it and charring the remains.

"Very good!" Malaki praised. "I see you favor evocation, or elemental magic. What of the others? Acid? Water?"

"I tend to use air and fire spells as my primary attack method, though I have dabbled in ice magic a little. I have never used any acid spells."

"I see. Well, acid does tend to be temperamental. You want to take care not to get any on you when casting. I think I know an ice spell that you might like, ya? Watch me."

Malaki closed his eyes and focused his energy inward for a moment, then he muttered a few magic words while rotating his arms in a flowing maneuver that almost looked like he was dancing. Then he opened his eyes slowly and inhaled deeply, and then pushed both hands forward with open palms while he exhaled forcefully. As he pushed out, ice and snow shot from his hands straight forward to the target almost fifty feet away. The target crumbled under the power of the ice and fell to pieces on the floor, and was quickly covered in snow.

"Now, I will teach you the words, and let us see what you can come up with, ya?"

The pair worked on the ice spell for a couple of hours, talking about the inflections in the words and the angle of the hand motions. When Malaki was satisfied at Arcus' progress, he left his pupil in the room alone for a moment and went to retrieve one of the magic tomes the dwarves kept. He brought it and some blank scrolls, ink, and a quill into the room and began flipping pages in the book.

"This is a useful spell for blending in for short amounts of time. I assume the elves taught you how to change forms, ya?" Malaki asked.

"Ya. Um, I mean, yes. Yes, they did," said Arcus.

"Very good. This spell here will do the same, but you can use it to change yourself or even somebody else, if they will let you, into an animal or even into another race, like an elf or a kedistam. The effects, unfortunately, last less than ten minutes, so you would have to make it count. Take this scroll and quill over to the table in the corner and copy it exactly. Do not make any error in your copy, or you will not be able to learn the spell."

Arcus nodded in understanding and carried the items to the desk as instructed. Malaki left the room to give him some privacy. Arcus spent the next couple of hours painstakingly copying every word exactly, making sure each letter had the proper angles and strokes. When he was done, he surveyed his handiwork and spoke the words aloud. He read the whole thing once, twice, and began the third time. As he did, the black words on the page began to glow gold, following along with his reading. When he was done with his third pass-through, the scroll was a blaze of glittering gold letters. The parchment then caught fire, and was destroyed in moments. Arcus thought back to the words and the paper, then he recited the words from memory one last time. This time he pictured being a dwarf with a full black beard, wearing black robes. When he was done, he closed his eyes, feeling a tingle course through his body. He opened his eyes and immediately felt disoriented. He was about a foot and a half closer to the ground than he'd been before. He turned and opened the door that led out of the training room, where he found Malaki at a desk in the front lobby area of the guild.

Malaki looked at him and smirked. "You make a fine dwarf, Master Arcus. Though you would never fool me. Come, let us sit and talk for a little while more, ya? The feast will be soon. Seems pointless to wander down to the tavern just to have to leave again so soon after."

"I thought this was a mage guild. Where are the other mages?" Arcus asked.

"They were here. They left a short time ago for the tavern to interview the refugees. I am the only one that stayed behind. It is their job to find out where the refugees came from, so that we can dispatch the warriors to escort them home."

"How will they do that, exactly?"

"Well, honestly, they will just ask. If any do not have a home, or if any – such as the children – do not remember where their home is, they will use divination spells to determine where to send them. The warriors could have probably handled it themselves, but it is best if we do it. That way, we can keep everything organized. Think of us as different muscles on a body. We mages are the brain, the warriors are the brawn."

After a few minutes, Arcus grew back into his normal self. They talked for a while longer, passing the time until the feast.

"…and this is the Grand Ballroom," finished Gunnarr with a sweep of his arm as he led Celeste, Tarnelius and Theri into the massive space. Dominating the room were four lengthy tables with hundreds of place settings and chairs, as well as a smaller table running perpendicular to the rest at the head of the room. People were scurrying to and fro as they hurried to get heavy trays laden with food into place on the table. There were huge platters of meat organized by body part. It looked and smelled like roast sheep, or perhaps goat. Also, there were trays of goat cheese, bread varieties, mashed potatoes, miniature cabbages, radishes, cloudberries, blueberries, strawberries, grapes and many other kinds of side dishes. There was dwarven ale, water, goats' milk, wine and some cloudy looking spirits Gunnarr called "aquavit", which smelled like fermented potatoes.

"We are to sit at this table, as guests of His Lordship," said Gunnarr, leading them with pride to the smaller table. "I wonder what is keeping Arcus and Malaki."

They made their way over to the table and took their seats along with many other dwarves. The dwarves were all smiling and joking together, laughing uproariously at intervals, which seemed to Celeste as if the entire room was echoing and pulsing. A short while later, Arcus arrived with Malaki. The mage gestured for Arcus to join his friends as he hurried to sit with the rest of the mages at a different table. The human refugees were also seated with the guild members. When everyone was present, two more dwarves entered the room and stopped on either side of the door. Each was armed with a ceremonial sword and a trumpet, and they wore guardsman clothes and purple sashes. They raised the instruments to their mouths as one and played a short fanfare. Then, a dwarf who was obviously the king entered, dressed in a fine suit and a purple robe the same shade as the guards' sashes. He walked a few feet into the room and stopped, seemingly for dramatic effect. He lifted his hands in the air and waited for complete silence before speaking.

"Thank you all for joining me today for this feast." Unlike many of the other dwarves, Lord Nickolai's was a very slow, unhurried drawl. "I am pleased that Brother Gunnarr is able to be here with us, thanks to the heroics of this group here at my table, in a place of honor. Celeste, Tarnelius, Arcus and Therinsalla, you have the heartfelt thanks of the dwarves. Please, everyone, dig in and enjoy!" With that, Nickolai walked to his chair – which was really a small throne more than anything else – and sat down, reaching for the goat ribs and grabbing a healthy portion. The room erupted with the sound of utensils clanking against plates and platters. Voices once more filled the air, as people joked amongst each other.

"I wanted to thank you for all your hospitality, Your Highness," said Celeste.

"This? This is nothing! This is the least I could do to show my thanks to you for helping one of my kinsmen. I heard what you did, by the way. Very impressive. Are all the elven druids like you in regards to ability?

"No. I have had centuries to work on my craft. Even of the others that are as old as I am, many have become complacent, or have branched out into learning other things. Tarnel, for example, has dabbled in anything and everything that he thought sounded interesting. He is still a powerful druid in his own right, but does not have the control or strength to summon some of the nature spells I do. That said, he is an excellent swordsman and tracker, much better than I could ever hope to be," answered Celeste.

"Ha! Who needs swords when you wield a tornado?" Nickolai scoffed.

"Part of being a druid is having respect for the forces you control. I cannot simply use a tornado spell and destroy entire ecosystems any time I choose. Besides, it takes massive energy to control it. I lost almost a full day recovering."

"Gunnarr here tells me that you are on a quest to Lumernia," said Nickolai.

"Yes, that is true, and we must leave early tomorrow morning," said Celeste.

"Lord Nickolai, would you be willing to assist us in our quest?" Arcus asked. "We are trying to stop King Liam from excavating the North Tombs and releasing an ancient evil."

"Why would you possibly need our help in what seems like a simple diplomatic issue? Seems to me you are capable of handling this without us, ya?"

"Axistra has told me I will need allies if I am to succeed. She has had a vision," said Celeste.

Nickolai's eyes widened. "The dragon? Why is she getting involved? I thought they had some sort of agreement to keep to themselves."

"They do; that's why she is sending us," answered Celeste.

"Then she is still getting involved. I wonder what the other dragons would think of that." Nickolai stroked his beard thoughtfully. "Gunnarr told me you have wings. Are you a herald?"

"My father was a herald of Melek."

"Ah, an angel of the very god reputed to have slain the moon itself. Interesting," he said. "I will tell you, times are changing, I feel the balances shifting, and whatever comes will change everything. I wonder what other heralds may be moving into place. I am sorry, Madame Celeste, but the safety of my people must come first, and we are safe here, inside this mountain, from anything that may come."

Celeste merely nodded and stared at her plate. Arcus spoke up, "We understand, Your Lordship. I just figured it wouldn't hurt to ask."

"Indeed, it never hurts to ask," Nickolai said. "Now, let us move on to more pleasant topics. Tell me about where you each come from. How about starting with you, Madame Therinsalla?"

Theri began talking about growing up in the south. Nickolai seemed enthralled by her stories, and interrupted her several times to ask her questions. The group had an animated conversation throughout dinner, though it seemed the elves were a bit withdrawn. Finally, the feast was over and many dwarves pitched in to help clean up. The four friends bade Nickolai goodnight when he eventually stood to leave with his two guardsmen.

"Tarnel and I will be staying outside the eastern gate. It is my understanding that Theri wishes to stay at Dagnar's tavern tonight. Where would you like to stay?" Celeste asked Arcus.

Arcus arched an eyebrow at her before responding. "Well, if it's all the same to you all, I'd rather sleep in a bed one final night, as long as we are staying anyway."

Gunnarr clapped his hands together. "Excellent! Let me escort these two outside and I will come and join you. Let us have a drink together. Looks like the mages are getting ready to take the others back to the tavern now. Why don't you go with them and I will catch up?"

The group wished each other good night, and then Gunnarr led the elves to the eastern door.

"Will you be joining us for breakfast in the morning?" Gunnarr asked.

"No, we need to be leaving pretty early. Please ask Arcus and Theri to be out around sunrise."

"Well, we cannot see the sunrise from in there, but I will tell them to come out early," said Gunnarr. "I guess that means this is it. Thank you, again, for rescuing me."

Tarnelius smiled and shook Gunnarr's hand. "Thank you for helping the others find their way back. I don't know what we would have done if you hadn't stepped up and offered to help when you did."

"And thank you for your hospitality," said Celeste. "Have a good night."

Gunnarr smiled and turned to walk back inside, shutting the door behind him and leaving the two elves alone.

Celeste moved over to where they had stashed their belongings that morning, picking up her bag and slinging it into place. "Shall we?"

"You want to head down to the trees?" Tarnel asked.

"Unless you have a better idea."

"Nope, that's the best idea I could come up with," Tarnelius said as he grabbed his bag and set off down the darkened path. "Good thing the other two decided to stay inside; I doubt they'd be able to see well enough to walk this path in the dark."

"Hmm. I'm not sure about Theri, I never asked her about her night vision or anything. She has never expressed any difficulty while on watch, though."

"Maybe," said Tarnelius.

The pair made it down the path to the tree line, where they settled on the soft pine needles.

"I think maybe we should take our rest as trees tonight. I don't expect any danger, but just in case there is an orc scouting party or something; they won't find us," suggested Celeste.

"Sounds fine to me, only I'm not tired yet."

Celeste gave him a bright smile that set his pulse racing, before standing up and walking out to the pool at the base of the waterfall. She stripped off her green gown that had become a dirty brownish color from all the traveling, and dove into the water. She surfaced a moment later and splashed water in his direction. Smirking, Tarnelius jumped up and stripped as well, before he ran to the water and jumped in next to her. She splashed him playfully, but he merely reached forward and grabbed her arms and pulled her to him to give her a heart-melting kiss. Then he released her and swam to the other side, at the base of the mountain. He searched a moment, until he found a slight indent in the rock-covered wall, where they could sit.

Celeste followed him over and sat next to him. "What's the matter? You didn't want to play?"

Tarnelius smirked. "With you, any time. But we've been drinking, and I didn't feel like treading water when all I really wanted to do was kiss you. Did you know that my fondest memory of us is a similar one? I often returned to it, in my daydreams, while I tended your garden at your old house. I was going to ask you to make the lifebond with me, that last time we went to the lake."

"Tarnel, please don't. Don't do this. You have no idea how much I regret leaving and losing centuries with you."

"But don't you see? It wasn't only your fault. I *should* have asked you then, in the water, like I wanted to. I chose to wait and ask for my father's blessing first. After that, everything fell apart. How could you have thought my feelings for you were anything other than those born of desperation when I offered to run away with you? I understand why you left. I can't even swear I wouldn't have done the same if the roles were reversed. I was so mad at you, but these last couple of weeks I've been thinking that maybe I should have been mad at myself as well.

Ultimately though, I always hoped that if I waited for you, eventually you would come back to me. When my divination spells failed, I wanted to search every square inch of every forest and everywhere in between. But, I knew that even if I did, I wouldn't find you unless you wanted to be found."

Celeste was silent for a moment. "I wonder if you *had* asked me at the lake if it would have made a difference. My heart says yes, I would have stayed. My brain says I still would have left. I don't know, and there is no way to find out."

"I think you might have at least heard me out, or might not have fought being found as much if you did go. That's how it's been playing out in my head anyway."

Celeste's eyes were sparkling as they reflected the starlight when she gazed up at him. "Tarnel, I'm so sorry. I wish I had never left."

"Hush. I'm sorry too." Tarnelius leaned forward and kissed her gently on the lips. He felt her shiver against him and he nibbled her lower lip before deepening the kiss, demanding entrance with his tongue. She opened to him and kissed him back with ever deepening passion. He ran his hands up and down her sides, feeling her curves, and moaned as she tangled her fingers in his hair. After several minutes they broke apart, gasping for air. "Celeste, we have to stop."

"Why?"

"Will you make the lifebond with me? Please, Angel, now. Tonight. Make the vows and join with me in front of Kamara and this pool and the native animals," said Tarnelius, gazing into her eyes.

"What? Where has this come from?" she asked.

"I realized, as we clung to each other last night, that I need you. I can't live without you. All I've ever wanted was for us to be together, and holding on to anger and hurt feelings wasn't constructive at all. I want to be everything you need, and all I need is you. Anyway, I can't keep kissing you like this. I have a weakness where you are concerned, but I want us to be together in every way before we are together physically. I lost you once and I don't want to lose you again. Once the bond is made, I'll always be able to find you," he said.

"You'll never lose me, I promise you that," breathed Celeste. "I swear to never exclude you from decisions again, or to act so impetuously. We've lost six hundred years because of my bad decisions, but I have learned from them. I'm not going anywhere."

"I want more."

"I do, too, but Tarnel, I don't even know if I'm able to make the bond," she said.

She saw him frown at her words. Celeste reached up to kiss him again, and rubbed her hand comfortingly over his face. "I do want forever with you. I do. We can still make the next six hundred years ours, or even longer than that."

"Then your answer is yes?" Tarnelius asked, the hope obvious in his voice.

"Yes, Tarnel. My answer is yes, though not right now. Not out here, on the road. When I give half of my soul to you, I want you to be the only thing on my mind. Let's do this the right way." She kissed him then, tangling her fingers in his hair and granting him the access he sought with his tongue. She sucked on his tongue, playfully, and he moaned in complete bliss.

Finally, Tarnelius pushed her off him and they broke apart, gasping for air. "Just because I want to wait to take the bond doesn't mean we have to stop what we are doing tonight," she urged.

"It does, Celeste. I don't *want* to stop, but like I said, I want our union to be complete and sacred; I want to be joined in soul and spirit before we join physically. If you want to wait, we will wait. As long as you swear to me your answer is yes, then I am the happiest man in the world. I've waited for you my whole life, so what is a few more weeks or months? When we kiss I feel my resolve weakening and I want to give in, but I don't want to have regrets later. I don't want you to have any regrets, either."

Celeste pushed away from him into the water and gazed up at him, her eyes hooded. "Are you sure that's what you want? It's only a ritual ceremony, and looking at you now I'm not convinced all of you is in agreement. Since I've promised myself to you, it's all only a matter of time anyhow."

"Obviously you don't just consider it 'ritual' or you would do it now. Yes, I'm sure."

"Then I suppose we should get dressed." Celeste swam away from him to the opposite shore where their clothes waited. She lifted herself up out of the water using her arms and bent at the waist to pick up her dress before sashaying into the trees.

Tarnelius remained at the shore wall for a few moments to watch her little show and sighed. Then, he pushed away from the wall and swam for a bit to let off some steam. When he was finished, he went to the shore and grabbed his clothes. He looked for her but only found a tall cypress, standing proud among the pines, that hadn't been there before his swim. He sat down and leaned his back against it, allowing his thoughts to wander.

"I don't understand why you aren't willing to bond with me now. We'd be stronger as a unit than as individuals." There was no answer. "But, I'm overjoyed that you have agreed. Truly. I've waited for you this long, I can wait a little longer." After a while, he shifted into a golden eagle and flew up to grip the upper branches with his talons and went to sleep in the boughs of the cypress.

"Celeste! Wake up," said a whisper of a voice.

Celeste opened her eyes and blinked up at the silvery scales and glowing blue eyes of Axistra.

"Where are we?" Celeste asked. "How did we get here?"

"You are exactly where you were, a cypress outside of Grimsgil. You are dreaming. I wanted to warn you, I had another vision. I saw a great evil taking hold of Lumernia, though I cannot pinpoint it. Something powerful."

"What does that mean?" Celeste asked.

"My visions are not always the whole picture. Still, I felt that I was being actively blocked, like whatever this evil is has been blocking divinations, which means it has to be powerful."

"Another dragon, do you think?"

"No, I do not. None of us would be foolish enough to interfere that directly. Besides, I have checked in on the locations of the other five, and they are all where I expected them to be. It has to be a lesser herald; some of them have grown quite powerful."

"Well, you are interfering by helping me, aren't you? The dwarf king said something to that extent and he was right. If you are helping me, couldn't one of the others be doing the same?" Celeste asked.

The dragon cocked her head as she considered this. "I suppose it is possible, but I am sensing the evil physically inside Lumernia. In either event, be on your guard. I saw danger in your future."

"I understand."

"Be careful who you trust there. I will give you a gift. Take this ring. If you need to speak with me again, crush the stone on the ring. Make sure you are somewhere safe when you do it, as you will immediately project to wherever I am. This ring can only be activated once, so don't use it unless there is an emergency." A small table with a pillow appeared in front of Celeste, with a ring set atop it.

Celeste reached out for it as Axistra said, *"Remember, be careful with it. And watch yourself and those you can trust. Peace be with you, child."*

As Celeste placed the ring on her finger, the dream and the dragon faded out and were replaced by another dream, a dream of Tarnelius.

Chapter Fourteen
No Happily Ever After

Celeste awoke before dawn and shifted her branches slightly. Tarnelius screeched and took flight, shifting back into his normal form as he landed. After he was safely on the ground, Celeste also shifted, withdrawing into herself as she shrunk down.

"You're lucky I remembered you were there before I shifted. That would have come as a shock to you when the tree you were perched on vanished," teased Celeste.

"Bah. I would have had time to fly off. It's not like you shift in a fraction of a second. Oh, and good morning to you, too."

"Are you saying I'm slow?" Celeste asked in mock anger.

"No, you're actually quite quick, but it still takes a few seconds. Calm down. Although, you should know that you're adorable when you are angry."

They caught sight of Theri and Arcus coming out of the door above them, and waving goodbye to someone whose voice they didn't recognize. Tarnelius leaned forward to give her a chaste peck on the lips.

"That's all I get?"

"Yes, that's all you get until you make the bond with me," Tarnelius said, smiling.

"That's blackmail."

"Hmm, so it is. I can live with that."

"What is this bond you're talking about?" Theri asked as they approached.

"You are earlier than we expected. Did you eat breakfast?" Tarnelius asked. "Where's Gunnarr?"

"Sleeping it off," smirked Arcus. "He thought that just because he is a dwarf, he could outdrink me. He lost. He didn't realize how much time I spent in bars with Joseph. Theri had breakfast. I figured I would just eat some berries on the way."

"Sounds good. Let's go then," said Tarnelius.

They set off. As they passed the pool at the point where it flowed into the river, Tarnelius caught Celeste's eye and smiled.

"What is this bond they were talking about?" Theri asked Arcus.

"Truthfully, you'd have to ask them. I only have a basic understanding. From what I understand, it's like a marriage and hand binding ceremony. The union is based on an old and powerful magic, and allows each of the pair to give half of their soul to the other. It does something else, too, but I can't remember."

Tarnelius jumped into the conversation. "The mated pair becomes bonded for life, each sharing the other's soul. As such, they become able to always know what the other is thinking and feeling. They can always sense where their mate is, no matter how well hidden they are, or what kind of magic masks them. It becomes like trying to find your own hand in the dark; you always know where it is, even if you can't see it. We elves often make arranged marriages for our children because it helps to ensure that our race survives. Especially when you consider that many wouldn't choose that path for themselves, as you lose all privacy. *All* privacy. We don't worry about love, because ultimately you can't feel someone inside you all the time and not love them. Well, I suppose it has happened, but it's very rare. I'm convinced I could have never loved Velonessa, even with half her soul inside me, because my entire soul was consumed by Celeste eons ago." He smiled at Celeste and took her hand. "I wasn't willing to take the risk on any account, even with my father using every trick in the book to force me." His face darkened and he shuddered slightly. "Elves bond for life, and never move on from a loss. Many are lost to the Fade after the death of their mate, unless there is something tying them here."

"What did your mother think about your decision to not marry the one they chose for you?" Theri wondered.

"My mother is dead. She died giving birth to me. I have no idea how she would have felt."

"Were your parents not bonded, then? Your father is obviously still alive," she asked.

"My parents were bonded, which is why my father never remarried. He has never been capable of loving anyone other than himself, so was less affected by the loss of his mate than the average elf would be. I think he sticks around to spite me, really. He does not want to give up the throne to his disobedient child. The joke's on him though; I don't care about being king, or even prince."

"This lifebond, is it druid magic? Like, can druids do it even if they are not elves? Or, can elves do it without being druids?" Theri asked.

"It is not druid magic; it is unique to our race. Only an elf can make a lifebond," answered Tarnelius.

Celeste sighed and pulled her hand away, staring at the ground dejectedly.

"What is the matter, Celeste?" Tarnelius asked.

"I tried to tell you last night, but I don't know if I can make the bond at all," she said. "I'm not a full elf. If I *can* do it, I will, and gladly, but I'm just not sure that I can. I know my parents could not bond."

"It's not like your mother fell in love with a human. Your father was a full-blooded herald. A seraph. In essence, he was purely a magical entity. Other than you, I have never heard of a herald being able to have any children at all. I don't have a single doubt that you will be able to make the bond if that is what you want. You can do anything you set your mind to. I've never looked at you as anything less than a full-blooded elf, one who happens to have more powerful magic than most."

"I – I really hope you are right," Celeste said.

"Hey," Tarnelius stopped her and lifted her chin to look into her eyes. "I am not worried about it. I know you can do it. *We* can do it, together."

He released her and began walking again.

"I'm glad you two have decided to kiss and make up," said Theri. "I could tell from the first time I saw you two together that you both missed the other and wanted to make up."

"Is that so?" Celeste said with a smirk.

"Definitely. I can read you like a book."

After progressing for a couple of hours, the trees thinned and ultimately vanished altogether. They were still climbing down the ever-lowering mountain range, but were finally out of the forest.

"Let's stay together. Theri, we won't need you to scout ahead. You'd be a huge target out there alone with no cover," said Celeste.

"Um, I kind of wasn't scouting ahead. I'm right here," she answered.

"Right. I know, I was only clarifying. Never mind," Celeste said with a sigh.

Suddenly, Theri stopped in her tracks and all her fur stood on end. "What the heck is that? A ghost in the middle of the day? Look, there, in the water!"

The others whirled around and sure enough, there was a person standing on the water, covered head to toe in black clothing. It was hard to tell, but Theri was right. The man in black was transparent, just like looking through a ghost.

"No," said Celeste. "Not a ghost, a projection."

"So this is all the mighty Axistra could muster to fight me? How insulting. I bet you don't even make it the whole way to Lumernia," said the figure with a deep voice that sounded hollow and echoed through each of their heads. "In fact, I bet I can see to that right now."

"He's lying; projections can't attack. They are, well, projections," said Celeste.

"Are you so sure about that, my mongrel friend? So sure you would stake your life on it?" The figure began to chant in some horrible sounding language. It was guttural and raspy and evil-sounding. None of them had ever heard any language like it before. Suddenly, standing before them, were two demons – a male and a female. The evil heralds were both very intimidating looking. The male was almost ten feet tall and had stereotypical red skin and bat wings. His head was disfigured and inhuman, with curving horns jutting from his forehead, and the face of a goat. His feet were cloven, and he wore heavy armor and carried a flaming broadsword. The female was a little over six feet tall and was scantily dressed, with a beautiful and statuesque figure, and her ivory skin was flawless. She had huge wings with soft and sleek black feathers. Her red eyes glowed mischievously as she caressed her whip, which was glowing a menacing red color as it hung coiled at her hip. She ambled toward Arcus and Tarnelius, who both took an instinctive step backward. The figure standing atop the river chuckled and vanished.

"Hello, boys. Look into my eyes. See what I have to offer you," the demoness purred. They didn't look up, but before anyone could blink, the demoness vanished from where she stood and appeared right in front of Tarnelius. "I said, 'look into my eyes,'" she repeated. Tarnelius looked helplessly at Celeste, who was glaring at the other demon. The demoness reached out her hand and tipped Tarnelius' chin toward her. "There now, do you like what you see? Oh, look at you. You're in *love*! Isn't that sweet? I can be so much better for you. I can be anything you want me to be, baby."

Tarnelius' eyes dilated as she spoke. Seeing this, she smiled at him. She glanced up at Celeste. "Don't worry about my pet. He doesn't bite unless I tell him to. Take a look over here; looks like your man wasn't so into you that he wouldn't change his mind at just one glance at a more *experienced* woman."

Celeste raised her hand, but the demoness was quicker. "Don't move, Princess. This is my show."

Theri lunged at her, but was frozen in her tracks as the demoness raised her hand in warning. "Ah ah ah. Down, kitty. No one invited you to the party just yet." She smiled at Arcus and pointed her finger. "Don't you get any ideas either, sugar. There will be plenty more of me to share when I am done with this one. You stay right there." Arcus stiffened in place as well.

She walked over to Celeste, gesturing to Tarnelius to follow her. "Ah, I can sense you are the one with most of the power. I can smell it on you. It's…intoxicating. Is that the aroma of *angel* blood I detect in your veins? Come here, Angel. Come watch." With that, she turned toward Tarnelius and kissed him deeply. His eyes dilated even more and he returned her kiss without thought. The demoness ran her hand down his torso, rubbing it over his stomach and lower abdominals. Tarnelius growled as his body responded.

Celeste squeezed her eyes shut and whimpered. The sound stopped the demoness in her tracks. She released Tarnelius and moved over to Celeste. "You resist my charms? How? Is it the *angel* blood? Answer me!"

"Maybe I would, if you'd give me a chance to answer!" Celeste retorted.

Quick as a flash, the demoness vanished and appeared behind her with a dagger that glowed the same infernal red color as the whip pressed to her throat. "I don't often need to wait for answers. My prey either does what I wish or is too enthralled to answer. Why are you so different? What are you?"

Celeste pushed her wings out with all her strength and pushed the demoness off her, cringing when the blade made a shallow cut into her throat as she knocked it out of the demoness' hand.

"Keep your hooks out of my *rakastan*, you whore!"

The two took off into the sky, drawing their weapons as they flew. As soon as their feet left the ground, the other three snapped out of the trances they had been placed in. Tarnelius looked into the sky in horror as the others turned to see the male demon draw his sword menacingly.

"Tarnelius! The other one! Look, quick!" Theri screamed.

Tarnelius drew both his swords and stepped protectively in front of the other two. He rushed forward to meet the demon head-on and became a whirlwind of swords.

Arcus and Theri ran around behind the hulking demon. Arcus shot a lightning bolt at the demon's back, which charred the armor at the impact location, but did little to slow down the demon. Theri launched herself at him, clambered up his back, and swiped at his head with her claws. Dark, almost black, blood trickled down from the deep gouges made by her claws. Tarnelius parried another hit and tried to find an opening to attack, but found himself blocked. Arcus reached forward and hit the armor with a freezing grasp, causing ice to form all around the back of the armor. Arcus kicked at the frozen armor, watching as a chunk of it shattered and fell off, but the rest of it stayed intact.

"Theri, come down from there. He's vulnerable to ice! I have an idea, but we'll need to disengage," yelled Arcus.

Theri scratched at him some more, her intent to rip out his eyes. Unsuccessful, she back flipped off the demon, and landed on her feet with grace.

They ran around to the other side, behind Tarnelius. "Tarnelius, you need to back off. I can stop him, but I don't want to hurt you. The spell is much more damaging than my fire spells," Arcus yelled.

"You've got to be kidding me!" Tarnelius yelled back. "Even if I did get away now, he'd just follow me or cut you down while you are casting. Figure it out!"

"Okay, Theri, I'm going to cast the spell and hold at the end. You'll see me freeze in place. I won't be able to talk to you or move from that position. When you see this, I need you to get Tarnelius out of the way, got it?"

"Um, I understand, but I have no idea how I'm going to make it happen!" she squealed.

"Like the man said, figure it out! Get ready!"

Arcus closed his eyes, drawing all his energy inward. He chanted the invocation and performed the motions just as he had learned back in the practice room in Grimsgil. Then he opened his eyes and inhaled sharply, freezing in place. Theri stared in shock for a moment at the suddenness, but then lunged toward Tarnelius.

"We have to get out of here, he's ready to cast and I don't know how clear of the area we need to be! Move!" She jumped back onto the demon, clambering up his armor and covering his head with her body. This gave Tarnelius a moment to turn and run. As he did, however, the demon's flailing sword caught him in the ribcage, striking deep. The sword was yanked from the demon's hand and fell to the ground. Theri leapt into the air and tumbled a safe distance away. Tarnelius gripped his injured side and ran a short way before collapsing to the ground. As soon as they were clear, Arcus shoved his hands forward, exhaling with force. Snow and ice burst from his hands and shot into the demon like a thousand icy daggers. As soon as the spell was cast, Arcus focused and began the spell again before the demon could recover.

Theri ran to Tarnelius' side to examine the wound. Tarnelius coughed in pain, a small amount of blood dotting his lips as he did so. Theri moved so he was propped up in an elevated position on her legs and stroked his cheek. "It's going to be okay, just hang in there. We'll get you fixed up, Tarnelius, I promise."

The demon fell to his knees as the second blast of ice and snow hit. Arcus stepped closer and cast the same spell he started with on the demon's armor, then cast another frost spell right in the demon's face. To Arcus' surprise, the demon disintegrated when hit with that last spell. His oily remains vanished in the snow.

"Arcus," Theri screamed. "Get over here!"

He turned and rushed to Theri's side. "He's hurt bad," she said. "I think it nicked his lung."

"Hang in there, old friend. I've got you." Arcus' hands flashed blue as he endeavored to pinch the wound shut. Nothing happened. Tarnelius coughed up more blood and gestured for Arcus to come closer.

"Tell Celeste that – that – I love her," he choked out.

"Stop that, Tarnelius. You're going to be fine, we'll get you patched up. Come on. Try to heal yourself. Together we can fix this." Tarnelius squeezed his eyes closed and attempted to focus, his hands flickered blue for a fraction of a second at the same time that Arcus tried again, but then he coughed up yet more blood and the light went out. He shook his head in defeat.

"It's ok. You're still going to be ok. Try not to move; you need to conserve your strength." Arcus tried once more in vain to heal him and cast a worried look at Theri. "We need Celeste. I hope she makes it in time."

Theri squeezed Tarnelius' hand and stroked his hair, trying to soothe him and keep him calm. Every breath was clearly a struggle for the elf.

Celeste and the black-winged fiend fought high in the air, oblivious to what was happening on the ground. The demoness snapped her whip and sought to bind her opponent. They both wore the marks of injuries delivered by the other, and blood fell from the sky like rain. Celeste flew higher and higher, then turned and cast a pillar of flame powered by her rage down onto her opponent, who cackled in amusement as she pursued her, snapping her whip again. Celeste drew her bow and shot her with an ice arrow, catching the monster in one of her glossy black wings. The demoness looked at her in shock as the ice began to spread. Celeste smirked and grabbed another arrow. She shot at the other wing, but missed. Celeste calmly nocked a third arrow and took aim, while the she-demon headed for the ground to land. Celeste released the third arrow, and struck her target on the other wing. Satisfied, she watched as both wings froze up and her enemy began to fall from the sky. They were too high for her to try any sort of safe landing, so the demoness merely phased out and attempted a blind landing on the ground. Celeste pointed to the ground where she stood, and started to chant. Ice walls formed around her on all sides, and grew to enclose the demoness. Celeste flew down and approached with her bow ready. She dismissed the wall, then released the arrow, catching her prey right in the heart. The evil herald fell to the ground in a heap. In mere moments, Celeste was on her with her sword drawn.

"Any other useless monologue before I kill you? This is for what you tried to do to Tarnelius." Celeste brought her sword down, beheading the demoness and watching in satisfaction as she disintegrated a moment later. "Ah, that's convenient. No need to clean up afterward."

Celeste stood up and sheathed her sword. Then she took a quick survey of her injuries and looked for the others. She quickly spotted them several yards away. Arcus and Theri were crouching over Tarnelius – she took off into a sprint to join them.

Theri was stroking Tarnelius' hair and whimpering. Arcus looked pale and he shook his head as she approached.

"No!" screamed Celeste. "No, this cannot be." She grabbed Tarnelius and pulled him to her, sobbing. "No, no, no, no! You can't be dead, you just can't! I only just found you again. We're supposed to have forever." She placed her ear to his chest and listened, her heart broken and her mind reeling.

They were supposed to have their happily ever after. He had asked her to take the lifebond with him. She should have said yes and bonded with him last night. Why, oh why, didn't she say yes? If she had given in, none of this would have happened. She would have known the moment he was struck and she would have known how seriously he was hurt. Tears poured onto his shirt as she stroked his hand, her head still pressed to his chest. Life wasn't fair; none of this was fair.

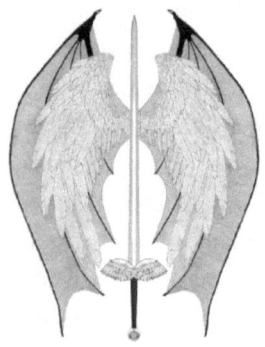

Chapter Fifteen
Hidden Dangers

Heartbroken, Celeste clutched the only man she had ever loved. Her body shook with convulsions as she sobbed. Her friends backed away, trying to give her privacy. Suddenly, Tarnelius twitched. It wasn't a big movement, but it was *definitely* a twitch. Celeste's heart lurched in her chest. She magically amplified her hearing, and placed her ear to his chest. After what felt like a lifetime, she heard what she was so desperate to hear – his heartbeat wasn't gone. It was there, slow and weak, but it was there. She chanted in desperation, her entire body glowing a bright blue color for a moment from the exertion. As they all watched, his wound began to knit and heal. Color began to return to his cheeks and he took a deep breath. Celeste held him tightly and cried even harder, this time with joy.

After a beat, he raised his hand and stroked her hair. She pulled back to look at him, catching his hand with her own and sniffled. "Don't ever do that to me again," she scolded.

"Celeste, my angel, I thought I was a goner. I tried my best to wait for you," he said in a weak and scratchy voice. "You saved me." He gave her a thin smile, his eyes twinkling.

She smiled through her tears. "You almost were a goner. You were down to minutes, judging by your heartbeat. Maybe less. Don't ever do that to me again. I can't survive without you."

Tarnelius gingerly sat up and kissed her swollen lips. "I'll certainly do my best, Angel." He ran his hand down her face and stopped at her still bleeding throat. "The dagger! It's a cursed weapon, like the sword." His hand flashed as he tried to heal her.

Celeste grabbed at her throat with her own hand and jumped to her feet as if he had stabbed her. "It's one of many minor injuries. I'll take care of it. We need to figure out what to do about the weapons they dropped. We can't just leave them lying around." She turned her back to him.

The whip, dagger and broadsword had all fallen to the ground before their owners had died. The armor the demon had worn had disintegrated with him. Celeste began healing her wounds while Arcus and Theri went to start collecting the weapons.

"What should we do with them?" Theri asked.

"I'm not sure, but I don't think we should keep them," said Celeste. "Besides, I don't know about any of you, but I don't know how to use a whip, and am not comfortable with a sword that big."

Arcus examined the dagger. "I could use this. It may come in handy."

"Take it if you wish, but I think we should destroy the lot of them. You never know what kind of evil curse could be imbued in those things," Celeste said.

"Shall I start working on a fire?" Theri asked.

Arcus looked up from examining the dagger. "No, ice will destroy them. They are born of fire."

Arcus reached into his bag, and tore a strip of cloth from his blanket to wrap around the dagger, before placing it carefully into the bag. Then he turned and pointed at the sword and whip, uttering a single word of magic. A line of ice shot from his finger. The two items froze over and then disintegrated, just as their owners had.

"Are you really okay now, Tarnelius?" Theri asked. "I thought you were dead. I saw you stop breathing, and felt you die in my arms. I'm so sorry you got stabbed. I feel like it was my fault, for blinding that demon."

"I'm fine now, and it's not your fault. On purpose, or on accident, that demon was gunning for me. I wonder if the female was his mate." He tried to catch Celeste's eye, but she refused to look at him.

"I doubt that particular breed settles for only one mate anyway," scoffed Arcus. Celeste glared at the two of them, then knelt down and started chanting. A transparent silver bubble formed over their heads and encased them all. It grew larger and larger, and when they could barely see it anymore, it vanished without popping. Celeste rose to her feet and said, "There, that ought to do it. Whoever that was who was scrying on us shouldn't be able to find us anymore; my spell will block them. Well, as long as you all stay close to me."

"I've never seen anything like that! Was that how you evaded me for all those centuries?" Tarnelius asked.

"Yes," Celeste said simply.

"How long does it last?"

"One day."

"You recast that spell every single day for six hundred years?"

"Yes. Now let's go," Celeste said. She took the lead, continuing east. The others fell in behind her.

"What's eating her, all of a sudden?" Arcus murmured to Tarnelius, who shrugged.

"She must be having trouble coping with my near-death experience. She seemed okay earlier, though."

"You men are really dense," interrupted Theri.

"What do you mean?" Tarnelius asked her.

Theri shook her head in exasperation and trotted to catch up with Celeste.

"I heard what you said," whispered Celeste. "Tarnel can hear us now, too. We have excellent hearing."

"Well, isn't that inconvenient when you want to have a private conversation with someone?" Theri snapped in exasperation.

"Look, to clear it up for both of you two men back there, Celeste is unhappy because of how easily she was forgotten as soon as the demoness showed up."

"But I –" started Tarnelius.

"Yes, yes. I know. She used magic to force you to give in to her. I know that, Celeste knows that. Ultimately though, you still gave in within seconds. It gives a girl a complex. Now, Celeste, it's over and in the past. You need to let it go because it will eat away at you if you don't. You both obviously love each other, so quit acting like children. You've known each other for too long to let something stupid like this taint what you have."

Tarnelius jogged up and grabbed Celeste's hand, turning her to face him. "What you don't understand is that I thought she was *you*. She did something to my head. As soon as she said 'I can be anything you want me to be', my mind fogged over, and she looked exactly like you. As soon as you broke her concentration I realized what I had done. If I had any desire for anyone else, anywhere on the planet, don't you think I would have had the time? It's only you. It's always been you. Don't you know that?"

Celeste cast her eyes down. "Of course I do. It just hurt to see you with her."

"You know, you'd feel much more secure if you would bond with me."

She gave him a small smile. "Just like how you wanted to do things right last night, I feel the same way. Though, I will think about it, if for no other reason than I would have known earlier that you needed me."

"There, that's all better," said Theri. "Now, let's go to Lumernia without all the awkward tension."

"How did you become so wise, anyway?" Tarnelius asked her as they walked.

"I come from a simple people. We feel the same emotions as everyone else, but aren't afraid to speak of them, the way I have noticed you all are. I'm sick of the tension. Life is easier if you say what you really think."

"Words to live by," smirked Arcus.

Theri fell into step beside him. "What about you, Arcus? Ever been in love?"

"Nope, I was raised around elves. There is something daunting about being surrounded by immortal beings that puts your whole life in perspective. If I want to reach my goals for myself, I can't be distracted by outside influences. Plus, you know, once I started hanging around with Joseph, he was always chasing after women. I tried that too, for a short time, but none of them ever seemed to be of the sort of quality you'd want to keep around, and I quickly became bored."

"I've been in love many times. Never found 'the one' though. Those two are lucky. I really am glad they made up.

Getting to watch the two of them sulk the last couple of weeks, while each of them snuck glances at the other when they weren't looking, was getting annoying," Theri said with a smile.

"We heard that, Theri," said Tarnelius.

"I meant you to hear it," Theri said with a grin.

Celeste stopped walking suddenly, almost causing Arcus to walk into her. "What is it, Celeste?" asked Tarnelius.

"Who was that guy?" Celeste asked.

"What do you mean?"

"Well, whoever that was, he summoned two powerful heralds like it was nothing. Who has the power to do that? Only a demigod, themselves, could summon the seraphs."

"But they are all gone," pointed out Tarnelius.

"I know, but that means the evil heralds have developed a hierarchy and chosen a leader. I can't say for sure that the good heralds haven't done the same, but I do know the seraphs pretty much operated independently after the war. If the demons have organized, and the angels haven't, that is going to tip the scales pretty horribly. We should hurry."

"Are you sure the seraphs haven't done the same?" Arcus asked.

"No, I'm not sure, but knowing what I do of them, I doubt they have. I don't remember even one of them being remotely power hungry."

"So if the side of good has angels, and the side of evil has demons, was there another side? One in the middle, following neither side?" Theri asked.

"There are heralds of neutrality. They are animal spirits for the most part. I've seen a few of them, but they keep to themselves."

"Accidentally start a forest fire. One will show up," muttered Arcus. Tarnelius chuckled.

"What was that?" asked Theri.

Arcus blushed, and Tarnelius spoke up to explain. "A few years ago, when Arcus here was barely fifteen, he set fire to the sacred tree. It was a magical fire, set by accident, because Arcus didn't know how to control his powers. Since it wasn't natural, the sentries that were on duty were having a difficult time putting it out. The great bear spirit, Karhu, appeared and put out the fire by absorbing it. Then he turned and roared at poor Arcus, who took off like he himself had been lit on fire!"

Celeste and Theri laughed. "It's not funny. At the time, I thought that massive monster was going to kill me," grumbled Arcus.

"Karhu isn't a monster; he was trying to protect the tree," said Tarnelius.

"That may be, but he was at least 16 feet tall! I was already panicking about what I had done as it was."

"Anyway," Tarnelius said. "If you noticed the scorch marks on the tree while you were there, that is the story of where they came from. The next time I saw our friend here was a few weeks ago, when he appeared right after you two did."

Arcus muttered, "I was too embarrassed to stay. I needed to find out who I was."

"You needn't have been embarrassed; we all knew it was an accident. Well, except for my father, who is a jerk, but that is another story entirely. We also understood why you left. I have to confess, I never expected to see you again."

"I saw a gigantic eagle once in the fringes of the forest near my tribe. Like, really gigantic. Standing on the ground, she was taller than I am, and I can't even hazard a guess as to how huge her wingspan was. Could she have been a spirit?" Theri asked.

"If I had to guess, I'd say that sounds a lot like Kotka. Yes, she is a spirit. What was she doing?" Celeste asked.

"Nothing. She just screeched and then took off into the sky. No one would believe me, when I told them what I had seen. I knew I wasn't crazy."

"Well, that remains to be seen," said Arcus.

"Oh, very funny," said Theri.

By nightfall, they finally made it out of the mountains. All around them, the ground became flat and grassy. The river still ran to their right, and the mountain range followed them all along their left. Their path, between the two, was smooth and clear. They built a campfire along the riverbank and set up the watch. Celeste sat down next to Tarnelius to watch the fire.

"What are you thinking about, Angel?" Tarnelius asked.

"Must you call me that?" Celeste asked.

"Yes, I must. You are an angel to me, and I like the endearment. Live with it," he answered with a wink.

"Well, anyway, I was just thinking, maybe when we get to Lumernia we could try to do the bonding ceremony. If we have the down time."

"We could do it here, out in the open, in front of all of nature. I don't mind as long as I get to have you," said Tarnelius.

Celeste smiled. "You'll always have me. I was thinking about what you were saying before. You were right, by the way. I do want to do this the proper way. I want the whole ceremony, the hand binding, and everything that goes with it. I want to give myself to you for the first time as a bonded couple."

"You shall have all that, and more. I will give you anything that is within my power to give. Though, I would bet we could teach the ceremony to Arcus and Theri, and they would help us do it."

"I'd love to have them help us with the ceremony; that's such a great idea. In Lumernia, we could have a private room though and not be out in the open, in hearing distance of our friends. Besides, there is another problem," said Celeste.

"What's that, *Rakastan*?"

"I don't know the words to the ritual. Do you? I can't teach them without learning it myself," Celeste said with a laugh.

Tarnelius smiled reassuringly. "Of course I do. I've presided over several ceremonies in the last six centuries. Remember, you're bonding with the Kayalost prince." He puffed his chest out in mock pride.

"Oh, excuse me, Your Grace. I forgot my place," she said with a giggle. "Seriously though, I never think about that. You're just Tarnel, my Tarnel. That's the only way I've ever thought of you."

"You have no idea how much it means to me that you only see me that way, instead of as my title. Anyway, do not worry about the ceremony. I'll take care of everything."

Celeste leaned forward and gave him a chaste kiss on the lips. "Despite all we have to worry about, I never worry now that I found you again. I love you, Tarnel."

Tarnelius' face split into a joyous grin. "And I love you, too, Angel."

The next week passed without any further issue or delay. Celeste made sure to cast the anti-divination spell every morning before they did anything else, and Tarnelius set about teaching the three others the bonding ritual, as he had promised.

"How effective would you say that spell actually is?" Arcus asked.

Celeste smirked. "Check with Tarnel, he'll tell you exactly how effective it is. Why do you ask?"

"I can't shake the feeling that we are being watched. I've felt eyes on us all this week."

"Not possible. It's just paranoia. Look around, to the left are the mountains, though they do end just over that last rise. To the right is the river, and beyond it more mountains. See? You can barely make out their peaks from here. We'd be able to see anyone watching us as well as they could see us, unless they are hiding in the mountains, but then they wouldn't be able to keep up," said Celeste.

"I know. That's why I was asking about divinations. Look, I'm sorry. I'm sure you are right. I am just feeling paranoid," said Arcus as they walked along.

"I think we are almost there, anyway. If we were being watched, don't you think whoever it was would have made their move by now? I think the outlying farms of Lumernia are just on the other side of those mountains. We should be able to see them soon."

Sure enough, by the time they were ready to stop that night, they had made it out of the mountain valley and in the distance they could make out many different farmhouses.

"Do you think we will be in Lumernia by tomorrow night?" Theri asked.

"Doubtful. We can't even see the great wall yet. Probably day after tomorrow," said Celeste.

"Too bad. I was hoping for a bed," pouted Theri.

Tarnelius smiled at her. "It's still a possibility. We may be able to find an inn, or even a farmhouse, where they would be willing to take us in."

"Oh, I really hope so," Theri said. "In my village, we usually sleep in trees, but I have found beds to be a most wonderful invention."

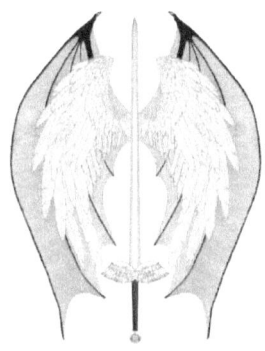

Chapter Sixteen
Under the Apple Trees

The night passed uneventfully, and the group packed up and got started, anxious to begin their day. They cast the spells to create the magic berries and to protect themselves from divinations, as had become the regular routine. Before long, they found a well-travelled foot path that ran slightly north, and away from the river. The path led them between the farmhouses they could only barely see the day before. Some were between them and the river, and there were more on their other side, to the north. There were farmers cultivating the soil for harvest and animals grazing in the fields. Children stopped and waved at them as they passed. More than a few adults stopped and stared at the group. They spoke in low whispers and pointed.

Celeste bristled. "What is it with humans and pointing? I'm sick of being the target of their gossip."

"Angel, in this case, my suspicion is that they are staring at Theri," said Tarnelius.

Theri grinned. "It's like they've never seen a kedistam before."

"They probably haven't," said Arcus.

By late afternoon, the group could just make out the top of the city wall in the distance. They decided to stop at a large plantation house, and ask if there was an inn nearby or if they could stay the night.

Tarnelius knocked on the door, which was answered by an elderly woman wearing a house dress. She had ice blue eyes, white hair and skin that had been wrinkled by many years in the sun.

"Can I help you?" she asked through the door, which she had only opened a few inches.

"Please, Ma'am, we only hope to ask for directions. Do you know of an inn nearby where we could rest tonight?"

"No inns around here. There's a bar the young people hang out at, but no inns. Nearest one is inside the city gates."

"Do you know of anywhere that might help us?" he asked.

"No," she said and started to shut the door, but just then Celeste stepped up. "Ma'am I see your fields are not cultivated and planted like the others. Why is this? Are you not farming any longer?"

"I don't see how that is any of your business," the woman scoffed.

"Well, it's just that I'm very good with plants. If you would be so kind as to let us stay here for one night, I would help you. Assuming, of course, that you still want to farm."

The woman sighed. "Look, times have become hard for us. We plan to sell this farm and move to the city soon. I'd hoped to have at least another year here, but my husband is unable to tolerate the pain of planting any longer."

Celeste glanced at Tarnelius. "We can help you. We are elven druids. If you bring your husband outside, Tarnelius here will try to heal him. I will take care of your crops. You will have a jump on all the other farms this year. Do we have a deal?"

The woman looked them over skeptically but then turned and yelled into the house. "Aengus, get out here *now*!" She stepped outside, shutting the door behind her, and looked the four of them over. "I don't know what you are doing here, and I don't care. My name's Roisin Walsh and my husband is Aengus. If you can really do what you said, you can stay here as long as you want." She peered at Theri, her lip curled in disgust. "Also, assuming your cat friend is housebroken and doesn't eat either of us."

Theri bared her fangs in contempt. "I am not a cat and I don't eat people. Furthermore, I found that comment about being housebroken to be just plain insulting."

"Theri, calm down. Let us handle this," said Celeste. "My name is Celeste, and this is Tarnelius. The gentleman dressed all in black is Arcus, and our kedistam companion is Therinsalla. I assure you, we will all be on our best behavior. You won't even know we are there."

The door swung open again, and an elderly man hobbled out. He was almost bald and was hunched over, leaning on a stick for support. He, too, had white hair and blue eyes. He was wearing long johns and was clearly getting ready to go to bed. "Roisin, what is this?"

"Aengus, these people are looking for a place to stay tonight. They say they can help us."

He lifted his stick in the air, and they could all see it trembling violently. "We are not an inn or a charity, and we don't need their help."

Celeste and Tarnelius both reached for him at the same time, their hands glowing blue. He tried to jump back but wasn't quick enough. They each caught him on the shoulder and their magic flowed into him. Roisin screamed but her cries stopped short when they released him and the old man stood straight and tall for the first time in years. He dropped the walking stick in shock and stared at them.

"H – how did you d – do that?" Aengus stuttered.

"Like I said, we can help you. Shall I head out to the fields now? Can we stay?"

"Young lady, for the first time in a decade my back is without pain. You are clearly an angel sent from the gods! Who would I be to turn you away?" Aengus exclaimed.

"Thank you very much, sir. Why don't you all go inside then, and I'll get to work. I'll be in soon," said Celeste.

"You can start tomorrow," said Roisin. "Just clearing the fields will take hours."

But Celeste was already walking out to the fields. They were overgrown with weeds and crops that hadn't been cut back the year before. It was a mess. Celeste walked out into the center of it all, watching as a couple of snakes slithered out of her way. She knelt down and placed her palm flat on the ground, and sat silently.

Back at the house, the others all crowded around the closest spot on the porch of the house to watch.

Celeste released her ivory wings, then she raised her hand in the air and slapped the ground. Her hand penetrated the soil and her arm buried in the ground up to her elbow. As they watched, the weeds and dying plants receded. They seemed almost to grow in reverse as they drew back into the ground and vanished. Then she plunged her other hand into the earth, and new plants emerged and flourished. Corn stalks raced up into the air, tomato plants emerged in their fields, and pumpkins sprouted a short distance away in their pumpkin patch. Apple trees shot into the sky from out of nowhere, as did plum trees and berry bushes. Bean stalks, carrots and potatoes each appeared where they had been grown in years past. In between everything, grass filled in and wildflowers flourished. The entire process took about an hour, during which time no one on the porch moved a muscle.

When everything was finished, it was dusk and the red moon had barely risen in the sky. Celeste stood up and swayed on her feet. Tarnelius leapt over the rail of the porch and ran to her, placing his arm protectively around her waist. He helped guide her back to the group on the porch.

"My gods, you really are an angel!" Roisin said.

Celeste smiled weakly. "The crops will be ready for harvesting tomorrow morning. The plants told me of all the love you two have shown them in the past. The apple and plum trees are my gift to you. Please, just don't tell your neighbors how this has happened until after we are gone."

The elderly couple both nodded. "Please, come inside. You look exhausted. I'll make up some of the guest rooms for you. Your secret is safe with us, and you can stay as long as you want. We'll tell them it was a miracle if they ask before you go," Roisin said.

"Three rooms, if you have them, please. Only I'm not going to sleep yet. Tarnelius and I are going to become bonded, first." She smiled up at him as he inhaled sharply. "Right here, under the apple trees."

"Are you sure you feel up to it now, Angel?" he asked.

"I've never been more sure of anything in my life," she said. "We've already waited so very long. Why make it longer and torture ourselves? I was being foolish."

"Bonded? What does that mean?" Roisin asked.

Theri clapped her hands together and hopped up and down in excitement. "It means they are getting married."

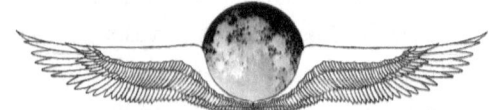

The old farmhouse was very large. It had belonged to Roisin's family for three generations. At one time it had been called home by many, including Roisin's grandparents, parents, aunts, uncles, cousins and hired farm workers. The halls had echoed with laughter and tears.

The master bedroom was on the second floor, though Roisin and Aengus had abandoned it years ago, when Aengus could no longer manage the stairs. There were six bedrooms in total on the second floor, and also a library. The first floor had three more bedrooms, plus a kitchen, dining area, family room and even an indoor bath house. Everyone had moved out of the old plantation house long ago, in favor of living inside the city walls. All except for Roisin and Aengus. Roisin escorted Celeste up to the second floor and showed her the master bedroom, hurrying to tidy up and change the bedding.

"Do you need a dress, dear? I'm sure my old dress is around here somewhere, though I'm not sure it would fit you."

"No, thank you, Roisin. I have one already. I just need to clean up a bit. Do you have some white material, though? I only need a couple of strips to bind our hands with."

Roisin stopped and stared for a moment. "What kind of ceremony do you elves perform? I've never heard of being tied up for a wedding. I do have some materials I like to sew with. I'll see what I have."

"We'll need two strips, please. If not, I'll tear the base of the dress I'm wearing now. This may not be white, but it will still serve its purpose."

Roisin finished with the room and pulled Celeste downstairs to the bathhouse. "Here, you do whatever you need to do. I'll go see about material."

"Where is Tarnel? I expected that he would be in here."

"He's already clean and getting dressed in the master bedroom. Aengus is trying to find him some clean clothes, I believe. Why did you think I kept you chatting for so long, dear? Your other friends are getting ready in their rooms, downstairs. We're giving you two lovebirds the whole upstairs to yourselves."

Celeste rummaged in her small magic satchel, pulling out the satin gown she had brought for her audience with the king. It was perfect. She smiled and laid the dress out for her to change into after she cleaned up. Then she removed her old clothes and cleaned herself in the bath, which was ingeniously set up with a piping system to filter river water through it; this kept the water clean and refilled at all times. After she finished cleaning herself, she also scrubbed her old clothes and left them to dry in the bath house. Then she slipped on her dress, pinched her cheeks, and summoned some of the magical berries. She ate a few of them, which helped to build up her strength and revitalize her, and broke open a couple more to smear the juice on her lips. Then she returned her bag to the master bedroom upstairs and went outside to the apple trees to wait.

Tarnelius and Celeste faced each other in front of the huge apple trees. Tarnelius had never felt happier at any time in his long life. He didn't know it was possible to feel this much joy. He gazed at his beautiful angel, as he took in the whole scene. He wanted to commit this image to his memory, forever. The moon had gone into hiding behind some heavy clouds, so Arcus had summoned some small white lights that lit up the area and reflected in her raven black hair as a bluish white. The ornate white satin gown she was wearing was the exact shade of her wings, which were on display. Around her pale neck hung a platinum chain bearing her mother's ruby hawk pendant. She was perfect, she completed him. She was his. Finally.

Celeste smiled up at him, her green eyes shining with joy. She knew she had made the right decision. Her heart skipped a beat when she saw the love in his eyes, as he met her gaze. He was wearing borrowed clothes; linen pants and a loose fitting white shirt that was untied at the collar. They fit reasonably well, and she was struck with just how handsome he looked, almost as if she were seeing him for the first time. His golden mane seemed to absorb the sparkling lights, making it glow. She reflected back on their history and couldn't believe how much time she had wasted leading up to this point, but was overjoyed at receiving this second chance.

The two stepped closer, until they were near enough to hold hands. As one, they each lifted their hands and grasped the other's, with their palms together and their fingers entwined. Theri stepped forward with the strips of cloth, and wrapped the material around their hands, binding them together with a knot. Roisin had really come through with the material. Her right hand was bound to his left in white satin, and his right to her left in white linen. Theri quietly took a few steps backward to stand next to Roisin, across from Arcus and Aengus. The scene was beautiful.

Arcus cleared his throat and spoke to Celeste, beginning the ceremony.

"Do you, Celeste, take Tarnelius to be your mate?
To be his constant friend,
His partner throughout life, and his one true love?
To love him without reservation,
Honor him and respect him,
Protect him from harm,
Comfort him if he is distressed,
And to grow with him in mind and spirit?
From this day until the end of days?"

Celeste beamed, seeming to glow from the inside out. "I do," she said.

Theri then smiled and spoke to Tarnelius.

"Do you, Tarnelius, take Celeste to be your mate?
To be her constant friend,
Her partner throughout life, and her one true love?
To love her without reservation,
Honor her and respect her,
Protect her from harm,
Comfort her if she is distressed,
And to grow with her in mind and spirit?
From this day until the end of days?"

Tarnelius gazed into her eyes, trying to express his deep joy and love for her by just baring his soul to her through his eyes. "It's all I've ever wanted, from the very first time I ever laid eyes on you when we were both children. Of course I do."

The two began to chant in unison. The ritual called for them to begin with the old elven language.

"Kattemme ovat forene!
Vi talereski lofte.
Bir gnist af raka, bragt til faenge.
Biz kaksi on oltava kuin bir.
Kalplerimiz tasma, rakaemme parlar sanli!
Emme hyvasky vi stan."

Then, they repeated their words, once more, in the common tongue.

"Our hands are joined, our souls unite!
We speak the ancient words.
A spark of love, brought to ignite.
We two shall be as one.
Our hearts outpour, our love shines bright!
We do accept the bond."

The couple stepped toward each other and kissed, joining their forearms together from their elbows to their fingertips. After a beat, Arcus and Theri stepped forward and carefully pulled the bindings off their wrists without breaking or untying the knots. They would keep the knotted material to signify that their bond was forever. As soon as they were free, the ceremony was over. Arcus and Theri dropped the ties at the couple's feet and the four witnesses offered their quiet congratulations. The four then stepped respectfully away, tiptoeing back to the house.

Tarnelius and Celeste noticed none of this. They were too engrossed in each other. As soon as they shared the symbolic kiss, they were both overwhelmed by the sensations they immediately experienced. Their souls had split and merged into one. They could both feel the all-consuming love, and hear the innermost thoughts, of the other. Celeste moved her arms up and around Tarnelius' neck, while his dropped to her waist. They deepened the kiss, their tongues exploring each other's mouth and twisting together in an erotic tango. Tarnelius moaned into her mouth in pure rapture. She trembled from the sheer emotion of it all. She knew that if elves died when they had nothing more to live for, she and Tarnelius would live for an eternity because they had each other; this was truly their happily ever after.

He broke off the kiss and inched back, trying to catch his breath and running his hands up and down her body in a delicious caress. *"Don't stop,"* she spoke inside his head. *"Don't ever stop."*

"Celeste, my angel. Don't ask me that now. I will never be able to refuse you. Come on, I'm sure the others are spying on us out here, and I want our first time to be in private, not out here in the open where anyone could interrupt us."

She leaned forward, offering her lips to him, pressing her body flush against his. He gave in and tried to give her only a brief kiss, but she reached up and tangled her hands into his golden hair, holding him against her. She moaned as she felt him straining against her and shivered as he caressed her wings.

He felt his control slipping as he kissed her with all the desperation of a starving man. They needed to get themselves under control or he would take her right there. When he felt her shiver he pulled back once more, running his hands again over her wings. She licked her lips and closed her eyes, breathing heavily. "Does that feel good, Angel?"

"Mmm," she answered.

He gave her a devilish grin as he stroked her feathery wings. "I had no idea your wings were so sensitive. Come on, we need to get inside. We'll have an eternity to get to know each other intimately, starting tonight. I promise I will always be exactly what you need, Celeste." He picked up the satin and linen bindings and took her hand. He led her away from the trees and into the house, up to their room.

After the ritual, Arcus went back out to sit on the porch steps. He pulled out the infernal dagger he'd kept from the demon fight. He carefully unwrapped it, admiring the red color that it still glowed. Suddenly, he heard the sound of a deep chuckle on the breeze, coming from the east. The hairs on the back of his neck prickled, and he stood up to see who was there.

Arcus examined the area, seeing nothing. The dazzling lights that he had created for the ceremony had been dismissed and the red moon now shone down ominously, creating shadows on the ground. Arcus never noticed the shadow come up behind him and walk literally right into him. His gray eyes flashed red for a moment, then he relaxed and went back to his bag to clean his dagger. When he was done, he removed the orc dagger he always carried from its sheath, wrapped it up in the cloth and placed it in his bag. Then he placed the infernal dagger in the sheath, to keep it close to him, and returned to his room.

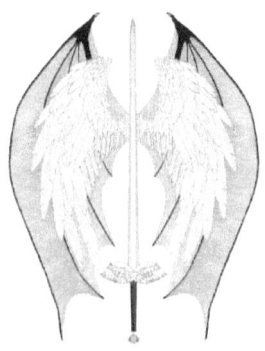

Chapter Seventeen
Mind Games

Tarnelius woke up to find his beautiful bride cuddled up against him. She was dreaming of him, he could tell from their link. The knowledge made him smile. He brushed her hair from her face with his fingertips, and kissed her on the cheek. She opened her eyes and beamed at him.

"Hi," she thought to him.

"Hi yourself," he returned.

"That's going to take some getting used to," she said aloud.

"Yes, it is. I'll have to try not to be too distracting with my thoughts of you throughout the day," he promised.

Celeste stretched and rose to her feet. She grabbed her spare traveling dress from inside her bag and carefully placed the satin one back into the bag, along with the tied ceremonial material. She brushed her hair and turned to find Tarnelius still lying in bed, his hands behind his head, staring at her.

She blushed at his thoughts. "Come on, get up. We need to get out of here before the neighbors see what I did, or we'll never escape this place."

"And how, exactly, would they force us to stay?"

"I don't know, and I don't want to think about it, so get up." She threw his bag at him, which he deflected with his arm, laughing. Then she left the room to go get the dress she had washed the night before, which she also placed in her bag. She found Theri at the table with Roisin and Aengus, happily eating breakfast and chattering away.

"Where's Arcus?" Celeste asked.

"My guess would be that he is still in his room. I haven't seen him," said Theri.

"Did you have a nice night, dear?" Roisin asked.

Celeste blushed a deep red and muttered an affirmation. Then she went to Arcus' room and knocked on the door. She frowned at the silence and tried to open the door, but it was locked from the inside.

"I'm sure he's fine," she heard inside her head.

She jumped in alarm. *"Don't do that! You scared me half to death!"* she thought back.

She frowned at the sound of Tarnelius' laughter. "I can't help it any more than you can," he said as he came down the stairs. "You project your thoughts to me, I respond."

"Well, anyway, he never sleeps in. I'm concerned."

"Come away from the door, my love. Let's have breakfast. I hear the farmers here had an early harvest," he said with a wink. "I'm sure Arcus will join us when he is ready."

Halfway through breakfast Arcus staggered in to join them. He looked worn out and drawn. His face and hair looked scruffier than normal.

"Is everything okay, Arcus?" Tarnelius asked in concern.

"Nightmares. I'm fine, just tired."

They ate their breakfast in silence, the mood dampened by Arcus scowling at them. When they finished, Celeste and Theri picked up the dishes and helped Roisin clean them.

"Thank you for allowing us the use of your house last night, and for breakfast this morning," said Celeste.

"Thank *you*, my dear, for everything. I wish you the best of luck in whatever you are here to accomplish. If you ever need a place to stay again, or if there is any other way we can help you, don't hesitate to drop by," Roisin said, while her husband nodded in agreement from behind her.

"Excuse me, son, might I have a quick word?" Aengus asked Tarnelius, who nodded and followed the old man into the family room. "I wrote this up for you last night. If you need any help while you are in the city or need a place to stay there, I want you to locate this address. This is my grandson's home, and the letter explains everything. He will recognize my handwriting and will help you."

"Thank you, sir," replied Tarnelius.

"I hope you two kids have a wonderful life together," said Aengus.

Tarnelius bowed in respect. "I'm sure we will, sir. I've loved her for over eight hundred years."

The old man inhaled sharply in surprise, but managed to maintain his composure other than that. The two went to rejoin the group.

Celeste and Theri gave the old couple a hug, while Arcus and Tarnelius settled for handshakes. Then they left, heading for the gate.

As they drew near, they became aware of vast numbers of knights all around them. Everywhere. Some stood in formation in the fields, as well as a large quantity of military style tents.

There were some standing along the side of the roadway, talking. A huge number of them waited to enter the city gates. The four friends joined the long line entering the city.

"Excuse me, sir," Tarnelius said to the knight in front of them, who was atop a dappled gray warhorse. "What is going on? Why are there so many knights entering the city?"

He turned the horse about. "King Liam has summoned us all for a special mission. How is it that you haven't heard? Where have you been?" Then he squinted into the sun, trying to bring the group better into focus. "Elves! Also, what are you?" he asked Theri.

"Kedistam," she answered.

"Whatever. Anyway, what are *you* all doing here?" he asked.

"We're here to see the king," answered Celeste.

The knight guffawed. "Well, good luck with that right now," he said as he turned his horse back around.

Tarnelius placed his hand on Celeste's shoulder. "Don't worry, we'll work it out."

"I wasn't worried," she said.

"You can't lie to me, Angel. Not anymore."

The line progressed rapidly, as very few of the knights in armor were stopped or questioned in any way. After only a couple of hours in line they found themselves at the front. Tarnelius had pulled his hood over his head. Celeste made sure her hair covered her ears.

"State your business here," said one of the gate guards.

"We have business with the king," said Celeste.

The guard looked up in surprise. "Do you have an appointment with him?"

"No, but he will see me."

"I doubt it, beautiful. Looks like you wasted your time." He raised his voice to be heard by the other guards. "Access de-"

Arcus jumped forward and snapped is fingers. *"Trust me, he will see us,"* Arcus chanted in his hypnotic voice.

The guard turned to face him and froze, locked in Arcus' stare. "I'm sure he will," he muttered.

"You will grant us access now, won't you?" he asked.

"Yes, yes of course. Access granted!" he shouted as he handed them each a card with the city seal stamped on it.

The group took their first steps into Lumernia. "You know, you are very useful to have around sometimes," Celeste joked to Arcus, who glowered but said nothing.

"Something is off with him, but I don't know what it is. He seemed fine last night," Celeste thought to Tarnelius.

"He does seem a bit quieter and angrier than normal, but it may be because he didn't sleep well. Try not to worry; if it continues I will address it," Tarnelius replied.

"Wait," she squinted at Arcus. *"The hilt of his dagger looks different…"*

"Arcus," said Celeste. "Are you carrying that demon dagger on you now?"

"What? Why do you ask?" Arcus frowned and looked down at his sheath. "I mean, I am; but why are you asking me that?"

"The dagger is evil, I'm almost sure of it. Please be careful with it. I'd really be much more comfortable if you kept it wrapped up in your bag, if you are unwilling to destroy it."

"Would you, Celeste? Would you be more comfortable? I'm sorry to be the one that has to tell you this, but not everyone around you is concerned with how *comfortable* you are," Arcus exclaimed, his eyes flashing red as he spoke. "Maybe you should take it up with your mate."

"Now, wait just a minute there," Tarnelius jumped in. Celeste put her hand on his arm to console him.

"Leave it," she said aloud. "He is probably right, don't make it worse."

"There is definitely something off about him. I think it's the dagger. Did you see his eyes change color? Either the dagger or something else has possessed him, or both. Don't antagonize him. I'm not sure what is going on, but we don't want to make a scene out here in public," Celeste thought to Tarnelius.

Tarnelius looked at her helplessly. *"Will he be okay?"*

"I'm not sure, but we'll do our best to help him. For now, let's just try not to set him off."

"I'm sorry, Arcus. I know you can handle it. I shouldn't have questioned you. Let's just go," Celeste said, smiling.

The city of Lumernia was enormous, and they were overwhelmed by the sheer size and complexity of it. The area just inside the gate was a market of sorts, with every kind of store imaginable. Several temporary tents had been set up that sold various blacksmith and leathersmithing items. These looked as if they had been set up in haste, most likely due to the demand caused by the increased number of knights.

The group stopped by one of the tents to ask a frazzled looking merchant for directions, and a general idea of the fortress city's layout. All around them was the bazaar area. Immediately ahead of them to the east was the city center, which housed the public parks, inns, pubs, taverns, places of worship and all of the official buildings necessary for keeping such a large fortified city running smoothly. Past that, at the easternmost point, was King Liam's castle. The castle was so large it could be seen from anywhere in the city, and even as far away as they were, they could see it looming in the distance. Northwest of them were the craftsman's guilds, where artisans created anything from women's fancy clothing to heavy armor. Between the north and east spokes lay the other guilds, which included the mage guilds and bookbinders. Between the western spoke, where they were, and the southern spoke was where they kept the livestock and the butchers. The merchant recommended avoiding that area, unless they absolutely needed to go there, due to the smell that always permeated the air. Beyond that, in the southeast section, were the residential areas. Each area of the diamond shaped city was divided by a lower city wall, and it was obvious that the city had been designed with clear planning. This was not a disorganized town that had continued to expand larger and larger in a disorderly fashion, as Izmar had. Instead, every building had its place, and every building was maintained with precision.

Thanking the merchant, they progressed to the east and entered the gate leading to the city center. From there, they entered the nearest inn, only to find it full of men sitting around and drinking. Celeste approached the man who appeared to be the innkeeper, a portly man with only a few wisps of hair left on his head, who was surveying a large number of harassed looking barmaids.

"Excuse me, sir, but we were interested in renting a room," she inquired. The bartender stared at her and the others in shock.

"Surely you must realize that everywhere is filled to capacity. Look around you, this is utter chaos," the man exclaimed. "Colleen, table five has been looking for you. Move, girl!"

"What exactly is going on here?" Celeste asked.

"King Liam has it in his head he is going to go after some holy relic, is what I've overheard from the soldiers. Then, when they get back, he is declaring war on the entire orc race. Going to wipe them all out, he is. Say, you aren't looking for a job for the next few months, are you? I think you'd make a decent barmaid," said the innkeeper.

"No, thank you, sir. If he is going to go after the relic first, why would he bring everyone here now? This city doesn't seem equipped to handle all these knights."

"Well, first of all, you're right and it isn't. Second, this is hardly *all* the knights. Actually, this is only the Rashnurian Order. I've heard that the Mithran Order is starting to arrive, but I haven't seen any come in here yet. The Saroshan Order hasn't had enough time to travel here. It will take quite a while to get everyone here and organized, so I guess King Liam decided to start things early."

"I see. Well, thank you for your time, sir. I'll let you get back to work," said Celeste.

"If you change your mind about that job, let me know. I'll be here."

Celeste gestured for the others, and they left the inn. "We can keep trying the inns if you guys want, but I suspect that the innkeeper is right and this whole place is overcrowded. I bet the troops that were too late for rooms are the ones that we saw with the tents outside the city."

"Do you want to look up Aengus' family?" Tarnelius asked.

"I hate to barge in on someone and just presume they will help, based on someone else's recommendation, but I suppose we'd better. The sooner we find somewhere to base ourselves from, the sooner we can get organized. Maybe his family will need healing or something, too, and then we'll have a way to pay him back."

The group headed out the southeastern gate leading to the residences. Outside the city center, things were considerably quieter. The wall itself seemed to muffle many of the noises overwhelming the city center and bazaar. There were still several knights walking around this area, but there were far fewer than anywhere else they had seen. There were also several commoners who probably lived here permanently. The group stopped a young woman carrying a basket full of clothing, to ask for directions. She pointed behind her and explained where the street was that Aengus had written down. Tarnelius bowed in thanks and they continued to where she had directed them.

They found the house easily enough, and Tarnelius went up to the door and knocked, while the others waited a few feet behind him. After a few moments they heard a masculine, muffled voice through the door. "Who's there?"

"You don't know me. My name is Tarnelius. I'm a friend of Aengus and Roisin Walsh."

"Are you a knight?"

"No," Tarnelius said, perplexed. "I can definitely say 'knight' is something I am not."

The door cracked open a little, revealing a thin man with brown hair and blue eyes that were the same shape as Roisin's. "I've already told those knights that they are not welcome in here. Rowdy bunch. They have no respect, not at all what you'd expect from paladins."

"As you can see, sir, I am no paladin. My name is Tarnelius, this is Celeste, Theri, and Arcus with me. None of us are knights. Your grandfather gave me this to give to you." He held out the letter and the man reached out and took it, a suspicious look on his face. As he read it, his eyebrows shot upward.

"This is not possible. There is no one on Altierra with the power to do what he described here."

"I assure you that it is not only possible, it is true," answered Tarnelius.

The man stepped out and scrutinized Tarnelius. "Lower your hood, sir," he said to Tarnelius.

Tarnelius did as asked, his pointed ears that marked him as an elf easily seen under his golden mane of hair. The man's eyes widened in surprise. He turned to look at the others, particularly Theri. He turned his eyes back to Tarnelius, hope appearing in his eyes.

"Can you help me?" he asked, his voice a strained whisper.

Celeste stepped forward. "What's wrong? What can we do?"

"My name is Conner Walsh, my wife is Fiona Walsh. Hurry, come inside; I'll explain." The group walked in and Conner shut the door behind them. "What I'm about to tell you cannot leave this room," he began. The others all nodded in agreement. "My wife, Fiona, is the love of my life. I moved out of the plantation for her, because she wanted to live here. She has a heart of pure gold, always helping others. One day, a few years ago, she was returning home after taking food to my grandparents' house when she found a blind leper who was begging outside the city. She tried to give the beggar money, but as she bent to give it to him, someone cut across her path and kicked at the beggar's money jar, spilling the contents everywhere. She hurried to help him, and when she reached out to return his money, he coughed and his spittle went right into her face and eyes. Time went on. I thought everything was fine. She never showed any symptoms. However, the lesions recently started to form on her face and arms. For the past few weeks I have kept her hidden here. She has lost her vision, and her voice is different now. I have her set up in our bedroom, and I have taken time off from work to help her. I don't know how long I can keep anyone from finding out, but I have to try. I won't let them take her away from me."

Celeste stared at him in bewilderment. "You live in a city full of paladins. Why don't you just take her to them?"

"Are you insane? They're the ones that would take her from me and make her live outside the city, begging for scraps."

"Why do you think they would do that? They are paladins, they should be able to heal her."

Now it was Conner's turn to stare at her in bewilderment. "Why on earth would you think an over-glorified fighter could help her?"

"Don't paladins receive healing magic from the old gods? Though they are gone, there were measures left in place to allow their children – us – to be able to use their magic. That's how we heal and cast other spells, using the magic Kamara gifted to her children."

"Well, they don't. Paladins are just fighters, and they are a disrespectful and judgmental lot. Can you guys help me or not?"

Celeste nodded. "We can help you. We will fix this, I promise. You don't have to worry anymore. Here is what you will need to do, though. First thing, we will heal her. Next, we're going to need to check you out, as well. Leprosy isn't really as contagious as people seem to think, but it is spread by body fluids, and I have to assume you have to have come into contact. Finally, we are going to need to clean this house from top to bottom. Do you have cleaning supplies, or can you get cleaning supplies?"

"I have a fair amount of lye soap. I've been washing my hands and face any time I come anywhere near that room. If I catch it, too, there would be no one to help."

"Good thinking. Now, why don't you show us where the basins and soap are? Theri and I will get started on preparing the cleaning water. Tarnelius, will you see to Fiona? And Arcus, would you be okay with checking Conner, after he shows us where the basins are?"

"That is fine," Arcus said, as Tarnelius nodded.

"I'll show you where the basins are, but maybe I should see to Fiona with you? I don't want her to become frightened. She can't see what is going on." Tarnelius nodded, then he and Arcus waited in the entryway while Conner escorted the ladies to the kitchen. After only a few moments, he returned and gestured for them to follow him down the hall. He stopped outside the master bedroom, which was at the end of the hallway.

"I'll wait out here," said Arcus, as Conner opened the door. The other two stepped inside, shutting the door behind them.

"Conner? Do I hear voices? Who is here?" Fiona asked, with a deep scratchy voice, from the bed.

"Do not worry, my love. This is Tarnelius; he is here to help you."

"What have you done?" she exclaimed. "He cannot help me. He will take me away, and banish me to live outside the city." Fiona began to cry.

"Madame Fiona, I assure you my intentions are nothing of the sort. I am a druid from the elven village of Kayalost; I am here to heal you." With that, he approached her. He laid his hand on her face. Fiona was stunned. Even her husband had been too fearful to touch her face. She couldn't see, so she had no idea how she looked, but she imagined the lesions were awful to behold. He began to chant in a strange language, and she heard Conner suck in his breath.

"What have you done?" Conner asked. "Why is she glowing that strange blue color?"

Tarnelius did not answer but instead kept chanting, repeating whatever it was he was saying over and over. Each time he began again, he put the inflection on a different syllable. The third time through his spell, her vision began to clear. She could almost make out the shape of her savior, his hand still on her cheek and forehead. With each word, each syllable, she could make out more and more until, finally, colors were returned to her. She could see that Conner was right. Tarnelius' hands were both glowing a radiant blue and they seemed to pulsate. Looking down, she could see that she was also glowing a blue pulsing color, though it was a lighter shade than his hands. Finally, he finished chanting and removed his hands, their color returning to normal.

"Madame Fiona, you are healed," the handsome elf said, breathing heavily. "I'll give you two a moment alone. Conner, when you are ready, you should go see Arcus so he can make sure you haven't caught it as well, and just have not yet become symptomatic. Then, we must begin cleaning this room." He bowed low and swept from the room. Outside, he nodded to Arcus, who was leaning against the wall. He entered the kitchen and found the soapy water the women had prepared with water from the well out back. He carefully washed his hands, then stood back out of the way, watching Celeste and Theri clean.

"Everything okay in there?" Theri asked.

"Yes. She was blinded because the lesions were actually in her eyes. She was still in the early stages, so she fortunately hadn't lost any of her extremities. I haven't even attempted any regeneration spells in quite some time, so I would have needed your help," he said to Celeste. "However, I should have warned Conner about the visual effects of what I was going to do. Since it wasn't a localized injury, I used one of the more ancient healing spells to heal her entire body. He was startled to see her change colors."

Celeste nodded as she cleaned. "Yeah, that's what I would have suggested. Don't worry about him being upset about the short-term color change, he'll get over it. You just gave him his wife back. How is Arcus doing with him, anyway?"

"They hadn't started yet when I came in here."

"Would you mind going back out? I don't want to leave him unsupervised. Matter of fact, I think until we figure out what is going on, one of us should be around him at all times."

Theri stared at her in bewilderment. "Who? Conner?"

Celeste frowned. "Great, was I talking out loud?"

"While you work this part out, I'll just be out there, then," Tarnelius interjected, before sweeping from the room.

Celeste sighed. "Theri, please don't say anything to him, but I think Arcus may have been possessed or something. I'm not sure. He has been acting strangely since this morning, when he started carrying that dagger around. When we first entered this city, and he snapped at me, his eyes flared red like a demon's. That's why I'm worried. I don't know if it's something as simple as taking away the dagger, or if there is something inside him fighting for control." Inside her head, Celeste felt Tarnelius thinking about what to do regarding Conner as it seemed he had contracted the disease. Arcus had found traces in his blood, but had never learned the ancient healing spells to encompass healing all of a person's blood and organs at once. *"Wait for me,"* she thought to him.

"Are you sure?" Theri gasped. "What can we do?"

"I don't know. This is beyond anything I can do. If I were a real herald I could fix him, but I'm not. I don't know where to find any of them anymore, either. We need to keep him as calm as we can, so that he has the easiest time possible staying in control. That said, we need to watch him and be ready to take him down if he loses that battle. I'm sorry, Theri, I don't mean to be rude, but I think that means Tarnel and I, because I don't think you are any match for him. Especially considering the goal would be to neutralize him, not kill him."

"I can handle him! Arcus wouldn't hurt me anyway."

"I doubt very much Arcus *would* hurt you, but whatever is riding around with him, fighting for dominance, sure would. If that thing gains Arcus' ability to wield arcane and druid magic, it could be bad for -"

"We're coming in," Tarnelius interjected inside her head. A few moments later the door swung open and Tarnelius stumbled in, assisted by Arcus, with both Conner and Fiona right behind them. Tarnelius appeared haggard. Celeste reached for Tarnelius, but he waved her away and stumbled to the basin to wash his hands again.

"Don't worry about me. It's just the magic taking its toll. It's been a long time since I've needed to cure any disease that complicated, much less do it twice. Probably some five hundred years ago, when several of the animals in the Kayalik Mountains suffered from a strange infection that caused them all to go insane and foam at the mouths, in fact. We used that spell then, but most of the infected animals were quite a lot smaller than humans, and there were many of us to cast it."

"I *told* you to wait for me," she sighed. "Why don't you go outside and rest for a little while? The rest of us can clean."

"No, Angel. I want to help. Just give me a moment to catch my breath."

The six of them all spread out, finishing the kitchen area in no time at all. Then they moved into the master bedroom. Celeste walked to the windows and removed the boards covering them, letting light and air inside.

"What is the best way to clean these sheets?" Theri asked.

"Burn them," answered Celeste. "We won't be able to get the material clean enough to guarantee there will be no reinfection. Her bedclothes too. Everything else needs to be washed. We'll need to change out the water from the basins often."

They started on their task, making sure nothing was missed. By the time they were finished with that room, they were almost out of soap, and had enough to finish maybe one more room. Celeste offered to go to the soap maker and get some more, as she also wanted to pick up some herbs. Conner gave her some money and told her where to go.

"Do you want me to see if I can pick up some more sheets as well?" Celeste asked.

"I'll need to get some more soon, but we have a few extra sets. I had been purchasing new ones regularly. Don't worry about it now," said Conner.

So Celeste was off, heading through the inner gate into the city center.

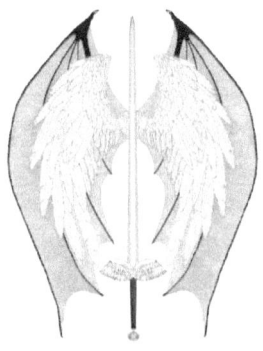

Chapter Eighteen
Flight of the Fallen

Celeste walked into the southeast quadrant of Lumernia, but something in the city center seemed to call out to her. She followed her instincts and veered east toward the castle, trying to tune out the many humans who all seemed to need to talk at once. The sheer volume level was very jarring to her. She pushed through the crowd and found herself standing in the middle of a manicured park. Children played all around her. Right in front of her were four white marble buildings. To the left of each of the doors on these beautiful buildings was a marble statue. Each statue was of a different paladin, and each one bore the symbols and trappings of one of the Paladin Orders. Three of the four doors displayed a matching symbol upon them. The building on the far left, however, seemed to be covered in an air of sadness. Its windows were covered with black boards, and a faded black cloth covered the door. The statue portrayed a male knight, his sword raised high in triumph. His shield, which was held carelessly at his side, exhibited an emblem of a longsword with large feathery angel wings where the guard should be. Celeste approached the statue and ran her fingers over the shield. She bit her lip and stared at the covered door for a moment, then decisively approached it. The door swung easily on its hinges when she pushed on it, as if it had been waiting for her.

Inside, all was dark, except for the light that beamed in from the doorway. The building seemed almost like it resented the intrusion of the fading sunlight outside. It took a moment for her eyes to adjust, and when they did, her heart dropped a little. This, indeed, was a temple to the demigod Melek. Every flat surface was covered in grime, as if no one had tended to it in centuries. The door had left a curving arc of cleared dust on the floor as if to demonstrate where it had travelled. She walked farther into the temple and saw that this room had been beautiful, once. There was a twin statue to the one outside, surrounded by seraphs. She might have been imagining it, but she would have sworn that one of the statues bore a strong resemblance to her father. It *had* been eight hundred years since she last saw him, though, so she couldn't be sure. The altar at the front of the room was draped in black, as were many of the other ceremonial items in the room.

She moved to examine some of the old paintings on the walls. Some were of paladins, others were of seraphs in flight. One painting had been covered. She approached it and tugged at the cloth, watching it fall to the floor. What she saw made her gasp in surprise. The painting portrayed Melek himself in full battle regalia under the light of the silver moon. He was surrounded by his heralds as they fought against Kuunkierto. The god of ultimate evil had been portrayed with the lower body of a large steel gray dragon, and the torso of a huge, gray-skinned demon with horns. His eyes glowed a menacing red and blood dripped from a gash in his side. Melek wielded his legendary sword, with wings extended from the cross guard. The plaque underneath declared, "*Melek's last stand.*" She had found the painting surprising because its presence here implied that the temple had remained active for quite some time after the death of the god. She gazed upon the painting a moment more before turning and pulling the cloth from the altar. Laying across it was a replica of Melek's sword. On the plaque here was written, *"Melek's sword was imbued by Aurinko, the Sun, giving him the power to defeat any evil."*

"Kamara help us," Celeste whispered. "He's going after the sword. That's what this is all about. He plans to take over all of Altierra and annihilate the races that disagree with him, starting with the orcs. That's why he is raising an army. I wonder how long until he comes for the elves and dwarves," she pondered aloud. "He's nothing but a common, power-hungry tyrant."

"What are you doing here?" exclaimed a voice from the door. Celeste jumped in shock, her wings popping free as she jerked to her feet. She had been so engrossed in the room's contents that she hadn't heard anyone approach. She whirled around to face the intruder, who had frozen in place.

"Celeste, are you all right?" Tarnelius asked in alarm.

"I'm fine. It's just a human that managed to sneak up on me. Don't worry," she assured him.

It seemed the female was every bit as surprised to see Celeste, as Celeste was to see her. She raised a pendant from around her neck into the air, and it began to glow with a bright, radiant light. The pendant was shaped into a shield with a lance crossing it. She stepped into the room and shoved the door as she did so. Her muscles strained as the heavy marble door didn't want to budge. Celeste frowned, as puzzled by the door as she was by the woman who now approached her.

"I'm sorry to have interrupted you, seraph. I was unaware that any of your kind was coming. I would never have intruded on your grief," said the woman, who still stared at her curiously. Celeste decided that now was not the time for modesty.

"It's quite all right. I should have been more alert to my surroundings, anyway. I don't usually startle that easily," she said.

The woman relaxed a bit. "My name is Siobhan Keating, paladin of Mithra. I – I thought you were a temple robber," she said with an embarrassed grin.

"This temple seemed to call to me, so I came. My name is Celeste."

She stood a few inches taller than Celeste, approximately the same height as Tarnelius. Her hair was a coppery red color and hung down to her shoulders. She had hazel eyes, and a healthy tan that attested to the obvious fact that she spent a lot of time in the sun. She was wearing a pale blue blouse and tan riding breeches. Celeste regarded her for a moment, and then looked at the pendant the woman was lighting the room with.

"That's a holy symbol," said Celeste.

"Um, yes. This is the symbol of Mithra, the shield and lance." She cocked her head as she looked at Celeste. "Were you one of his? Melek's, I mean."

"No. I mean, yes," Celeste sighed. "It's complicated. Look, it was nice to meet you, but I have to go. My companions are waiting for me, and I still didn't get what I came for from the shops."

"There are more here like you?" Siobhan asked.

"Like me? Um, not exactly. I'm very sorry, I have to go." Celeste moved to the door and reopened it, watching as it swung easily on its hinges again. Then she frowned and shut the door just as easily. She turned to look at Siobhan. "Wasn't this door stuck a minute ago?"

"Not stuck. It just hadn't been opened in years, and it's heavy." Siobhan moved past her and strained, trying to open the door. "Then again, I think maybe you were right and this temple *was* calling to you."

Celeste retracted her wings and opened the door again. The two walked out, then Celeste shut the door behind them before she carefully arranged the faded cloth back into place over the door. She turned to Siobhan and spoke. "Would you mind walking with me, Paladin of the Mithran Order?"

"I never said I was in the Mithran Order. I said I was a paladin of Mithra, and yes, I will walk with you." They walked through the nearby gate into the southwest quadrant of the city.

"What's the difference between the two? It seems like semantics to me."

"Lip service, basically. Look, with all due respect, you should be aware of the difference by now. I know, back when the gods were still here, paladins were paladins and we were all granted powers accordingly, but these days the real ones are few and far between. It seems that every generation brings fewer and fewer into our ranks. I suspect one day there will be none of us left." Siobhan waved her arm toward the masses all around them and curled her lip in disgust. "Just look at them. Most don't even pretend anymore. They are grown children playing dress up in the trappings of a knight, and I see most of them can't even be bothered to carry their fake holy symbols."

"How many real paladins are left now?" Celeste asked.

"Maybe as many as a hundred or so altogether, maybe less. I know there are many more paladins of Mithra than either of the others, but we have scarcely more than fifty left of us, not counting the squires."

"What do you know of King Liam's plan?"

"He intends to destroy the evil race of orcs and lead us into a new age of goodness. At least that is what I have heard, and why we were called here. We have yet to have an audience with the king, though we have been trying for a few days now. All of our requests have been refused. Maybe I will know more later on today, when we again try to meet with him. Do you know anything more, seraph? What are your thoughts?"

They arrived at the soap maker's, and Celeste broke off their conversation to purchase the soaps needed to finish cleaning Conner and Fiona's house, then they set off for the bazaar and the herbalist, cutting back through the city center.

"I feel that King Liam is a tyrant. My intent is to stop him and anyone in my way," Celeste said quietly to Siobhan.

"Our king is a lot of things, but I'm not so sure I would go so far as to call him a tyrant," Siobhan said indignantly.

"He speaks of annihilating entire races. Today the orcs, tomorrow the tumasi, I am sure. Who then? The elves and dwarves? Neither race will go down without a fight that I'm not sure he is prepared to handle. That is something only a tyrant would do." Celeste paused in her speech for a moment. "And, in his decision to do anything to accomplish his goal, he will unleash an evil so ancient I'm not sure anyone will be able to withstand it."

"What are you talking about? What is he doing?"

"He seeks Melek's sword, which was lost in the Deity War, in the north. Opening the holy tombs could release Kuunkierto, who would then rule the world uncontested."

"That can't be true. Kuunkierto was killed," Siobhan scoffed.

"You can't kill the moon, Siobhan. Kuunkierto was defeated, not killed. Somehow, he was trapped inside the tombs. The moon turned red. It didn't disappear."

Siobhan fell silent, lost in thought.

"There's something else I wanted to ask you," Celeste said as they approached the bazaar. "What do you know about demonic possessions, or evil weapons?"

"You think the king is possessed?" Siobhan asked, dismayed.

"No, unrelated situation. Although, as a side note, I have heard there are demons here, even in the king's court. They could be a corrupting influence. Anyway, call me curious."

"Easiest way is to kill the host. After the demon moves in and takes over, the victim rarely survives without being tainted, anyway."

"So no one attempts to merely exorcise demons these days?" Celeste asked.

"Like I said, the host rarely comes out unchanged. Look, I see evil, I destroy it. I suppose, if the situation warranted, channeling holy power into the host would be enough to knock the demon loose. That's the official way of performing exorcisms, anyway. I've done it before, though not often. Not all paladins can do it, even true paladins. Plus, like I said, it rarely works out as intended. Exorcisms are not as easy for us as for you seraphs. You were built for it, we weren't."

Celeste made her purchase of lavender flowers and juniper leaves, then turned to leave. "Is there any other way?"

"Not that I know of. What are you doing with all that anyway? Lavender, juniper, soap? Is there a plague upon this city that you are trying to ward against?"

"No, no plague. These are just good to have on hand. I should really be going now. Thank you for talking to me. It was nice to meet you," Celeste said.

"You also, Celeste." The two shook hands, then went their separate ways.

Celeste hurried back to Conner's house, knowing she had been gone for much longer than she should have. It was dark by the time she made it back. She hurried up the front walk, pausing when she saw Tarnelius snoozing under the tree out front, clearly exhausted by all the spell casting. She smiled at the sight of him, then entered the house, realizing as she did so that Tarnelius' presence outside meant that no one was keeping an eye on Arcus.

She flung open the door and rushed inside, dropping her packages by the door. She moved with caution into the kitchen as she looked for the others, but to no avail. Then, she checked the rest of the house. No one was in the master bedroom, or the nearest guest room. She was about to start panicking by the time she checked the next room. She pulled the door open and found the four of them in the last room. Theri, Conner and Fiona were standing behind Arcus, watching in fascination as he used magic to clean up all around the room.

"Oh, Celeste, you're back," called Theri. "Turns out we don't need that soap after all. Arcus figured out how to use magic to clean the rooms. This is the last one," she said with a grin.

"And, it's finished now," Arcus said, bowing. He spoke another word of magic. A strong breeze blew through the room and removed all traces of dirt from the people inside. "There, that should do it. Now we are also clean. That should help fight any reinfections."

"Thank you, Arcus," exclaimed Celeste. "It looks great in here. I brought lavender and juniper back from the herbalist to help fight disease. Since it looks like everything is well in hand here, I'm going to go see to Tarnel."

"I'll cook something for dinner," Fiona said with a huge smile. "I can't thank all of you enough. You have given me – us – our lives back. I can't believe how excited I feel to be able to do something as mundane as cooking." She laughed as she skipped from the room.

"I agree, thank you so much. This is better than my wildest dreams. I owe you everything. Please, stay here for as long as you like," Conner said, as they all exited the guest room. "Unfortunately, I only have two guest rooms, but you can share, or one of you can sleep in the great room. I could find some cushions to place in there."

"That option would probably be best. Arcus and I can draw straws for the bedroom," said Theri.

"You can take it," offered Arcus. "I'm so tired from not sleeping last night, I could probably lie down on hot coals and still be unconscious in seconds."

"Thanks, Arcus," grinned Theri.

Arcus wandered into the great room with Conner, while Theri went to help Fiona in the kitchen. Celeste walked back out the front door, and lowered herself to a seated position next to Tarnelius, against the tree.

She hated to wake him; he seemed so peaceful. She reached out and took his hand and caressed it. The evenings were balmy this time of year, and it was a beautiful night. The red moon was at its fullest, and there were no clouds, so the stars twinkled brightly in the heavens. She leaned her head against his shoulder and stared up at the moon, regretting that she had not had a chance yet to try to drop in on the king. Not that she knew what she would say when she got to see him, but she knew she would have to make the effort, and soon.

Tarnelius squeezed her hand. "Don't worry, it'll come to you. I'll be right there at your side, along with the others. You won't be alone."

"That sounds like an old catch phrase Melek's heralds used to say. 'You never fight alone,'" she sighed. "I'm sorry, Tarnel. I was trying not to wake you."

"I could hear you worrying. Besides, I shouldn't be sleeping now. I came out here to wait for you and get some fresh air. Then, the next thing I knew, you were sitting next to me. How much is left of the cleaning?"

"It's done. Arcus found a way to clean everything with magic while I was away."

Tarnelius sat up straight. "I forgot about Arcus. We need to get back in there, we left him unsupervised."

"We should go back in, yes. I don't think we have anything to worry about tonight; he seems perfectly calm. I was worried when I returned earlier, but so far, he has acted like his old self. Besides, we'd hear if there was anything going on inside," said Celeste. She stood up and brushed the dirt from her dress. "Let's go in and see if Fiona needs any help." Tarnelius rose to his feet and took her hand, and together they crossed back over the threshold into the house.

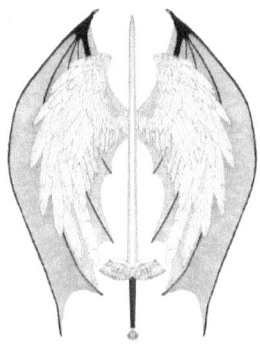

Chapter Nineteen
Nine-Tenths of the Law

Hours later, Celeste and Tarnelius both bolted up out of bed. They hurriedly threw their clothes on, and bolted from the bedroom into the great room. Their arrival found Arcus on the cushioned floor, where he screamed and writhed as if he were in agony.

"Arcus, what's happening?" Tarnelius yelled over the cries. When there was no response, he moved to Arcus' side and turned him over. Theri and Conner both entered the room, alarmed expressions on their faces.

"He's asleep," remarked Tarnelius. He began to shake him. "Arcus. Arcus, wake up!" Still, Arcus kept shouting and crying out in pain. He didn't respond to Tarnelius' attempts to wake him.

"What's happening to him?" Theri asked, her eyes wide with worry.

Celeste chewed her lower lip. "I'm not sure." She walked over and reached toward him. Her hand flashed blue as she tried to heal him. As her hand extended, Arcus' eyes snapped open and he grabbed her wrist. His eyes glowed an evil red color, and they bore into her with malevolence. He yanked her toward him and in a flash the dagger was out and pressed to her throat.

"Stupid bitch, Arcus isn't home right now," said a hoarse version of Arcus' voice.

"Let her go," exclaimed Tarnelius. Helplessly, he stared at Arcus and Celeste in horror.

"What is it with you demons, and holding this dagger to my throat? It's getting old," hissed Celeste.

"Well, the obvious difference is that the last one was unwilling to carry out her threat," Arcus answered as he cut a shallow slice into her neck. "Slow and painful, that's the best way. Then I can savor this. I want to hear you beg for your life, so I'll leave your vocal chords intact for now."

"What do you want, demon?" Celeste gasped, as she felt the agony from the red hot knife penetrate her skin.

"Ah, there's a good question. You see, I'm the exterminator. My master wants me to stop all of you from getting in his way. As I remove your head from your shoulders, I also remove the head from the snake that is this group."

"Who is your master?" choked out Celeste.

"Oh, well, since you're going to die anyway, I'll go ahead and tell you. Yeah, right. Do you think I am stupid? Keep asking questions so that I am forced to kill all the others too, though. I won't mind. Do you think young Arcus here will kill himself after he finds out he has killed all his friends and doomed the world? I sure hope he does." The demon cut a deeper gouge into her flesh and blood gushed from her throat.

"There is one th – thing you are forgetting, demon," forced out Celeste, her voice nothing more than a pained whisper.

"What's that?"

Celeste pushed her wings out from her body with all her strength, shoving Arcus away from her as hard as she could, losing more blood from the exertion and falling to the floor in her weakened state. The dagger flew through the air and hit the wall to their left. Conner ran over and grabbed it. As soon as Celeste was clear, Theri leapt right over her body and tackled Arcus to the floor. The two rolled across the floor and ended with Theri on top of Arcus, pinning him to the ground. Arcus struggled, but he was caught fast in Theri's grasp. Every time he tried to move, Theri's claws would extend and press into his skin as a threat of worse.

Tarnelius had rushed to Celeste's side the second she had broken free and knelt beside her. He pressed his fingers to her bloody throat and his hand flashed as he tried to heal her. Nothing happened, and she continued to bleed heavily. Tarnelius roared in agony as he realized she was going to die and he couldn't do anything to help her.

"Tarnel," came Celeste's voice in his head.

Tarnel lifted her in his arms. Tears formed in his eyes, making her shimmer in his vision.

"Kiss me," Celeste thought. Tarnelius let out a strangled sob.

Not wasting any time, he leaned down and kissed her for all he was worth, as he was sure it would be the last time. As he did, he felt a tingling sensation running through his veins and a wave of exhaustion ran through him. *"This is it,"* he thought. *"The Fade is coming for me. I can't live without you, my love."* He opened his eyes one final time to look upon her before he gave in, and what he saw almost stopped his heart. Her eyes were open, her forehead creased a little as she focused. More than that, she was glowing. A second glance proved that he was, too. Realizing now what she was trying to do, he kissed her again, lending his strength to her spell. Then he tried to heal her again himself. He reached inside himself to find her and drew from her own magic to add to his spell. When they were done, she was healed, and they were both exhausted from the effort.

They stood back up together, and approached Arcus and Theri. Celeste retracted her wings and knelt on the floor near his head.

"You've got him, Theri?" asked Tarnelius, feeling apprehensive of having Celeste so close to him now.

"He can't move, which limits most of his spells. I've got him."

"This is impossible," said Arcus in that evil sounding voice. "I killed you, I know it."

"You and your master underestimate me. You underestimate all of us. But I'm done talking to you. Bring back my friend," said Celeste.

"Never! I finally gained control and I'm going to keep it. I like this body; so powerful, so much potential."

"Arcus, I know you are still in there! Fight him, fight this. Gain back your body, gain back your control. You are better than this," Celeste said. Then she reached forward and tapped him on the forehead as a flair of red light jumped from her fingertips onto his head.

Arcus cackled defiantly, but the red of his eyes began to fade, then darken back. Within a minute or so they had returned to their normal gray color.

"Theri –" Arcus said.

"Let him up," said Celeste.

"No!" snapped Arcus. "No, I can't be trusted. He's not gone. I can still feel him inside me. I need to be tied up. Celeste, I am so sorry," he said in a tormented voice.

"Let him up," repeated Celeste. "Arcus, you are strong enough to fight him. I know you are. You can do it. I think we will have to tie you up while you sleep until we come up with a way to get rid of him permanently, but you can do this." Theri released him, and rolled away.

"I – I can feel him inside me. He is screaming and fighting me even now." Arcus clenched his eyes shut for a moment. "Can you help me? Please, Celeste?"

Celeste lowered her gaze, unable to meet his eyes. "I'm sorry, Arcus. I can't. I promise you though, we will find a way."

Conner still stood there with wide eyes, gripping Arcus' dagger. "What exactly is going on?"

"It seems we've picked up an unwelcome guest. Give me that dagger, please, there is one thing I can try," said Celeste.

Arcus' eyes flickered and he stiffened up as Celeste took the dagger. "Steady, Arcus," said Celeste. "You've got this." She spoke a word of magic and the dagger froze over and disintegrated. Arcus gripped his head and moaned, dropping onto the bloody cushions and breathing heavily.

"He didn't like that," Arcus gasped.

"He's still there?" Celeste asked.

Arcus nodded in agony. "He's really angry."

Celeste sighed. "That complicates things. I was really hoping he was tied to the dagger." She chewed on her lower lip. "I need to find Siobhan. In the meantime, you'll need to stay awake. I was thinking we could just tie you up, but the more I consider it, the more I think that when you are asleep is the only time your strength of will is lowered enough for him to take over. Once he has you, I'm not sure rope would hold you, so you'll need to stay awake."

"Who's Siobhan?" Arcus asked.

"She is a paladin of Mithra. I met her today," answered Celeste. "The only trouble is, I have no idea where she is."

"We talked about that. I know you have some ill-conceived notion that paladins are some sort of holy warriors, but they have no powers other than to be able to wear that heavy armor without collapsing," scoffed Conner.

"You're wrong. This one is different. She carries the symbol of Mithra and speaks with sadness at what the paladin order has become. She will help us, if I can find her again. The essence of her goddess, which remains here on Altierra, has blessed her."

"What does that even mean?" Conner asked. "'The essence of her goddess'? All the gods are gone."

"Yes, they are. However, there are traces of each of the gods still here, if you know where to look for them. The magic Tarnelius used to heal you and your wife, and the magic I used at your grandparents' house, was a gift from the gods. Only true servants can wield the divine powers left behind for us."

"And you think this paladin is one of those servants?"

"I'm sure of it. She bore the holy symbol, and it responded to her wishes."

Conner frowned, at odds with what he was hearing versus what he knew to be true. He knelt down and picked up a white feather that was tipped in red blood. "And what are you, Celeste?"

"I am just me. Don't worry about it. You should try to get some sleep. Go back to your wife. We will need to stay with Arcus to keep him awake; we can't take any chances. I will start searching. Best to find her sooner, rather than later." Celeste took a few steps but was faced with a wave of dizziness and nausea. With a gasp, she stopped to catch her breath.

"Are you okay?" Tarnelius asked, concerned.

"I lost a lot of blood, that's all. Can you guys clean up in here while I go look for Siobhan?"

"I don't like you going alone right now," Tarnelius said.

Arcus sighed and magically cleaned up all the blood the same way he cleaned the rooms earlier. "I'm so sorry, Celeste. I wish I had some way to fix this."

"It's not your fault. I'll be back soon."

"How are you going to find her?" asked Arcus.

"Well, logically, as a member of the Mithran delegation, she arrived later than the Rashnurians. Since the Rashnurians are swarming the inns, she is likely based outside the gates. I just need to find the tents, and other items that bear Mithra's symbol, and then I can ask around."

"Sounds like a solid plan, except we're coming with you," said Arcus.

"Hmm, a mage playing host to an evil demon walking right into a camp full of true paladins. I can't see even one single thing wrong with that plan, assuming that you have become suicidal," snorted Celeste.

Arcus sighed. "At least take Tarnelius with you. I'll never forgive myself if anything happens while you're out alone, in the dark, in the weakened state I put you in."

"Tarnel needs to stay up with you. I'll be fine, and stop blaming yourself," answered Celeste.

Theri spoke up. "I'll stay with Arcus. It'll be fine. You two go find this paladin."

"But –" started Celeste.

"No buts. Everything will be fine here. If his eyes even hint toward changing color I'll just pin him down again until you come back. Go, now, shoo!"

So Celeste and Tarnelius left together. They transformed into birds and flew up and over the city wall, heading northwest.

The vast quantity of tents set up outside the city was overwhelming. They circled and swooped through all the different encampments, and finally settled on one camp that was smaller than the rest. The flags all bore the symbol of a lance crossed over a shield. This particular camp had only about twenty-five tents set up, and was set back a few miles northwest of the city gate. Almost fifty horses in all different colors grazed nearby, not tied up but seemingly uninterested in leaving. There were two men sitting around a campfire on watch. The two birds landed right in front of them and shifted back to being elves. The men jerked to their feet, drew their swords, and raised their holy symbols high.

"I really do wish people would stop pointing sharp objects at me. It's getting old," said Celeste. She released her wings and stood there, radiant, in the light of their holy symbols. Her pale skin, black hair and ivory wings made her the perfect image of an angel.

Tarnelius regarded the two men with interest. "You were definitely right. These are real paladins."

"Let's speed things up, shall we?" Celeste said. "I'm looking for Siobhan Keating. Is she staying in this camp?"

The man on the right, a paladin with short brown hair and brown eyes, stared at her in shock and dropped his sword to the ground. "A sacred herald," he exclaimed, astonished. He looked at the other man, who was younger and thinner, with brown hair long enough to reach his chin, and nodded to him. He sheathed his sword and scampered off into the camp.

"Apologies, herald. I had no idea you were here, or that you would be dropping in on us in the middle of the night like this. My name is Ryan. My squire is Cayden. He will be right back."

Tarnelius regarded her in amusement, but said nothing aloud. *"Herald, huh?"*

Celeste smiled warmly at the knight as she waited in silence. *"It's not like it's a total lie, just go with it."*

After several minutes, Siobhan and Cayden came rushing back to join them. She was wearing her full plate armor and all her knight insignias and trappings. Apparently, Cayden had helped her to dress before returning with her. "Celeste, I did not expect to see you again so soon. Especially in the middle of the night. What is the matter?"

"I need your help, Siobhan. I apologize for the time, but will you come with us?"

"Yes, I will, but first tell me what is going on, and who this is with you," Siobhan said.

"Oh, I am terribly sorry, that was rude of me. Siobhan, this is Tarnelius. Druid prince of Kayalost and my bonded mate. To put that more simply, my husband," she said with a smile as Tarnelius bowed low to her. "Tarnelius, this is Siobhan Keating, paladin of Mithra. As to what is going on, it is of a sensitive nature and I would really prefer to speak in private."

"I keep no secrets from my brothers- and sisters-in-arms," she snapped.

"Of course not, and you are more than welcome to fill them in, after the situation has been dealt with. Please, Siobhan, I need your help to save *my* brother-in-arms."

Siobhan's eyes widened in surprise as she realized what was happening. She nodded once to Ryan. "Please ask Katie to take the tent down when she awakens. I'll be back as soon as I can. I'm sure it won't delay our plans, so make sure the campsite is disassembled when the sun rises."

Siobhan turned and gestured for Celeste to lead the way. After they had travelled a short distance, Siobhan asked, "Um, can I know what is going on now? Also, where are we going?"

"Back into Lumernia, of course," answered Celeste.

"How? The gate is shut tight until morning. I'll not break in like a thief."

Celeste paused. "Is it? I didn't notice earlier. No problem, I can fix this." She began looking all around them, as if searching for something.

Siobhan furrowed her brow as she started to become angry. "Celeste, what is going on?" she demanded, stressing every word.

Celeste sighed, and turned to face her. "Look, the story is long. Very long. I *will* tell you everything you wish to know, but for now let's keep to relevant issues. Our friend and companion, a good man named Arcus, has been possessed by a demon. When he falls asleep, the monster is able to overpower his strength of will and take over. We need you to exorcize him, please."

"First of all, I told you before, exorcisms are a waste of time. The host never ends up untainted. Second, all *you* have to do is channel your herald power into him to force the demon out. Why do you need me?"

"I knew it wasn't a good idea to lie to paladins," thought Tarnelius. Celeste shot him a look.

"Actually, you said 'rarely', not 'never'. Our friend is worth the attempt." Celeste finally found what she was looking for, and hurried over to a tall tree. "Here we go, this will do nicely." She looked at Tarnelius for affirmation, and he nodded to her.

"Madame Siobhan, will you take my hand, please?" inquired Tarnelius. She frowned at him in suspicion, but did as he asked.

Tarnelius spoke a few words of magic, running his hands up and down the trunk of the tree. A golden door lit up on the trunk and slid open. Tarnelius pulled Siobhan inside and the trunk closed behind them. Celeste counted to ten and then followed suit, stepping through the tree to see the other two standing in front of Conner's house, waiting for her. Siobhan looked shocked, but was standing in stoic silence.

"As for why I can't do it myself, my mother was an elven druid in the elven village of Kayalost. My father was a herald of Melek. I inherited some of his traits but not all."

"You're lying," hissed Siobhan.

"I'm not. That is the truth."

"Heralds are made of holy magic. They do not have desires of the flesh, nor do they have offspring."

"Only part of that sentence was true. Look at me," she released her wings. "Look at me for the answer. You know it to be true. Now, please, I'm sorry I allowed you to believe I was a full herald, but I really do need your help. The man inside is suffering, and you have the power to help him. I can beg."

Siobhan sighed a deeply aggravated sigh, and allowed herself to be led inside. Theri and Arcus were sitting on the cushions, playing with dice. Siobhan regarded the two of them in surprise as they jumped up to introduce themselves. Arcus looked deep into her hazel eyes, hoping she could really help him as Celeste had said. She was beautiful, more beautiful than anyone he had ever seen before, even in her silver armor. He worried she wouldn't be up to the task.

He grasped her hand in greeting, jumping a little at the small jolt of electricity that hit him when he touched her hand.

"You must be the paladin. My name is Arcus, and this is Theri," he said. She waved and grinned a toothy grin.

"Siobhan Keating," she replied. "You must be Celeste's friend that she is so worried about. Let's see what we are dealing with." She raised her holy symbol in her left hand and placed her right hand on Arcus' chest over his heart. There was a flash from the holy symbol and she stared at him in concentration.

"There is definitely a demon in there," she said. "It puts an evil taint on your aura. I may be able to remove it, but I make no guarantees. The process may kill you, or may change you. The demon may leave you tainted. Are you willing to accept these risks?"

"Tonight I tried to kill a friend. No, not me, him, with my body. I don't even know what I'm trying to say, everything is becoming blurred. All I know is I can't live like this, and I can't stay awake to fend him off forever. Please, help me. I will take the risk. I will take any risk," Arcus said, with desperation in his eyes.

Siobhan regarded him silently for a full minute, waiting for his resolve to weaken. When he remained firm in his decision, she turned to Theri, Celeste and Tarnelius. "Leave us," she said, then paused. "Wait, Celeste, would you be so kind as to bring me some good, strong rope? Then you can leave."

Theri and Tarnelius moved down the hall toward the bedrooms. Celeste remained where she was, without any sign that she had heard the question.

"Is there something confusing about my request for rope? Did you not hear me?"

"I heard you. I also don't think you are fully aware what you are getting yourself into."

"Enlighten me," snapped Siobhan.

"You need us in this room. Arcus, tell her what you are capable of."

Arcus frowned in bewilderment, then his eyes widened as he realized what she was talking about. "I have been trained by the elves as a druid. Rope will not hold me; I can shift forms into something either larger or smaller and escape. In addition, I have been learning to cast my arcane spells while shifted into animal form. I haven't figured out a lot of it yet, but I did maintain a spell that causes fire to run up and down my arms as I shifted into a bear. If the demon is able to tap into potential as well as actual learned ability, it could get ugly fast."

"If he shifts, you'll need us here, Siobhan. You won't be able to help him if you are dead with your throat ripped out."

Siobhan sighed. "Fine, you can stay, but we will need to take extra precautions, because we don't want the demon to jump hosts before I've got him caught in my channeling spell. Just so you know, I'm not really concerned about him shifting, but I suppose the extra help wouldn't be such a bad thing." She stared at Celeste. "Are you sure you are up for this? You look very pale. Much more so than you were when I met you yesterday."

"I lost a lot of blood getting my throat slashed open. I'll be fine."

"You'll need to be better than fine, or you'll be a target."

Celeste frowned at her. "You forget who I am. A demon would not be so foolish as to try to possess me. My seraph blood would destroy him. It would actually do us a favor if he did try. I will go get the others," she said as she walked down the hallway.

As soon as she left, Siobhan turned back to Arcus and asked, "All right, now tell me how this happened."

"Honestly, I don't know. Last night, or I suppose actually night before last since it's almost morning now, I was sitting outside, on the porch, after Celeste and Tarnelius' bonding ceremony. I remember pulling out the dagger I had taken from the demon Celeste had killed, to examine and clean it, and I heard what I thought was laughter on the air. That's where things get hazy. I looked for the source of the noise but didn't find anything. I remember deciding to carry the dagger in my sheath, and then I went inside. I couldn't sleep all night. I was plagued with nightmares about killing my friends and myself in horribly gruesome ways. Yesterday was mostly normal except that I kept feeling like there was something inside me, just below the surface, fighting for dominance. I felt out of control and confused. I went to sleep hoping things would be better after a good night's sleep, but awoke to find that I had no control of my own body. I tried to move, tried to fight, but had to watch from the back of my own head while my body tried to kill Celeste. I thought I had succeeded; there was blood, so much blood. I thought she was dead, but Tarnelius brought her back. Then, I fought with everything I had to gain control back. That's it, that's the whole story. Now, will you *please* set about fixing me? Get him out," Arcus begged.

"So, long story short, this monster has been inside you for less than two days?"

"Yes," sighed Arcus.

"Where is the dagger?"

"Celeste destroyed it; she hoped the demon was tied to it." Arcus winced at the memory. "He was furious, I could feel it."

"The dagger came off a demon," Siobhan pondered. "Did it do anything?"

"It glowed a horrible red color, and if you were injured from it, the wound would not heal. Only Celeste seemed to have any luck healing it with her magic. Neither Tarnelius nor I were able to heal the wounds inflicted by the dagger," said Arcus, as Theri and the two elves returned to the room.

"Okay, I understand. Now for the big decision; I wonder if we should take this outside. Inside might lead to the house being burned down, but outside has us potentially creating a light show for the neighbors in the middle of the night. If we go back outside the city itself, we are in full view of way too many warriors."

"How about the Temple of Melek? No one goes in there anymore, judging by the dust. The windows are blacked out. If there is a fire, we can keep it under control, even if there ends up being minor damage," Celeste asked.

"I don't know," Siobhan hesitated. "I would worry about anything getting destroyed in there."

"If Melek were still with us, he would want to help us. I'm sure of it. I swear I will not let the building be destroyed," promised Celeste.

"Let's do it. Arcus, will you be able to stay in control long enough to get into the temple? I doubt very much that demon will want to go in there; it's hallowed."

Arcus clenched his jaw in determination and nodded once.

"In fact, I should go first. I can prepare a holding spell on the floor to help contain him once you are in place, so he can't run away with you once we draw him out," said Siobhan. "Give me a ten minute head start and all of you come together." With that, she swept from the house.

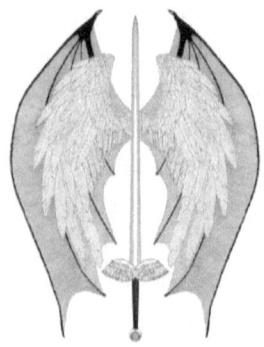

Chapter Twenty
Welcome to the Party

As soon as Siobhan left for the temple, Celeste collapsed onto the cushions next to Arcus. He jumped up like she had struck him and moved away from her.

"I'm not angry with you, Arcus," she said.

"Well, you should be. That's not why I moved, though. This demon has heard every word and he is very angry. I think I'm getting a migraine from him struggling and fighting. You being so close makes it worse. He makes me want to reach out and throttle you just to make the pain in my head stop."

Tarnelius went to Celeste's side and sat down next to her. He took her hand and caressed it. He cast the simple spell to create some of the magical berries they had been eating on the road for so long. "Here, these will help the dizzy feelings until your body can make more blood. It's all going to be fine, don't worry." She smiled at him in thanks, before taking and eating them.

After that, they waited in silence for the ten minutes to pass. Arcus paced back and forth, rubbing his temples. Tarnelius held Celeste to him and gently kissed the top of her head. Theri sat on a chair silently, lost in thought.

Finally, they got up and travelled to the temple. Tarnelius and Theri each stood beside Arcus, and Celeste led the way. As they reached the park, Arcus stopped and moaned. He doubled over and grabbed his head in agony. Tarnelius and Theri came closer, trying to decide if they needed to bodily move him, or if they should wait. Celeste stepped farther out of the way.

"Arcus, are you all right? Can you go on?" Tarnelius asked.

Arcus shook his head. Then he retched and vomited spectacularly, all over the ground. The other two jumped back out of the way as he did. "Nooo," he moaned, as he continued to hold his head. "I am the one in control." He retched a few more times. Tears and sweat ran down his face from the effort and exertion. "You will not take me," he wheezed. Finally, he stood up and looked Tarnelius in the eyes. "I won't make it." He gagged again. "I'm sorry, old friend. I'm not strong enough."

"Don't say that. You *are* strong enough. We all believe in you," Tarnelius encouraged him.

"No, I'm not. I cannot move my own feet anymore. I don't have the strength. I – I can't go on. I need your help, please," he begged. "I'll keep fighting him for control, but I need help."

Tarnelius nodded once and gestured to Theri. The two of them each stepped around the vomit on the ground and grabbed an arm. "Don't touch me!" Arcus snarled, thrashing. His eyes flashed red for a moment but then darkened back to gray. "Hurry, please," he pleaded.

They pulled Arcus across the park and into the temple on the far left. The door was already open, and a light flickered from inside. As soon as Celeste entered, Siobhan pointed to a circle surrounding a star drawn in charcoal on the floor. "Get him inside the circle, quickly, and be careful not to smudge it."

Theri and Tarnelius carried him toward the circle, but he started to struggle violently. Magical energy shot off him, in every direction, as he fought them with everything he had. Siobhan rushed forward and grabbed his feet. Together they maneuvered Arcus into place without causing damage to the marks on the floor. Then, they backed out of the circle, leaving him there, alone. He jumped up and turned to run toward the door, but the effects of the circle stopped him, holding him in place.

Siobhan cast another couple of spells on the circle, causing the marks to light up in different colors with each spell. Then she took both Tarnelius' and Theri's hands and spoke a word of magic, causing a red spark to travel to each of them. Celeste hurried to shut the door, then she and Tarnelius shoved the benches against the walls.

Arcus lay on the floor, and clutched his knees to his chest as he shivered. Siobhan knelt in his line of sight and smiled encouragingly. "You did great, Arcus. I'm very impressed you made it all the way here. You can let go now. Relax. Stop fighting."

Arcus shook violently, but didn't say anything.

"Take a look at this symbol here for a moment." She removed the pendant from around her neck and held it up. "Look closely." The pendant lit up and glowed a brilliant white color. Arcus' eyes throbbed and he squinted against the brightness. The light became brighter and brighter; it felt like his blood was boiling under the heat from the necklace. It began to make him angry. He envisioned snatching the pendant away to break it into a million pieces, before he would rip this infuriating woman apart, bone by bone. He'd start with her thumbs, and then her fingers, and then –

"That's enough of that," she said. The light abruptly went away. She smiled. "Welcome to the party, demon."

Arcus' eyes were a brilliant red. He stared at her with hatred and implied threats. "Well, aren't you a pretty thing. No wonder dear Arcus was practically panting like a dog who saw a bitch in heat. Pathetic, really. Though, I bet your hair would look even better coated in your blood when I rip it from your scalp." He stood and lunged for her, but she held up the pendant again, which glowed a soft white color. It pushed him back down onto the floor.

"Flattery will get you nowhere, demon," she growled. "Now, why don't you tell me what you want with Arcus?"

Arcus glared at her holy symbol before answering. "Like I told them, my master doesn't want them interfering in his business. See, he has big plans. Big plans that involve ruling the world. These fools aim to stop him, so I will stop them."

"Who is your master?"

"Wouldn't you like to know?" Arcus snarled.

"I would, actually, otherwise I wouldn't have asked." The light increased on the pendant ever so slightly, causing him to cry out as it seemed to pierce straight through his brain. "Tell me, if you want the pain to stop."

"I like pain; I'm a demon. I'm used to pain, but since you seem to really want to know, I'll tell you." Arcus cackled with mirth. "It's your precious king."

"King Liam?"

"Liam is the key. The one who will change the world and make us strong. He is not my master; he is the puppet dancing for my master's whims." Arcus began to cackle, the sound horrible to hear. His hands lit up in flame and he began to shift once more into an enormous black bear. He rose up on his hind legs and swatted toward Siobhan, but she was out of reach. The bear snarled and his eyes rolled back. Suddenly, a fireball shot from his paws right toward her. It caught her full in the chest, but her armor seemed to absorb it and she remained upright and calm as she raised her holy symbol high into the air. Celeste hurried to cast spells to put out all the minor fires that had erupted all over the building.

The bear cried out as the light grew painfully bright. He snarled and cast again, causing bright explosions of color to erupt from the remaining fires. Theri wasn't prepared and yelped, as the light was so bright that it blinded her. Celeste had been facing away from them as she was extinguishing the flames, so hadn't been looking in the direction of the explosions. Tarnelius had immediately squeezed his eyes shut when he saw the fires begin to spark with color. Siobhan was looking at Arcus, not the fires, and wasn't affected at all.

She stepped closer, dangerously close, her arm holding her holy symbol stretched out in front of her. "We've had enough of this foolishness, demon. Now be gone!" she exclaimed.

The bear bellowed as the light became brighter and brighter, until he couldn't stand it anymore. Even with his eyes clenched shut, he couldn't take the brightness. The light began to break up before his vision, and he felt like he was getting pulled in a hundred directions all at once. He fell to his knees in agony and shifted back into Arcus. He pushed out with his arms as hard as he could, and let out a horrible, pain-filled scream that echoed loudly around the room. Suddenly, the boarded-up stained glass imploded, spreading across the room. Several pieces bounced off Siobhan's armor, landing with an ineffective tinkling sound. One shard embedded deep in Theri's neck, and she collapsed to the floor with a strangled scream. Several other shards landed within the circle, and Arcus grabbed the largest piece he could reach.

"You won't take me without killing him as well, you bitch!" Arcus snarled at Siobhan. With that, he slashed his wrists vertically along the large brachial arteries, his blood spreading across the floor. He switched arms, continuing to gouge deeply into his forearms.

Tarnelius and Celeste ran to stop him. "Do not cross the lines into the circle!" Siobhan yelled. "You mustn't enter the circle until the demon is destroyed." Tarnelius stopped short and stared at his bleeding friend, a tortured look on his face.

Celeste glared at her and ran into the circle, wasting no time in knocking the glass from Arcus' hand. She dropped to her knees in front of Arcus, and reached out to him, her hands glowing blue. Arcus grabbed her hand, his arms still gushing blood, and twisted her arm with a superhuman strength.

He glared down at her, his eyes still glowing an evil red. His blood dripped onto her skin and clothes, covering her. "Celeste, why did you leave me? Why did you never say goodbye? My death was all *your* fault, for leaving me alone." It was Arcus speaking, but it was her mother's voice. Her eyes widened in horror, but she continued to struggle, caught in the demon's gaze. "Now this boy's death will be on your shoulders. He can't hold on much longer. You let me die, and you're going to let him die, too."

"No!" Celeste bellowed, as she forced herself to her feet and shoved Arcus back.

"Celeste, get back!" yelled Siobhan, as a bench lifted from its place along the wall and flew toward her. She was quick to duck, but Tarnelius was hit hard in the back of his head by the bench and he collapsed to the floor with a thud. Celeste screamed in agony.

Arcus cackled in mirth and reached down to the floor to pick up another glass shard, but he seemed unsteady on his feet. Celeste snarled in fury and tackled him to the floor, her wings springing free to help carry them harder and faster to the floor. With the circle broken because of Celeste's entrance, they tumbled hard to the floor, no longer contained by the holding spell. As they landed, the light faded from Arcus eyes, and he lay still underneath her. Something that looked like Arcus' shadow rolled clear, and stood up next to Arcus and Celeste, her feathery wing cutting through his incorporeal body. He almost seemed to be going through the motions of breathing heavily, but no sound came from him.

Celeste's hands flashed blue as she gripped Arcus' still-bleeding forearms, sealing the wounds right as Siobhan lunged for the shadowy demon. The evil herald was faster, though, and dove into the unconscious body of Tarnelius, who was only a few feet away. A moment later, he opened his red eyes and sat up with a groan.

Celeste jerked to her feet and off Arcus like someone had stung her. She held up her index finger to Siobhan as if to say "wait one second" before locking eyes with the red eyes of the demon that stole her mate's body.

"*Get out of my* rakastan's *body, you evil parasite.*" She came across loud and clear in the demon's head.

"That's a nifty trick, bastard half-angel," Tarnelius said aloud, while Siobhan watched in confusion.

"*You should have picked the kedistam, demon,*" thought Celeste. "*Not my* rakastan."

"Oh, and why is that?" Tarnelius asked.

"*Because Tarnelius is carrying half my soul. Half my angelic soul.*" With that, she gestured to Siobhan and then concentrated on combining her magic and strength with

Tarnelius' and focused as hard as she could to channel as much positive and healing energy as they could muster. Tarnelius gave a strangled scream and fell back to the floor, unconscious again, as the demon was forced back out of his body. Then, Siobhan was on him, forcing the shining holy symbol directly into the center of his incorporeal form, right where his heart would be. The shadows of the demon began to rupture. Cracks formed and filled with light, which grew in intensity until the demon exploded, his shadowy shards bursting through the room and vanishing into nothing.

Celeste dropped to Tarnelius' side and stroked his hair, her hands flashing blue as she felt the huge ostrich egg sized knot on the back of his head. She murmured to him in the old language as she waited for him to wake up. Siobhan ambled up to Theri and placed her hands on her neck and face. Siobhan's hands and forearms took on a golden glow. She removed the glass from Theri's neck and finished healing her wounds and restoring her sight. Then, she returned to Celeste and Tarnelius.

"Hold him still," said Siobhan. She furrowed her brow in concentration, focused and unmoving.

"He's unconscious. It's not like he's going to move," she answered.

"No need for the attitude. This would never have happened if you hadn't broken the circle. Anyway, I see no evil on him, so the demon left no taint behind that I can see. He was only in there for a few seconds, so the chances were unlikely, but better to make sure."

"I had to break the circle. Arcus was going to die and you were going to do nothing to stop it."

"Please. He would have fallen unconscious long before he died. Any of us could have saved him after the demon was out. I wasn't worried. You shouldn't have panicked, and you should have done what I said. This was why I tried to send you all away for the exorcism." Siobhan turned and walked over to Arcus, leaving Celeste on the floor with Tarnelius.

She watched Arcus, still unconscious on the floor, for a few moments, before placing her hands onto his forearms. Celeste had healed him somewhat, but she had been rushed, and the job was not finished. The wounds on his arms looked like injuries that had been healing for a few days. Siobhan's hands again took on that golden glow and the marks faded away to nothing. A small amount of color returned to Arcus' cheeks. His face twitched as he started to wake up.

"Sit up slowly; you've lost a lot of blood. I don't need you passing out again on me," Siobhan said. "The demon is gone. You were lucky; I see no hint of evil left in your aura. It looks like you shouldn't have any lasting damage." Arcus started to nod, but then thought better of it and just sat up very slowly as he had been told to do. Theri ran over to help him into a sitting position, then gave him a big hug.

"Are you all right?" Theri asked him.

"I – I think so," Arcus answered gruffly. He cleared his throat. "I think I will be, at least."

Siobhan stared at them for a moment, and then moved to put the benches back where they belonged. When that was done, she walked back to the group, who were all still near the circle. "Is he still injured?" she asked, referring to Tarnelius.

"No, I've healed him. I'm not sure why he won't wake up. He's alive and his heartbeat is strong, so I guess he'll wake when he's ready. That was a pretty hard hit to his head, it hurt me pretty badly just through our link. There was blood building around his brain. I've healed the damage, but it will take a little while for everything to end up back where it should be. Head wounds are tricky."

"All right. Well, in the meantime, would somebody now like to fill me in on what is going on?"

Celeste nodded. "Okay, we definitely owe you that much. What exactly do you want to know?"

"Well, I can't possibly know that until you tell me, so start at the beginning."

Celeste smirked. "All right. Well, more than eight hundred years ago –"

"Not that far back," snapped Siobhan.

"Fine, I assume you know your history anyway, being a paladin. Suffice it to say Kuunkierto was defeated and trapped in the north, and a lot of people died. Well, I was living alone in the forest, north of the Nehir River, when I received a summons to the Silver Dragon's castle. Have you heard of Axistra?"

Siobhan nodded, so Celeste continued. "All right, good. Anyway, she'd had a vision of King Liam opening the holy tombs to the north, and releasing Kuunkierto from his prison. I had thought he was dead, but like I told you yesterday, you can't kill the moon. If he is released, he will be the only god on Altierra and will rule uncontested. Axistra also had heard that there was a herald here, corrupting the king. We intend to find the herald, eliminate him, and try to convince King Liam that opening the tomb would be a very bad idea. When we arrived here, I found out that he intends to go after Melek's sword. The sword had the power to entomb Kuunkierto in the first place, but my personal opinion is that there is no one alive today with the strength to wield the sword. Not against him, at least. King Liam's goal seems to be to destroy the entire orc race. My guess is that he will then turn a greedy eye toward the tumasi, and that the elves and dwarves will not be far behind if we do not fall into place at his command. Only the human and kedistam races will be left unscathed. This must not be allowed to happen."

"Wait one minute there. Why should we not destroy the orcs? They are evil and their existence is a plague on this land," argued Siobhan.

"I'm with her on that one; we should let the paladins kill them," agreed Arcus, as he smiled at Siobhan.

"Let me put it into perspective for you both. If you ask an orc if they are evil, they will tell you no. They will tell you humans are evil. The tumasi will do the same, they will say the kedistam are evil. If Kuunkierto is allowed freedom, the first thing *he* will do is eradicate all the humans and kedistam. Then, he'll probably come for the elves and dwarves, unless we bow to his will. Only the orcs and tumasi will remain. Sound familiar? Good and evil diametrically oppose each other, and both are needed to maintain balance. If evil tips the scales, all will be lost to chaos. If good wins, the world will be lost to tyranny. Either way, we lose."

"I disagree. Goodness and tyranny are not the same thing," said Siobhan. "Goodness does not have to lead to tyranny. As long as laws are in place and everyone follows them –"

"Right there is your problem. Who sets these laws? Humans? King Liam? Think hard about your training, what you learned of the gods. You know that if Mithra were here she would show mercy. If Mithra were here, perhaps she could control a society of only good beings, without it becoming tyranny – except she wouldn't, because she would show mercy. Mercy and forgiveness are the ultimate act of good. That includes mercy for all races, not only the 'good' ones. The other gods felt the same. Tedavia, goddess of healing, would allow her gift to be used for all. If a tumasi broke his leg, would it not heal? Sevda, goddess of love, shared her gift with everyone as well. So the law becomes, 'it's not okay to be an orc, by penalty of death'. What if the next law is to punish stealing with death?

Stealing is, inarguably, an act of evil, but at what point is the line drawn? A hungry child steals a loaf of bread, so he must die? That isn't justice. Enforcing unfair laws is a form of tyranny. Once the orcs and tumasi are eradicated, the elves and dwarves would be the new 'evil' races that oppose him. We aren't his idea of good, so we must be evil, right? What if King Liam decides next to exterminate the elves simply because we will never conform to his laws? Is that justice? There must always be a balance," finished Celeste.

"In the south, we have many problems with the tumasi as a whole, but as a child I played in the woods with a tumasi pup. There was nothing evil in him. Their ways are different, and he has probably done things I would consider evil by now, but to him maybe they weren't. Or, on the other hand, perhaps that tumasi pup grew up and did not become evil at all. I like to think we all have the free will the gods gave us. Each of us, individually, has the ability to choose to do great good, or great evil, in our lifetime. King Liam should not have the right to judge an entire race without knowing all of them," added Theri.

Siobhan furrowed her brow as she considered their words. "Tell me about each of you. The truth, Celeste."

"I told you the truth before. My father was a herald of Melek. He died over eight hundred years ago in the Deity War. I am around eight hundred and fifty years old – give or take a few decades – and was raised in Kayalost with my mother, who was a full-blooded elf. Tarnelius was my playmate as a child, and we loved each other our whole lives. Due to an unfortunate, uh, misunderstanding, we were separated for over six hundred years, but are together now and bonded. Arcus was also raised in Kayalost, after his parents were murdered by orc raiders in our forests. Theri is from the Southlands and she is here simply because she was asked to come by her people, and she feels our cause is right."

The room fell silent as Siobhan considered everything Celeste had told her. After a few moments, Celeste asked her, "Would you be interested in helping us talk to King Liam? He may take us more seriously if we have the support of one or more of the paladins."

"I'm not sure you do have my support, and it doesn't matter anyway, because we are leaving today to return home, so I cannot help you. Regardless, I will think about what you have said; I am not sure I agree, but what you have said does make a certain amount of sense. I will speak with my brothers- and sisters-in-arms, to get their input. They are everything to me, you know? My entire family have been paladins of Mithra for as many generations as I can remember. It's always been so easy, good versus evil. Black and white, never any gray. Maybe we were mistaken all this time," said Siobhan. "It's a shame about those windows. They may have been boarded up for centuries, but they were undoubtedly beautiful once. This whole temple looks like a warzone. Broken glass everywhere, and covered in blood. In a strange way, it seems almost poetic." She went to the door and pulled it open, struggling with its weight. "The sun is out. I should be getting back to my camp."

"Didn't you just arrive? Why are you leaving so soon?" Celeste asked.

"The king issued a general summons for all the knights of the realm, but he has excluded *us* from his plans. He wants us to fight for him, but treats us no better than untrained foot soldiers. My brethren and I were already on the fence about this mission to begin with because, although we answer to the king, we really have no place among his play-acting knights. We were actually surprised he bothered to send for us at all. Anyway, he meets regularly with the others, but treats us as if we are plague-ridden. We have requested several times to meet with him, but all our requests have been denied by the king's vizier. We don't need to be given the run around by a non-paladin mage who can't even be bothered to tell us himself. He sent a servant with a letter written by him bearing the king's seal. We have better things to do and people in our homeland to protect. Anyway, it was nice meeting all of you, I guess. You've at least given me a lot to think about. Farewell."

Arcus shakily stood up and went to the door after her. "I can't thank you enough," he said as he held his hand out to her to shake.

She ignored his outstretched hand and seemed to almost look through him as she answered. "Not a problem. It's my duty to vanquish evil. You were right to come to me. Good day." With that, she started off down the path leading to the bazaar and out of the city. Arcus stared after her. When he could no longer see her, he returned to the others and sat on the floor near Celeste and Tarnelius.

Celeste carefully climbed out from under Tarnelius. She retracted her wings and walked to the door. As she pushed it closed, she noticed that the door again moved easily for her. She idly considered the implications of the door's behavior for a minute, then decided that it must have something to do with the building recognizing her seraph blood. She returned to Tarnelius and the others, to wait for him to wake up.

"Should we go back to Conner's house?" Theri asked after a short time.

"We could, but we are safe here. We might as well wait, rather than carry him all the way back with people staring at us," Celeste answered.

"I don't know about the rest of you, but I could use a nap," said Arcus. "This blood-covered floor is starting to look very comfortable." He looked around him at the mess all over the floor. "You know, it's amazing how much blood a body actually holds. I'm having trouble reconciling there being this much blood everywhere with my being alive right now."

"I know exactly how you feel," said Celeste.

"Celeste, I truly am sorry. I wish there was some way I could go back and undo what happened," Arcus said in a raspy whisper, overcome with guilt.

"It wasn't you, Arcus. You need to stop apologizing for what that monster did."

"It was still my body."

"Stop it. I'm too tired to argue with you. Just know that I do not hold you responsible; but, if you are going to insist on taking blame, I want you to know that I forgive you."

"I'm going to go sleep on one of the benches," Theri said, jumping up. Arcus stood and followed, smiled in thanks at Celeste, and agreed that the bench was a better idea. Celeste made sure the floor area she and Tarnelius were occupying was free of glass, then she lay down with him, making sure to keep his head cushioned against her body rather than on the hard floor. They all fell asleep within minutes.

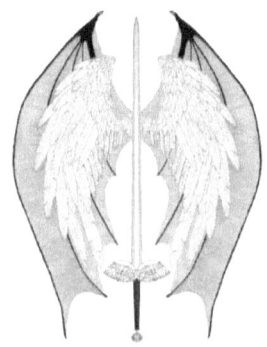

Chapter Twenty-One
Warning Unheeded

After they all woke up a couple of hours later, around midmorning, they cleaned up the temple. Tarnelius used his magic to repair the stained glass windows, while Arcus used his cleaning spell to remove the blood and grime from the room. Despite Siobhan's comment about the destruction being poetic, Celeste could not bear to leave the old temple in such a state. After everything was spotless, the group returned to Conner and Fiona's house.

"So...looks like you can definitely cast spells while shifted," Theri said to Arcus.

"Well, the demon sure could. I've never really tried to cast like that before."

"It was still your body and your magic. I'll bet you can do it. You just have to have faith in your abilities. Work on it; there's a lot to be said for casting while shifted. No one would ever suspect the house cat of being up to anything magical," added Celeste. "We need to clean up, and get our stuff together, so we can go and try to meet with the king."

"Anyone know what happened to our hosts? I'd like to apologize for disturbing them last night," said Arcus.

Celeste cocked her head slightly. "They're in their room. Probably best if we try not to disturb them."

"Ah, understood. Well, they just got their lives back. We should get out of here, give them their privacy," said Arcus. He spoke the words of magic that caused the gentle wind to blow through the room, cleaning all the blood and dirt off each of them and their clothing, while leaving the clean smell of wildflowers behind.

"How did you learn to do that?" Celeste asked.

"It's just a little spell I've been working on while we've been traveling. I finally figured out what I had been doing wrong yesterday while we were cleaning the house. Handy little spell, isn't it?"

"Definitely," answered Celeste. "Too bad you didn't figure it out sooner; we all could have stood to be cleaner while on the road. Come on, let's go." The group separated to get their stuff ready so that they could leave.

Celeste walked to her room and dressed herself in the white satin gown she had married Tarnelius in, packing the rest of her belongings in her small magic bag.

"Are you all right?" she asked Tarnelius, who had sat on the edge of the bed, his eyes downcast. He'd been quiet since they had woken up.

"I'll be fine, don't worry. I'm just not at my best right now. It feels like I have a lot of pressure in my head. At least it doesn't really hurt anymore, thanks to you," he said as he gave her a chaste kiss on the lips.

"That's all I get?" Celeste asked.

"Mmm, the others are waiting for us. Besides, there's the matter of the pressure in my head, remember? I'll make it up to you later. Let's go." They picked up their belongings and joined the others outside the house.

"How are we going to get into the castle?" Theri asked as they set off.

"Well, first thing, let's try the front door. If that doesn't work, we'll see what we can come up with then," answered Celeste. "We'll just 'wing it'."

They crossed into the city center and turned east toward the castle proper. They crossed the courtyard and approached the front gate. There were several guards posted outside the gate.

"State your business," said the nearest guard.

"We come from Kayalost to speak to King Liam," said Celeste.

"Kayalost?" The guard turned to look at the others in confusion. "That isn't one of the delegations ordered to come here. In fact, it sounds like something from the Kayalik area."

"It is," affirmed Celeste.

"That area is controlled by the elves. His Highness has nothing to do with them. He is too busy right now to see you," said the guard.

"He will want to see me," stated Celeste.

"I doubt that very much. His Highness is very busy. You should come back another time."

Celeste released her wings and flapped them over her head. "I represent the seraphs. He will want to see me. Now let me in at once."

The guards scrambled backward out of her way and stared at her in shock as they opened the gate without another word of argument. Celeste swept inside with the others close behind. She stowed her wings after she turned the first corner and was out of sight of the gate.

They strode purposefully down the hall as they wondered where they should start their search. Even though they had gained access to the castle, they were pretty sure it wouldn't be as simple as just bumping into the king in the library. They walked through the large hallways, peeked into rooms as they passed by and listened outside doors that were closed. They checked the central courtyard and found many knights outside on the benches, who talked in loud voices. Some were in full armor and seemed to be set up for mock battles. They crossed the courtyard and entered another door. Across the hall from the door that led to the courtyard was a huge, ornate, gilded door. This door was easily twice the size of any other door in the castle they had seen so far, and the others were not small by any stretch of the imagination.

The group stood outside the door, and tried to decide what to do, when it opened. A tall and slender knight, who wore the armor and insignia of a high-ranking Rashnurian Knight, walked out and continued down the hallway, with hardly a glance at any of them. Celeste and Tarnelius made eye contact and pushed the door open. Then, they all entered, as if they lived there themselves.

The room itself was massive. Each of the four walls contained a mural that depicted one of the four demigods the paladin orders were based on. In front of each of the walls was a statue of the founding member of each order, standing proudly at attention. Next to each statue was an altar. The altar and statue in the back of the room were each draped in black cloth, which hid them from view. There were row after row of benches that looked like church pews, in four distinct areas. The two areas in the center were filled almost to capacity, while the section to the far right – near the door – had only a handful of knights in attendance. The section on the far left was empty. The front of the room displayed a raised dais with a podium. The mural behind the podium depicted Rashnu in full plate armor standing in judgment over the heralds of evil, bearing his rod and scales. A speaker was addressing the room in a loud voice. The acoustics in the room were quite remarkable. As large as the room was, sounds seemed to bounce from wall to wall, and made it easy to hear the speaker. He wore ornate Rashnurian full plate armor, as well as a long purple cape that fanned out behind him, and a massive crown Celeste was sure had to give him a headache if he had to wear it for more than a few minutes. Along the wall behind the speaker six armed guards stood at attention. Celeste walked in silence to the back of the room, and stood next to the covered statue. Tarnelius and the others slid into seats near the door.

"We will take what is ours and come back to claim the lands away from the lesser races. We cannot fail; justice is on our side! We shall claim victory!" King Liam exclaimed.

Celeste removed the cloth covering the statue and altar, watching it slide to the floor in silence. The king noticed her then, and stared at her in silent surprise for a full minute. Those in attendance all turned to look at what held the king's attention. "Guards, grab that woman. I want to know why she dares defile Melek's shroud."

"I? I am not the one defiling anything of Melek's. You are the one who seeks to disturb his rest after eight hundred years," she called back in a strong, commanding voice. The room erupted in whispers. The guards began to close in on her, but she raised her hand at them in warning. "Do not touch me, mortals. I'll not be manhandled by you. I come to represent one who can no longer represent himself." With that, she released her wings with a flourish and lifted into the air. She flew to the left side of the room and sat down in the front pew of the empty left section. She perched on the edge to allow room for her wings to remain out behind her.

King Liam stared at her still, his shock at her interruption evident on his face. The whispers increased into loud murmurings as everyone stared at her, pointed at her, and talked about her. Celeste tried not to fidget. She knew she had to remain strong and show these humans no weakness.

"And what does Melek's representative have to say about my plan?" King Liam asked.

Celeste stood back up and waved her hand dismissively. "This meeting is adjourned, as I must speak to King Liam in private. You all may go. You will be summoned again when you are needed."

"You do not have the authority to dismiss my meeting, young lady."

Celeste turned back to face him. "Very well. I will speak to the group, as a whole, then. My father was a Sacred Herald of Melek. He died over eight hundred years ago in the Deity War. You have been deceived, you have all been deceived. Your ruin, and the end of the world, awaits you in the Holy Tombs."

The room erupted with the loud voices of the Paladin Lords.

"Order! Bring this room to order this instant," Liam bellowed. The volume lowered but did not silence completely.

"What is the meaning of this? How dare you come in here and interrupt my council meeting with this foolery?"

"In fairness, Your Highness, I did try to dismiss your meeting. I have come hundreds of miles to speak with you, but no one from your gate guards to you, yourself, seems to want to take me seriously."

Liam was seething, but he turned back to the room and bellowed. "Meeting dismissed. I will send for each of you later this afternoon to finish up, so do not go far." A few of the knights began to argue, but Liam silenced them with a glare and pointed to the door.

The delegation of high-ranking knights all stood and filed out, staring at the newcomer for as long as they could, without seeming too obvious.

The king gazed at her in silence while he waited for the room to clear. After several minutes, the only people left in the large theater besides Celeste and her friends were King Liam and the six guards.

King Liam frowned at the other three. "Didn't I say the meeting was adjourned? Get out."

"They are with me, Milord. Much like the guards behind you are with you."

"Right, fine then. What is this all about? Why is a seraph here now – and is that a kedistam?" Liam stared at the three still seated on the long benches in the Saroshan section.

"Like I said, I – we – have come a long way to warn you to cancel this mission. You must not disturb the Holy Tombs. I have been sent by the great dragon, Axistra. She has had a vision of what is to come."

"And what has the dragon seen of my future?" Liam asked, a mocking tone to his voice. "No wait, don't answer that. I'll tell you about my vision. Perhaps we *are* talking about the end of the world, but if we are, we are talking about the birth of a new one. We're talking about power and leadership. We're talking about the elimination of all the evil of this world and bringing it to heel. We're talking about a new beginning, of a world where humans and the angelic heralds can work together to restore order."

"At what cost? The gods you claim to remember, and whose memory you still serve, would not have wanted you to annihilate their children. All six of the great races were created by the Three, not just the humans," said Celeste.

"Ah yes, but you are forgetting that two of those races were created by the ultimate evil. Why shouldn't we destroy them?"

"Because, among other reasons, such a venture would release Kuunkierto from his prison," answered Celeste.

"You've been listening to fairy stories. Kuunkierto is dead. He has been for many centuries. Even if he were not dead, once I have Melek's legendary sword, I will slay him myself."

"You can't be so arrogant as to think you can slay one of the Three with Melek's sword when you are nothing but a mortal. Not when so many that were much stronger than you have tried before and failed!" Celeste yelled.

"You will not speak to me in that insubordinate tone! Watch what you say before I have you all arrested," snarled King Liam.

"I'll not be arrested. I warn you now that I will bring this castle down around your ears before I let any one of you lay a finger on me or those under my protection. Now, you need to listen and pay attention. You have been tricked by someone in this castle. Someone you trust has been whispering great evils in your ear. Kuunkierto is not dead. You cannot kill the moon. Axistra has seen your fate, and sent me to warn you off your current path. Axistra has seen that if you go to the north to retrieve the sword you will start a chain reaction that brings about your own destruction, and the end of the world."

"What would Axistra the Silver care about humans, anyway? All she cares about are her elves. Speaking of which," the King walked closer to her, reaching out his hand to pull her hair back from her ears. Tarnelius leapt to his feet and rushed toward them with a snarl. "You are an elf, not a herald. Why should I believe anything you say?"

Celeste held her hand up to stop Tarnelius. "I am both. You should listen to what I say because you know that Axistra and her kin are the closest thing to gods left in this world. She may favor the elves, but that does not mean she would lead you astray. Kuunkierto's freedom would mean your death, and the kedistam's, and quite probably her death and the deaths of her kin, followed by the elves and dwarves. You should also listen to what I say because I am well over eight hundred years old and was there the night the moon changed from shining silver to hideous red. If there is anyone whose council you should be seeking, it should be those who remember," answered Celeste.

King Liam said nothing further, pondering what she had said.

Celeste decided to press her advantage. "The dragons are limited by the same pact the demigods made all those years ago, when they swore not to get involved in the lives of mortals. The fact that she became involved enough to send us to warn you and sway you from your path should speak volumes. She has seen a demonic herald disguised as someone you trust here inside your walls."

"Who? Who is this herald?"

"I don't know yet. Someone you trust. Someone with power. Perhaps an adviser?" Celeste asked.

Something changed in King Liam's expression that looked a lot like recognition. His lips curled in a grin that didn't quite reach his eyes.

"Yes, yes of course. I will interview them all. I will have my paladins interview them as well. I will find this imposter. Madame Seraph, I'm sorry, but you never told me your name."

"My name is Celeste."

"Well Madame Celeste, thank the gods you came in time to warn me. Of course, I will immediately change my plan of action, now that I know the truth, starting with finding and eliminating the herald. Now, I need to recall the paladin lords so I can tell them the change of plan, then I will bring in all my advisors so that we may judge them. Why don't the four of you join me this evening? We will have dinner together. I'm sure this whole messy business will be sorted by then."

"Really, Milord, there's no need to put yourself out. We don't need –" began Celeste.

"Ah, but I insist. You will be here at sundown, all of you. We have much to celebrate. Now, please allow me to get started on my task. I trust that you can show yourselves out. I thank you again for coming to warn me." With that, he gestured toward the door, an expectant expression on his face.

Celeste sighed. "As you wish, Your Highness." She turned and started for the door, signaling to the others, who followed her out.

As soon as the four strangers left the room, King Liam turned to his guards. "You there, Sean, I need you to go find Vizier Tarryn and send him to my chambers. As soon as I finish this meeting with the Paladin Lords, I will need to speak to him in private." The guard saluted and marched from the room, not wasting any time.

As soon as they made it out of the castle proper, Theri cleared her throat. "Celeste, you don't honestly think he's going to cancel his plans, do you?" she asked.

"No."

"Then what are we doing?" asked Theri.

"What could we have done? He could not have been more transparent if he were made of glass. He was dismissing us.

There was nothing I could say to convince him, and nothing we could do, short of an assassination attempt."

"Assassination is probably better than the end of the world," Arcus pointed out.

"I haven't ruled it out, but in the castle is neither the time nor the place."

"Well, we aren't planning on walking into that obvious trap he's setting for us, are we?" asked Tarnelius.

"Unless you have a better plan," said Celeste.

Tarnelius stared at her in shock. "You can't be serious."

"Look, if we do not show up, we show him we are afraid of him and we show him we aren't strong in our beliefs. Also, if we do not show up, we miss the chance to try to find the herald ourselves."

Siobhan stared at the campsite, not really seeing it. All the tents had been pulled down and the pack horses had been loaded. Her squire, Katie, kept herself busy by fastening Siobhan's riding cloak to her shoulders and saddling her own horse. Katie was slender, with her dirty blond hair cut into a pixie style.

"Milady, will you be summoning Apollo? We should be leaving soon," Katie asked.

"What's that? Oh, yes, you are right." A second later, there was a tall palomino stallion standing next to Siobhan. She reached up and stroked his soft nose as she looked around to see what was left to do. To her amazement, everyone else was already packed up and ready for her.

"Is everything all right? You've seemed distracted since you returned from the city this morning."

"Yes, everything is fine. I'm just wondering if we are doing the right thing." Siobhan sighed. "Do not concern yourself. I recently met some people in the city who have a different view than what we've always been taught and I can't help but wonder if they may be right.

"Mount up," Siobhan called to the others. "It is time we return home. Let us return by way of Beinn-anbas. Perhaps we can do some good with this trip, rather than just write it off as a waste of time."

The other paladins nodded in agreement as they mounted their horses. The squires also mounted up and led the pack horses with lead ropes.

Beinn-anbas, Siobhan thought to herself. *Well, at least we'll see if the rumors have been true.* The name roughly translated to "Hills of Death", and was located several days' ride northwest of Lumernia. It was named for the undead that were always present in the area. The knights had received reports from travelers in the nearby city of Gormloch that there had been more and more activity from the undead lately, particularly at night. The Paladins of Mithra would send patrols on occasion into that area to clean house, but it had not been very long since their last patrol, and there was no reason for them to increase in number as fast as the reports would suggest.

Liam burst through the doors into his private chamber, a servant hot on his heels. He yanked the crown from his head and shoved it onto its cushioned pedestal. He marched to his armor stand and stretched his arms out without a word. The servant ducked all around him, and frantically untied and removed his cape and his armor, piece by piece. He carefully placed the armor on its stand, which looked like a carefully constructed statue when he was done. Liam waved his hand dismissively and the servant ran from the room without speaking even one word.

Now that he wore only the soft padded garments that knights typically wore under their armor, Liam walked through another door in his living quarters leading to a sitting area that contained a darkened alcove with a shelf holding a few bottles of wine. Most of his wine was stored down in the wine cellars, but he enjoyed having a few bottles within easy reach. Liam started to walk to the alcove, but paused when he noticed Tarryn sitting in the high-backed armchair with its back to the door he'd entered. Tarryn was wearing white mage's robes bearing the Rashnurian rod and scale symbol. His unlined face, black hair and dark brown eyes, that were almost indistinguishable from black, made it difficult to determine the mage's age.

"Oh good, the guard found you. We need to talk," said Liam.

Tarryn looked straight ahead, unblinking. He raised his hand to take a sip of the glass of thirty year old sherry he had helped himself to while he waited. Liam walked to another shelf and selected a wineglass with an ornate silver stem. He poured himself a glass and also took a sip. He savored the delicious flavor as he swirled the drink around his tongue. Satisfied, he took his glass to the chair opposite Tarryn and sat down.

"Excellent choice, one of my favorite vintages," he said. "So, I had some surprising guests show up for my meeting with the Paladin Lords."

Tarryn continued to gaze at him in silence.

Liam cleared his throat before he continued. "There were two elves; one was a full elf and one was a bastard half elf with wings and a superiority complex. There was a scruffy looking human and a kedistam, too. The half-elf spoke of an apocalypse, and how someone who works for me was trying to trick me, just as you said she would. How did you know they would come?"

"I always know, Liam. I always know. The elves fear change, and they love to cause mistrust among friends simply to keep progress from happening. They fear what you will be able to do."

Liam stared back at him. "Seriously, how did you know? I've never known you to be a seer."

Tarryn smirked. "One of my assistants heard the half-elf speaking to a paladin near the herbalist's yesterday and told me about it."

Liam paused. "There isn't really any chance that Kuunkierto really is still alive, is there?"

"Utter nonsense. The moon is covered in his blood that poured from him in his death throes. He is dead. Now, what have you done with our guests? Did you have them arrested, as I told you?"

Liam tossed down the last of his wine before he answered. "No. She threatened to bring the castle down around my ears, and I believed her. She seemed to tremble with power."

"Damn it, Liam! So you let them leave?" Tarryn demanded, his anger palpable. His glass exploded in his hands and, ignoring this, he stood up and grabbed his staff to lean on as he paced. The staff was a burnished gold with a clear oval shaped crystal held fast on the top. Inside the crystal was a large golden key.

"Calm down. They'll be back. I invited them to dinner tonight," said Liam.

"And what makes you so sure they will return? No offense intended, *Your Highness*, but you aren't exactly the most suave man out there when it comes to hiding your intent."

"They will be back. I have ordered it and they will come, if for no other reason than for curiosity. I'm sure they have some notion they will be able to find their hidden demonic herald, if they have access to those close to me. Speaking of which," Liam paused. "They said Axistra the Silver warned them of what was to come. The dragon had a vision of the end of the world and that a demonic herald was here, in the castle, in disguise, and acting as my adviser. How could they think that could happen and we wouldn't know about it? Rashnu's power would alert me if there were such a creature hiding here."

Tarryn laughed coldly. "I agree. I don't think anyone in this castle could be a demon. I'd be able to sense it with my magic, as could you with yours. Besides, this mission was conceived between myself and you, so I suppose I would be the most likely culprit if there were a demon here, disguised as your advisor."

Liam laughed at this. Tarryn was his most trusted friend and ally. If it weren't for Tarryn, he would have never learned the ways of Rashnu and come into his paladin powers. There was no way he could be a demon. "Well, let's hope that is not true. We are all in big trouble if you are a demon."

Tarryn smiled at him. "That is true. Lucky for everyone I am not. Now leave the half-elf and her friends to me. I will take care of them."

"Why are you so concerned with them anyway?" Liam asked.

"People like them stir up trouble. They stir up discontent among your followers. It is the way of man to always question authority and if you let them stay, they will chip away at your control until you have a full mutiny on your hands."

"What do you plan to do with them, then?"

"I will prepare a standard anesthetic, opium and hemlock, which I will enhance with a bit of magic and slip into their food or drink. After they are in a deep sleep, I will send some servants to carry them back to their people, or perhaps even to Gormloch. I have a friend near there who would tend to them. I swear that no lasting harm will come to them. It is not my way."

Liam sighed. "All right. You win; do as you wish. I will make sure no one interferes. I'm not sure I like this, but you have never given me any reason to doubt your wisdom in the past, and honestly, I don't have a better plan anyway."

Tarryn bowed to his king and then excused himself from the room to begin his preparations. He created the potion exactly as he described, as well as cast a glamor spell on it to make it clear. Then he bottled his concoction and went to the dining hall as the servants had just finished the place settings at each table. After checking to make sure no one was around, he coated the clear sleeping potion onto the inside of each of the four wine glasses at the king's table that were marked with the placard reading, "guest".

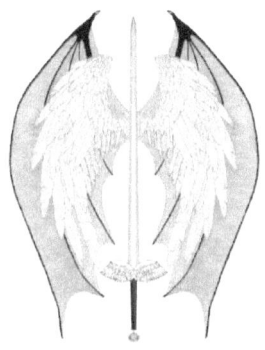

Chapter Twenty-Two
Dinner Plans

"You must be the guests King Liam told me about. Come in! I will show you to your table. My name is Tarryn, and I am the royal vizier." Tarryn beamed at them and bowed low. "Oh, I almost forgot, if you have any weapons with you, you will need to stow them in the next room. We want to make sure everyone here is safe."

"We come unarmed, sir, as you can see. My name is Celeste, and these are Tarnelius, Arcus and Therinsalla."

"Excellent. Right this way, then." As the group started to walk past him, they froze in surprise. Theri wasn't expecting the sudden stop and walked right into Arcus. "Oh, I apologize, I should have told you. This room is shielded by an anti-magic field. If you are feeling any dizziness or discomfort, I assure you it is only temporary," said Tarryn. "As soon as you step back out of the room, it will be gone."

"Why would the king need such protection?" asked Celeste. "I do not like this. I feel we are being set up."

"Taking away a caster's magic is the same as taking away a warrior's sword. It's simply to keep everyone safe."

By now, the small room was beginning to fill up with the other guests. There weren't many coming; it looked like only a few of the Paladin Lords from each of the orders. Celeste and Tarnelius glanced at each other. *"I do not like this,"* Tarnelius thought to her.

"I don't either, but what can we do?"

"We should just leave. We have little to no chance of finding the herald without any magic anyway," he thought.

"We can all shift, except Theri, who still has her claws. Anti-magic fields never affect that ability. I'll still have my wings, which I can wield as weapons in a pinch, to protect us. We can't give up trying now," Celeste answered.

"All right, but I still think this is a bad idea; I can feel it." Tarnelius walked over and sat in one of the chairs the vizier was gesturing to, marked "guest". Celeste sat down next to him and the other two sat on the other side of the table. Tarryn also sat down next to Celeste, his staff on his other side, against the table. His hand rested on it, as if he were afraid it would fall if he let go.

"That's an interesting staff head," Celeste remarked, staring at it.

"Oh, this? You can get one just like it at the mage guild. They aren't very expensive. It helps me keep my balance and just looks nice."

"The key emblem looks familiar, somehow." Celeste squinted at it, trying to remember.

"I just find it odd that the key is sparkling like that inside the crystal," remarked Tarnelius. "Since that appears to be a magical effect, and there is an anti-magic field here."

"It's only a trick of the light, helped along by a gel material that makes it look – oh, the king is here." Tarryn grabbed his staff and used it to help lower himself to a kneeling position. The rest of the room followed suit and kneeled as well. The group exchanged glances and then followed suit.

"Thank you for coming. We are gathered here today to celebrate new alliances and friendships, as well as a new age of order," Liam said. "Please rise, and enjoy the humble offerings of this castle."

A servant came and poured a sweet red wine in the king's glass, then continued around the table using the same bottle to fill the other glasses. Tarryn raised his glass in a toast, and said, "To our king, a true paladin and visionary. Long live the king." He took a long drink of his wine, and the others did the same.

"A new age of order?" Celeste remarked as the servants all carried plates of food to the four tables. "I thought you had decided against going to the north."

"I had considered it. However, I have decided that the benefit of gaining the sword far outweighs the nonexistent risk of waking a dead god."

"Do not underestimate his power," warned Celeste.

"There is no power there; the moon is dead. It is covered in the blood that was spilled hundreds of years ago. You worry too much; I know what I'm doing. Eat up, the food is good," he said between bites.

Celeste placed her empty glass on the table, noticing her hand shake as she did so. She shook her head, trying to clear it, but her ears seemed to be ringing. The anti-magic field was apparently tearing her apart. Combine that with trying to talk to this foolish human, and she knew that Tarnelius had been right. They should have gone. They had no chance of finding the demon. She tried to mentally reach out to him, but she felt a block. She couldn't hear herself think, much less hear his thoughts. She stood up suddenly, realizing she had interrupted something Liam was saying. She shook her head again and turned to walk toward the door, anxious to escape the anti-magic field.

Then there was darkness.

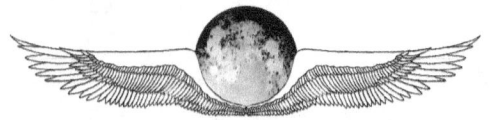

As soon as Celeste hit the floor, chaos ensued. Tarnelius rushed to her side and held her to him. Tarryn jumped to his feet, staff in hand, followed by the king and the Paladin Lords.

"Holy Rashnu, is she dead?" Liam yelled above the din. "What could have happened?" Tarryn knelt alongside Celeste on the opposite side from Tarnelius. "She isn't dead, is she, Tarryn?"

Tarryn tried to pull Celeste away from Tarnelius, but backed away as the elf snarled at him like an animal. They were then distracted by a loud clanking sound as Theri collapsed onto her plate. Arcus stood up and began backing away toward the door. "What is this? What have you done? She is a druid; druids cannot be poisoned. Kamara protects us, I don't unders –"

Arcus made it just to the other side of the door and collapsed as well. One of the paladins rushed to his side, while several others milled about nervously. From the crowd came a lone voice, "The plague! The strangers have brought plague with them." The paladin at Arcus' side jerked his hand back in fright and ran away from the room, followed by the others. Soon, the room had cleared out, leaving only Tarryn, Liam and the four foreigners. Tarryn gave up on his attempts to see to Celeste, as

Tarnelius was still growling at him. He went out to the entryway and dragged Arcus back inside the room. He placed two of his fingers to his jugular for a moment.

"This one is still alive; his pulse is slow but steady. He is asleep. I am sure the others are too," said Tarryn.

Liam walked over to Tarnelius. "May I see to her, please? I want to help, only to help." Tarnelius' eyes were bloodshot and wary, but he allowed the king to touch her wrist. "Yes, she is alive. I can feel her heartbeat as well. I'm so sorry this happened, Tarnelius, is it? She will be all right, I promise you."

Tarnelius blinked his eyes but said nothing. He exhaled heavily and his eyes rolled back in his head as he collapsed, still holding fast to Celeste.

Liam sighed. "Are you sure this was necessary, Tarryn? I feel awful about it."

"Your Highness, do not worry. As you can see, they are still alive and unharmed. Go back to your paladins and assure them that everything is fine. Tell them that the foreigners are unwell, and are being sent home. I will take care of everything. This way is better, I promise. The worst is over, and now your plan is safe from the mutiny they would have caused."

"But –"

"Liam, you either trust me or you don't. Go, time is short."

Liam turned and strode from the room.

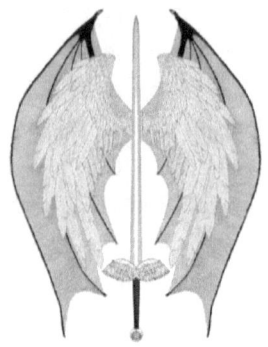

Chapter Twenty-Three
A New Direction

Siobhan and the rest of the paladins steered the horses off the road into the grassy pasture. They had been travelling for only a day and a half, and were still over one hundred miles away from the southern edge of the Dacre River. On the other side of the river was the border to Beinn-anbas. The path they had chosen would lead them right into the fabled Hills of Death on the way home. They dismounted and let the horses graze and rest. The paladins' mounts did not require as much food as regular horses and so could travel farther in a day, but they were limited by their pack horses, and by the squires' horses.

Siobhan sat down near a large bush blossoming with beautiful purple bell-shaped flowers. They pulled out some of the dried trail rations they each carried, and ate a little bit. After close to a half an hour had passed, they collected their horses and remounted, prepared to start again. Siobhan stopped Apollo short just as she was about to direct him back onto the road. She held up her hand. "There's a wagon approaching at a fast speed.

Let's wait for them to pass so we don't hinder them." They all turned to look, and sure enough, there was a horse-drawn wagon not far off, only a little more than a mile in the distance. As the wagon got closer and closer, the paladins' horses started to become antsy. Apollo reared up angrily, his front hooves flailing in the air. Siobhan attempted to soothe him, then turned to look closer at the wagon. It was being pulled by four black horses, and two men sat up in the front. She stared at them, and as she tried to see what it was the horses saw, her paladin senses kicked in. An evil red aura became visible all around them.

"Demons," Siobhan exclaimed. "On my command, be ready to charge. Kill the humans and the horses, they have also been possessed. No prisoners."

Siobhan paused, waiting for them to get a bit closer. "Now," she bellowed, and urged Apollo into the road as she drew her sword. She was aware of several of her brethren following her into the road, while several others ran alongside in the field. They converged on the wagon from two sides, and made short work of cutting down all the demons.

"Why would they bother to possess horses?" Katie asked when she caught up with her.

"If the horses are possessed, they don't need to worry about them being rested. Plus, regular horses would have been too frightened of the demons to be controllable."

"What shall we do with the bodies?" Ryan asked.

"Burn them," answered Siobhan. "Maybe the wagon as well, but let's take a look at what they were transporting in such a hurry."

Ryan organized a cleanup crew who spread out to find materials to make a funeral pyre. Meanwhile, Siobhan and Katie dismounted and moved around to the back of the open air wagon to find out what they carried. Siobhan removed her helmet and set it on the back of the wagon so she could see more easily.

The back of the wagon contained four long, thin, rectangular, wooden boxes. They were poorly made and some of the wooden boards didn't quite meet. Each box was held together with nails, and each was bound by thick ropes. Squinting to try to look inside one of the boxes, Siobhan thought she could make out a body.

"Great! Have the demons been responsible for the undead increasing in numbers? It looks like they were bringing fresh bodies."

"I've never seen them use animal corpses before, though," said Katie.

"Animals?" Siobhan looked at the box she was pointing at, just in time to hear a muffled thumping sound come from inside, like something in there had shifted. Siobhan frowned for a moment, then her eyes widened. "Open that box at once!"

Not waiting for Katie to actually carry out her order, Siobhan drew her sword and slashed the ropes. Then she wedged the side of the sword into the corner and pried the box open. Sure enough, inside the box was Theri. Her hands and feet were bound, and her mouth was gagged. She blinked at the sudden change from darkness to harsh sunlight.

"Open the other boxes," Siobhan ordered. She reached into the box and began to untie the knots binding Theri. Katie offered her a small dagger. The other paladins hurried over to lift the other boxes from the wagon and place them on the ground. That task done, they began to cut the bindings on the boxes, so they could open them.

Siobhan took the offered dagger and carefully cut away the ropes and gag. That was when she noticed that Theri's eyes were bloodshot.

The other boxes contained the other three that Siobhan had met in Lumernia: Celeste, Tarnelius and Arcus. All of them were bound and gagged, and none of them were conscious. The paladins set to work freeing them from their bindings, and then attempting to revive them. Siobhan extended a hand to Theri, and helped her to sit up.

"What happened to you?" Siobhan asked.

Theri squeezed her eyes closed for a moment, trying to focus. "I – I'm not sure. The last thing I remember was walking into the dining hall to meet King Liam. I think he drugged us."

Katie and Siobhan stared at her in surprise. "You think King Liam drugged you and sent you out of the city with demons?"

Theri frowned. "Demons? I don't know anything about… I just woke up and heard fighting. Oh, I'm so confused. My head is pounding."

Siobhan watched her in sympathy. "I'm going to go see to the others. You stay here and try to stay calm. We'll figure out what is going on, don't worry."

Theri sighed. "I think I'm going to be sick. I'm not going anywhere." She rested her head on her knees and groaned.

Siobhan patted her on the back gently, her hands taking on a golden shine. She didn't know what had happened, but if Theri was sick, she knew she could help. If she *had* been drugged, she would need to wait for her body to eliminate the drug naturally. Siobhan hoped there had been a mistake, that Theri was just confused by whatever had happened to her, but she couldn't deny that the evidence before her seemed to support the kedistam's claim. She hoped the others would be able to shed some light on the situation, if they were even still alive.

"Any luck waking them up?" Siobhan asked her brethren. She moved among them, and finally stopped next to Celeste. At the chorus of "no" that answered her, she added, "They are all still alive, aren't they?"

Cayden, the squire, nodded his agreement. "Yes, Captain. They are all alive, though their heart rates are dangerously slow."

"We'll need to keep trying. I'm not sure what caused this, but we have reason to believe these people have been drugged, which means there isn't much we can do as far as healing them. Try lifting their feet a bit." Siobhan frowned a little as she considered. "Cayden, go get some of the blankets from the pack horses." He jumped up and hurried to obey.

Just as he was coming back, laden with blankets, the human started coughing and gasping. Arcus jerked onto his side and tried to curl up but his knees hit the side of the box. Siobhan hurried over to Arcus and knelt down next to him.

"Cayden, fold the blankets a little, and prop them under the other two's feet. Arcus, can you hear me?"

Arcus coughed again and nodded. He opened his eyes a tiny bit, looking up at the beautiful face of a redheaded angel. Upon closer examination, he realized it was actually the same paladin who had saved him from the demon. He squeezed his eyes shut again. "What set off the stampede that ran over me?"

"There was no stampede. What is the last thing you remember?" Siobhan asked.

"Let me think. After you left, we met the king. He insisted we come back to have dinner later. There was a mage there, and an anti-magic field. I remember Celeste collapsing and I recall so much yelling, both inside my head and out. It was deafening. I remember thinking we had been poisoned, but druids are immune to poisons, so that can't be. How long were we unconscious? It was dusk when we went into the castle and it's bright now."

"I last saw you early yesterday morning, so you can't have been out for too long. Hours, not days. Why would you think someone would poison you?"

"Who knows? They wanted to shut us up, I suppose. Geez, being hung over doesn't hurt this bad," complained Arcus. "Wait, what about the others? Are they all right? Where am I?"

"Theri is awake, but the two elves are not yet. You're on the road leading to Gormloch. You were in a wagon being controlled by demons."

Arcus groaned again. "Demons. Why is it always demons?" He peered up at her, nervous. "There's not another one inside me, is there? I don't feel one, but everything hurts, so who knows? I can't focus."

Siobhan stared at him for a moment as she checked for any sign of evil taint on him. "No, not this time. I'm glad you mentioned that, though; I should check the others."

Arcus relaxed and rolled with difficulty onto his stomach, still in his box on the ground. "Thank Kamara, because I don't think I could survive another exorcism right now."

"Do you want a hand up?"

"No, I'm going to lay here and focus on not losing yesterday's lunch and try to hide from the sunlight." Arcus' voice was muffled from talking into his arms.

Siobhan gently laid her hand on his back to try to heal him, surprised to once more feel the same spark she had noticed the morning before, when he shook her hand. He seemed to feel it too, even through his tunic, because he jumped a little. After she healed him, she got back up and walked over to where the two unconscious elves were still laying. She glanced over to check on Theri just in time to see her throw up over the side of the wagon. It appeared she had climbed out of her box but her stomach wasn't ready to be mobile. Siobhan turned away.

Honestly, if this was either a drug or a poison, out was better than in.

"Antoine, go see to the kedistam, and check her for demonic possession while you're at it," she commanded. Antoine ran over to do as he was told.

"Their heart rates have improved slightly, with their feet elevated," Cayden reported.

Siobhan nodded as she scanned them for demonic presence, not finding any trace of evil on them. "We need to get moving. We can't stay here in the middle of the road with a wagon and a bunch of poorly made caskets on the ground." With a thought, she dismissed Apollo back to the celestial realms he inhabited when she didn't have need of him. "Cayden, unpack four of the pack horses and secure them to this wagon. Their loads can also go in here. Katie, please assist Arcus out of his crate and into the wagon with Theri. Then see about also getting the two elves out of their boxes and into the wagon. Make a pallet with blankets. Ryan, why don't I see a funeral pyre yet? The rest of you, form groups and help the three I placed in charge with their projects. Oh, Ryan, you can use the crates and severed ropes for kindling."

There was a flurry of activity as everyone hurried to do as she commanded. Within minutes, a fire was burning, and they were carrying the demon-possessed humans and horses to the pyre. The elves had been placed on blankets in the wagon, and Arcus had actually managed to climb in under his own steam, though with many complaints. Katie jumped up onto the driver's seat, and Siobhan climbed in the back with the others, promising to come up front to help drive the wagon if she was needed. Siobhan directed Katie to keep to the center of the paladin group, so she waited for half of them to set off before she urged the wagon forward, while the other half of the group fell in behind them. With a snap of the reins, they were off.

Siobhan watched her fellow paladins who were riding behind her, and checked on the two elves often. Arcus was alternating between burying his face in his hands and staring at her, for some reason. Theri seemed to be feeling a little better as she was actually looking around at her surroundings and moving semi-normally.

"Where were they taking us?" Theri asked after they had been traveling for almost half an hour.

"How should I know?" Siobhan answered. "I'm not privy to the demons' plans." Theri fell silent and Siobhan sighed. "What I do know is that this is the road to Gormloch. A little farther than that is Castle Mithra. Also, before we reach Gormloch, we cross the hills known as Beinn-anbas, the Hills of Death. No one *lives* there exactly, but it is possible that they were taking you there."

Arcus joined in. "Why do you think they would take us there?"

"Same answer as before, though the Hills are the only stronghold of evil this side of the mountains."

"Not including Lumernia, of course," challenged Arcus.

"Lumernia isn't an evil stronghold."

"Isn't it? I don't even know what exactly happened to us, but I do know a demon possessed me, there were more driving us out of the city, and there are who knows how many left there unchecked." Suddenly his eyes widened. "We have to go back," he said.

"We aren't going back," answered Siobhan.

"No, we *have* to go back. We have to stop King Liam, we have to stop the demons. Wait, why are you taking us down the path away from the city? This seems like the same path the demons were taking us down."

"What are you accusing me of, Arcus?" Siobhan asked in a frosty tone.

"I'm not accusing you of anything. I am telling you what we must do. The fate of the world is at stake, yet you are preventing us from doing what we need to do to save it."

Theri rolled her eyes. "This isn't helping, Arcus. Besides, it doesn't matter now. Siobhan is helping us, and Celeste and Tarnelius are still out. Like you said, we don't know what happened, but what I do know is if Celeste and Tarnelius know the trees there, it shouldn't be too hard to get back once they wake up. Stop fighting like children. I don't want to have to listen to it."

Celeste moaned, and her hand twitched as she found and gripped Tarnelius' hand. Siobhan, Theri and Arcus all stopped and turned to watch the elves. Theri slid down alongside Celeste and nudged her shoulder.

"Celeste, wake up. Please wake up; we need you right now." Celeste moaned again and drew her hand over her face to cover her eyes.

"Theri?" Celeste asked in a weak voice.

"I'm here," Theri answered.

"Where are we?"

"I'm not sure. We're in a wagon, travelling somewhere west of Lumernia. Siobhan and the paladins are here."

Celeste frowned a little, then rolled over, throwing her arm around Tarnelius. She pushed herself up a little and opened her eyes, looking down at him. "Tarnel?"

"He's not awake yet. Arcus and I have been up for a while," answered Theri.

"What do you remember, Celeste?" Siobhan asked.

She frowned in thought. "Give me a few minutes to collect my thoughts. My head feels like it's full of rocks." She squirmed, reaching her right arm down the collar of her dress, trying to reach under her left arm. "Drat, it's shifted behind me. Theri, could you give me a hand?" Theri reached down the back of her collar and struggled a bit, eventually drawing Celeste's small magic bag out, as well as a long strip of material. Celeste squirmed some more as she pulled on the material she had used to bind and conceal the bag, to finish removing it.

"I'm surprised they didn't notice this under your arm," Theri said as she passed over the bag.

"Whatever happened to us back there, I guess this at least proves they didn't strip-search us or anything like that while we were unconscious. There's a silver lining, at least. Plus, it's a good thing they *didn't* find this, as it contains all our equipment. Although, had they searched us in the middle of that anti-magic field, it would have just appeared to be an empty bag anyway."

Putting the bag down beside her, Celeste stroked Tarnelius' jaw and traced his ear with her fingers. Then she sat up a little more and placed her hand over his heart, leaning down to kiss him. At first nothing happened, but after a moment she could feel his heartbeat increase under her hand, then he twitched and responded, kissing her back. His hand came up to cup the back of her head. She broke away, smiling down at him as he opened his eyes, his unfocused gaze trying to find hers.

"Hi, sleeping beauty," she said to him.

He gave her a weak smile. "That's my line."

Siobhan cleared her throat. "I'm glad you are all awake. Now maybe we can figure out what happened. I'll fill you in on what I know. My brethren and I are headed home by way of Beinn-anbas, the Hills of Death, where we intend to look into reports of increased activity from the undead. We were just getting ready to leave, after we'd rested the horses, when we saw a wagon approach at speed. It was being drawn by four demon-possessed horses and driven by two possessed humans. We cut them down and found you in the back. Now, have you any idea why this is?"

Celeste chewed her lower lip. "What day is it?"

"We last met yesterday morning before we packed up and left, if that is what you are asking."

Celeste nodded. "Everything is hazy, but I'll try to put the pieces together. I remember returning to the castle for dinner. I remember meeting the vizier. The room had a strange feel to it. Tarryn said it was because of an anti-magic field covering the room. I remember Liam saying he was going to go ahead to the north despite my warnings, and then the room went out of focus. I couldn't hear what anyone was saying. I couldn't hear my own thoughts. I panicked, then everything went dark."

"After you fell, I panicked too," Tarnelius confessed. "I couldn't hear my thoughts either, or yours. I didn't know if you were alive or dead. I was worried, and couldn't focus. All I do remember before I blacked out is someone who told me you were still alive."

"I wonder what happened to us, though," Arcus mused. "It couldn't be magic, it couldn't be poison."

"The only other thing I clearly remember is Tarryn's staff. It looked so familiar, and the answer is right there, just out of reach. I can almost feel it," Celeste said in frustration.

"It *was* a strange staff," Tarnelius agreed. "I don't care what sort of make-believe answer he was about to give us about tricks of the light; it was definitely sparkling. The key was almost pulsating with magic."

"Key?" Siobhan asked, intrigued.

"Yes, gold staff with a clear oval crystal containing a golden key," answered Tarnelius. "Very striking, very mysterious."

"The golden key locked away inside a crystal is a symbol of Raziyl, god of secrets," said Siobhan.

Celeste gasped. "Kamara help us, you're right. I bet that was actually Raziyl's real staff, too." She looked at Tarnelius in horror.

He shook his head. "Raziyl would not have left it behind. I agree the staff does meet the description, but I see no reason for it to still exist on this plane of existence."

Theri stared at them in confusion. "Is anyone interested in sharing what they are talking about with me?"

Celeste spoke up. "Raziyl, the god of secrets, possessed a magical staff. It was golden, and contained a key encased in a crystal. Anyone that came within the crystal's range lost the ability to cast any kind of magic."

"They also lost any gifts given to them, such as the ability to shift – good thing we didn't try that – or the ability to see good or evil auras, for example. In addition, it granted the demigod the ability to still use his own magic, even as everyone else's was being suppressed. Anti-magic field my foot," Tarnelius added bitterly.

"I bet that is why we felt so off, too; the power of the staff was messing with us. The more I think about it, the more it makes sense. It all makes sense. Tarryn is the demon, and the staff hides him from the few paladins that would be able to see him for what he is," Celeste said.

"Would this staff also suppress our poison immunity?" Arcus asked.

"Probably it would, yes. Though I don't think we were poisoned, Arcus. If we were poisoned, we would never have woken up. I don't know why he didn't just kill us when he had the chance, but he must have had a reason," answered Tarnelius.

"Tarryn was the one that denied our requests to see King Liam," added Siobhan.

"Which also makes sense. He wouldn't have to worry about you finding out what he is if he keeps you away," Celeste said.

"But he wouldn't need to worry about it with the staff, if it truly is the real thing."

"The staff is probably limited to only working when it is being held by the mage who activated it. Many magic items are able to be activated or deactivated, and stop working immediately if dropped. Plus, it would be too risky for him that one of you would recognize it. Let's face it, *you* recognized it from just a description."

"I still don't understand how a demon would get hold of it in the first place," said Tarnelius. "Why wouldn't Raziyl have taken it with him?"

"I suspect there's no answer to that question."

"So, shouldn't we part ways here and head back to Lumernia?" Arcus asked. "Seems there is a demon we need to kill."

"No," Celeste said after a moment. "No, we should go to the north, to the tombs."

"Why wouldn't we just go take care of this now? We can go back through the trees," argued Arcus.

"Ooh, I know this one," interjected Theri. "It's because there are too many knights back in Lumernia, isn't it?"

"Yes, that, but the demon will have the home field advantage there. He will have who knows how many possessed allies, and he may be half-expecting it anyway. Even if we manage to kill him, Liam is still determined to go; you heard what he said. We will need to beat them there, and expose the demon's identity to Liam where there are fewer warriors in the way," said Celeste.

"What do you know of the tombs?" Siobhan asked.

"Very little," Celeste confessed. "I know that there once was a castle to the north. I know that during the war, many of the gods died, mostly the ones who embraced neither good nor evil, as they were the first to arrive on scene to oppose Kuunkierto's rule. He threatened the balance, so the druidic gods showed up to fight him. Eleven were lost in that great battle, which included two of the evil ones. Finally, Melek showed up with his seraphs, his sword gleaming with Aurinko's blessings. The battle was fierce and bloody. With Melek's last bit of strength, he brought the castle down on top of them all and sealed it tight, using his sword's magic."

"How would someone open the seal?"

"Well, according to the stories, only someone blessed by one of the four paladin gods would be able to open it," said Celeste.

"Well, that explains what the demon is doing in Lumernia among the paladins, but it doesn't explain why he didn't try to corrupt an actual paladin," mused Tarnelius.

Siobhan sneered. "A demon showing up in Castle Mithra would have to be a suicidal demon, indeed."

Celeste nodded. "Like I said earlier, it's too risky that a real paladin would recognize the staff, and without the staff they would recognize what he is in seconds. No, better to choose a weak-willed warrior pretending to be a paladin to open the seal." She paused. "Except that wouldn't work, because they would have to actually be blessed enough to be a real paladin to touch the seal." She trailed off, confused. "I actually have no idea what he is doing. Back to the original question, though, I do not think he poisoned us. I suspect he put some powerful sleeping spell on us, or perhaps drugged us." She nodded to herself. "Probably both. That would explain both the speed we were knocked out and the amount of time we stayed knocked out. It would also explain this horrible 'floating brain' sensation I still have, and I know Tarnelius still has. How about the rest of you?" They nodded.

Tarnelius added, "I think, for argument's sake, we have to assume he is the man in black that projected himself to us on the way there."

Celeste's eyes widened. "Oh no, that means –" She stopped talking and immediately started chanting. A transparent silver bubble began to form. It wavered for a moment but burst. Celeste sighed and began again, in a more determined voice. The bubble again formed and expanded larger and larger until it could barely be seen any longer, then it vanished without popping.

Siobhan stared. "What the –"

"It's an anti-divination spell," said Celeste. "Keeps people from magically watching us. I may have been too late. I sure hope not."

"I still don't understand why the demon would drug you and send you this way," said Siobhan.

"Me neither. I don't know why he wouldn't just kill us," said Celeste.

"Now our conversation is going around in circles," said Tarnelius.

"Siobhan, will you and your people help us? Will you please come with us to the north to stop the demon?" Celeste asked.

"We will have to discuss it, and we will have to get permission. I will consider it on one condition."

"What's that?" Celeste asked.

"We will arrive in Beinn-anbas in a few days. If you help me clear out the undead, I will speak to my brethren on your behalf."

Celeste sighed. "I wish we could, but can't you understand that we are limited by time? We have to get there before Liam does."

"I know that he wasn't planning on leaving for several days yet. He was waiting to speak to the Saroshans before leaving," said Siobhan.

"We can't know that his plans haven't changed."

"True, but I doubt he would have changed his plans. He was going to select a few from each order to go with him. The Saroshans have several sorcerers among them. I do not think he would give up the chance to choose a few of them. Either way, those are my terms. Also, just so you know, the path to the north will lead you right through those hills anyway."

"I think we should stick with Siobhan for now," Arcus murmured. "Since you've decided we're headed north, to the tombs, anyway."

Celeste looked to the others for a moment before she nodded. "All right, we will help you."

"Excellent." Siobhan stood up, and her armor clanked softly. "I'm going to go up front to check on Katie. You should all rest up; you need to get whatever they drugged you with out of your systems." With that, she climbed up to sit next to her squire.

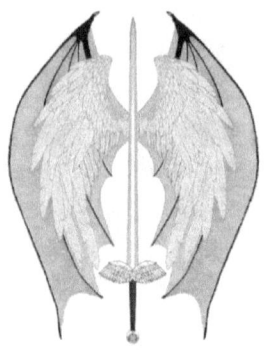

Chapter Twenty-Four
Blinding Darkness

Tarryn was in a horrible mood. First of all, those meddlesome Mithran knights had all up and vanished on him. He couldn't stand them anyway, but at least with them wasting time out in the Lumernian fields, he knew where they were and what they were doing. Worse, he had tried to find them via divinations, but his attempts had all failed. On top of that, he had lost contact with the men he had sent to take his cargo to Beinn-anbas. The last time he had been able to make contact with them was three days ago, on the morning after he had sent them out. He was kind of concerned the two problems were connected, but he consoled himself with the knowledge that the most direct way to Castle Mithra would have taken them well north of the road he had sent his servants on.

Even if those Mithrans have gotten involved, it soon won't matter. We'll be on the road and harder to find, he thought to himself.

More and more of the Saroshans were arriving by the hour. Soon would be the last of the war council meetings, then they would choose which of the men from each order would accompany them to the north. If all went well and Liam was cooperative with his decisions, they should be ready to go in less than a week. Tarryn fully intended to encourage expediency, and hoped he could decrease the wait time to two or three days.

Liam. The man drove Tarryn crazy. He treated his status the same way a child playing dress up would. He loved to rule because he loved the attention it brought him, but he wasn't strong enough to actually make good, solid decisions. If Tarryn didn't need him to open the seal, he would have rid the world of him long before now. He did have his uses though. He was a trusting man, and far too gullible for his own good. Tarryn had been pulling the strings on his Liam-puppet for several years now, as he formulated his plan and slowly transformed Liam from being a second rate warrior king to being a real paladin king. If his plan was going to work, he would need the help of a real paladin, and most of them were too nosey and meddlesome for him to keep under control.

He sprinkled some more sand into the basin of water in his room and focused on it. He spoke the name of his contact in Beinn-anbas. "Valen." The water swirled around and around, changing in color and brightness until it settled on an image of a room lit by candlelight. In a large, elaborate armchair in front of an old, ornate desk, sat Valen. His hair was a glossy black and was tied back in a ponytail. His skin was sickly pale, as if he hadn't seen the sunlight in years. His eyes had been at one time a light chocolate color, but due to his curse had dilated to where the iris was covered by the solid black of his pupils. He was writing on a formal parchment with a long, black feather quill. *At least this scrying bowl still works*, thought Tarryn. He focused harder on the image, imagining himself there, in the room. He closed his eyes and spoke a word of magic. When he opened his eyes, he was standing in the room, just behind Valen. As usual with his projection spell, everything looked transparent to his eyes, just as he knew he appeared transparent to any who saw him.

Tarryn cleared his throat, but Valen did not even pause for a moment in what he was working on. Without looking up, he said, "I did not expect any interruption tonight. As you can see, I am busy right now, so make it quick. Why are you here?"

Tarryn arched an eyebrow. "I send you gifts and this is the greeting I receive?"

Valen looked up then, placing his quill in the inkwell. "Ah, you look different dressed in white. Well, *my lord*, to what do I owe this unexpected visit?"

"Have my men arrived yet with their cargo?"

"No, sir. None have come here. I also walked these lands last night but saw no one. Well, no one of consequence, anyway."

Tarryn looked at the parchment on which Valen had been writing. "Interesting shade of ink."

"I find that many things are better when they are written in blood. Letters are taken more seriously. Scrolls penned in blood are far more potent. Blood is power."

Tarryn nodded once. "I'll try to check back soon to see if they have arrived. I will be leaving for the northern tombs in a few days, or at least I will be if I can get that fool of a king moving by then. Since my men have decided to take their time getting there, they will be unable to make it back to me in time to make the trip. Therefore, they are no longer useful to me, and you may do as you wish with them. Likewise, the four prisoners they carry are yours, as my gift to you. The only requirement I have in regard to their care is that you not allow them to escape. Careful with untying them; they are powerful. Three of them are druids."

"Ah, a challenge. That will be a nice change. The people that I find travelling from the nearby towns are so…unexciting."

"Don't underestimate them. Farewell, Valen," Tarryn said as he vanished.

His spirit rejoined with his body back in his quarters, Tarryn tried once more to locate the men he had sent, but again the water swirled and found nothing.

The Mithrans stopped early that same evening, just before passing around the southern edge of the Dacre River at its source. There was a small natural lake, a reservoir, at the border of Beinn-anbas, created from the water that drained off the elevated hills. Siobhan explained that the hills themselves were very marshy and wet because it rained here almost daily. She arranged her group into eight patrols of six each, and instructed them to spread out and destroy any of the roaming undead they found when they entered the hills the following day. She decided that she and Katie would join the four outsiders as a ninth patrol. Then, later, they set the watch and all went to get some rest.

Their rest was cut short, however, as they were all jolted from their tents by the sound of screaming, coming from Beinn-anbas. The paladins hurried to call for their armor and the squires raced to assist them. Celeste, Tarnelius, Arcus and Theri jumped from the wagon they had been using as a make-shift tent by covering it with blankets, and took off in the direction of the screaming. Siobhan and Katie, who had been on watch, hurried to follow after them, leaving the others behind to catch up.

They ran as fast as they could, but were hindered by the ever present fog. Celeste and Tarnelius shifted into large cats. Celeste became an Amur tiger, while Tarnelius shifted into a huge liger. His golden mane, the same color as his normal hair, darkened to black near his shoulder blades and gave way to tiger stripes. After a few seconds, Arcus shifted as well, into his black panther form. Theri trotted along with them, easily keeping up. Siobhan and Katie fell behind, as they could not see as well to keep up, and Katie seemed a bit alarmed by the way the others changed form.

"A liger, Tarnel? I thought your big cat form was a lion," Celeste spoke inside his head.

"I guess your tiger is influencing my forms. What can I say? Besides, this hybrid liger is much bigger and stronger."

The four cats raced into the night, squinting into the fog and following their senses of smell and hearing, and trusting their instincts. Suddenly, the sound they had followed stopped. The group slowed down a tiny bit but continued forward, finally coming to a demolished campsite. The tent was ripped, pieces of it strewn about with all of the campsite owner's other belongings. Kneeling in the wreckage was a scrawny looking monster who was devouring someone's bloody shin, which had been separated from the rest of its body. The monster, which resembled a zombie but was faster and more agile, was chewing with a contented look on its face, and its mouth was much wider than what seemed normal. When it saw the cats, it rose to its feet and bared its teeth – several rows of them, like a shark's – then it spit at them. The saliva fell well short of the group, but where it fell the ground frothed and boiled.

Tarnelius charged at the creature. He leapt onto it and knocked it down. As the pair rolled on the marshy ground, Theri hopped after them to try to figure out how to jump in. Suddenly, Tarnelius roared in fury and reared back. He shook his head as though trying to clear it and made a strangled noise.

"Arcus, do something," urged Celeste, still in tiger form. "He's been blinded. Theri, get back, don't let it get close to you." She rushed to Tarnelius' side and stood between him and the undead monster protectively.

Wasting no time, the panther began to make strange noises, like he was trying to talk. Shaking his head in frustration, he rose to his hind legs and let out a mighty roar. As he dropped back down, a huge ball of fire shot from his paws and hit the monster in the chest, which knocked him backward.

The creature let out an enraged shriek as it flailed, trying to put out the flames. Arcus stared at it in shock. Theri tumbled back toward Arcus to avoid being caught in the creature's death throes. Celeste shifted back into her normal form just as Siobhan and Katie caught up.

As Siobhan paused a second to assess what was happening, she drew her sword and charged in. Her blade flashed in the moonlight as she swung her sword. She had lined up the swing to separate the monster's head from its body, but it moved and all she caught was an arm, which dropped to the ground with a thud. Arcus roared again, and small glowing bolts shot toward his target at the same time Katie let loose an arrow, which narrowly missed and shot right past the burning creature.

Tarnelius was in agony. His face felt like it was on fire and he could not see anything. He was acutely aware of Celeste's hands on him as she tried to heal him, and he worried about what was going on that he couldn't see. Celeste attempted to calm him with her thoughts, but he was having none of it in his panicked state.

Siobhan swung her sword again, this time cleaving the cadaverous monster in half at waist level. It dropped to the ground but continued to writhe and scream. Arcus was quick to step forward and between his fiery spells and Siobhan chopping the thing to bits, they were successful in destroying it, turning it into ashes and dust.

"Tarnelius, shift back so I can get a better look at the damage." Celeste was still trying to soothe the big cat, but he kept rubbing at his face with his front legs. Healing him should have worked, but it didn't seem to have any effect.

"What happened?" Siobhan asked as she and Katie came striding up. Tarnelius shifted back and they all gasped as they saw that his once handsome features had been melted away. His cheeks looked sunken as the acid had eaten away part of his cheekbones. His eyelids had been mutilated and had fused shut. His nose seemed to be missing a chunk out of it. The only bright side was that the injuries all looked healed over as if they had happened months ago. Tarnelius dropped to his knees and moaned.

Celeste reached for him. Her hands flashed blue and lit up the darkness as she tried once more to heal him. "That nasty thing had acid spit. I've healed the injury, but the damage is still done. I'll have to prepare a regeneration spell, and those take time as I will have to commune with nature and the spirits first." She bit her lip. "I'm so sorry, Tarnel. I can't help you to see now. I will help you back to camp and will prepare the spell first thing in the morning."

"How bad is it?" he asked in a tortured voice.

Celeste merely gave him a kiss on the side of his face that hadn't been as badly mangled, and didn't answer. She helped him to his feet and held on to his arm so she could lead him.

Tarnelius sighed. "It's okay, Celeste. I can take it. I can hear your thoughts anyway. I appreciate you trying to spare my feelings, but you don't need to worry. I love you too, Angel."

Siobhan stepped forward with her holy symbol and placed her hand on his head. Her right arm began to glow gold as she channeled her holy power into him. After a moment, she pulled her hand away and sighed. "On the plus side, there isn't much to see out here in the dark in this gods forsaken place anyway."

Tarnelius frowned slightly. "I can see a bright glowing light right there," he pointed right at Siobhan's glowing holy symbol.

Celeste smiled. "Well, *that's* something. Thank you, Siobhan, I think you restored his sight; he just can't open his eyes. That, at least, is an improvement."

She started to lead Tarnelius back to camp, but was stopped by Arcus. "I wonder what would possess someone to camp here," he said. "Looks like they won't make that mistake again."

"We were too late," Celeste said with a sigh. "Which means this whole thing was for nothing."

"Not exactly nothing; we destroyed that monster," corrected Siobhan.

Celeste began to lead Tarnelius back to camp, but was stopped by the unmistakable sound of Siobhan's sword being drawn once more. "What now?" Celeste asked.

"I'm not sure. Something big is coming. Something evil." Siobhan squinted into the darkness toward the south, back toward their camp. She raised her holy symbol, but it only seemed to reflect back at her in the fog. "I can't see anything physical, but I can see the aura of evil coming. Be ready."

Celeste led Tarnelius back out of the way, toward the decimated camp they had just left. "Stay down, don't move. I'm not going to play around with this thing." She cast her spell, and her eyes rolled back in her head. Storm clouds built overhead, lightning flashed in the sky.

She turned to take on a defensive position, releasing her wings. Tarnelius spoke to her inside her head. *"Please be careful,* Rakastan. *It's killing me that I can't see."*

Arcus shifted back and squinted into the mist, moving over to stand near Siobhan. They all waited.

From out of the darkness emerged a larger and deeper darkness. A giant, thirty feet tall, that seemed to be the embodiment of blackness itself. The only features they were able to easily discern were its glowing red eyes.

Celeste pointed up at the shadowy form and bellowed. Lightning flashed and struck it, causing it to pause for a moment. Lightning flashed all around it, revealing the monster's full form for a moment. The creature then pointed his shadowy finger back at her, and a black beam of darkness shot out and struck Celeste in the heart. She groaned and sank to her knees. The storm clouds faltered and dissipated.

Siobhan charged forward, striking the monster in its shins. Black, sludge-like blood poured out from the gash, but it otherwise did not react. The shadow creature remained eerily silent as they fought.

Celeste struggled back to her feet and recast her spell. The storm clouds began to gather once more. Katie shot her bow, her arrow driving deep into the monster's leg.

The shadowy form stepped closer, kicking Siobhan away as he walked. She flew through the air and crashed several feet away, dazed. He reached down toward Katie, who turned and ran. He managed to catch her bow as she turned, snatching it away. Arcus quickly chanted his spell, shoving his arms toward the monster as snow and ice shot out at it, but it didn't seem to react to the cold at all.

Celeste pointed once more at the monster, and once more lightning danced all around him. The monster paused, his irises vanishing into the darkness as he closed his eyes for a moment, seemingly dazed.

Siobhan picked herself up and looked around for her sword, which had been knocked from her hand. Katie had made it a safe distance away, and drew her sword as she turned to regroup.

The monster crushed the delicate bow in his hands and continued ever closer. He pointed once more at Celeste, and again the black beam shot out and connected with her. She screamed as she once more lost her concentration. The magic he was using was pure evil. Death magic. Every time she was struck with it, she could feel the bony hands of Death, himself, on her spine. She once more fought off the sensations and rose back to her feet. She realized the monster had come ever closer, to get to her, and she needed to draw him away from Tarnelius.

As Arcus shot lightning at the monster, Celeste decided to act on her decision. She rose into the air and flew right up toward the glowing eyes. She yelled and shouted and tried to confuse it, as she drew her rapier from its sheath. Siobhan and Katie charged back in and attacked.

The monster did not focus on Celeste in the air. Instead, his red glowing eyes locked onto Tarnelius, who was backing away. He could hear and feel the fighting close by, and instead of waiting to get trampled, he was trying to retreat, which was proving difficult with his lack of vision. The monster stepped toward him, almost crushing Siobhan and Katie, who both dodged out of the way. He reached down to grab at Tarnelius –

Only to grab Theri instead as she dove forward to push Tarnelius out of the way. Theri had realized what was about to happen, and tried to tackle Tarnelius and roll both of them out of harm's way, but instead was caught by her tail and then grabbed and lifted with the monster's other hand. He picked her up, slowly, into the air, to examine his catch. She fit easily inside his massive hand, which seemed much too large for his body.

The others redoubled their efforts. Siobhan and Katie attacked with sword and holy symbol. Seeing the bright light, Celeste began casting as fast as she could while Arcus shot a ball of fire at the creature's legs. Blood dripped from high in the air onto the ground in large pools. Theri could not be seen. Celeste finished her spell and the sky was suddenly illuminated bright as day. It appeared the sun itself had been summoned by Celeste's spell. The light was so bright. So painfully bright. The sun burned away the mist, and struck them all. Everyone screamed except the shadow monster, who was still silent. The light grew brighter still, as well as even more hot and painful. The shadow monster exploded into ash, dropping Theri to the ground with a sickening thud. Then, as quickly as it appeared, the light was gone, and none of them could see a thing. Celeste dropped to the ground, using her wings to slow her descent, but still landing awkwardly on the ground with a loud thump.

"What the hell just happened?" Arcus gasped. "I can't see."

"Sunburst spell. I didn't *want* to risk casting it because it would blind us all and I had no way of knowing if it would do the trick or not, but that creature did seem to have an aversion to the lightning. I figured chances were good it would work. Even if it didn't, it was starting to look like we were all going to be dead anyway, so it was our best shot. Everyone okay?"

Siobhan channeled her holy magic on herself, curing her blindness and healing her injuries. Then she moved to Celeste to do the same. As she approached, she caught a glimpse of Theri on the ground and inhaled sharply. "No, Celeste. I'm so sorry, but not everyone is okay."

"Who's hurt?" Celeste asked, frantic. "Tarnel?"

"Not any more than I was," Tarnelius answered. "How are Theri and Katie? They are the only two I haven't heard speak."

"I'm okay," answered Katie.

Her vision restored, Celeste jumped up to see what Siobhan had seen. "Theri, no!" She ran to her side.

Theri's body was mangled beyond recognition. The monster had crushed her in his hand before he exploded. Celeste tried to heal her, but nothing happened. She felt all around the body, checking for any signs of life, but nothing was there. Theri was gone.

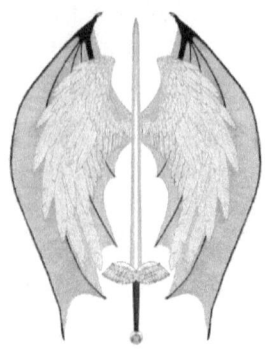

Chapter Twenty-Five
No Greater Love

Siobhan healed Katie and Arcus, then she went to help Tarnelius over to Celeste. He dropped to his knees next to her, pulling her away from Theri so he could comfort her. Celeste beat on his chest as she tried to pull away, sobbing and inconsolable.

"Shh, *Rakastan*. I'm here. I'm so sorry about Theri," Tarnelius murmured as he grabbed her hands. Arcus stood on Theri's other side, and stared down at her with a look that was a mixture of shock and horror. After a few moments, Celeste stopped fighting and just embraced Tarnelius, holding on as if her own life depended on it.

After several minutes of this, Siobhan gestured to Katie and they stepped closer to the others. "We have to get out of here, before more of those creatures come. We have already lost Theri, and for all intents and purposes, Tarnelius. He is in no condition to fight. We need to regroup. Katie and I will carry your friend's body out of this cursed place." Celeste didn't move, only cried harder.

Arcus moved around Theri to get to her and Tarnelius. "Celeste, I think Siobhan is right. We need to get out of here; we are no match for these things right now if any more come. You need to get up." He helped Tarnelius get her to her feet. "Come on. Theri wouldn't want you to die here, mourning her loss. We still have to get to King Liam. Besides, you don't want us to get ambushed here again. I have a bad feeling that this place is truly cursed; I can feel it. If we don't get Theri out of here, I worry she would come back as one of *them*."

At that, Celeste nodded and stood up the rest of the way. She bowed her head, unable to look at her fallen friend, and took Tarnelius' arm. She led him back the way they came, back toward the camp. Arcus followed them, and Siobhan and Katie brought up the rear, carrying Theri.

The group returned to the campsite, only to find it abandoned, with half of the horses missing. Siobhan and Katie exchanged glances before setting Theri down on the ground. Celeste led Tarnelius over to their wagon to rest and then climbed in after him. Arcus sat on the ground near Theri. He stroked the little bit of fur he could see under all the blood. After several minutes, he reached forward and unhooked her magic belt before carefully sliding it out from under her. Siobhan paced toward the Hills and back to the camp, clearly anxious.

After a while, Arcus sighed loudly and began building a funeral pyre. He gathered all the small branches and dried grass he could find, then lifted Theri up and placed her onto it. Seeing what he was doing, Celeste got up and led Tarnelius over to the pyre.

Tarnelius reached forward with his hands, and groped his way along until he found her body. He stroked the matted fur on her crushed head and murmured in the old language. Finally he said, "Thank you, my friend. You saved my life, and I will always remember you."

"What was it you said before that?" Arcus wondered.

Celeste sniffled loudly as she suppressed a sob. "He said, 'There is no greater love than from he who lays down their life for a friend'."

Tarnelius raised his head, his eyes still fused shut. "It would have been me, had she not shoved me out of the way. I couldn't see it, but I could feel that monster's ice-cold hands near me as she was pulled away. It was just – just so fast. I'd hoped she had jumped free, but clearly, I was wrong." Tarnelius roared out his frustration and ran his hands over his face. "This is all my fault. None of this would have happened if I hadn't gotten myself blinded by that first monster."

"You can't know that," argued Siobhan as she walked over to join them.

"She was my best friend," said Celeste as she broke down in tears. "My first and only friend in hundreds of years. Oh Theri, what am I ever going to do without you? Of all of us, you were the only one who was here because you really just wanted to help. You were content to take things as they came. You had such a pure heart and such a good spirit; you were truly the best of us. I'm going to miss you so much." Celeste broke off, the tears overcoming her again. "What kind of a healer am I, if I couldn't even save my best friend?"

"Don't beat yourself up. You saved us all," said Arcus. "If you hadn't cast that sun spell, we would all be dead."

"But why couldn't I have tried it sooner? Then Theri would still be here."

Siobhan sighed. "You guys need to stop blaming yourselves. We all did the best we could under the circumstances. Death is a risk of battle. Theri knew that, as did we all. Yes, she was a good person and saved you, Tarnelius, but all this moping and blaming yourselves does is tarnish her memory and her sacrifice. Remember her for her deeds, remember her for who she was, and continue living. Carry the memory of who she was and what she did with you. Then she will live forever through your hearts and memories."

Arcus cleared his throat. "Well said," he choked out, his voice thick. He cleared his throat again. "Anyone have anything else to say?" The others shook their heads, so Arcus pointed at Theri and spoke a word of magic. Fire shot from his hand and set the pyre ablaze. They all stood in respectful silence as the fire consumed her, and carried her into the next stage of her journey.

When all was said and done, a brokenhearted Celeste led Tarnelius back to the wagon and helped him to settle, before she began preparations for the regeneration spell. She knew there would be no rest that night, not that she could rest in the state she was in. Somehow, she was going to have to push thoughts of her lost friend from her mind, so she could focus. Tarnelius needed her, but every time she shut her eyes to meditate, she could see Theri. She saw her the first time they met in the castle in the clouds. She saw herself insisting on going after her when she had been captured by orcs. She whimpered as she remembered her at the bonding ceremony. The memories overwhelmed her, and the tears threatened to overtake her.

Tarnelius stirred next to her. He reached up and groped around until he found her hand, which he squeezed. "I'm so sorry, Angel. I wish I could fix this. Part of me wishes she hadn't jumped in the way."

"Is that supposed to make me feel better? So, part of you would prefer to be dead, leaving me without *you*?"

"I didn't mean it like that. You know I didn't mean it like that. I just wish she were still here," he answered, his voice breaking.

Celeste lay down next to him, burying her face in his neck. "I know. I need to focus on preparing for this regeneration spell, but every time I close my eyes I can still picture her. I can see her grinning at me, in her infuriating way, as she introduced herself. I was so awful to her that first night, but she still stayed by my side. I recall her stuffing her face with Arcus' stew in Grimsgil, and I remember how we joked around about her having wet fur. I can't believe she's gone."

Tarnelius stroked her hair, soothingly. "I know what you mean. I remember when the demon stabbed me, she was right there, trying to keep me calm, encouraging me to hang on. The demon wasn't even destroyed yet, but she still stayed with me, not wanting me to be alone. I can see her binding our hands at our bonding ceremony. She was so full of life, so caring, but with an understated strength. You should have seen the way she tackled Arcus after the demon made him slice your throat."

Celeste trembled in his arms, tears still streaming down her face and soaking Tarnelius' neck and shirt. "I saw her holding him down after we got up. Thank Kamara she was able to do that, or we would all be dead now. I'd doubted her strength. I doubted her, when she has been the one saving us this whole time! I miss her so much, already."

For a while, they just held each other, both seeking and giving comfort. Then, right as Celeste was about to get back up to begin her meditations again, she heard the sound of Siobhan clearing her throat.

Celeste sat up and looked at her. "Yes?"

"I need your assistance. Katie and I are going back."

"Going back? In there? Have you lost your mind?"

"No. The others aren't back, as you can see. I have no idea where they could have gone, since we headed toward the screams and they never found us. Something definitely isn't right."

"Tomorrow we will go back. In the daylight. After I get Tarnel patched up."

"No, we need to go now. Do not forget that I am in charge, and I cannot leave my men behind."

"It's suicide. You may be in charge of them, but you are certainly not in charge of us," snarled Celeste, as Arcus hurried over to find out what was going on.

Siobhan watched his approach. "If you will not come with me, I will go on my own. Or maybe your mage will want to come with me."

"Where?" Arcus asked.

"Back to those cursed hills," scoffed Celeste.

"I need to find the others," clarified Siobhan. "I requested assistance."

"No, you demanded assistance for a suicidal mission. We have already lost Theri, and you want us to sacrifice more. Tarnel can't come; he cannot see. I need to prepare to cast the spells to fix him."

"Which is why I am now asking the mage."

"He has a name."

Siobhan sighed. "Look, you are upset and you have become unreasonable. I'm done with this. Arcus, will you come with me?"

Arcus stared back at her, torn with indecision. "Look, I want to help you, truly I do. Maybe we can check around the perimeters and see if we find anyone? I really don't think we can take down any more of those shadowy things on our own."

Siobhan growled in aggravation and turned on her heel to stomp to Katie. Arcus caught her by the arm as she turned. She yanked her arm away and shoved him hard; he fell hard onto the ground from the force of her shove. "Just so the two of you know, I would come with you if the tables were turned."

Celeste leapt to her feet and swung her arms in a wide arc as she spoke a word of magic. A powerful gust of wind shot toward Siobhan, knocking her off her feet. Celeste jumped off the wagon and marched straight to her, fury in her eyes. "Now you listen to me. They have been gone a long time now, over an hour. At this point they are either lost or dead. If they are lost, hopefully they found a place to hole up for the rest of the night. If they are dead, rushing out after them like you are in a hurry to die also will help no one. Now, I'd like you to think with that armor-plated head of yours. Think hard, and realize that you can't help them right now. During the day, the shadows will recede and the mist will burn away. Then, we will find them. I will go with you, but I will not commit suicide for you. I will not allow Theri's death to become meaningless. You need to be patient and not go running in half-cocked. Understand?"

"Yes," spat Siobhan. Arcus came over and extended his arm to give her a hand up. She ignored him and rose to her feet before stomping away toward her tent. Arcus hesitated a moment and then followed her. Celeste returned to the wagon and Tarnelius and began her communion with nature.

"Why are you following me, Mage?" Siobhan asked.

"Because I want to make sure you don't go off by yourself. It's really okay if you call me Arcus, by the way. I don't mind."

"Well, I'm not going until dawn. I'm not sure I agree with it, but Celeste's logic was true enough. That answer should suffice. Goodbye."

"I will stay here just the same. I won't let you go by yourself if you happen to change your mind."

"*You* won't let *me*. You? How would you stop me?" Siobhan stepped right up in his face, in an obvious attempt to intimidate him. She was taller than him by about four inches and she tried to use that fact to her advantage.

Arcus looked up at her, his gray eyes locked onto her hazel ones. He licked his dry lips slowly before answering. "I have my ways."

Siobhan leaned forward, almost touching him. He could feel her breath on his face and his heartbeat sped up. Her eyelids fluttered for a moment before she closed them. A few moments later she opened them again, only to find that he was gone. She looked all around, not seeing any trace of him at all. With a sigh, she turned and entered her tent.

Out from behind a nearby tent hopped a small grackle. The grackle remained still for a moment, contemplating what had just happened. Then he flew up to land on top of one of the nearby tents, which was in full view of Siobhan's.

"*What was that all about?*" Arcus wondered to himself. He stayed perched up there for the rest of the night, just in case she came out. He spent the time thinking about the loss of his friend and trying to get the fiery, redheaded paladin out of his mind. "*I'm sure what happened was just in my imagination. That must be it; my mind is all messed up after losing Theri and is seeking comfort. She is a paladin, and one that is a royal pain to boot, with no regard for anyone other than herself and her precious knights. She wouldn't be interested in me, and I definitely should not be thinking of her in any way other than as a metal-covered fighter.*" Thoughts of her kept playing in his head, however, toying with him, and making him feel guilty for thinking of anyone other than Theri on that night.

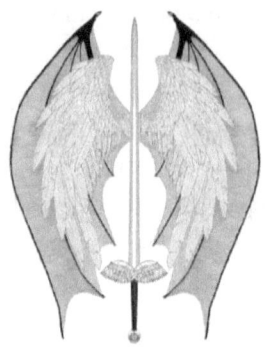

Chapter Twenty-Six
To Death's Door

A few minutes before dawn, Celeste completed her meditations and cast her spell on Tarnelius. The sunken bones in his cheek started to heal and reform, his eyelids healed, and his nose turned back into its normal shape. Within about two minutes, he was back to looking like his normal, handsome self. He blinked his eyes as he focused on Celeste, and then gave her a huge smile before standing up. He grabbed her and gave her a deep kiss.

Celeste smoothed the hair from his face. "There's the man I love." She smiled.

"Oh? You didn't love me the way I looked a moment ago?" He pretended to look wounded, knowing her true feelings.

"I missed your eyes," she murmured as she gave him another kiss. "You know that I love you regardless of how you look."

"And I you, Angel. More than mere words can express." He smiled at her, his eyes crinkling. After a moment, he sighed, his expression now sober. "Well, I suppose we should go find Siobhan and head back out." Tarnelius took Celeste's hand to lead her that way. They passed Katie, who was stroking the nose of a dappled gray horse. As they approached Siobhan's tent, a grackle flew down and landed in front of them, before shifting into Arcus.

"She's been in there all night. I made sure she didn't leave alone."

Celeste didn't comment, and merely stared at the ground. Tarnelius watched her with concern before stepping toward the tent. "Siobhan, if you are ready, we can head out to go find your group."

Siobhan shoved the tent flap open and walked out, still in her armor. Her eyes were red and puffy and her hair was disheveled, but still she had a determined look on her face. She turned and marched back toward the hills, signaling to Katie as she went. The others followed behind her in silence.

The group walked back to where their fight had been the night before, but there were no traces of any scuffle. With the sun up by now, the mist had burned away and they could see much better. The first thing they all noticed was that the tattered tent and human remains were gone. The monsters they had fought were nowhere to be seen. There were no skid marks in the marshy ground, or blood, or anything to show there had ever been a fight.

"This is where we were, right?" Tarnelius asked. "I would swear this was the direction we came."

"It is," answered Siobhan, confused.

Celeste knelt down, placed her hand flat on the ground, and concentrated. "This is the place. The local fauna's memories are fragmented, but enough is left that I can tell that we were here without a doubt. I don't see any of the knights coming through here, but entire hours have been wiped out."

"Let's keep looking," said Siobhan. The group continued on. Soon, they crested a large and rocky hill, and they paused to get their bearings. Siobhan frowned. "Where did *that* come from?"

From atop this hill, they could see several other hills spread out in front of them. Settled on a distant one was a large castle that appeared dark and ominous from this far away.

"I don't see the knights anywhere," said Arcus.

"I don't see *any* signs of life at all," added Celeste. "No animals of any kind, not even any birds." The group continued to stare out at the castle and the hills and valleys between them in silence for several minutes.

Siobhan frowned. "Well, I guess we should check it out. That castle is the closest thing we have to a lead. There were no castles in Beinn-anbas, last I saw."

"That's a long way, though. What about the horses?" Celeste asked.

Her eyes widened as she turned to look at Siobhan and saw a huge palomino stallion appear out of nowhere. Siobhan stroked his velvety nose and said, "Apollo, please stay with the horses back at the camp. Keep watch over them, and if trouble arrives, please urge them to flee the area. Stay together. Do not worry about the tents and wagon. Do you understand?"

The beautiful animal bobbed his head and stamped his foot. Siobhan waited for him to turn and go, but he stayed right where he was. "Apollo?" Siobhan said with uncertainty after several moments, wondering what was wrong.

"He's beautiful, Siobhan," breathed Arcus. "May I try to speak with him?" At her nod, he stepped forward to approach the stallion, being careful to display respect as he locked eyes with him.

"You can hear me?" Apollo asked in Arcus' head.

"I can. Did you have something you were trying to tell Siobhan?"

Apollo heaved a deep breath. *"I worry about her. These hills are cursed. I can feel it. I've been here with her before, but I've never felt this curse before. The hills are trying to confuse you. Why are you here now? I know we were to clear out the undead, but everyone is gone."*

"We are trying to find them."

Apollo reared up on his hind legs and neighed. *"Onyx told me that his rider went into a large castle with many of the others, but I know of no castles near here so I told Onyx he was wrong. Now I see a castle where there should be no castle. I feel that these hills are trying to confuse us. I hope you are able to find them. Tell me which direction to go to return to the pack horses."*

"Due south out of the hills. It's not far; only about three or four miles. Keep the morning sun to your left and you'll soon find the road and the lake at the base of the first hill. The camp is near the lake. Stay safe."

"You as well, and promise me you will keep Siobhan safe. I care about her a great deal."

"I will, I swear it."

"What is your name?" Apollo asked.

"Arcus."

"Arcus, see that you keep that promise, or I will find you. Tell her she knows how to call me if she needs me. Farewell." Apollo broke eye contact with Arcus and stepped around him to Siobhan, nudging her with his nose affectionately before turning and galloping off.

"What was that all about?" Siobhan asked.

"I think I just got threatened by a horse," Arcus said with a smirk.

"What?"

"He says the hills are cursed. He made me promise to keep you safe and told me to remind you that you know how to call him."

"Strange. We have all known Beinn-anbas has been cursed for many generations. I wonder why he would warn us like that now."

"He says it's different. He kept saying something about the hills trying to confuse us. He seems like quite a remarkable animal, very intelligent. Much more so than any other animal I have ever spoken to. Also, do you know of a horse named Onyx?"

"That's Ryan's horse. Why?"

"Then we are heading to that castle. He says Onyx told him his rider and several others went into a castle. Let's go."

"I never would have thought of asking Apollo what happened," Siobhan said, chagrined.

They all began walking. As they walked down the north side of the hill they had started on, they lost sight of the castle. As they crested another hill, they stopped in surprise because they discovered that the castle was now much farther west than it had looked before. Turning around, they realized the hill they had left also seemed to have moved. They were no longer sure which of the hills they had started on, or which direction they were travelling. Bewildered, they continued toward their destination. When they crested the next hill, they couldn't find the castle at all. Turning around, they finally found it behind them, and worse, it didn't look any closer than when they had started.

"This is insane," Siobhan grumbled.

Celeste released her wings. "I'm going to fly there slowly and stay just above and ahead of you. Keep up with me and I will keep track of the castle. If we start getting separated at all, let me know, Tarnel. I'm going to be mostly focusing on that castle. You guys need to focus on keeping *me* in sight and not worry about the castle."

With that, she took to the skies. Celeste flew very slowly, but the others still needed to jog to keep up with her. After only a couple of hours of travelling like this, they arrived at the castle, and Celeste landed and withdrew her wings. From up close, they could see that the castle actually seemed to be made of some shimmery, black shining material that seemed almost like glass. It reminded Celeste of Axistra's castle in the clouds, except that one was blue. Unlike Axistra's castle, nothing on this one made it seem at all transparent, and there were no windows to be found at all. Thinking of Axistra's castle reminded Celeste of Theri, and she whimpered and shook herself to snap out of it.

"That was much easier," Siobhan said, by way of thanks.

"I can see what Apollo meant by 'the hills are trying to confuse us'," added Arcus. "So now what?"

"Now we go in," said Siobhan.

"Great. Is your intent to just go knock on the door and hope for the best?"

"Do you have a better idea?"

"Hmm, so here we are in the middle of the creepiest hills I've ever seen, in front of a spooky black castle, and you think politely requesting entrance is the way to go?" Arcus asked in disbelief.

"We don't know why this castle is here or where it came from. It doesn't have to belong to a monster."

"Are you entirely insane or merely naive?"

"I'm not sure how to answer that question."

Arcus stared at her in shock. "I think we should find a stealthier way in that doesn't announce us to every evil monster lurking inside."

"Sneaking in is cowardly. I'm not afraid, and you shouldn't be either."

"It's not cowardice, it's smarter. Do you see evil coming off the castle?"

"I see evil everywhere around this area. It's hard to focus on specifics."

"But you could see the evil aura of the monsters over the general feel of the area last night," Celeste interrupted their conversation.

"Yes, that had a specific shape and location to it. Here, it's everywhere. It's kind of tough to explain."

Celeste knelt down and placed her hand on the ground. "I think the knights were here. I can see bits and pieces, but the memories of the earth here are still very fragmented."

"What would cause that?" Siobhan asked.

"I don't know, something with strong magic." She kept focusing on the ground, her brow furrowed. Suddenly her eyes widened and so did Tarnelius'. "No, that's impossible."

"What is it?" Arcus asked.

"Vampire," said Tarnelius. "She saw a vampire."

"A vampire? I always thought those were just myth and legend," said Arcus.

"They used to be very real. A long time ago, when the six dragons were new to their powers, they experimented with rebirth and resurrection. The good dragons, Seratrix and Aanhextrios, learned how to return the dead to life. The neutral dragons, Axistra and Khellendriox, learned how to reincarnate their dead. They could bring the spirits of their fallen back into an entirely new body. The evil dragons, Crusiliux and Tarextros, could not do either of these things. Instead, they learned to bring false life back into their dead. Thus came the vampires. They were powerful monsters with immense magic that survived by stealing the life forces of others. Each of the dragons taught those of their line these spells. Those of Kuunkierto's line could create the vertassa, which are like vampires in that they have to drink blood to survive, but are much less powerful. Much less intelligent, too. Those of Aurinko's and Kamara's lines were taught resurrection and reincarnation magic, respectively. However, mortals were never able to fully cast them in the same way. That's why, *if* you can find a magic user powerful enough to cast the resurrection spells, the magic is limited. The returned parties only survive for weeks, or months, or maybe a year if you are really lucky. Ultimately, death takes them all, and it's just one more thing the dragons won't do anymore," Celeste said bitterly.

"But, what about the vampires?" Siobhan asked.

"Oh yes, well, during the Deity War, vampires fought alongside Kuunkierto and the evil demigods with their heralds. They were very powerful and highly skilled with magic. Though the evil dragons did not learn to cast real resurrections, the mockeries of life that they did create were far more powerful than their mortal counterparts. Part of the truce that came afterward included the destruction of all these walking dead monstrosities. The evil dragons demanded that if they gave up their creations, the other sides would too. Thus, everything they had learned to do was undone. Those they had brought back died again, and all the walking dead were destroyed. Mortals could still use the magic they had learned, but the dragons no longer cast these spells. Looks like one slipped through the net, though."

"See, Siobhan? This is a vampire's castle. Clearly, the smart thing to do would be to not go in the front door like a bunch of fools," said Arcus.

"I doubt we have a choice," mused Celeste. "I don't actually see any way in other than the door, and we have to assume the paladins are inside there."

Tarnelius looked up at the sun, directly overhead. "Looks like it's about midday. If we are going to do it, we should do it now."

"Let's at least circle the whole thing and make sure there is no other way in," suggested Arcus.

So they approached the building with caution. When they got within about ten feet of it, the door swung open with a loud creaking sound. They all froze, staring at it in alarm before turning as one, and walking the other direction to check for other entrances. The glossy wall was smooth and unmarred as they circled around, finding themselves back at the door, where they started, which was now closed.

"There can't just be one door and no windows to this thing. What if there were a fire?" muttered Siobhan.

Celeste bit her lip and went to examine the door. As she approached, the door once again opened for her, revealing a well-lit front entry and great room with beautiful antique furniture. They all stared into the room, its beauty at odds with their views of the evil that surely dwelled within.

"Either come in or stay away, but my preference would be to shut this door soon," came a masculine voice from inside.

Arcus sighed. "Great. Who wants to be the first to step into the creepy trap?"

Celeste stepped forward, but Siobhan pushed her way in front of her to lead the way in. She stepped into the entryway, surprised at how cool it was inside. The others joined her soon after, and the door swung shut.

"Welcome to my home. I have been expecting you," came the voice, smooth as honey. "Though, honestly, I expected your escorts to be a little different."

"What are you talking about?" Siobhan asked, turning to look around the room to find the source of the voice. "Show yourself at once!"

The voice chuckled and a dark mist gathered in the center of the room. The mist formed a human shape and gained more and more substance, until it became solid. In the span of a second, a light-skinned human male with long black hair tied in a ponytail and deep black eyes devoid of any color was standing before them. He was wearing an expensive looking tailored outfit that was also all black. The man appeared to be in his late twenties, but held an air of authority and power about him.

"Forgive me for my rudeness. The sun is very bright on my eyes, plus I do like to make an entrance. My name is –"

"Vampire," snarled Siobhan. She drew her sword and charged at him, her weapon flashing gold as she swung. At the moment it would have connected, he vanished back into mist, rematerializing off to the right.

"No, my name is Valen, actually. I'll thank you to put that stick away while you are in my home, young lady. You wouldn't want to get hurt."

Siobhan charged him again, and again he reverted back into mist just as she would have struck him. He smirked at her, after he reformed. "I can do this all day, you know, but eventually *you* will become tired."

"Siobhan, wait," said Celeste. She turned to Valen. "What do you mean you were expecting us?"

"Ah, someone is on the ball. What might your name be, my seraph friend?"

Celeste's eyes widened. "How did you know I am a seraph?"

"First, your name, if you please."

"Celeste."

He bowed low to her. "Pleased to make your acquaintance, beautiful Celeste. I knew you were a seraph because I can see it in your eyes. I can see it in your stance. Everything about you screams power and goodness. You are like the sun, painful for me to behold. As for how I came to expect you, I was warned of your approach, though I expected my old friend to send his minions, not paladins. Certainly not real paladins. No matter, though. I will deal with him later."

Tarnelius stepped in front of Celeste, taking on a defensive posture.

Valen chuckled. "Ah, my elven friend. You are no match for me. Stand down; your woman is capable of defending herself." He turned to Arcus, cocking his head in puzzlement before turning to Siobhan and Katie. "Someone else with power. What is your name?"

"I'm not speaking to such an abomination. You shouldn't even exist."

"And yet I do, and speaking to me with such insolence does nothing but make you sound like a child. No matter, I heard the seraph call you Siobhan, so that is what I will call you as well."

With that, he vanished and reappeared next to Katie. "Such beautiful skin. Such youth and beauty. Ah, and look at you, so new in your training that you are still smart enough to fear me. I can smell it; it's intoxicating. Why don't you head on downstairs to my chambers while the grown-ups talk. The stairs are down that hall, on the left."

Katie trembled, a tear trickling down her cheek. She looked at Siobhan and shook her head.

"I think you misunderstand me. I said, 'Go downstairs. Now.'"

Katie's eyes dilated and she moved to comply, but Siobhan stepped in front of her to stop her. As the two struggled, Celeste pushed past Tarnelius to approach Valen. "Why are you doing this? What do you want from us?"

"My dear, what would make you think that I wanted something from you? Perhaps I'm just happy to entertain. However, suffice it to say I do not trust Tarryn. He is up to something, and I want to know why he is sticking me with his dirty laundry. In this case, perhaps the enemy of my enemy is my friend."

Celeste's face darkened. "Are you responsible for the evil monstrosities roaming the hills outside?"

"They are my children. It gets so lonely out here."

"They murdered my friend. Nothing can make me help you."

"It's such a shame. Working with me could forward your own agenda." Valen regarded Siobhan and Katie in silence for a few minutes before sighing. "Or maybe I was wrong. Siobhan, if it's that important to you, she may stay. Come here, my dear." Katie stopped struggling and immediately turned to walk to Valen, who led her a little way from the elves. He slowly caressed her cheek. "So beautiful." Suddenly, he jerked his arms toward the group and they slid backward against the walls. They all struggled against their invisible restraints, but were held fast to the wall. Valen returned to Katie, looking at her with tenderness.

He kissed her gently on the lips before moving down her jaw, kissing her as he travelled. When he reached her neck, his fangs elongated and he swiftly penetrated her vein, drinking deeply. Other than the initial surprise as he pierced her, Katie made no negative reaction. She closed her eyes and moaned in bliss as the toxins in his fangs took over her blood.

"No!" Siobhan exclaimed in agony. "Katie, fight him!"

"Enough of this," Celeste murmured. Her eyes rolled back in her head as she chanted softly.

After a short time, Valen released Katie and she dropped heavily to the floor. Valen regarded his other captives as he wiped a stray drop of blood away from his mouth. "Which one of you should be next? Tarryn told me not to underestimate the lot of *you*, yet here you are, under *my* control."

Siobhan glared up at him in defiance. "Take me next, you monster, and I hope you choke."

It was then that Valen noticed Celeste. He approached her, trying to hear what it was she was chanting. "And what do – oof!"

Arcus spoke a word of magic and a bolt of electricity shot out of his trapped hand and struck Valen in the chest. The vampire vanished for a second, reforming almost instantly as he grabbed Arcus by the throat, choking him. As Arcus gasped, Valen suddenly became aware of a feeling of pressure that was steadily building in the room. He cocked his head, confused, as he watched Arcus turn steadily blue. Suddenly, the roof and top floors of the castle exploded, and he was yanked away from Arcus and the rest of the group, into the far wall. Only Celeste remained standing, as everyone else sagged to the floor, Valen's hold on them severed. Celeste raised her arms and the cyclone lowered to the wall on the opposite side, where Valen was crouched. Sunlight streamed in from the noonday sun. The storm knocked that wall out and lifted the vampire in its windy grip, flinging him across the room. Finally, Celeste dropped her arms, allowing the storm to dissipate. Arcus was the first to recover, jumping to his feet and hitting Valen with a fireball. Siobhan and Tarnelius stood up and raced over to him, drawing their weapons. Tarnelius arrived first, slicing at the vampire with both weapons so fast his arms were a blur.

Siobhan raised her sword once more, the magic golden glow consuming it. "I will smite you, you monster, for Katie!" She brought her sword down with more force than even she was expecting, slicing Valen's head clean from his body. Then she quickly recovered her weapon, bringing it down again to pierce the beheaded vampire's heart. Just as she brought it down, he seemed to dissolve away into nothing. Her sword embedded deep into the floor.

She yanked it out and spun around, frantically searching the room as she waited for Valen to reappear. They all looked around for a while, but there was no sign of the vampire.

"Do you think we killed him? Where did he go?" Siobhan asked.

"I have no idea. I hope so," answered Celeste.

"I beheaded him, but then he vanished." Siobhan looked around the room trying to find Katie. She finally located her on the outside of the ruined castle; she had been blown out through the ruined wall. Siobhan examined her, noticing the withered appearance of her skin. "She has been sucked dry. There is nothing left. Farewell, my friend. You would have made an excellent knight." Siobhan knelt next to her, two single tears slipping down her face as she struggled to maintain her composure. Arcus crept up next to her and placed a gentle hand on her shoulder to offer her support. Siobhan turned and flung her arms around him, almost knocking them both over as she cried, silent sobs wracking her body. Arcus looked shocked, but stood and patted her on the back, nonetheless.

Celeste and Tarnelius turned away from the unlikely pair and headed toward the stairs, which were now exposed to the sun. Celeste dragged her feet as she walked, and Tarnelius slid his arm around her to help support her. She leaned into him, but aloud said, "I'm fine. Really, it'll be okay."

"The last time you cast that spell you lost consciousness for a whole day. I'm not convinced I believe you."

"I'm just a little tired. This time I only controlled the storm for less than a minute. Last time was for much longer."

The pair crept down the stairs, noticing as they opened the door to the next floor that it was also well lit. The door opened up into a grand bedroom containing a huge four-poster bed.

"Ha, not what I expected," chortled Tarnelius.

"What did you expect?"

"I don't know, a coffin perhaps? Something dark and cold and barren. Do you have any idea why we were suddenly able to hit him?"

"The sun dazed him. He was too confused to react. If it hadn't been for the sun, things would have turned out much differently."

The two searched the room. They found several gemstones, rings and necklaces, which Celeste scooped up and slid into her bag. Tarnelius began to rifle through some books on a shelf, and grabbed one that seemed to shimmer with magic. He stuck that one under his arm and continued searching. Another book that he grabbed seemed heavier than it should be, and when he pulled it, a hidden panel in the wall opened with a clicking sound. Tarnelius handed Celeste the magic book, which she placed into her bag. The two stepped through the secret door into a dim hallway. A few feet in, they discovered two large dungeon cells, one on either side. Inside each cell were some of the missing paladins, nine on one side and eleven on the other. They all jumped to their feet when they saw the elves.

"Celeste, Tarnelius, thank Mithra you are here," exclaimed Cayden.

"Do you know where the key is?" Tarnelius asked.

"That bloodsucking monster has it. Where is he?"

"Not here for the time being. Not sure if he is dead or will be back. Rust spell, Tarnelius," instructed Celeste. They each positioned themselves at one of the cell doors and cast together. As they chanted, the metal bars corroded under their touch, the rust spreading out to cover the entire door until it looked like the bars had been submerged in water for years. "Stand back," Celeste said before they each kicked in the cell doors. The paladins caught the doors and lowered them to the floor, stepping onto them to leave.

"Where are the others?" Celeste asked, taking a quick inventory of those she remembered.

"Gone, ma'am. Several died to monsters on the way, and of those who made it here, the ones who didn't fall under his spells were killed last night. He gave their bodies to some other monsters that reeked of death, and the monsters ate them," gasped Antoine, his voice hoarse.

"So you all came here together? You didn't split up?"

"No, ma'am. We all came here together. We were trying to find you, but seemed to be going around in circles."

Celeste nodded. "Let's get back to Siobhan. The stairs are back that way, through the vampire's bedroom," said Celeste.

"I'm so sorry about Katie," said Arcus.

Siobhan took a shuddering breath and pulled away, her eyes downcast. "I'm sorry I lost control like that."

"What do you mean?"

"Katie knew the risks when she agreed to be my squire. Still, I feel as if I failed her. Regardless, I'm not normally one to cry, ever."

"You don't have to be made of ice. It's okay to thaw a bit and let the people that care about you see that you are merely human, like the rest of us."

"You care about me?"

"I – you saved my life twice now. Once from the demon, and again when we were trapped in the wagon. How could I not?" Arcus frowned a little, confused about what Siobhan was implying.

"That's not what I meant, I –" suddenly, Siobhan's eyes widened. "Arcus, I need you to set Katie on fire. Now."

"What? Why? We haven't built a pyre yet. We should wait for the others."

"Don't you see? She – oh, you really can't see. She has an evil aura surrounding her. It's faint but growing. Please, I don't know what will happen but it can't be good. I won't – I can't fight her."

Arcus nodded once and spoke the words that caused fire to shoot from his hand and set Katie's body on fire. Siobhan turned away and refused to watch. Arcus sighed and gathered her in his arms before pulling her face down to his. He kissed her gently on the lips, a chaste kiss. A promise. She trembled in his arms as she returned the kiss.

"I do care about you, Siobhan," Arcus murmured, as he brushed her hair back from her face and tucked it behind her ear.

Then he stepped away from her to watch Katie's body burn to ash and make sure the fire didn't spread.

By the time the fire had almost burned itself out, Celeste and Tarnelius had emerged from the wreckage, followed by what was left of the Paladins of Mithra. Celeste looked exhausted, but she was still moving under her own power.

Siobhan did a quick count in her head. There were only seventeen paladins left, not including herself, and three squires. Less than half of what they had when they entered Beinn-anbas the night before. Those that were left looked pale and drawn, their spirits broken from the horrors they had witnessed.

While the knights told Siobhan what had happened during the night, Celeste gestured to Arcus to come and speak with her and Tarnelius. She reached into her bag and withdrew the jewelry they had picked up, as well as the book.

"I was hoping you could tell me if these things were anything worth keeping," Celeste said.

"Sure, I'll take a look at them later, when we get a chance." Arcus' eyes were locked onto the book. He flipped it open and his eyes widened. He slammed the book shut and looked over at the two elves in surprise.

"This, however, is worth far more than what I suspect this jewelry is worth. Apparently, our friend Valen decided to keep a spell book filled with spells."

"He was an arcane caster? I suppose that makes sense, since he was created by the dragons, but I wonder why he didn't cast anything when we fought him," Tarnelius wondered.

"I suspect he would have, but he really wasn't expecting us to fight back like we did. He thought he had full control over us by taking away our freedom of movement. He underestimated all of us, and especially Celeste. He really never saw that cyclone coming." Arcus stuffed the book and the jewelry into his satchel and returned to Siobhan.

With the excitement dying down, Celeste felt her strength beginning to wane, and she leaned more heavily into Tarnelius. He held her to him as they listened to the others talk.

"We need to get back to the horses," said Siobhan. "I think we have done enough here for now, and we have certainly suffered more than enough casualties. We will return to the camp and rest tonight. Tomorrow we will ride hard, skirting around the edges of Beinn-anbas. We have extra horses now. If we trade them off as we go to keep the horses as fresh as we can, we should be able to be in Gormloch after two days' worth of riding. Any comments? Questions?"

At the sight of everyone shaking their heads, she started toward the elves. "Let's go, everyone. Celeste, will you fly ahead and lead us out?"

Celeste started to push away from Tarnelius to release her wings, but he pulled her back into him. "No, she cannot. We'll have to come up with another plan. She's exhausted from the tornado spell, and frankly it's amazing she's still awake at all right now."

"Tarnel, stop fussing, I can –"

"Absolutely not," he said.

"I can fly overhead as a bird," offered Arcus. "It may not be necessary, though. The hills didn't try to stop us from leaving last time."

"I don't want to take any chances. I just want out of this horrible place," said Siobhan.

"Captain, what if we summon our mounts? We would make it much faster while mounted. There are only a few of us that would have to double up," Ryan sadly suggested, his voice breaking on the word "few".

"Great idea. Mount up, everyone. Celeste or Tarnelius, one of you ride with me on Apollo. The other go with Ryan and Onyx. The rest of you, double up as you can."

All around them, beautiful horses were appearing out of thin air. The horses either knew what had transpired, or they sensed their masters' melancholy feelings, because they all seemed reserved and sad, as well. Siobhan was about to call for the elves again when she saw Tarnelius shift into a horse himself. Arcus helped Celeste to mount, and then he shifted himself into his peregrine falcon form and flew over to land on Siobhan's armored shoulder.

"Well, all right, then. Miseil, you're with me. Cayden with Ryan, and Aiden go with Antoine. Everyone ready? This is the bird we need to not lose sight of for any reason. Let's go."

Arcus flew into the sky, circling around as he got his bearings to determine which way was the correct way to the camp. Then they were off, the horses maintaining a brisk canter to keep up with the bird.

Deep inside the castle, far below the cells the knights had been kept in, Valen made it to his coffin. Still in mist form, he entered it and spread out inside, knowing that as long as nothing happened to disturb his rest, he would be okay and would be back another day. He knew he would never underestimate the druids again, and wished he had heeded Tarryn's advice.

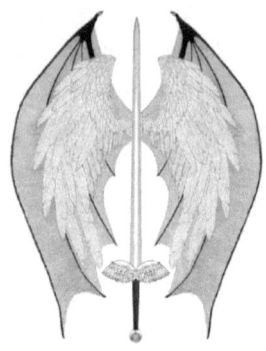

Chapter Twenty-Seven
Fears of the Fearless

Celeste gripped Tarnelius' mane as he raced on, because she had no barding or reins to hold on to. *"I'm pretty sure flying would have been less exhausting than focusing on not falling off,"* she thought to him.

"I won't let you fall off. Don't worry, I've got you."

After only about an hour and a half, the group arrived back at camp. They all dismounted and dismissed the horses they had ridden in on so they could recover. Celeste and Tarnelius headed to the wagon to rest.

Arcus landed near Siobhan and shifted back. "How can I help?"

She gazed at him, looking utterly broken. "What?"

"With the tents?"

"Oh, oh yes. We need to take down the extras. Don't worry about it, we will get it. You should rest up with your friends."

"I don't mind helping –"

"I said we've got it, Arcus. Just go away. This is not your problem, so stay out of it," she snapped at him, her tone harsh.

He sighed. "I don't know why I ever thought things would be different now." Arcus turned on his heel and stomped over to the wagon, where he found Celeste fast asleep. Tarnelius was holding her head cradled to his chest and he held up a warning finger to his lips to signal Arcus to be quiet. Not wanting to intrude, Arcus decided to walk around the nearby lake to clear his thoughts. As he walked, he pulled out the vampire's spell book to try to figure out what spells it may contain.

There were some mages that could cast spells by reading how to do it in books, and they could change out their spells every day by simply reading and learning new spells. Arcus could learn arcane spells by either reading how to cast them, or by someone teaching him how to do them, but either way, once they were learned he knew them forever. He couldn't manage to learn as many as those that learned daily from books, but he knew more than enough. He sat down at the shore and flipped through the pages, noticing the strange shade of brownish ink that had been used. On closer examination, he realized the book had been written in blood. *Figures*, he thought.

He rifled through his satchel until he found a quill and a scrap of parchment and started scribbling notes. The spells were all written in the dragons' native language, as most arcane spells were, but he had learned how to read and write in that language while back in Izmar. Most of the spells were various enchantments, but there were a few elemental spells, and he made notes on these so that he would know which ones to learn. He was so engrossed in his task, that he was startled when Siobhan came and sat down next to him. She had removed her armor and was just wearing riding breeches and a loose fitting blue blouse. He realized he had never actually seen her without her armor before, and he struggled to keep his eyes on his book.

What is the matter with me? Arcus wondered. *Why am I so drawn to her? She is infuriating and cold. I never know whether she is going to be happy to see me or whether she will lash out at me. I need to stay away from this female.*

"It's hard for them, you know? They saw horrible things last night, the stuff of nightmares. Many of the squires had never been out here before. They didn't know what to expect, and now they don't know how to say goodbye," began Siobhan.

"Hmm," said Arcus, still thumbing ineffectively through his spell book.

She sighed. "So now you aren't speaking to me?"

Arcus set his book down. "I'm speaking to you. I just don't know whether to expect you to snap at me or not. I can't help but notice that if the others are around you treat me as if I am beneath you, and if we are alone you want to chat with me. I'm not sure it's worth the headache."

"What do you want me to say, Arcus?"

"Are you ashamed of me?"

"No, of course not."

"Good, because all we've shared is one kiss. No need for shame just yet. If you're already ashamed of me, maybe it's best if I steer clear before we both end up emotionally invested."

Siobhan picked up a smooth rock and flung it into the lake, watching it skip. "Look, I don't know what I'm doing. I'm supposed to be in charge, but I feel like a failure. I feel this connection to you, but I know I should stick with my own kind, especially because we need to rebuild the Mithran paladin order."

"I see."

She sighed. "I just feel confused, and lost. Plus, you and your friends are going to continue north, and I need to stay at Castle Mithra."

"First of all, some of the Saroshans mix arcana with their religious power. It's not unheard of. Next, you said you would help us if we helped you."

"I said I would ask for permission. That was before everything changed. I have to report back to Castle Mithra. I need to answer for all these deaths. I doubt I will be allowed to go."

"Then just come with us. They will forgive you. Especially when they find out what we are doing."

"I – I can't."

"Wrong, you won't. Just like you won't lower your defenses enough to give us a chance."

"You're right."

"Damn right, I am. Why not? What are you so afraid of?" Arcus challenged.

"I'm not afraid of anything."

Arcus stared at her in silence.

"Fine. I'm afraid of you. Are you happy now? I'm afraid that you might be the one man who is different from the rest. The one I could let my guard down around, who wouldn't use me to gain power. I'm afraid I might fall in love with you, and that you might leave. I saw your strength of character and your strength of will as you fought off the demon that very first time we met. I saw the pain and compassion in your eyes as you told me what you had done – what you had been forced to do." She took a deep breath and threw another rock into the lake.

"Hey," Arcus reached over and turned her face toward him, before rising up onto his knees to lean over and kiss her deeply. She returned the kiss, melting into him for a few moments. His scraggly beard scratched her face, but in a pleasant way. After too short a time, she pulled away with a sigh.

"Why would you just assume I would leave you?" Arcus asked.

"Because you will. My place is with my paladins. Your place is saving the world with your friends. Then who knows where you will go? I doubt it would be to Castle Mithra just for me."

"You really have this all planned out, don't you? Why don't you just come with us, and we'll see where things lead?"

"I can't. I already told you," she sighed. "This was a mistake. I should go."

Arcus reached out and grabbed her hand. "Stay, please. Don't push me away."

She sighed again, but remained where she was.

"Why does everything have to be about 'my place' or 'your place'? If you really wanted to, we could forge a whole new path that is 'our place'."

She leaned forward to kiss him one last time. "Because, ultimately, you aren't a paladin. You'd never be comfortable among us, and you would never fit in. I don't deny that I feel a strong connection to you; when we touch I can feel the sparks. I care for you, but it's not enough. It's not our destiny to be together."

She stood up and started walking away.

"Destiny is what you make it," muttered Arcus to himself. *I sure know how to pick them*, he thought. *We don't even have a relationship yet and we are already breaking up. Joseph would be so impressed.* Without another word, he picked his book up and attempted, without success, to regain his focus.

Siobhan stomped the short walk back into the camp. She noticed Celeste was up from her nap, so she decided to head over to the two elves so she could officially let them know that she would not be returning with them.

"Where's Arcus?" Celeste asked, as she approached.

"Just over that rise at the lake, studying some book. I wanted to talk to you."

"Okay, how can we help you?"

Siobhan sighed. "There's no easy way to say this, so I'll just be direct. I won't be able to come with you to the tombs."

Celeste's eyebrow shot up. "Why not? We had an agreement."

"I'll have to answer to the head of my order for all the deaths that happened under my watch when I was not around to defend them. It is unlikely they will allow me to go with you now."

"Well, then forget about them. Send any of your paladins who are not ready for such a journey back there to explain, and you can just come with us. We fight well together, and we need you."

"Arcus suggested much the same. However, I cannot."

"Not even to avenge the deaths of your people?"

Siobhan frowned. "How would I do that? We already killed the vampire. At least, I hope we did."

"We didn't kill the demon. The demon that was sending my friends and me to Valen. The same demon who likely set Valen up there with that castle. He still lives."

"You don't know that the demon was in any way involved with placing him there."

"I know that you said the castle wasn't there the last time you came through here. I know that Tarryn knew Valen was there, and knew enough to think he could get away with sending us to him. Liam's vizier *is* the demon responsible for the deaths of your men, even if he only intended our deaths and not theirs."

Siobhan growled in frustration. "None of you seem to realize how much I want to come with you. I do, but going back is my responsibility. I have no choice. Not even for Ar –"

Celeste arched her eyebrow at Siobhan's sudden stop. "What about Arcus?"

"Nothing. He wants me to come, too, that's all."

"I've seen the way he's been looking at you. He's hero-worshiped you, ever since the exorcism."

"It doesn't matter."

"How do you feel about him?"

"It doesn't matter."

Tarnelius jumped in. "Actually, it matters a great deal. Arcus is a good man and my friend. I've known him since he was a small traumatized child who had just seen his parents murdered in front of his eyes. He is slow to make friendships and although I have no idea what he was doing in the few years that he was gone, I would think it's safe to say that when he told us shortly before Celeste and I were bonded that he'd never been in love he was telling the truth. I, too, see how he has looked at you since his exorcism. I also see that you have been cruel to him at times. Sometimes you are vindictive, and sometimes I see you looking at him the same way that he looks at you. Don't play with him."

"I'm not –"

"Don't play with him," snarled Tarnelius. "If you care for him, then be good to him. Don't mess with his head."

"Look, it's not any of your business, but it doesn't matter because, as I told him, my place is with my people and his is with you. Even if that were not true, he would never be happy living among paladins. I have no intention of playing with him."

"Did I ever tell you why Tarnel and I were separated for six hundred years?" Celeste asked. "I know I told you that we were, but I don't think I told you why." Siobhan shook her head.

Celeste continued. "Well, without getting into too many details, I thought that I was losing Tarnelius forever because we were not fated to be together. I thought that he would choose duty over me, and then I was afraid that he wouldn't when he should. I decided to take the decision away from him and left. I left and hid myself away for hundreds of years and refused to be found, only to discover what a fool I had been and how much pain I had inflicted on both of us for nothing. He is my soul mate, my *rakastan*, and I would give anything to be able to take back what I did and have that time together that we lost. I thought, at the time, that I was doing the right thing, but I could not have been more wrong. Don't make my mistakes. Don't give up on something before it's even begun."

"Well, that's easy for you to say now that things obviously worked out. I have no such guarantees, and my life with the paladins is important to me. Now if you'll excuse me, I'll be returning to my group to organize the watch. Why don't the two of you take first watch tonight?" Without waiting for an answer, she turned and walked back to the tents.

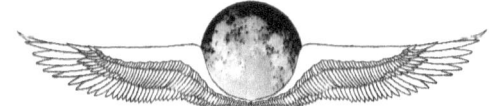

The next morning, everyone awoke and pulled down the tents. They loaded up the wagon and the horses and set off, skirting around the eastern edge of Beinn-anbas. The two-day trip passed uneventfully, and the second evening found them riding up to the gates of Gormloch. Siobhan and the paladins led their pack horses into the paddock area and unloaded them, storing their belongings in a nearby warehouse. That done, they headed to a large inn called "The Golden Griffin," where the innkeeper was quick to hand out keys for the rooms and make arrangements with the cook to prepare dinner, despite the late hour it had become. The Paladins of Mithra were held in high regard in Gormloch, as they were frequent visitors and, even when not traveling through the city, still kept things safe simply by being so near. Though the city was nowhere near as organized as Lumernia, crime rate was low and in general the people were happy.

After the room arrangements were sorted out, Siobhan requested her paladins to all squeeze into her room for a talk about what was to come the next day. She asked Celeste if she would bring Arcus and Tarnelius down to the dining area alone, so she could speak to the paladins in private.

"Theri would have loved this place. She loved getting to sleep in beds instead of on the road," mused Celeste, as they sat down at a table to await the others.

"That's true," agreed Arcus. "I miss her. She was really the life of our group."

"I wonder if there is anyone in the south we should notify about her death," said Tarnelius.

Celeste was watching Arcus, a concerned look on her face. "Hmm, you know, you're right, Tarnel. We should look into that when this is all over." She reached forward and nudged Arcus' arm. "Hey, you've been quiet these last two days. I know your book has been interesting, but you need to snap out of it."

"Sorry."

"Anything you want to talk about?" Celeste asked.

"No."

"Leave him be, Celeste," murmured Tarnelius.

Celeste sighed. "Arcus, we know about Siobhan."

Arcus looked up at her in surprise.

"I mean, we've seen how you look at her."

Arcus lowered his gaze back to his hands, which were folded on the table. "It's nothing. Don't worry about me."

"You're my friend, Arcus. Why wouldn't I worry?"

"Because there's nothing to worry about. What would she want with me? What do I have to offer her? She told me I wouldn't fit in among her friends, and she is right. I need to get over it already. I just feel like – like she tricked me. Made me feel like she cared, but really, the only one she cares about is herself."

Celeste patted him on the hand. "You're wrong, Arcus. You have a lot to offer."

"So says the married elf. Look, really, I'm fine, and I'd prefer to just put this whole business behind me. I liked myself a lot better when I was the detached one watching Joseph throw himself at women."

"Yes, but –"

"Celeste, leave the man alone. Seriously. Let it go," said Tarnelius. Arcus nodded his head to him once in quiet thanks.

"Fine."

The trio fell silent while they waited for the knights to emerge down the stairs. They ate dinner, a simple but delicious fare. The cook was familiar with trading with the elves and had sent over a vegetarian plate for them, and for Arcus as well when he requested it. Afterward, they each retired to their rooms.

Arcus cast a spell that created a small floating ball of light and returned to his spell book. He was interested in a couple of complicated spells that were similar to spells he already had, but much larger in scale. He was distracted by a soft rapping on the door. He looked up in annoyance and cleared his throat. "What is it?"

Instead of an answer, there was merely another series of light taps. Arcus sighed and stood up to go open the door. He jerked it open and started to snarl, "What?" but stopped short when he saw Siobhan on the other side. She was once more dressed in breeches and a low cut green button-down shirt. She hadn't said a word to him since the fight at the lake, and had barely even looked at him.

"Can I come in?" Siobhan whispered.

He held open the door for her and stepped aside. As soon as she had passed him, he shut the door and turned to look at her. She was staring at the little ball of light he had cast. She placed her hand through it and expressed surprise that it wasn't hot.

"What's this about, Siobhan?"

She straightened up and looked him in the eye. "I've decided to place Ryan in charge of the remainder of the paladins. He will lead them into Castle Mithra tomorrow and tell them what I have done." The last part was spoken in a whisper.

He continued to watch her, surprised at this turn of events. "Does that mean you will come with us?"

She nodded. "If you still want me. I mean –" Her eyes grew round. "If you still need me, um, to come with you. You know, all of that sounded much better in my head," she finished with a sigh.

The corner of his mouth twitched a little. "I knew what you meant."

"So does that mean you do?"

A lock of her red hair was in her face. It was taking an immense amount of control for him to not go to her and brush it behind her ear. He knew if he did that they would end up kissing again, and he worried she would just rip down all his defenses again. He met her eyes and realized she was waiting for an answer. He cleared his throat. "Yes, we would love to have your help. I have a feeling we can use all the help we can get."

"What about you?"

"What about me?"

She approached him slowly, her hazel eyes locked on his gray ones. She placed a hand on his chest and felt his racing heart. She relished that thrill of electricity that ran through her body as she touched him. "Do *you* want me? Please Arcus, I need to know now, before I risk making myself an outcast."

He took a shuddering breath. His head told him she was nothing but trouble, that she would break him. His heart didn't care; it wanted her. He nodded his head, not trusting his own voice.

She smiled and lowered her head down, kissing him hard, possessively.

Yes, he knew she would definitely break him, and at the moment he couldn't care less. Who was he to fight the passions that threatened to consume them?

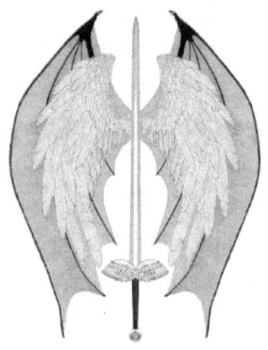

Chapter Twenty-Eight
Second Thoughts

"Goddess, it's morning!" Siobhan yelped as she jumped from the bed and frantically threw her clothes on.

"Is that supposed to be a problem?"

"I can't let them see me here," she answered, her tone distressed.

"Once again, I'm experiencing that paranoid sensation that you just might be ashamed of me."

Siobhan didn't meet his eyes. Instead, she whispered, "This was a mistake. I'm not someone who normally…"

"Neither am I," answered Arcus.

"Right, and I'm supposed to believe that after last night? You…you seduced me!"

"I did nothing of the sort. Note whose room we are in. *You* came to *me*."

"Regardless, this was still a mistake and it can't happen again."

Arcus stood up and grabbed her arm, pulling her to him. That dratted spark was still there, and she stared at him with frantic eyes.

"Why did you come to my room last night, if this was a mistake? What was your intent?" His voice was quiet, rumbling and dangerous.

"I wanted to tell you I would honor my promise to come with you. I wanted to tell you we could give us a try and see where things go. I wanted to take it slowly, and now it's too late, and we've ruined everything."

"Nothing is ruined. I can't even tell you I'm sorry because I would be lying. Now, you need to calm down. I can see myself falling for you, but you need to stop with this randomly running hot and cold business. You asked me last night if I wanted you, and I do. What do you want, Siobhan? Can you see yourself falling for *me*?"

"I wanted to find out, but not like this. What happened last night, it can't happen again. I'm sorry. Everything *is* ruined."

"Why do you think that?"

"Because now that we've – I mean, I didn't want to rush things, and now you'll expect us to… We'll just have to, you know."

"I know you did not just say that to me," he growled. "Do I strike you as the type of man who would force you to do things you don't want to do? What kind of men have you been with?"

She pushed away from him and walked to the door. "I just wanted everything to be different with you. I have to go, I'm sorry." She opened the door as quietly as possible and snuck out into the hallway.

Arcus stared at the door in frustration.

"Damn it," he exclaimed, as he slammed his hand down on the small table he had placed his spell book on. Fire burst from his hands upon impact and ignited the table. Reacting at once, he shoved his precious book off the table and grabbed the pillow to beat the fire out. He shook his head; it had been a long time since he had lost control of his magic like that. He took a deep breath to calm himself and cast the spell to fix the table. It wouldn't do to leave the furniture covered in scorch marks.

He had been right; she was definitely going to break him.

After he had regained control of himself, he gingerly picked up his satchel, afraid that he would set it on fire as well. Then, he picked up his book and located his clothes. He cast the spell to clean them and packed his stuff away into his bag. He took a final look around the room to make sure he hadn't missed anything, and then he headed down to breakfast. He paused by the innkeeper to turn in the key, and then went to sit with Celeste and Tarnelius, who were already at a table, eating breakfast.

"Morning," said Celeste.

He nodded to them but didn't say anything.

The two elves exchanged glances, but went back to eating their breakfast of native fruits and breads. After a few moments, a waitress brought Arcus the same.

Before long, the paladins were all back in their armor and at the tables for breakfast as well, Siobhan arriving with Ryan, deep in conversation. She excused herself and approached their table, smiling at Celeste.

"Sorry for our tardiness. I hope you haven't been waiting long. It takes a while to get ourselves into our armor, especially without squires. Though, I'm sure you noticed that yesterday," she rambled, being careful to not make eye contact with Arcus.

"It's no problem. Tarnelius and I are early risers, and Arcus only came down a few minutes before you did."

"Did you hear about the change of plans?" Siobhan asked.

"Change?"

"Yes, um, I've placed Ryan in charge. He will lead the paladins into Castle Mithra in my place. I've explained that I am needed in the north with you."

Celeste and Tarnelius exchanged surprised glances.

"Are they all going back, except for you?" Tarnelius asked.

"Yes. I don't wish to lead any more to their deaths, and if we are going up against a powerful demon I don't think any of them are ready. Apollo and I are at your service, and hopefully when all is said and done, I will still be welcomed in my home."

"You will be. I can always go flash my wings at them and explain how you helped save the world," Celeste said with a wink.

Siobhan smiled at that. "I may hold you to that, Celeste. Well, since I've given up captaincy, I should go see if our new leader needs my help." She turned and walked off to sit next to Ryan. A waitress hurried to bring her a plate of food.

Celeste took a long drink of water before she set her cup down with a clunk and smirked at Arcus. "Okay, spill it."

"Spill what?"

"Don't play coy with me. She has changed her mind about coming with us. Plus, she asked if I had heard yet, meaning one of us already knew. It wasn't us so, it must have been you."

"I don't want to talk about it right now."

"Why not? This seems a positive step."

"I just don't. I hope she does come with us; we could use the help. Part of me won't be surprised if she changes her mind again when we reach the bridge to Castle Mithra. Don't get attached."

"Attached? Is that advice for you or for me?" Celeste asked with a frown.

Arcus merely glared at her, and ate his food in silence.

After breakfast, they returned to the paddocks and collected the horses and wagon. Ryan decided to leave all their equipment loaded on the wagon after acquiring some new saddles to replace the ones they lost in Beinn-anbas. He offered horses to Arcus, Tarnelius and Celeste for their journey. Miseil and Aiden were assigned to drive the wagon.

Arcus looked up at his horse doubtfully. "I haven't had much practice riding," he confessed.

Tarnelius laughed as he mounted his. "You can either ride the horse or be the horse. Your choice, but you may get tired after all the running."

"Don't tempt me. I guess I'll give this a try. We'll call your idea 'Plan B' and use it if this doesn't work out." Arcus locked eyes with his horse to have a talk with him. Tarnelius laughed again and urged his horse out of the paddock to join the others.

Soon, they were all assembled, and Ryan led the way north toward the Mithran Bridge, riding point. Castle Mithra was just on the other side of the Joki River, across the bridge. The road was well maintained, and they covered the distance in only a few hours, arriving by lunchtime. Siobhan steered her horse off the road, to the right hand side. Arcus and the two elves followed suit. They wheeled their horses about to face the knights. Ryan dismounted and saluted Siobhan, followed by the others. They remained frozen in place until she returned the salute, a sad smile on her face. Then they all led the horses across the bridge, where they remounted and continued on toward the castle.

Siobhan watched them go for a moment, then she urged Apollo back onto the road and into a gallop. The others looked in her direction in shock. Arcus growled in irritation and jumped off his horse, shifting into his peregrine falcon form and streaking after her. Tarnelius caught the reins of Arcus' horse.

Arcus soon caught up with Apollo and overtook him. Flapping a good distance ahead, he dove down and shifted back, standing in the road and forcing her to slow down and stop.

"Going somewhere? You know none of our horses come anywhere close to being able to keep up with Apollo," said Arcus.

She shrugged. "Part of me was worried I'd turn back if we hesitated, another part of me was worried they'd come looking for me. That could still happen, so we need to keep moving."

"We need to wait for Celeste and Tarnelius. Anyway, we won't let them take you, and I doubt Ryan will let them try."

She nodded at the truth of these words. Ryan had been briefed on where she was going and why. He could be trusted to defend her decision. The truth was, racing along with the wind in her hair made her feel free from everything, including her heart and the weight of her decisions.

"Arcus?"

"Yes?"

"I – I am sorry about the way I've treated you."

"Don't be sorry. Just fix it. Commit to a decision, and stick with it. I get whiplash trying to keep up with the back and forth."

"One of the first magical abilities we get as a paladin is the ability to never fear anything. I haven't felt fear since I was knighted. My faith shields me from it."

"Fear is sometimes a good healthy reaction that sparks an ability to do incredible things. Fear can also help keep us alive."

"And yet it can be debilitating and cause us to freeze up in battle. Fear can kill us. So when you asked me what I was afraid of, my answer was true when I said I feared nothing." She locked eyes with him. "But, against all reason, I do feel fear around you. I fear falling for you, and yet I know I'm falling at every moment. I fear something happening to you and tearing us apart. I go back and forth because I'm trying to keep you at arm's length to protect my heart. I'm afraid of my fear."

Arcus was stunned. He stared up at her, in amazement at her confession.

"Siobhan, I –"

"Your friends are coming."

He fell silent and turned to see Celeste and Tarnelius trotting up to them. Tarnelius was leading Arcus' horse. Arcus accepted the reins back with a nod of thanks when they caught up and remounted before steering his horse next to Apollo. Tarnelius and Celeste rode up on his other side as they continued on.

"There is only one more major city between us and the old ruins. We may want to see about exchanging your horses there, or else leave them behind and continue without them. The city of Mordun is about one hundred miles north of here. From there, we will have around three hundred more miles to get to the north outpost. I don't know if there are any settlements up there currently, but from what I recall from studying the old maps the Melekian Keep used to be up there, which would be the castle you mentioned before," said Siobhan.

Celeste nodded. "That makes sense. I think you are right, and that was their territory. I vaguely remember being brought to visit once with my father. That was when I was a small child, before the war. The last time I was there, the land had not yet frozen over. Everything was green."

"Well, it's frozen over now. That is why we will need to find horses raised from that area. They will have thicker coats and be used to it. We will also need to pick up some cold weather gear for ourselves and Apollo. Have you put any thought into what our plan is?"

"No, I really don't have one. I kind of figured the answer would come to us when the time came," said Celeste.

"Well, that's a good way to get us all killed. I thought you were supposed to be leading us."

Celeste turned red, but didn't answer.

"Well, do you have a better idea?" Tarnelius snapped.

"Not really, but perhaps we should think of one. Let's see. So far we know that Tarryn is behind all this, and that he is powerful. We know he has a staff, probably a relic, which tips the odds heavily in his favor."

"The only thing I don't understand is what he wants with Liam. If he's so powerful, why doesn't he just go alone?" Arcus mused.

"That's actually a very good question," said Tarnelius.

Arcus arched his eyebrow. "I've been known to ask those, from time to time."

"Well like Celeste said earlier, Melek used his dying breath to ensure that the seal he created to lock Kuunkierto away could only be opened by a true paladin, one who could channel energy from their holy symbol. Tarryn is *not* a paladin, and therefore could not open the seal alone. That said, Liam is not a true paladin," said Siobhan.

"Are you sure about that?" Arcus asked.

"Liam is a figurehead. He's a fighter at best, and not even a good one of those. True paladins would never allow themselves to be fooled by a demon. I suspect Celeste was right when she suggested that Tarryn wouldn't see us in Lumernia because we would know him for what he was," said Siobhan.

"I have no idea why Tarryn would need Liam, then. Maybe just for appearances' sake? Bah, that doesn't make sense either," grumbled Celeste.

"Unless he was trying to get one of the Saroshans? After the Mithrans, they have the highest percentage of real paladins. No, that can't be it, because they would see through him, same as we would."

They rode on a few more miles, lost in thought.

"Oh, back to what we were discussing," remembered Siobhan. "We'll need to get the staff away from him, or else we will all be severely weakened. I think that needs to be a priority."

"Okay, but how will we accomplish that without magic?" asked Tarnelius.

"We'll need to catch him unawares, and simply grab it away. I could always charge in on Apollo and attempt to disarm him. I am actually quite good at disarming my opponent from horseback. It's a valuable skill in jousting and swordplay. Once the staff is away from him, we'll need to keep it as far away as possible from the battle. Then you guys can drop as many spells as possible onto him."

"What about Liam?" Tarnelius asked.

"I think he will fight with us once that monster is exposed for what he is," said Siobhan.

"I doubt it," muttered Celeste.

"Let's cross that bridge when we come to it," said Arcus.

They continued to discuss various possibilities as they travelled up the north road, following the Joki River. Celeste created some magical berries and they all ate them. They stopped for the night when the sun began to set at a well-used campsite a short distance from the road. The temperature seemed to be a little cooler than normal here, but wasn't yet near being classified as cold. They ate more berries and shared some with the horses, then Siobhan dismissed Apollo to rest until the next day.

"We left all the tents on the wagon," complained Siobhan.

"We tend to sleep under the stars most nights anyway. It's much easier to travel light without tents," said Arcus.

"Regardless, we'll need to remember to get a couple in Mordun," said Siobhan.

"Oh, come on, is it so bad out here? I'll let you share my bedroll," Arcus answered with a wink.

Siobhan swatted him playfully. "It's going to be very cold soon. We'll need them."

"I'll keep you warm." Arcus grinned.

Her face darkened a little. "We'll still need tents. We'll need some sort of shelter against the cold and you should probably try to conserve your magic wherever possible."

"It's a good idea, Siobhan. We'll get some if we can," said Celeste. "I can carry them inside my bag anyway."

They set the watch, Siobhan taking first watch, which passed without event. She went to wake up Arcus for his turn when she realized she was being watched by a pack of wolves. She left off trying to get Arcus' attention and drew her sword. The wolves growled at her in warning as she stalked toward them. The lead wolf charged toward her, his pack close behind, but stopped short at the sound of a barked command.

"Stop!"

Siobhan turned her head a little to see that Arcus was up and approaching, his eyes locked on the wolf leader.

Arcus continued toward the large white and gray wolf, neither of them looking away. He stepped in front of Siobhan and pulled her behind him, displaying a protective stance. After a few moments, the wolf leader lowered his head and turned to disappear into the darkness, his pack following behind him.

"How did you do that?" Siobhan asked.

"The elves taught me to understand and speak to the animals."

"But that was like something else entirely. Those hungry wolves were going to eat the horses and probably any of us they could sink their teeth into, and you changed their minds."

"I did nothing of the sort. Those wolves were just passing through. They had just eaten a large deer they had brought down. They saw you draw your sword and thought you were attacking them. I merely cleared up the misunderstanding, and they went on their way."

Siobhan considered this revelation for a moment. "How could I have known?"

"You couldn't. Going forward, though, you should know that just as Mithra's heralds would recognize you for what you are, animals the world over recognize the three of us as being touched by Kamara. They recognize us as their defenders, and treat us with respect. You never need to worry about wildlife when you travel with me."

"I will remember that. I'm sorry."

"We both have a lot to learn about each other. You should get some sleep. I'll take over the watch."

"I'm not tired anymore. I'd like to stay up with you."

Arcus smiled at her and sat on the ground a fair distance away from his friends. Close enough he could keep an eye out, but far enough that he wouldn't disturb them by talking. He patted the ground next to him and she sat down, her armor clanking as she moved.

"I always thought paladin armor would be noisier."

"This is a special material, designed to be lightweight and more easily worn than regular steel. It's called 'mithril' and is favored by my order."

"Still, it can't be comfortable to sleep in."

"I don't generally sleep in it, and you're right, it isn't. It's tough to get all the ties in place, though, so I figured I'd just try to deal with it for a little while, since I no longer have a squire."

"Teach me what to do. I'll help you."

So she told him where all the ties and snaps were, and together they managed to get her armor off her. Underneath, she wore the traditional padded under-armor preferred by the knights. She settled back down next to him and smiled.

"Tell me about yourself."

"Not much to tell."

"I don't believe that; a human among elves is rare."

"My parents and I were travelling east from Izmar when I was a small boy. I think I was around five years old. My mother was sick and we were trying to find someone who could help her. Looking back, I think she must have had sorcerer blood too, but her power was untamed and was tearing her apart. She would hear voices and think there were people everywhere, when there was no one. She would sit still and unblinking for hours, and when she would come to, she would tell us of people and places she had seen. My father thought she had become crazy. She began to waste away to nothing, because she started to refuse any food, preferring to be in her imaginary places with her imaginary friends.

"Anyway, we were travelling east through the forested Kayalik Mountains to find someone who could heal her, when there came a crashing sound, through the trees. My father shoved me away behind a large rock, and a moment later a group of orcs charged through and attacked. They shot my father full of black-tipped arrows, and when he fell they grabbed hold of each of his hands and feet and ripped him apart. Literally to pieces, right in front of me. I remember my mother screaming in fright and horror. I wanted to help her, but I was afraid, and I didn't know what to do. I remember what they did to her too, though I try not to. Despite how horrible what they did to my father was, I still can't bring myself to describe what my mother went through. Suffice it to say that when they'd had their fun, they stabbed her and carved out her insides.

"I knew I would be next, and I had never been so frightened in my life. It was only a matter of time until they found me, but I knew if I ran they would find me sooner. I just squeezed my eyes closed and prayed to anyone that would listen. That's when I heard the sounds change. The orcs screamed in fear and I opened my eyes and peeked back out to see Tarnelius and his sentries fighting the monsters that had killed my family. I didn't know who they were. They were killing the orcs, but for all I knew, they could be even worse. Tarnelius found me though, hiding behind the rock. He brought me back to the elf village of Kayalost, where he and the other elves took me in as one of their own. They taught me their ways and I lived happily among them as a fellow druid.

"One day, soon after I turned fifteen, the arcane magic took me and I set fire to one of their sacred trees. I fled in fear, returning to Izmar, where I was luckily found by the owner of the Izmar School of Sorcery. I learned from them for a few years, until the day came that I had to flee the city and again sought the safety of the elf village."

Siobhan had been listening in silence, her chin on her knees. "How awful. I'm so sorry you went through all that. It's such a heartbreaking story, especially when you consider you were so young, so innocent. How did you end up such a good man after that?"

"I'm hardly a good man. At least not compared to your goodness. I try my best, most of the time, but sometimes the darkness takes me."

"Why did you have to flee the city?"

"I killed a man."

"What?" Siobhan asked in alarm.

"Yes. It was an accident, mostly. My best friend was always in trouble. He couldn't keep himself and his urges under control, and some guy and his friends took exception to him making a play for their woman. Joseph was a sorcerer as well, but he had poor instincts. He was well on his way to getting himself killed by that guy and his friends when I interceded. Ultimately, though, I overdid it and zapped one of the man's friends, stopping his heart. We had to leave in a hurry, and even then the city guard almost caught us."

Siobhan frowned. "I wish you hadn't told me that part."

"It's important to me that you know who I am. I am not perfect, and I am not a paladin. You were right. For you, I will do my best to be who you need me to be, but I'm not goodness and purity embodied. I have darkness. I interrogated an orc who had kidnapped Theri. I tortured him with the same knife his kin had used on my mother. I do not regret that. I suspect I will always hate the orcs. Can you blame me?"

Siobhan thought for a moment before answering. "No, not for that, I suppose. I can't understand how you felt, but I can sympathize. Do you regret killing the man in Izmar?"

Arcus sighed. "It was necessary, because I needed to save my friend. Yes, though, I do regret killing him. It was an accident. I didn't think."

"Well, remorse and repentance counts for a lot," said Siobhan in a soothing tone. "Although, the shame here is that you said it was the man's friend. So, likely, he wasn't doing anything wrong other than trying to help *his* friend, who had actually been wronged."

"One could argue that the man's girlfriend wouldn't have bothered with Joseph unless the man wasn't good to her. Maybe he was beating her, or perhaps he was unfaithful. Izmar is a seedy place, full of sailors with no morals. The fact that his friends backed him up meant nothing."

"Well, I could argue that you're basing that theory on circumstantial evidence." Siobhan sighed. "Under different circumstances, I would insist that you turn yourself in to the guard to face the consequences of your actions. If you are truly remorseful and did not mean for it to happen, they should show leniency. I suppose that in this case, you are more useful here than running back to the guards."

"Have you ever been to Izmar?"

"No, I haven't. Why?"

"If you had, you'd know that their guard is corrupt. There are no paladins nearby to keep everything running smoothly. The town is lawless and dangerous. Those that offer the biggest bribes are the ones that are favored by the law."

"That sounds awful. I can't imagine living in a place like that. Look, I suspect that we are never going to see eye to eye on topics such as this. We can fight over it, or we can accept each other's differences and move on from them. I'd be lying if I said I'd rather you were there in prison instead of here with me."

Arcus gave her a small smile and put his arm around her, drawing her closer. "See? We can learn and be adults. I haven't repulsed you too much, have I?"

"Maybe a little, but as long as you're promising me that you really do feel remorse for what happened with that man and make a clean start from this point, I'm willing to overlook it."

He kissed her deeply, trying to express with his mouth what his heart wanted to say. Finally, he gave up and decided to just say it.

"Siobhan, I – I don't tell many people the details of that day. In fact, you are the first person I have really given details of any sort to, since it happened. I only ever tell people that my parents were killed by orcs, but no details of what happened. I wanted *you* to know though, because... because I want you to know everything about me. I've fallen in love with you, and I know it's crazy, because we haven't known each other long, and have only recently decided to try things out between us, but I wanted you to know. I've never felt this way about anyone before, never knew these feelings were possible."

Siobhan stared at him in shock, blown away by his confession.

"Say something, Siobhan. Anything. Don't leave me hanging like this."

"I – I love you too, Arcus. I agree that it's too fast and that it's crazy. This overwhelming passion I feel for you keeps me off balance, and I don't know how to deal with it. I've tried to deny how I feel, but this pull I feel between us is too powerful."

Arcus' heart swelled and he kissed her again. After a few minutes, he broke away and smiled at her. "Your turn."

"My turn? For what?"

"Tell me all about you."

"This was your plan all along, wasn't it?"

"You started this conversation, so no."

Siobhan chuckled. "Well, my story isn't anywhere near as tragic or dramatic as yours. My parents were paladins of Mithra, as were their parents and theirs before them. Honestly, as far back as I can trace, my family has always served Mithra. When I was a teenager, I was squired to a knight who thought he would gain a higher standing among us if he won me over. He was so sweet at first. I fell in love with him, and before I knew it, he was no longer the nice guy I had once thought he was. Once he had a taste, he took advantage of my naïve nature, forcing me to allow him to do things to me that I didn't want to do. He told me it was my duty as his squire. He lost his paladin powers and his horse early on, because once a paladin turns from the path of goodness they are stripped of their powers, but no one noticed this until the day my father caught him. Then he was stripped of his rank and banished. I thought my father was going to kill him, but he finally stepped aside and allowed our legal system to do its job. Since then, I've had a hard time trusting, and never let anyone in. Until you, at least."

Arcus was trembling with rage, but was trying to not show it. He turned to her and took her face in his hands, forcing her to look in his eyes. "I understand now what happened this morning. Please know that I am not that bastard, and I would never do anything to hurt you or break your trust. I am content to just bask in your radiance and wait for you."

Her heart melted and she gave him a huge smile, the love showing in her eyes.

After a moment, Arcus cleared his throat. "So what happened to him?"

"I don't know. He left and went somewhere else. Why?"

Arcus twitched a little, apparently struggling with his answer. Finally, he said, "No reason. It's probably better that you don't know where he is. Come here, I need to kiss you again."

"You need to?"

"Like I need air to breathe."

They kissed again and again, lost in each other. At some point, they became aware of the sound of someone clearing their throat nearby. They jumped apart in surprise and stared up and Tarnelius and Celeste, who were both watching them.

Siobhan turned as red as her hair, and Arcus smiled up at them. "Did we wake you?"

"No. As you know, we don't sleep as long as you need to. We just woke up and figured we'd relieve you from watch duty," said Tarnelius.

"Thanks," said Arcus. He rose to his feet and held his hand out to Siobhan. "Come on, it's their turn to snuggle here on the ground. Let's get out of their way."

Siobhan wouldn't look at either of them as she stood up, her face flushed a deep red. Arcus paused, waiting for her to look at him. "Hey, don't worry about it. Theri and I have been stuck watching the two of them act exactly the same way for weeks. They aren't judging, or at least they'd better not be." He smiled over at the two elves. "Good night you two."

Arcus led her over to where they'd spread out their blankets earlier in the evening. He lay down and stared up at her, expectantly. Siobhan looked nervous as she glanced back at the elves. "Arcus, I'm really not comfortable with –"

"Relax. It's late, and I'm tired. I'm sure you must be as well. These heart to hearts are really draining. Besides, I said I would never force you into anything. If you want to move your stuff over by them its fine by me, but I'd really like it if you stayed and just slept near me."

She smiled and stretched out next to him, and they both drifted off to sleep.

Chapter Twenty-Nine
Best Laid Plans

The next evening, the four of them rode into Mordun. They checked the three horses into the stables there and found an inn, where they rented three rooms. They ate dinner, and Arcus identified the jewelry they had taken from the vampire's castle, before they went to sleep. The next morning they got up, ate breakfast, and headed out to the shops to find some cold weather gear. Arcus and Siobhan headed out to look for warm clothing and blankets for all of them and for Apollo, while Celeste and Tarnelius went to look for horses.

Unfortunately, although the traders of Mordun were more than happy to trade some of the horses to the elves, none of them were really suitable. Celeste and Tarnelius checked each of them and determined them all to be too old and tired to make such a long journey in the conditions they would require of them. Better for them to live out their days here, happy and taken care of, than being forced to carry riders to the frozen north. They sold off their horses and tack to the stable master and went to find the other two.

Arcus and Siobhan had picked up several heavy fur jackets, as well as other winter clothing.

"The other two will not be happy about this," mused Arcus, as he held up a large bearskin jacket.

"Would they be happier with freezing to death?"

"Possibly. We'll just tell them the bear died of natural causes."

Siobhan's lips thinned. "Why would you lie to your friends?"

"It may not be a lie."

"You don't know that it's the truth, and you made it up from nothing. Therefore, even if it's true, it's still a lie."

Arcus frowned. "You can't be serious right now. Why would it even matter?"

"It matters enough that you would choose to lie about it to your friends who trust you."

Arcus sighed. "Whatever. Let's just pick up this stuff. Celeste has the magic bag, not me, so we'll have to lug all this around until we find her."

Arcus carried the heavy clothes for the four of them. Siobhan picked up three tents, as well as fur covers to be placed over the tops, and a heavy blanket for Apollo.

Without another word to each other, the pair found the vendor and started bartering on price. In the end, Arcus talked him into accepting a large ruby from the vampire's castle that Arcus assured him would set off a silent alarm in the owner's head if anyone entered the building the gem was placed inside. Arcus taught him how to set it up and how to activate and deactivate it, then they left with their merchandise.

They'd no sooner left the shop than Celeste and Tarnelius hurried over to them.

"No horses?" Siobhan asked.

"No, none of the ones here are up to making the journey. We'll have to go on foot. That's a shame, because it will slow us down," answered Celeste.

"Though there is another option," added Tarnelius. They all turned to look at him.

"Well, Siobhan has Apollo, who is the fastest and strongest horse I've ever seen. She could ride, and the rest of us can shift into something that moves a little faster. We could always maximize our winter coats for warmth when we shift, or choose an animal built for cold."

"Like a snowy owl," added Arcus. "What a good idea." He smirked at Siobhan. "Looks like we won't be needing all these clothes after all."

"Oh, let's put all that stuff away. Come over here, out of the way," said Celeste. She wandered into a small alley.

"How long should it take us to get to the northern passage?" Arcus asked.

"Well, assuming we don't run into any issues that slow us down, Apollo should be able to make that distance in five to seven days. We should reach the frost line a couple of days before we get there."

Celeste opened her bag and folded each jacket inside it, then placed the tents inside. She arched her eyebrow at Arcus when she saw all the fur, but didn't say anything.

"Lucky thing you had that bag and thought to bring it," remarked Tarnelius.

"Tell me about it. When I was a child I used to play with this bag, trying to fit half the house into it. Who knew it would become so useful?"

Siobhan summoned Apollo and rolled up the winter blanket she had grabbed for him before tying it to the back of his saddle.

"Does he really stay saddled and battle ready all the time?" asked Arcus.

"It's complicated. When you shift, all your clothing and gear merge into you and cannot be seen or taken from you by any means, for as long as you are in animal form. When he goes back to the celestial realms, his belongings vanish or merge into him. I've never really been clear which, but when he comes back his stuff is always there."

Arcus nodded, satisfied with that answer. Once they had all their things stowed away, Celeste and Tarnelius both shifted into snowy owls as Siobhan mounted Apollo.

"I can't wait to see you shift into an animal that isn't black," Celeste said to Arcus, her beak clicking.

"You still need to teach me how to talk while shifted like that," said Arcus.

"Tarnel doesn't know how either, so don't feel bad. It takes practice."

Arcus focused inward and pictured being a snowy owl. He focused on how it would feel to be a snowy owl, then he opened his eyes when he heard light laughter from Celeste.

He looked down at himself. He had done it right; he was a snowy owl. Whereas the two elves had become white as snow itself, he was covered in black feathers. Still mostly white, but with quite a lot of black mixed in. He hooted in amusement and took off into the air, landing on Siobhan's shoulder. Siobhan directed Apollo out of the city, and pulled away from the Joki River to travel due north, while the two solid white owls took off ahead.

"You can go fly with them if you want," Siobhan said. "I don't mind riding alone. I have Apollo with me." Arcus cocked his head and squeezed her shoulder a little with his talons.

Celeste and Tarnelius circled each other in the air. They could move faster than Apollo, so they didn't worry about falling behind. They circled and swooped and dove through the air, making sure to keep Apollo in sight. After a while, Arcus took off to fly with them, occasionally returning to ride with Siobhan.

They travelled that way for five full days. On the fourth day they found the snow, and the air became noticeably cooler. The group dug out their cold weather clothes to wear from that point on. The sixth day, in the early afternoon, they finally approached the North Passage. The three owls had been circling through the skies, when Tarnelius whistled the alarm. The owls spread out and took in the scene below them before they dove back down to where Siobhan and Apollo were riding. The three druids transformed back to their regular forms, and Siobhan immediately stopped Apollo.

"What's happening?"

"They are here, at the crossing," Tarnelius answered. "We were almost too late. Good thing we didn't walk."

"Did either of you see Liam?" Celeste asked.

Both of the men shook their heads. "I saw the boat carrier they had all those horses pulling," offered Arcus.

"Yeah, judging by the size of the rig they had pulling it, the boat could only hold about twenty men or so. They will have to bring it back and forth. Liam probably would have been on the first boat."

"And Tarryn?" Siobhan asked.

"Oh, he was there. I could make him out easily. He was the one wearing wizard robes in the cold and carrying the obvious looking staff," said Celeste.

"Then it looks like it's show time," said Siobhan.

The group crept forward as close as they dared, leaving Apollo behind and hunkering down in the snow to watch.

Tarryn loudly barked orders at the men and seemed to be in an ill mood. The knights were scrambling to do his bidding. They had been working on erecting a campsite and were breaking apart pieces of their wagon to try to get enough of a dry platform to build a fire. From what the four of them could understand, they'd had some sort of delay getting across the channel, which was making Tarryn angry.

"Do you need a distraction?" Celeste whispered.

"Not unless you can distract them without alerting them to your presence. I'd rather them see me and be struggling to react than have them on alert. Just be ready to charge in as soon as I've separated him from his staff."

"Tarnel, your eagle form will be more suited to speed and being able to lift things. Let me cast a spell that will help you withstand the cold for an hour so you can fly overhead, out of sight. Be ready to swoop down and grab the staff, or shift back and defend Siobhan if things go badly. Arcus and I will hang back and await our moment."

"Can you cast it on Apollo too? He's moving okay, but I think he'd be able to run better if it weren't so cold."

"Sure."

The group backed up and returned to Apollo to prepare. Celeste cast her cold resistance spell on Tarnelius and Apollo. Tarnelius kissed Celeste goodbye and took off into the sky, climbing rapidly. Celeste also cast a few protection spells on Siobhan and Apollo as she mounted up and readied her sword.

"Wait," said Arcus.

He fished around in his bag. "This was Theri's belt. I saved it. The Grimsgil dwarves gave it to her and told her it would make her as strong as a giant. I was going to give it to Tarnelius, but I bet you could get good use of it now." He helped Siobhan to loop it around her slender waist.

"Thank you," Siobhan said. "I can actually feel it working. Are we ready now?"

"Just one more thing," Arcus said as he pulled her down toward him and gave her a small kiss. "Be careful out there. In case everything falls apart, know that I love you."

"I love you too, Arcus. Stop worrying. I know what I'm doing."

"I can't help it." He patted Apollo on his neck. "Your turn to take care of her for me, old boy. Be careful."

She spurred Apollo into a gallop and took off, sword ready. The pair ran north to the crossing almost soundlessly on the snow. She was almost on the group before they looked up to see what was coming for them. The men scrambled to avoid being trampled by the huge stallion. They stared on in shock, as her sword flashed in the light of the midday sun and her holy symbol began to glow brightly on her chest. A couple of the men from the Mithran order gathered their wits enough to call out to her to inquire why a fellow knight was charging into their midst. Siobhan ignored them all and kept right on running. Time seemed to stand still as she approached Tarryn. Her holy symbol glared blindingly bright and then winked out as she drew near. Apollo shuddered and seemed to pale in vibrancy a little. Tarryn's only reaction was to turn toward her and glare in vague surprise.

"Foolish girl," he began to say as she reached him. She lowered her sword and thrust it upward with no magic to back her up. Even the belt that Arcus had given her failed in that moment. All she had was the strength she was born with. She hit the staff with her upward swing as they flew by, not even bothering to take the time to attack Tarryn personally, her only concern the staff. It flew from his hand, high into the air. It flew gracefully through the air, the light from the key inside the crystal dimming and going out as it hit the ground over thirty feet away. Siobhan's holy symbol burst back into light. Apollo seemed to regroup, and he turned about as nimbly as if this had been a joust. Siobhan saw a golden streak dive from the sky and grab the staff, flying to the south. As she turned to focus on Tarryn, she was surprised by a huge black whip that came out of nowhere and struck her in the chest. She was knocked from Apollo to land heavily in the snow.

She rolled to the side, her sword still held fast in her hand. She gasped for breath and jumped to her feet, sure that whatever had hit her had broken a few ribs. She turned to face her attacker and almost dropped her sword from the surprise.

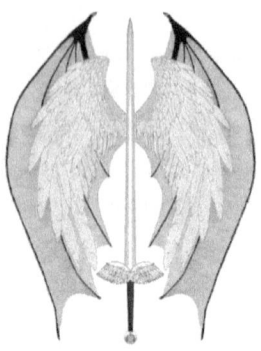

Chapter Thirty
Foolish Girl

Celeste felt hope rise in her chest as she saw the plan unfold exactly as they had intended. Siobhan disarmed the mage with ease. Tarnelius had grabbed the staff and, even now, flapped toward them as fast as he could. She and Arcus both ran forward, spells on their lips. Storm clouds gathered overhead. Just as she was ready to begin her lightning assault, she saw something that caused her to stop in her tracks. Arcus slowed down but managed to continue moving at least. The storm clouds vanished as fast as they'd appeared.

As Arcus and Celeste watched, Tarryn seemed to stretch and expand. A long black tail emerged, ripping the white robes to shreds. The tail thrashed from side to side, knocking over several shocked knights and dislodging Siobhan from Apollo. Still he continued to grow and grow. Huge horns sprouted from his head, which had expanded on his ever-lengthening neck. Massive black wings exploded from his back.

"Fall back!" Celeste screamed, as loud as she could. "Dragon! He's a freaking dragon! Get out of there, Siobhan. We can't hope to win. It's Tarextros!" Tarnelius dropped the staff and shifted back in midair as he was landing next to her.

Siobhan heard none of what she said; she was staring at the dragon. Knowing she was about to die, she dismissed Apollo from the fight, raised her sword high in the air, and ran toward the onyx dragon.

The great beast swiped at her with one of his massive claws, knocking her down and opening a bloody gash from her chest to her abdomen. The claw easily rent through her mithril armor. She fell to the ground, but still grasped her sword in defiance.

"You foolish girl. You cannot stop me. Death himself once feared my presence. I no longer need the staff anyway, nor do I need any of these knights. Liam is the only one that I need, and he is safely on the other side, miles from here," the dragon's voice rumbled through the air.

Tarextros took a deep rattling breath and opened his massive jaw. A glimmering purple glow could be seen forming in the back of his throat, right before he lowered his head toward Siobhan and breathed blazing purple fire at her.

"No!" Arcus yelled as he hurriedly cast a spell on Siobhan. A large, green, glowing box appeared around her, shielding her from the dragonfire. Enraged, the dragon dropped onto the box and tried pulling it apart with his massive claws. "Get out of here. Head to our last camp," Arcus shouted to the elves.

Without waiting to see what they would do, he vanished from sight while the two elves stared in astonishment. A split second later, he reappeared inside the magical cage he had erected. He grabbed hold of Siobhan as best he could and the pair of them vanished, just as the dragon ripped apart the cage.

Celeste and Tarnelius watched in horror as Tarextros laid waste to the paladin army. Every instinct told them to run as the dragonfear rolled over them, but still they stayed and watched with morbid fascination. Most of the men were running and trying to find a place to hide. A couple of them turned to try to fight him. It didn't matter what they did; the carnage was horrible. The dragon breathed fire on many, sent many more flying with a simple snap of his tail, crushed some, and simply ate others whole. There was no escape.

"I need to talk to Axistra," whispered Celeste.

"How?"

"I have a way. Let's get back to Arcus. You can see if he needs help while I contact Axistra."

The two turned into their eagle and hawk forms and sped back to the south as fast as they could, the staff held between them in their claws.

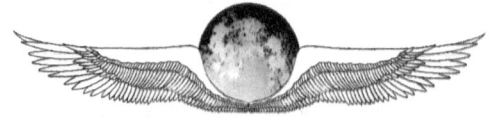

Arcus and Siobhan appeared back where they had spent the previous night. He lowered her gently to the ground, and assessed the damage.

"Hang on, Siobhan. I've got you."

"Arcus?" Siobhan asked, in a weak voice.

He ripped the armor off her as fast as he could, cutting himself on the sharp edges without even noticing.

"Arcus," she said again.

"Yes?"

"You saved me," she finished.

He reached out and began to heal her, trying to seal the huge gash.

"How could I not?"

"You came for me, even though I was about to be eaten by a dragon."

"Of course I did." He continued healing her.

She grasped his hands with her own, placing them on her belly. Her arms glowed bright gold, her holy symbol flashed. The gold merged with the blue of his hands and together they finished patching her up.

"You really love me, don't you?"

"I said I did. You didn't believe me?"

"Saying it is one thing, showing it is another." She sat up slowly, wincing in remembered pain more than existing discomfort.

"Does it still hurt? I'll keep going."

"No, it's fine. I'm fine, thanks to you." She leaned forward and kissed him. "I thought I was staring at my death. I never thought you would risk your own life just to save mine. I never expected there to be any way to save me." She laughed a little. "For the moment, anyway. Soon, we'll all be dead."

"Probably."

"I mean, a dragon? How can we possibly defeat a dragon?"

Arcus didn't answer; he just gripped her hand. Around an hour later, the two birds flew in, the staff gripped between them. They dropped it and shifted back, breathing heavily.

Tarnelius looked at the two humans in concern. "You both okay?"

"For the moment," answered Arcus.

"Okay, I'm going to contact Axistra. We can't possibly be expected to do this alone now. I don't know what will happen, but from what she told me, I had to do this from a safe place. If anything happens, I won't be able to help."

With that, she smashed the stone on the ring Axistra had given her during her dream.

The world went black.

When her vision cleared, Celeste found herself back in Axistra's audience chamber in her castle in the clouds. She felt confused and disoriented as she gazed upon Axistra, noticing none of the fear she felt when she was normally in the dragon's presence.

"Axistra," Celeste said, to gain her attention.

The dragon's head snapped around to locate Celeste. She stood up on her massive legs and spread her wings.

"Celeste, I hoped that you wouldn't have need of me. I assume the fact you are here means bad news. Has Liam reached the seal?"

"Not yet, but no doubt he will sometime very soon. Axistra, Tarextros is there!"

"What?"

"It's true, I saw him myself. He just killed most of Liam's delegation."

"Impossible. I would have sensed him with Liam. I have checked. He is in his volcano in the south."

"Search my memories or look for him now. He somehow had Raziyl's staff; that's why you didn't know. We have it now, but I worry it's too little and too late."

Axistra's eyes began to glow an even brighter blue than normal as she stared at Celeste, viewing her memories.

"Axistra, I have to get back to the others. I have no idea if he is looking for them. What do we need to do?"

"Yes, you need to go back. Pursue Liam. Tarextros is no fool. If he thinks Liam has the power to open the seal, then he does. He won't change forms again if Liam is nearby; he'd risk not being able to get in. Stall him, help is on the way."

"Th –"

The world went black again.

"– ank you," Celeste said as she came back to her own body in the snow.

The others were all staring at her.

"Axistra is coming," Celeste said simply.

They all cheered. Celeste told them what had been said so they could plan what to do next.

"So, we are to go back there and chase after a fool and a dragon on *purpose*?" Arcus asked, incredulous.

"Axistra seemed sure that Tarextros will not reveal himself again until the seal is opened. He cannot risk losing Liam."

"I still don't get what Liam will do to open the seal in the first place," grumbled Siobhan.

"Tarextros obviously knows, or he wouldn't go to this much effort," said Celeste.

"I guess that's true. So I suppose we should get going. Do you feel up to traveling, Siobhan?" Tarnelius asked.

"Yes, I'm fine. Arcus fixed me up. Only thing is, how are we going to get across the channel? We have no boat and, unlike you, I can't fly."

"That reminds me. When did you learn to teleport, Arcus?" Celeste asked.

"It's one of the spells I've been studying in my book, actually. So was the magic cage. I'm really glad they worked; I hadn't tried them before."

"You and me both," Siobhan said with a grin.

"So, can you teleport across the channel?" Celeste asked.

"No, I have to be familiar with the area or the spell won't work."

They all thought for a moment.

"We could fly overhead and land. I could take a good look around and teleport back to get you," said Arcus.

Celeste flexed her fingers inside her gloves, trying to maintain circulation. "That could work. Can you teleport more than one person at a time? That way we don't have to leave her unguarded."

"What's that supposed to mean?" Siobhan interjected.

"Only as much as I can carry, so no. Wait. Yes, I can, if you guys are shifted into something small, like birds."

Celeste nodded. "That will work. Why don't you two men go and take a look around, and teleport back when you are done?"

"Let me take a look at this staff first," said Arcus. He walked over to it and lifted it into the air. Nothing happened; the crystal at the top remained dark.

"Is it broken?" Siobhan asked.

"No, I just don't know how to activate it." Arcus tried several command words in the language of magic, but to no avail. After he exhausted all his ideas several minutes later, he finally gave up and handed Celeste the staff.

"You think I will have better luck?"

"No, I think you are the one with the magic bag. Come on, Tarnelius, let's go."

The two men leaned over to kiss their women goodbye, and then shifted and flew off, soaring high into the sky to reach the air thermals and increase their speed.

They soared over the battle site and marveled at the carnage. The once white snow was covered in sparkling red blood. The large wagon that once pulled the boat had been burned away, leaving a huge melted crater in the thick snow. There were bodies of horses and men strewn everywhere, left to rot. Some were in horrible disfigured positions, others had been scorched away, leaving nothing but partially exposed skeletons.

The dragon was nowhere to be seen.

The two birds circled around a couple of times and then continued north, over the channel. Crossing it took almost half an hour even at the speeds they were travelling.

The pair landed on the other side and looked around to make sure no one was around before shifting back. They shivered in the freezing temperatures and pulled their hoods down farther over their faces.

"Remind me to get Celeste to cast her cold protection spell on all of us later. It was so much better while that was working. I think I've been spoiled," said Tarnelius.

"Definitely. I had no idea anything could be this cold. Should we go get the women and bring them here, or keep going until we find the ruins, do you think?"

"Let's keep going. Maybe we can find Liam."

"I say if we find Liam, we should just kill him. He can't open the seal if he's dead. Much less bother," said Arcus as he shivered.

"Don't tempt me."

They shifted back into snowy owls and took off, heading for the ruins. The temperature dropped even further, the nearer they drew to it. Soon, they were trying to fly through a thick blizzard. The pair flew right above Liam and Tarryn, as well as about twenty knights that were with them. They were trying to pick their way through the snow, but it was so thick and powdery that walking was difficult. The two kept flying, finally approaching the ruins, which were situated on a hill. They circled around the old castle, scoping out the area. The castle seemed to have fallen in on itself, and the top was barely recognizable as having once been a castle. Gray steam rose from the structure, high into the sky. Any snow that entered the steam melted away instantly. Ice floes branched out from the castle walls.

The pair flew up to the collapsed roof, and landed on the wreckage. The brickwork was unnaturally warm, given the current climate. The inside of the castle was shining, like it was wet. The top floor had either collapsed or rotted through, but the debris was gathered on the bottom floor. The two owls hopped from the wall and flew down inside. In the floor of the main room, stationed in front of the front door, was a circular raised dais bearing an image of a knight wielding both a holy symbol and a winged sword. Magic pulsed from it, creating the heat that warmed the castle and melted the snow. On the north side of the room was an ornate stone altar to Melek, still standing proud after all this time. The engraving on the altar read, "You never fight alone."

They flew back out through the roof and landed on the south side. Arcus shifted back, so he could thoroughly examine the area. The cold was even more biting now that they had been warm, almost seeming to punish them. Snow covered Arcus' clothes and hair. When he was satisfied with his mental image of the area, he gestured for Tarnelius, who landed on his shoulder, and together they teleported back to the camp.

"So what is the general plan? Do we even *have* a general plan?"

Celeste shrugged her shoulders and brought the heavy blanket she was huddled under closer to her chin. "I have no idea. 'Stall them,' were my instructions. How are we to stall a dragon?"

"And for how long?" Siobhan finished.

"Exactly. I guess we'll just wing it. If it's our destiny to die, then we will. At least we'll know we tried. If we do nothing, we'll die soon enough, anyway. Regardless, I don't see how any plan of attack could work. We're just going to have to keep them talking, and try to prevent them from reaching the seal."

The two sat in silence for a while longer, contemplating their futures.

"I always thought, deep down, that this would be easy," mused Celeste. "That there was no way we could fail. I never thought there would be a dragon involved in destroying the world. I should have. I'd asked Axistra about it early on, but I never really believed it to be possible."

"We will win. I can feel it."

"How on earth can you feel that?" Celeste asked, incredulous. "You were almost roasted and eaten today."

"Yes, but I wasn't. I feel stronger than I have ever been. I feel...happy. You know, he changed *my* destiny in there by coming for me, right at the feet of that monster. I've never known anyone that would do that for someone before."

"Who are you? This doesn't sound like the Siobhan we've come to know."

"Almost getting killed changes one's outlook, I suppose."

"I guess that's true. Tarnel almost dying caused me to change my mind about bonding with him while on the road."

"See?"

They fell back into a companionable silence.

After almost an hour, Siobhan looked to her broken armor. "It's a shame about that. I've had that armor forever; it's like my second skin. It's been in my family for generations."

Celeste stood up, wrapped her blanket around her shoulders, and walked over to it. She picked it up and examined the broken pieces. "Yeah, this is some serious damage to the breastplate and whatever this part is called."

"That's the plackart."

"Okay, the plackart. Anyway, I don't know enough about metal working to try to fix it. Though, after this is over, my people may be able to fix it for you. They love working on magical items. Oh, actually, ask Tarnel when he gets back; he would have a better idea."

The pair continued to wait patiently, until Arcus reappeared with Tarnelius on his shoulder. They were covered head to toe in snowflakes, and Arcus was shivering heavily.

Celeste's eyes widened, and she yanked her blanket off her shoulders and placed it over Arcus. Then she grabbed Siobhan's from her outstretched hand and wrapped that around him too. Tarnelius shook the snow off his feathers and shifted back.

"There's a blizzard on the other side of the channel," Tarnelius said, after he had gained control of his vocal chords from shifting.

Arcus continued to shiver. "We will need some of that cold protection when we go through there, for sure. Though, on the plus side, the inside of the ruins is quite warm. We saw what's left of the paladins. Looks like it's just Liam, Tarryn and about twenty men. Judging by the difficulty they were having with walking through the snow, it will probably take them a couple of hours."

"I wonder what the story was for what happened to the rest," mused Celeste.

"My guess? That *we* killed them," said Arcus.

"Did he even see all of us?"

"Doesn't matter; he saw Siobhan, and while we might not be linked to her, he got a good look at me when I teleported in. At least, there is a good chance he did. While we are on the subject, can we just kill Liam? It really will make things easier."

"No," Siobhan and Celeste said together.

"Why not?"

"Because we aren't murderers." Celeste stood up and gestured to Tarnelius. "Do you think this armor is salvageable? Should I bother keeping it for her?"

"I think we could be murderers for the sake of the whole world," argued Arcus, while Tarnelius went to examine Siobhan's armor.

"So, it's all right for us to murder Liam, but not all right for him to destroy the evil races? What is the difference?" Siobhan asked.

Tarnelius gave a low whistle as he took in the damage to the armor.

"First of all, if he wants to destroy the orcs, I have no problems, remember? Just not by destroying the rest of the world in the process. Next, with Liam gone, there is no one here who can open the seal."

"No one except me, anyway."

"I think I can mend it enough so it's at least wearable *now*. It won't be as strong as usual, but it will do. I have no doubt that either the dwarves or the elves could fix this, though. Shall I try fixing it now, or would you rather wait?"

"Well, *you* aren't going to open the seal anyway, so that is a moot point," said Arcus.

"Yeah, but do you think he won't come after me and try to force me if you take away his pawn? He's a freaking dragon. I have no doubt he would find a way. Who do you think would be easier to stop if it came down to it, him or me? We need to keep Liam alive as long as possible, and besides that, I won't be a murderer. I would lose Mithra's power and Apollo if I did. Plus, you promised you'd be what I need, and I definitely do not need you to be a murderer. *Again.*"

Tarnelius watched them for a moment, and wondered if he was going to get an answer on the armor. Finally, he decided to just get to work fixing it.

"That was fighting dirty," Arcus grumbled.

Siobhan smiled at him and stood up to give him a kiss on the cheek. "But you know I am right."

Tarnelius finished casting his spell on the armor. "Finished!"

"You fixed it?" Siobhan asked. "Thank you so much."

"Like I was saying, it's nowhere near as strong as it was, so be careful. It can definitely be reinforced and made to be as good as new after this is over. This material is really quite easy to work with."

Arcus helped Siobhan fasten her armor back in place. "There you go, all better. Are we ready?"

The others all nodded.

"No we aren't. Celeste, cold protection, please," said Arcus.

Celeste quickly cast the spells to protect each of them from the elements, and then Celeste and Tarnelius shifted into owls. They flew up to land on Arcus' shoulders, he grabbed hold of Siobhan, and they all teleported back to the ruins.

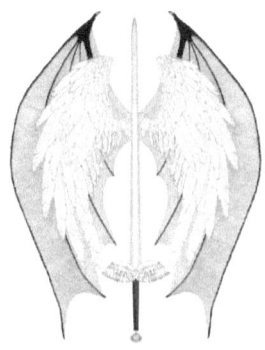

Chapter Thirty-One
Broken Oaths

The group reappeared on the south side of the ruins. The wind was whipping the snow around, making visibility difficult.

"Where's the seal?" Siobhan asked.

"Inside the castle, on the other side of the front door. You can get there from the roof access, or by just opening the door, assuming it still opens."

Celeste approached the front door and touched the handle. Just like the temple door in Lumernia, this one swung open easily for her. She stepped inside, the others following close behind her.

As Arcus had described, the interior of the castle was pleasantly warm, despite the lack of roof. Celeste approached the dais and examined it. Her eyes widened.

"That's Melek's sword," she said.

"Looks like a picture," commented Siobhan.

"It does, but if you concentrate on it, you can see it come into focus. This is some sort of illusion magic. The sword is right there, waiting to be grabbed. Probably the way it works is that someone has to channel holy energy into the platform to release the enchantment enough to grab the sword."

"The sword is the key," said Tarnelius.

"Knowing the way Melek worked, I would bet that the sword would only relinquish itself to the same person that channeled their holy power. In other words, Liam will have to channel power and then he himself will have to grab the sword. That's only a guess and I may be wrong, but that's my thought. It recognizes the one that frees it."

"That makes sense based on the picture, too," said Siobhan. "The paladin is wielding both at once."

"Thank you for figuring that out for us, though I already suspected all of that. Please step away. We'll take it from here," came a snarling voice at the door.

The four of them all jumped in surprise. They looked up to see Tarextros, in his human disguise, and the rest of the knights filing in the door.

"What's the matter? Didn't expect me so soon? Well, I saw the two of *you* flying overhead and knew I needed to speed things along. It's really a simple matter to clear away the snow."

"Where's Liam?" Celeste asked.

"Don't you worry your little head about Liam, my mongrel friend. I'm keeping him safe from the likes of you. I won't let you murder him, like you did the others. Men, attack," he snarled to the knights, who drew their swords.

"Don't listen to him. He's an evil dragon," yelled Celeste, as the men all charged as commanded. Tarnelius and Siobhan drew their weapons and took defensive stances.

Tarnelius' swords flashed as he parried and thrust, spinning around to deflect attacks from all sides. Siobhan combined her holy magic with her sword, and she focused on disarming as many of the knights as she could. She sent her current opponent's weapon flying across the room before shouting to her friends, "Look into their eyes; they are not themselves. I think the dragon is controlling them."

"Try not to kill them, if possible," commanded Celeste.

Arcus pointed to a group of five knights who were trying to retrieve their swords, *"All of you, stop moving."* The entire group froze in place.

Celeste nocked her bow and shot an arrow into a knight's leg. Ice travelled up and down, freezing him in place. He howled in pain. Celeste calmly drew back another arrow and shot another in the leg. She screamed in pain as she was stabbed in the back. The knight withdrew his sword and went for another attack, but Arcus was too quick for him and zapped him in the face with electricity.

Tarnelius continued to parry blow after blow, struggling not to attack outright. Siobhan was doing the same, and still she knocked weapon after weapon from the knights.

"I was wrong; it actually looks like most of them are possessed. I can see the evil taint, now that I've had a better look," Siobhan added.

Arcus seemed to be moving much faster than normal. "I'm done with this. Try to get them into the corner, by the others," he yelled.

Tarnelius and Siobhan redoubled their efforts to push the knights back the way he said. Celeste looked around to find Tarextros, but he had vanished. She shot another in the leg, watching with satisfaction as he froze in place.

Arcus cast a spell toward the possessed knights. A small bead of fire shot from his finger and vanished near them. "Get as far away from that corner as quick as you can," he yelled.

"Not you, though," he said to the enemy paladins, who still struggled in the corner. *"All of you, stop moving now."*

They froze in place and, a few seconds later, a fiery explosion rocked the castle from the point where the small bead of fire had vanished, bringing down the far wall near the knights.

"Take cover," shouted Siobhan. Bricks and various rubble crashed down all around them. The group ran back to the opposite side of the large room, trying to dodge the falling structure.

"All right, Arcus, exploding the unstable structure is a bad plan," Tarnelius yelled as he ran.

"I was jealous of all the fun Celeste has had destroying buildings. What can I say?"

Before the dust had even settled, another loud explosion shook the foundations of the ancient fortress. The group dove for cover underneath a large section of wall that had fallen, holding it up to prevent more rocks from crushing them.

Siobhan backed up to peek over the wall to see what was going on. "The dragon is back. He's destroying the building." She ducked back down to join the rest in holding up the wall.

"My gods, what have I done?" Liam's voice rang out. "I trusted you all along, and all along you were this? How? You – You trained me to be a paladin!"

"Get the sword, your majesty," gasped a nearby knight. He was one of the knights that had been shot by Celeste, and his leg was still frozen over. From the sound of him, he was near death. "Get the sword. With the sword you can defeat him."

"No, Liam! Do *not* grab the sword. We will find another way," screamed Celeste.

Liam stood there, torn with indecision. The dragon roared and breathed a huge cloud of purple fire into the air. His massive wings stretched out, and his tail struck another small part of the castle that was still standing. The cold began to overtake the warm air that had previously been held inside the castle, though the seal still pulsed with warmth.

Liam knelt down and held his hands up in the air. "Great Rashnu, use me as your vessel. Help me to defeat this great evil. I had no idea what I was doing. Forgive me, please." He held up his symbol with the golden scales and channeled Rashnu's holy power.

"No!" All four of them jumped away from the wall they were using as a shield and lunged for Liam. Arcus shot lightning at him, but the dais itself seemed to block the magic. The rest were running for him when he reached down and grasped Melek's sword, withdrawing it from the dais.

The dragon began to laugh, a deep, evil laugh. Celeste reached Liam first and tackled him to the ground.

"What have you done?" Celeste shrieked at him.

"Let me up. I'm trying to save us, you fool."

"You've doomed us all!"

A great rumbling sound shook the ground beneath them. Celeste's eyes widened and she jumped to her feet to get away. Siobhan, Arcus and Tarnelius were quick to run after her.

Liam stood up and lifted the winged sword high in the air. "I will slay you, evil wyrm. Though I may die, I must make restitution for –"

He was cut off as a massive, smoke-gray hand reached from inside the dais and grasped Liam, squeezing him tightly and dragging him inside the platform. Liam didn't make another sound, not even to scream. The sword fell to the ground with a clatter.

Celeste rushed for it, releasing her wings and grabbing it. She rose into the air, brandishing the sword at the dragon.

"You foolish mongrel. You cannot hope to defeat me now," the dragon boomed.

"Defeating you is my only hope," she said. "We are all doomed to death anyway, so the best I can do is take you with me. It's my destiny."

The other three ran out into the snow toward the dragon, brandishing sword and magic. Tarextros breathed another huge cloud of fire at Celeste, but she darted away to safety. He stood on his hind legs and grabbed at her, but again he missed. Celeste never saw the long tail snapping at her from behind, though, and she was knocked through the air under its great weight. She fell from the sky still gripping the sword, and the dragon was quick to drop down his clawed hand to crush her and pin her in place. With the last of her strength, she raised the sword above her so that his hand came down right on top of it. Tarnelius cried out in agony, as he felt Celeste's pain through their link.

Tarextros roared from the pain the sword inflicted. He shook his forearm and tried to dislodge it. He thrashed and bellowed, as he knocked Celeste away and into the wreckage. He was so caught up in the sword that was stuck in his arm, he never noticed the silver clad elf and human dressed in sparkling gold that appeared out of nowhere.

Siobhan and Tarnelius slashed at the dragon's legs, trying their best to avoid getting crushed in the process. Arcus fired off spell after spell, but nothing seemed to penetrate the dragon's thick scales. None of them noticed the two newcomers, either.

Tarextros finally dislodged Melek's sword and flung it away from him. Already, he felt weaker from the sword's effects.

"Grab the sword, paladin," yelled the elf. She was dressed head to toe in silver, and had silver hair and blue eyes.

The human, who was dressed head to toe in gold, with golden blond hair and green eyes, began to shift. He grew larger and larger, sprouting a tail and massive wings. Just like Tarextros, his neck elongated and his head grew massive. His scales were a gleaming gold, and looking directly at him was like staring at the sun.

"You've broken your oath, brother," the gold dragon said.

"It doesn't matter, Aanhextrios. The only oaths that matter now are the new ones that my master and I will make together."

A dark gray, shadowy figure, larger than any of the dragons, rose from the floor beneath the dais. The lower half of his body was the shape of a dragon, while his upper body was almost human in shape. He had massive horns that extended from his head, like a demon's. His massive wings, which sprouted from his shoulders, blocked out the setting sun. The god raised his arms in triumph, and gazed out upon the world with eyes that glowed an evil red color.

Aanhextrios looked at Kuunkierto's massive form, and lifted himself into the air. Roaring a battle cry, he rushed at Kuunkierto, only to be yanked back as Tarextros bit him on the neck. The two of them took to the air, fighting with magic, fire and claws. Dragon blood fell on the three mortals like rain.

Axistra hurried to transform into her dragon shape and flew into the newly awakened god, her force knocking him back only a small step. The dragon clawed and bit and slapped with her tail as best she could, but was flung from the sky and onto the ground.

Siobhan ran to find where the sword had landed, while Tarnelius hurried to find Celeste. Arcus chased after Siobhan, to help her find the sword.

Axistra recovered quickly and launched herself back at Kuunkierto, but again she was flung away like a rag doll with a mighty hit from the god's arm.

Tarnelius found Celeste lying on the ground, broken and bleeding. Both her wings were broken, as well as multiple other bones. She was barely alive and had gone into shock.

"Celeste, I am here with you. Don't die, Angel. We need you right now." He began healing her, setting her bones as he went, though it pained him to do so.

Siobhan and Arcus searched among the snow and rubble, but with only a vague idea how far the sword had flown, finding it in the snow seemed a monumental task.

Aanhextrios and Tarextros fought in the air, tumbling through the skies. Tarextros bit his brother again on the back of the neck, rending his claws down the gold dragon's back. He roared and flipped his body around, shoving Tarextros with all his strength. Once free, Aanhextrios breathed golden fire at his foe, and snapped at him with his tail. The flames caught Tarextros full in the face, and he roared in agony, before snarling a word of magic. A massive hand formed around the gold dragon, squeezing. He began to fall from the sky, struggling and casting counter spells. He broke free of the spell but didn't manage to stop his fall in time. He crashed to the ground. Aanhextrios rolled onto his feet and rose back into the sky, casting his own attack spell.

Huge fiery meteors rained down from the heavens, and hurtled toward Tarextros. He tried to escape, but the meteors were too fast and too big. They crashed into him, knocking him from the sky. One of the meteors caught him in his left wing, burning and ripping through the leathery membrane. He roared in pain as he fell heavily to the ground, more meteors falling around him. When they stopped, Aanhextrios leapt atop him, grabbing his head and ripping it back. His claws made huge gouges across the black dragon's wings and back. Finally he cast another spell, and Tarextros turned to solid stone. With a mighty swing of his tail and a triumphant roar, he broke the Tarextros statue into pieces.

Axistra fought the great evil that had emerged from behind the dais for all she was worth, but didn't seem to be having much effect. She cast fire spells and lightning. She tried the meteor spell that Aanhextrios had used. Nothing seemed to do much to slow him down. Wherever Kuunkierto stepped, the snow melted, and was replaced by crumbling black and brown rock. Everywhere he had been seemed darker than before, as if the world was dying around him. The massive dragon seemed only an annoyance to him as he stretched his wings and took in the outside world.

Arcus shouted in triumph as he grabbed Melek's sword. He tossed it to Siobhan, and the two of them ran toward Kuunkierto. Siobhan brandished the sword, bringing it down into the god's foot. He kicked at her as he walked, and she flew through the air, landing heavily, the wind knocked out of her.

Siobhan stood up and tried to gather her wits before running back. Arcus cast his lightning and his cold spells at Kuunkierto, but the god didn't even look at him. Siobhan hurried back with the sword, pausing when Axistra launched through the air, landing near her.

"Axistra, I have Melek's sword," she screamed. "Take it!"

The dragon was breathing heavily. She shook her head. "I can't," she gasped. "Only a paladin or angel may wield that sword. Or one of the paladin gods." Siobhan noticed Axistra's foreleg was bent at a horrible angle, obviously broken. She stood up and shook herself off, clearly in agony. Once more she launched herself at the evil god, latching on and attacking ferociously.

Having won his fight, Aanhextrios also launched himself onto the massive god. The pair of them managed to push Kuunkierto back a few steps. Working together seemed to have better results, and Kuunkierto was taking notice now. He stomped his foot on the ground, and the world rippled beneath him from the impact. Snow flew into the air and away. Craters formed where his foot struck. The ground began to take on the appearance of the moon's surface. The dragons were ripped from him by the vibrations and Arcus and Siobhan both lost their balance, falling to the shaking ground.

Ignoring the chaos, Tarnelius had managed to fix most of Celeste's broken bones, and now he was trying his best to wake her up. He reached deep into himself to find the place that was her.

"Come on, Celeste, come back to us."

"Tarnel?"

"Celeste!"

"Everything hurts," she said.

"I'm so sorry, Angel. I did my best to patch you up, but battlefield healing never seems to be as good. Celeste, they need us. Well, they need you, especially. We have to make things right."

"How, Tarnel? He's out, we're done."

"Well the dragons haven't given up, so neither should you." He stood up, lifting her into his arms so she could see.

"Dragons?" Celeste exclaimed as she took in the sight of the gold and silver dragons fighting Kuunkierto. "My gods, we may have a chance after all. Let me go."

She painfully took to the skies, flying toward the fight. Tarnelius ran after her as fast as he could.

She landed next to Siobhan, who had risen back to her feet and was hacking unsuccessfully at Kuunkierto's heel. Siobhan looked at her in shock. "Celeste, you're alive?"

"For the moment. Give me the sword."

Celeste grabbed the sword and returned to the air. Axistra flew backward through the air, trying to catch herself with her wings. She launched herself once more into the thick of it, knocking him back another couple of steps. Celeste flew between them, stabbing Kuunkierto hard in the chest. She recovered the sword and stabbed again, dodging his flailing arms as he tried to reach through the dragons to get to her. Finally she flew up in his face, driving the sword hard into his eye. Kuunkierto roared his pain and fury as he stumbled backward. Dark blood poured from the wound onto the ground. Magic sparked from him, sending lightning and dark blue flame hurtling into the heavens. As he fell back, flailing about in agony, he managed to pry the dragons off once more and he struck Celeste. They all flew from him, landing hard. Axistra landed hard on her wing, which broke under her weight. Axistra did not get up again, though she cried out in pain as she landed. Aanhextrios picked his broken and bleeding body up off the ground and prepared to launch himself at the god once more. Celeste did not make a sound or move at all after she was struck down. The sword fell from the god's eye and landed at Siobhan's feet.

Aanhextrios realized what he must do. "Be ready, paladin," screamed the gold dragon. He launched himself high into the air, way above the god's head. When he reached enough altitude, he dove down with all his strength, pleased to discover that Kuunkierto had been finally pushed back onto the dais. As he dove, he summoned his meteors, he dropped snow and ice spells, and he channeled as much of his power as he could manage downward, onto the god.

Seeing this, Arcus added his own ice spells, pummeling Kuunkierto with as much downward force as he could manage. Axistra screamed out the words to her spells, from her place on the ground, and also added her meteors. Aanhextrios collided hard with the god on his downward dive, forcing his claws into the god's weak point, his injured eye. Together, with all their combined magic, they forced him back down inside the dais. The gold dragon and Kuunkierto all vanished at once with a blinding flash of light.

"The sword, Siobhan!" Axistra shouted. "The portal remains open!"

Siobhan held the weapon high in the air, bringing it down with crushing force onto the seal. The sword merged with the picture, but instead of letting go, Siobhan kept pressing. The seal began to sink lower and lower into the ground, where it was soon covered by the earth itself. Finally, when she could no longer reach down to press it in any farther, and the seal itself could no longer be seen at all, she released the handle and struggled to pry her hand from the rock. Arcus hurried over to her and cast a spell, which turned the ground to mud. Once she was free, he patted the mud down to fill the hole and cast a counter spell, turning the ground into smooth, solid black rock that still resembled the moonscape.

The pair of them fell backward onto the ground, their breaths coming in heavy gasps.

"Is it really over?" Arcus breathed.

"I can't believe that worked," said Siobhan, incredulous.

Tarnelius was on the ground, cradling Celeste to his chest. Tears fell freely down his face onto hers. He lifted her into his arms and carried her to the others.

"Is she –?" Arcus couldn't bring himself to finish the sentence.

Tarnelius nodded without a word. He kissed the top of her head and walked to the altar he had seen at the north side of the building. By some miracle, it had remained intact. Rubble was strewn all around, but nothing had harmed it.

"You never fight alone," he choked out, as he laid her on the altar.

"Here lies the last herald of Melek," said Siobhan as she and Arcus followed him to the altar. "And the best. Your name will be sung in song and legend for generations to come, my friend."

Arcus couldn't think of anything to say at all, and merely stared at her body, laying lifeless and broken on the altar. There came a loud noise behind them, and Arcus and Siobhan whirled around.

Axistra was rising slowly to her feet. She shifted back into her elven form, crying out when her broken bones reset themselves as she shifted. When she had shrunk back down into a silver haired elf woman, she cast a healing spell on herself, and looked around at the wreckage.

"Axistra," breathed Siobhan. She hurried to the elf's side. "Axistra, can you do anything to help her?"

"I cannot bring her back. I'm sorry."

"Why not?" Tarnelius snarled as he spun around. "She died fighting *your* battle. Your battle that you should have fought yourself. She had no business here, fighting a dragon and a god. None of us did. Now I've lost her, so soon after finding her, and it's all *your* fault."

"I can merge her soul into another body, but it's complicated because you have half of her soul. She lives on in you even now."

"And half of me is dead; I can feel it. The best half, the half she carried."

"I'm sorry, Tarnelius, I wish I could change things. This was her destiny."

"No, her destiny was *with me*. To have forever with me. And now you have the nerve to tell me that you won't even try to save her."

Arcus approached his friend, and placed a hand on his shoulder. "I know it hurts, my friend. Maybe the dragon is right, though, and this was her destiny. If it was, don't take away from what she did by saying that it wasn't fulfilled. She saved the world; she and the gold dragon, and all of us. We saved the world, because of their sacrifices. If she hadn't stabbed him in the eye with Melek's sword when she did, things would have turned out very differently."

Tarnelius moaned in agony and turned back to the altar. He grasped her hand and clung to it.

"The snow is thawing. It will be a little while before this stuff dries enough, but would you like Siobhan and I to begin trying to find materials for her pyre, so that you don't have to?"

"I can help, also –" began Axistra, but she was abruptly interrupted by Tarnelius.

"You don't get to speak, dragon. You stay out of this moment. We do not need your help," he bit out, then he sighed. "It doesn't matter, Arcus. Once she is fully gone, sent on to the next stage of her journey, I will die too. I can feel it. I won't be leaving this place; there is nothing left for me here."

Siobhan watched the elf, her heart breaking for him. "Tarnelius, please don't say –"

"Let it go, Siobhan. Come on, let's give him some private time with Celeste. We'll go see what we can find."

Tarnelius knelt before the altar and stroked her cheek. He smoothed her hair out as best he could, and memorized every feature. He felt out of sorts. Half of himself had died, while half of her lived on inside him, even as he gazed at her dead body. He was hurting and confused, and didn't know how to move on. He didn't even know how to stand up, at this point. "I'll see you again soon, Angel. This won't be the end for us. If you can't come back to me, then I'll come to you. Don't worry."

Suddenly, he gasped in shock and scurried quickly away from the altar. Celeste had lifted into the air, and hovered as if someone was holding her there. Axistra hurried to his side, and also stared at Celeste in astonishment. Siobhan and Arcus also came racing back to see what was going on.

"What's happening?" Tarnelius demanded.

"You can't see him?" Axistra asked, incredulous.

"See who?"

"It's – it's her father. I can't believe it. This is impossible."

A brilliant light flashed from Celeste's body, originating from the red hawk pendant hanging from her neck. She began to breathe deeply, in and out. Color returned to her cheeks, and all the broken bones and abrasions were healed. After the light flashed, they could all make out the form of an angel, clutching Celeste to his chest as if she were a baby. His wings were fully extended and brushing the ground, and he had hair the same shade of black as hers.

"You never fight alone," he said. His voice was deep and echoed, as if it came from another plane. "My Celeste, I knew you could do it. I always knew you were destined for greatness. I couldn't be more proud of you." He set her back down on the altar with a smile and a nod to Tarnelius. "Take care of her, young man. This is not where her story, or yours, ends." Then, with another flash of light, he was gone.

Tarnelius rushed to her, lifting her in his arms.

She opened her eyes and smiled at him. "Tarnelius, I dreamed I saw my father. It was the most beautiful dream. I was in a strange world filled with light. There were heralds everywhere and everything sparkled and glowed. He said he was proud of me."

She brushed away his tears. "Why are you crying? Everything is fine now; he told me so."

"Yes, Angel. Everything is fine now."

He set her down and she took his hand, taking in the sight of her friends and Axistra. "What did I miss?"

"Well, Aanhextrios flung himself into the portal, dragging Kuunkierto with him. He sacrificed himself to save the world," said Axistra. "The cycle is broken. Everything is going to change. Normally, if one of us dies, we are reborn to the mortal races until we come of age and take our place as dragons again. It's rare, but it has happened to Khellendriox. If Aanhextrios is trapped down there, he may be gone forever, upsetting the balance."

"I'm not so sure that he *is* gone," said Arcus. He pointed to the sky. They all looked up to see the newly risen red moon shifting colors. It changed from its normal ghastly red color to a dark orange. From orange it changed to a bright yellow, and from there it became a beautiful gold color, triumphantly shedding light over the world.

"Does this mean what I think it means?" Celeste asked.

"Well, I'm not sure, but it sure looks like it means that Aanhextrios has become the moon," said Axistra with a huge grin.

"How is that possible?" Celeste asked. "How could he defeat Kuunkierto?"

"We may never know, but the evidence is in the sky."

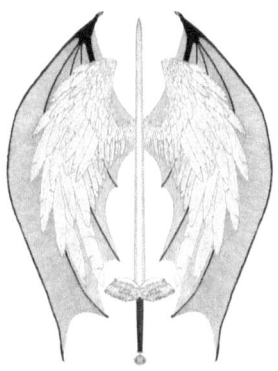

Epilogue
New Beginnings

The cold receded in the northern wastes, though despite the best efforts of the nature spirits, the plants would not reclaim the area. The land continued to look like a barren wasteland resembling a crater-filled moon.

Arcus teleported everyone back to Kayalost, where they were greeted with a lukewarm reception. Despite the evidence in the sky of what they had done, they found the world mostly unchanged. Tarnelius and Celeste soon realized that they felt like strangers there.

Arcus then took them to the Mithran Bridge at Siobhan's request, and accompanied her to her people. Ryan had explained what had happened to the best of his ability, making it clear he felt Siobhan had not abandoned them in Beinn-anbas at all. She was accepted back with open arms, and she and her friends were treated with honor. While they were there, she and Arcus got married in an official paladin wedding. Celeste learned how to perform their ceremony and gained permission from the Mithran council to officiate.

Arcus went through the paladins' library to read all he could on Raziyl, so he could learn to control the staff. He made plans to someday build a sorcerer school just outside Castle Mithra, where he could teach any with the gift. The first person he would extend his invitation to when the school was built would be Joseph, if he could find him, he decided. He hoped he might even find one or two talented enough to learn druid magic as well, combining them as he had.

Celeste and Tarnelius created their own forest near Castle Mithra so they could be close to their friends. Celeste used her magic to make the trees grow large overnight as if the forest had always been there. They built themselves a home and made plans to fly to Celeste's old forest to the north of the Nehir River to talk some of the animals into returning with them.

About ten months after Theri's death, they decided the time had come to seek out Theri's family to tell them what had happened to her. They packed up their travel gear and Arcus brought them all back to Izmar, so they could hire a ship to the south. They had no idea how to find her family, but felt it was important to at least try.

Meanwhile...

"Come quickly, Chika is going into labor!" Kwesi shouted to the shaman in excitement.

The shaman grabbed his herbs and remedies with a heavy heart. Chika should have given birth at least three months prior, but all attempts to induce her labor failed. He didn't see any way the pups could survive. He only hoped his friend survived, herself.

The pair hurried out into the night air. No matter how many times he had seen it in the last ten months, the old shaman could not get used to the golden moon shining in the sky every night. They arrived at her hut, drawing the curtain aside. Sure enough, the female tumasi was breathing heavily with the exertion of the contractions. The shaman began to prepare a poultice from the herbs he had placed in his leather skin bag, which he then slathered on the female's belly. He turned to light his various incense candles, and he'd no sooner lit the last one than Chika let out an ear-piercing screech. A scream of such complete agony, he was sure it would wake the dead from as far as three generations back. Then her scream cut off, the sound being replaced by a shrill whine of a newborn pup. The shaman grabbed up the child, shocked by how large he was. Poor Chika was lying in a pool of blood, a look of terror frozen on her dead face. The shaman hurriedly cut the cord and cleaned the infant's fur, trying not to look at Chika. At least the baby had survived; that was something.

"Maaa!" the baby cried, his strange golden eyes wide open. The shaman looked at him in bewilderment. Tumasi almost never had a litter of one, and their newborns couldn't even open their eyes, much less speak. Also, their kind never had eyes that color and shape, the pup's eyes almost looked reptilian and were the shade of molten gold – the same shade as the new moon. Young Kwesi whimpered, as he went to Chika and stroked the fur of her head. "Maaa!" the baby insisted. The shaman sighed, and placed the baby on the ground next to his mother, noticing as he put the baby down that he had a strange birthmark on the solid black fur of his back. It looked almost like a raised tattoo of bat wings that were folded to his back and sides.

The pup reached out a tiny hand and placed it on Chika's chest, which immediately started to rise and fall. Chika sat up with a loud, pain-filled gasp. She grabbed up her baby and cuddled him, breathing just one word, "Rextros."

The End.

<u>Appendix</u>

<u>Races</u>: There are six major races in the land of Altierra. Two born to each of the three original deities. While each race was created to reflect the principles of their creator, they were also granted free will and are able to decide whether to follow the principles of one of the others, if they so choose.

Elves: Children of the earth; guardians of Altierra. Elves have taken up Kamara's cause after the fall. They, above all other races, have learned to tap into the powers of the earth released after the death of the neutral demigods. Their great lifespan and wariness of the other races has made many grow apathetic. Elves never age and are considered immortal. However, after several hundred years, some of them seem to lose their will to live. When this happens, they become more and more tired and withdraw into themselves, eventually falling asleep and never waking up again. This is called "being lost to the Fade." Still, elves' great memory and skill support their task as protectors of Altierra. Elves all have large, otherworldly, green eyes, with hair color in varying shades of blond.

Elves inhabit forested areas. There are large villages in the Kayalik Mountains, as well as the Silver Isles. There is also a smaller village on the southern continent.

Many elves are forced into arranged marriages. They are ruled by customs and traditions, which dictates proper elven decorum. They tend towards formality, and as such do not often have intimate relationships unless they are married, which they call being bonded. The bonding ceremony is a ritual that, when complete, binds the two together, forever. Each of their souls is split and shared with the other. They then gain telepathy in regards to each other, as well as the ability to experience one another's emotions, and to always know how to locate their mate. If one is killed, the other is usually not far behind, as they lose half of themselves at the same time.

Dark Elves are another of Kamara's children, though they prefer to live underground. Unlike their cousins, their skin is dark in color, and they have bright red eyes. They are able to see in the dark as if it were as bright as day, and due to this, have difficulty with the brightness of the outdoors.

Dwarves: Some call them Kamara's prodigal sons, because they seem to care nothing for nature. Dwarves seek to be left to themselves as they delve and tinker in their mines. Their greatest joy is creation and construction. Unfortunately, this leads them to build only for the sake of building, while they ignore the consequences of their actions. Many a great dwarven discovery has been tainted by evil and found its way into the arsenal of the orc hordes. Most dwarves tend toward agoraphobia, making them uncomfortable outside of their mountain homes.

Humans: These possess the most diversity of any race, and have founded cities and villages throughout most of Altierra. They show great drive and curiosity, exploring and settling as they go. Despite being children of Aurinko, they can also be strongly influenced by Kuunkierto, and as such have a great capacity for evil. Humanity's greatest flaw is their propensity for arrogance, so even the greatest armies of good can unwittingly cause great evil. Humans vary widely in appearance and can adapt to perform any profession or skill.

Kedistam: The kedistam resemble the larger feline species in bipedal form. They call themselves Aurinko's firstborn. Kedistam are noble yet savage. They prefer a simpler life on the southern continent in jungle villages, and as desert nomads. They are wild but not cruel, and show kindness and mercy unless crossed. Many embrace the path of druid or shaman and count the elves as allies.

Tumasi: Where orcs are wild and savage, tumasi are cunning and organized. They, too, crave power, though they also respect order. They know their place in the great pack, but work and scheme to improve their station. A small number of them are able to see the strength of good, and to that end, seek peace and order. Tumasi mainly dwell on the southern continent. They resemble bipedal forms of the various canid species: wolves, jackals, or foxes.

Orcs: The hordes can be chaos incarnate. The orc nation seeks power that brings misery to all they conquer. Unfortunately for them, their chaotic nature tends to tear down any progress they make as tribes fight for power within the horde. The one thing orcs recognize is strength, and they even respect natural forces. This has allowed the druids to easily keep them in check and out of their woods. Orcs mostly inhabit the southeast desert areas.

Classes:

Druids: Those blessed by Kamara, or any of her children, with nature magic are known as druids. They are the primary healers that still remain in Altierra. Most druids are elves, as they are the race most likely to follow the path of nature and balance, though they may be found among any race. Their spells mostly channel through them in natural colors such as blues and greens. They wear very little armor, as metal separates them from their communion with the earth. Many do not bother to carry, or learn how to use, weaponry. Often, they will choose an animal to accompany them, as they are able to speak to them through telepathy. Druids are shape-shifters; they can take the form of animals or, in some cases, plants. Their magic encompasses the power of nature, allowing them to control the weather, wield natural elements, as well as heal others.

Paladins: True paladins are rare. These are holy warriors serving the memory of one of four paladin deities. Once they have completed a lengthy training period, they are knighted and gain powers granted to them by the essences of their gods. They wear heavy armor and are expert swordsmen. In addition, they are gifted the ability to channel holy power through the symbol of their deity, which they wear around their neck. They have the ability to use healing and protection magic, which shows as a flashy gold or silver color when channeled. However, in most cases, they do not have to cast; the magic just flows out of them as they will it. When they are knighted they receive an intelligent magical steed from the celestial realms to serve as their companion. As time goes on, this animal becomes even more powerful.

If a paladin knowingly commits any act of evil or behaves in a way that would go against the laws of their deity, they lose their steed and their magical abilities immediately. They then become warriors.

Warriors: These are a very diverse group. They are often trained in the use of many different weapons and armors. Some warriors take an intellectual view on their training, wishing to learn many different styles of combat. Others become warriors out of necessity, and as such are more inclined to learn as they go. Many are strong, using their brute strength to overpower their enemies, while others make up for lack of strength with grace and finesse. They do not wield magic of any type.

Many warriors are "false paladins." These men and women call themselves paladins, and in fact, think they are paladins. However, they do not uphold the laws of the paladin deities and have no magical abilities at all.

Sorcerers: Wielders of arcane magic, all sorcerers have been blessed by the dragons. This is not a class someone could learn merely by studying; the mage must be born with the ability. Once the sorcerer comes of age, the powers begin to manifest. This is the time when a sorcerer is able to tell what kind of magic they naturally specialize in. Some are seers, and are especially skilled in divinations. Others wield elemental magic, compulsions, enchantments, or necromancy. Once the mage becomes aware of his or her abilities, it is important that they become trained in its use. An untrained sorcerer is dangerous to themselves and others, as their magic becomes wild, prone to unpredictability during times of emotional duress.

Once the mage begins training, they are able to memorize a certain number of spells. Although the kind they specialize in will always be more powerful, they are able to learn spells of other types if they so choose.

There are a few mages that do not permanently memorize spells, but instead read books daily to learn spells. Each day they have to reread them and relearn them, even if they knew them the day before. This has an advantage in that they can cast a broader range of spells from day to day, but limits them in that they actually must take the time to learn every day or they cannot cast at all.

Sorcerers rarely carry weapons other than staves. They also may carry a dagger, which is easily concealed beneath their clothes. They do not wear armor, as it limits their freedom of movement, making the intricate movements required for casting more difficult.

Scouts: Those that choose the path of the scout are masters of stealth and expert skirmishers. They know where and how to strike to have the most effect. They are usually dexterous, and are able to reach their opponent's vulnerable areas with skillful use of acrobatics. They are excellent trackers and can find and disable traps with ease. They only wear light armor and are often proficient in the lighter weapons.

Rangers: Like scouts, rangers are expert trackers. They specialize in either archery or by learning to fight with weapons in both hands. They are stealthy and skilled at blending into their surroundings, unseen and unheard, making them excellent hunters. Rangers are at home with nature, just as druids are, and often create bonds of friendship with a companion animal in the same manner. They train extensively on learning the weak points of particular, oft seen, types of enemies, and are skilled at defeating them.

Clerics: True clerics are very rare in Altierra, though there are many charlatans who will try to trick the populace into believing their fake herbs and potions will help them. True clerics have been blessed by the remaining essences of the gods that once ruled over the land. Like paladins, they channel healing power and protections magic through a pendant bearing their chosen deity's symbol. Their spells are more powerful than a paladin's, but they lack the combat training. Because of this, they tend to use simpler weapons, but can wear pretty much any kind of armor.

Cyfuniad: This is the newest class in Altierra. Cyfuniads are sorcerers that are able to blend their arcane power with the divine power of a druid. In order to manage to balance both aspects, the spellcaster must be highly adept in both trades. They continue to learn both kinds of magic as they go, and eventually learn to merge them both seamlessly, casting arcane spells while in an animal form, for example.

Deities:

The Three: Altierra, and the heavens above, were conceived by the Three. First, they made the Great Dragons and the demigods. Then, they formed the land, sea, and the stars in the sky. In the twilight of the world, the Three brought forth their favored races: Aurinko created humans and kedistam, Kamara made elves and dwarves, and Kuunkierto, the orcs and tumasi. They then joined with their creation and left the lesser gods to finish their work.

Aurinko: Greater god of order, light, and good. He was said to become the sun and bring light to the world.

Kamara: Greater goddess of nature, balance, and neutrality. She joined with Altierra and became the very land itself.

Kuunkierto: Greater god of the night, darkness, and evil. He became the moon to rule over the darkness.

Demigods: Other than the dragons, the demigods were the first children of the Three. Each one reflects an aspect of their god and was granted immense power. The demigods in turn helped complete Altierra and governed it before the war. They and their heralds were physically in the world and dwelt with the children of the Three. Many even brought forth other lesser races in an attempt to mimic the Three's creation. Most demigods do not use arcane magic, these being powers of the dragons. They have their own divine powers and can grant energies to their followers. Few true devotees of the gods remain in Altierra, and as such a true cleric or divine paladin is a strange sight.

When Kuunkierto returned to the world, his first strikes were against Kamara's children. Most fell before any organized resistance could be mustered, which kept them from allying with the armies of good. Tulpar and Demirei were able to rally with the followers of Aurinko, and together they were finally able to defeat Kuunkierto and his minions. After the war, the remaining deities left the world, making a pact to leave the mortals to forge their own destinies. Heralds could still intercede between mortals, and devotees could worship and possibly gain powers, but they would no longer directly interfere with the world. As time passed, the gods became more legend than memory to the shorter lived races, and very few truly devote themselves to their service. As the elves are the only race long lived enough to remember the gods, most others have forgotten and divine power is mostly thought of as myth in everyday life. Most elders of the various churches are not truly clerics and have no powers granted.

Followers of Aurinko:

Rashnu: The greater paladin god of justice, discipline and light. Chief of good demigods and allied closely with Mithra and Sarosh. Appeared as a king in full armor, with his rod of lordship and judgment scales. His followers were humans, paladins, knights and judges.

Mithra: She was the paladin goddess of honor, loyalty and truth. Also associated with Tulpar, lord of the horse. Appeared as a knight on a white charger. Her symbol is a lance and shield. She was revered by horsemen, paladins and constabulary.

Sarosh: The paladin god of order, obedience and repentance. It is said he learned magic from the dragons and many of his knights also practice the arts. He often appeared as a wizened old man or a squire. His symbol was an upright staff crossed with a pair of swords.

Melek: He was the paladin god of protection and chivalry, and was known as the Great Angel. He was mankind's guardian and fell, in their defense, to end the Deity War. His symbol was a winged longsword.

Mertlek: Known as the god of bravery. He was often called reckless and carefree, but was fiercely loyal. He appeared as a muscular man or giant white tiger.

Tedavia: She was the goddess of healing and restoration. She knew no violence and sought only peace and rest for all. She did not hold her power back from any, that all may find healing freely. It is said that she released her power unto Altierra when the gods left. Her symbol is two crossed palm branches.

Mikail: The god of hospitality, kindness and generosity. He often appeared as a fat monk or a happy bartender. He was the brother of Tedavia, and he opposed violence and sought peace and mirth. His symbol was a cup of mead.

Sevda: Called the goddess of love. She brought joy, light and love to all. Her gifts were given to all mortals who sought it. Her symbol was an outstretched hand.

Minions of Kuunkierto:

Sevash: The god of war and strife. All who relish conflict bowed to him. Even supporters of good secretly called him the necessary evil. He appeared as a dark warlord, clad in heavy armor and wielding an axe and mace. The crossed axe and mace was his sigil.

Salgin: Plague, pestilence and disease were this god's domains. He loathed Tedavia and sought to undermine her with infection and sickness. He appeared either as a pale rider on a sickly horse or as a horde of vermin. His symbol was a rat skull.

Nefreti: The goddess of hate and spite. She loathed Sevda for her gifts of love and compassion. She appeared as a howling black jackal. Her symbol was a dagger thrust through a heart.

Aeshma: Twin sister to Nefreti, she was known as the goddess of wrath. She embodied anger and rage. She was impulsive and reckless, frequently striking out without thinking. She appeared as a rabid wolf or a raging barbarian.

Yalamar: Known as the prince of lies, he infected mortals' minds by spreading falsehoods and deceit. He was petty and vain, seeking to twist the truth and ruin lives. He often appeared as a serpent or a tall human with a benevolent appearance. His symbol was a coiled serpent with its forked tongue extended.

Indara: She was the goddess of panic and fear, and fed on the misery caused by her brethren. She was one of the few evil Demigods to die in the war.

Aazap: Known as the lord of pain. Like his sister, Indara, his power was enhanced by the other children of Kuunkierto. The two of them were both less powerful demigods, and acted more like servants to their greater brethren. He, too, fell in the war.

Children of Kamara:

Tengri: The god of the sky. He controlled the winds and returned water to Okanus with his rain. It was said that his death was the cause of great storms as his power has no master. His symbol was a storm cloud.

Orman: Known as the lord of the forest, and the father of woodland spirits. He sought the balance of life and death above all, closely associating with Umay and Azraiyl. His power was released to the druids when he fell in the war. His symbol was a baobab tree.

Okanus: The god of oceans and seas. The currents and tides were commanded by him. The deep ocean was his kingdom. He fell with his brothers in the war and now his powers rage unchecked in the oceans.

Deniz: The lesser god of rivers and lakes, and the lieutenant of Okanus. He collected the waters from the land to send back to the seas. He fell at his master's side.

Hayvan: The lord of all land animals, he created the great animal spirits. Of these, it is unknown how many fell with him during the war. However, their progeny became the dumb beasts of today.

Kartalia: Known as the goddess of birds. She was the wife of Hayvan. Creatures of the air were her children. The great air spirits were her servants. She fell at her husband's side.

Baalin: The god of fish and whales. His children dwelled in Okanus' and Deniz's realms, though Hayvan was his lord. He did not survive the war, dying alongside Okanus and Deniz.

Tulpar: The lesser god of horses and hooved creatures, and the servant of Hayvan. Tulpar was one of few neutral gods to survive the war, as he was protected by Mithra. It is believed they left together after the pact. His power is still seen in unicorns, pegasi, centaurs, minotaurs, and satyrs. His symbol was a running stallion.

Demirei: He was the god of earth, stone, and mining. He cared little for mortals, and was far more concerned with his mountains and underground caverns. However, the dwarves shared his passions and he shared many of his secrets with them. Though they are not his children, he is known as the Old Dwarf to many. His symbol is a black mountain.

Kavesh: The god of metalworking and smithing. Known as the inventor, Kavesh embodied creativity and practice. The workshop and forge were his temple. His works sometimes conflicted with the more natural gods of his order, as he strove for new creations above all else. His symbol was an anvil and hammer.

Umay: The goddess of fertility and rebirth. Though she is a goddess of Kamara, she often dealt with Sevda, Mikail, and Tedavia. This was her salvation, as she was with them at the beginning of the war and thereby under the protection of the armies of Aurinko.

Sakima: She was the goddess of music and bards. She gave her gifts to all races equally and all songs gave her joy. She was revered by bards of all races.

Azraiyl: The god of death. The reaper. Many marked him as evil, but his job was merely to complete life's cycle. He was neither vicious nor cruel, only taking those whose time has passed. He dwelled alone and was untouched by the war.

Raziyl: The god of secrets, seer of the hidden. His specialties were the secrets and hidden lore of the world. He maintained great control, keeping his powers safe as both good and evil sought his knowledge to upset the balance. He was believed to have survived the war. His symbol was a golden key locked in a clear crystal.

Aydin: Called the god of knowledge, or the old scribe. To him, knowledge and ideas were the ultimate power on Altierra. He collected lore and stored it in a massive library hidden on his island, whose location was known only to him and his younger brother, Raziyl. He was lost in the Deity War and his library remains hidden. His symbol was an open tome.

Heralds: All of the deities created heralds to assist them and their mortal creations on Altierra. The Three created the dragons. Their children created the angels, demons and nature spirits. All are considered immortal, as they are immune to the ravages of time. However, they can be killed.

Dragons: Six great dragons were the first creation, even predating the demigods. They acted as heralds of the Three, with a pair aligned with each god. They are truly immortal, for if they are slain, their soul is reborn as a child to one of the greater races. The race seems to be whichever is favored by the dragon. The child is obviously different, with great power even from birth. When they reach maturity, they fully realize who they are and become the great dragon, reborn. Dragons are shape-shifters and can take many forms in addition to that of their favored race. They have also spawned many children over the years including drakes, dinosaurs, wyverns and sea serpents. All arcane magic comes from the dragons.

Aanhextrios: This male dragon of Aurinko favors humans. His scales are brilliant gold, and his lair is hidden in the glacial isles northwest of Izmar.

Seratrix: She is the sapphire colored dragon of Aurinko. She favors the kedistam and makes her lair in the south jungle.

Axistra: The female dragon of Kamara has shining silver scales. Elves are her favored race. She dwells in the Castle in the Clouds, hidden far above the hills south of elven lands.

Khellendriox: The male dragon of Kamara dwells in the mountains south of the dwarven capital, as they are his favored race. His scales are a sparkling emerald.

Crusiliux: This female dragon of Kuunkierto favors the orcs. She dwells on the islands south of Lumernia. She is the one dragon whose location is widely known and, though she ignores them, some of the black orcs worship her.

Tarextros: He is the onyx dragon of Kuunkierto. His scales are black as the deepest night, and his favored race are tumasi. His lair is in a volcano in the deep south.

Vampires: True vampires are not heralds of any sort, but were created by the dragons of Kuunkierto. They can appear to be from any race, as they are but corpses reanimated to unholy life. The vampire is not the person they were in life; their souls are replaced by the spirit of a demon. They steal from the life force of others, in the form of blood, to keep themselves strong and to be able to recharge their powers.

Vampires are skilled in dark magic, especially if the original host was also skilled in magic. Regardless, all vampires possess the ability to phase into mist at will. In this form, they are incorporeal; they may not cast spells or manipulate items unless the spell is one that may be performed by force of mind alone. Vampires are sensitive to the sun. They may walk outside during the day, but they are severely weakened by the sun's effects. This penalty is eliminated by shifting into mist form.

All vampires are able to use mind-affecting spells, and they can create different types of lesser undead from the bodies of their victims. When one of the evil dragons creates a vampire, they choose an item that was important to the mortal host during their lifetime. The item, known as a phylactery, sustains the unnatural life required by the vampire. If a vampire is slain, they revert to mist form and seek out this item, which is hidden away inside their coffin. Once there, they are able to regenerate in a few days' time until they are strong enough to leave their tomb and feed themselves. The practice of creating vampires has been forbidden, and all of the known existing ones were destroyed.

Vertassa: The vertassa are similar to vampires, but were created by the mortal races. These beings crave blood to survive, and will hunt with single-minded purpose. They do not have any magic, but do possess supernatural strength and speed. They are allergic to the sun and die immediately if exposed to it. They may also be killed by being stabbed through the heart, or by being beheaded. They are created using specific rituals, which are cast over a body that has been dead for no more than one week. In addition, they can procreate by draining the blood of their victims, and then giving their own blood to them to drink.

Angels: The heralds of Aurinko's children are classified as angels. They are powerful beings and are blessed with gifts from their creators. Most, like the Seraphs, Devas and Archangels, have large feathery wings in white, silver, or gold.

They wield god-granted magic such as healing spells and protection magic, and most are skilled with martial weapons such as swords. There are a few species that are smaller. One notable species, the Custos angel, has no solid form and appears as a ball of light. While once there were organized angel armies, most angels today are elusive creatures who can only be found if they allow it. A very small number of them hide among Altierra's people, with their wings cloaked to keep themselves secret. Unlike the dragons, if an angelic herald is killed, he or she is not reborn. Their numbers have been greatly reduced since the Deity War.

Demons: These creatures of darkness, including the Archdemons, Barzuls, and Spikels, once served the children of Kuunkierto. Most are hideous to look upon. They are often tall and intimidating. Their faces often resemble a mockery of a human's, but may resemble other things. They may have the head of a goat, or cloven hooves. They may appear cat-like. Many have leathery bat wings. Some, like the Eyrenals, are beautiful, and have feathery wings in black or red that appear very similar to their angelic counterparts. Yet another, are the Shadack demons, the least common of all the races. They appear as incorporeal shadows and have the ability to attempt to possess a mortal. Doing so may be dangerous for them, however, because if their host dies while they still inhabit their bodies, they are destroyed themselves. The Eyrenals are the only race of demon able to retract their wings and blend in, but very few ever choose to do so. Demons are often proficient in martial weapons and dark magics, including life-draining spells or mind control enchantments. Their weapons are imbued with the unholy power to drain life from a being, and only the most powerful healers have any hope of healing the wounds these weapons inflict. Like the angels, they do not resurrect when destroyed, and their numbers are also much smaller than they once were.

Nature Spirits: Kamara's children created nature spirits for themselves to act as their heralds. Most are various animals, but no species has more than two spirit animals among them. These creatures are massive in size, usually between ten and twenty feet tall regardless of size of their non-spirit counterparts. They are all very strong and will defend the natural world with force when necessary. There are also other nature spirits, such as dryads, nymphs, and other fae. All of them, animal and fae alike, are gifted with the ability to wield nature spells similarly to a druid, including healing and elemental magics. The fae races are also adept at mind control. Like their counterparts, they never age but can be destroyed. It is unknown how many of the nature spirits are still alive today, as very few participated in the Deity War and remain in hiding. Not many are aware of their existence at all.

About the Authors:

D.S. Schmeckpeper (a.k.a. Dottie and Steve Schmeckpeper) live in Florida, USA. They are a husband and wife team who work together to create the Land of Destiny series. Both have loved the Fantasy genre for many years and have wasted way too much time playing fantasy-based games. Dottie was a vocal performance major in college, before she decided a liberal arts major was not for her. Ironic, huh? They have two wonderful twin boys, who are three at the time of this publication. They are the light of their parents' lives. Steve does the artwork and comes up with many of the story concepts. Dottie brings the ideas to life. When not working, writing or drawing, the pair love to take their children to Florida's many amusement parks, and can often be found there.

If you've enjoyed this book, please consider leaving a review and/or rating on the site you purchased it from. Authors, especially Indie authors, depend on feedback from our readers to help us improve. Thank you very much.

Check us out on Facebook to see upcoming news, excerpts and more of Steve's artwork!

https://www.facebook.com/DestinysWings

Also, on Twitter!

https://twitter.com/DS_Schmeckpeper

Coming Soon:

Book two in the Lands of Destiny series:

Destiny's Flame

Chapter One
Accountability

Pop!
Izmar.

Where it all began. Had it really only been a year since he had last set foot here? Arcus released his beautiful wife, Siobhan, to stand under her own steam. The two parrots on his shoulder squawked and took flight. After circling around, the birds shifted into his friends, Celeste and Tarnelius, as they landed. Siobhan handed him the staff she had been holding.

Arcus looked around and tried to get his bearings. They had teleported outside, in an alley that was only a block away from the Dragonfire Tavern, a bar that he and Joseph used to frequent. Arcus furrowed his brow as he thought about the last time he was here.

"What's wrong, Arcus?" Siobhan asked, concerned.

"Nothing, Shiv. It's just been a while. Come on, let's get out of this alleyway before some idiot thinks it would be a good idea to try to mug us."

Tarnelius smirked. "Are you actually worried about being mugged, Arcus?" The elf adjusted his hooded cloak, attempting to hide his ears.

"Not at all. I just don't want Siobhan to have cause to be mad at me for using 'unnecessary force.'"

They walked out of the alley and approached the docks, dodging people as they moved here and there, loading and unloading the ships.

"Let's split up," Celeste said. "Why don't the two of you check out the south wharf, and Siobhan and I will take the north."

Arcus nodded. Breaking off toward the south wharf, he and Tarnelius approached a man who was barking out orders in front of a large carrack. The man stood about as tall as Tarnelius, but was very bulky and muscular. His head was shaved, and he was almost covered in tattoos. The carrack bore the name *"The Southern Hope."*

"Are you the captain of this vessel, sir?" Tarnelius inquired.

"Aye. Who wants to know?"

"My name is Tarnelius, and this is Arcus. We are trying to book passage to the southern continent, on the kedistam side. There are four of us altogether, including ourselves and our wives."

For a moment, the man silently scrutinized them. "I don't transport passengers. This is a trading vessel. The seas get choppy out there, and I don't need any lubbers puking their guts out on my ship. Besides, it's bad luck to have a woman on board. Two would be twice as bad."

"What if one of those women were able to control the weather and guarantee smooth sailing? Besides, we can pay you."

He cocked his head to the side as he considered this. "Seventy-five gold pieces each, to be paid when you board. Also, I want her to prove this claim before we leave."

Arcus' eyes widened. "That's insane. I happen to know that the normal passage to the southlands is never more than thirty gold."

"If you want aboard this ship, you have to play by my rules. Feel free to see if anyone else will sail you to Gallabat; it makes no difference to me. Just make sure you are here before high tide tomorrow morning, if you are coming along. Good day, gentlemen."

"Wait, you never told us your name. How will we look for you?" Tarnelius asked.

The man yelled back over his shoulder as he strode up the gangplank, "It's Stone."

Arcus and Tarnelius continued down the wharf, to see if they would have better luck elsewhere.

"We found someone with The Southern Hope *who will take us. They will charge seventy-five gold each, and want you to prove you can control the weather, before we can board. They leave tomorrow,"* thought Tarnelius to Celeste.

The two of them had married, or become bonded, almost eleven months prior. The bonding ritual split their souls so that they each carried half of the other's. Among other things, this allowed them to communicate even when they weren't together.

"That's more success than we've had. We were shot down by six captains. Most do not travel that way. Apparently, the captain from the seventh one frequents one of the nearby bars. It's called the Dragonfire Tavern. We're going to try to find him. Whenever you two are done, why don't you meet us there?" Celeste answered.

Tarnelius and Arcus approached several other vessels, without success. The other captains to which they spoke did not cross the Gulf of Galgendor. Most of them commanded Galley ships, intended for river travel or following the coastline. *The Southern Hope* was, by far, the largest ship in the port. Discouraged, the pair turned to go find the women.

Izmar was a sprawling city that had started as a small port town. Near the docks, there were several bars and inns. From there, the buildings spread out a lot more haphazardly. In the northern part of town, there was a large keep where the Lord of Izmar lived. There was a sorcerer school to the east. In between, there were many residences, other businesses and even more bars. The city was kind of seedy, and the law tended to favor whoever offered the biggest bribe.

Leaving the docks behind, Arcus and Tarnelius approached the tavern district. "Celeste said they were in a bar called the Dragonfire Tavern," said Tarnelius.

Arcus' eyes widened in alarm, "the Dra –"

"Arcus, is that you?" came a feminine voice behind them.

Arcus spun around. Standing behind him, with a look of surprise on her face, was a short young woman with curly brown hair and chocolate colored eyes. She was slender, and wore a dark blue dress with silver embroidery on the neckline and sleeves.

"Victoria?" he asked, astonished.

She flung her arms around his neck. "Arcus! It *is* you. I've missed you so much."

Arcus stiffened and tried to disentangle himself.

Tarnelius smirked. "I'll just be waiting in there with your wife, and mine, too. See you soon." He strode away, purposefully.

"Tarnelius, wait!" Arcus yelled, but Tarnelius ignored him.

"So, this is awkward," said Victoria.

"What is?" Arcus snapped.

"You're married now? You? I was sure you'd be single forever. You certainly never gave me, or any of the other girls, a second glance in school. Is she a sorcerer, too?"

"No, she isn't, she's a paladin."

"Huh. So that's what you're into. Don't you find the warrior type to be emasculating?"

"Not that it's any of your business, but no, I don't."

"You still hanging out with that loser, Joseph?"

"I haven't seen him since we left. Listen, I really need to go; my wife and friends are waiting for me in there. It was good seeing you." Arcus turned away, pretending not to notice the way she was pouting. He walked toward the Dragonfire Tavern, feeling nervous. The last time he had been inside this bar, he had gotten into a fight and "accidentally" killed his opponent. He didn't want to go in there, but he had no way to get his friends out if he didn't. He could wait, but then he'd be stuck out here with Victoria. He sighed. Maybe, if he kept his head down, the bartender wouldn't recognize him. He opened the door.

He looked around to try to locate the others. He found them seated in the corner farthest away from the bar. That was something, at least. Trying to not draw attention to himself, he walked straight over to them. Sitting down in a chair with his back to the bar, he glowered at Tarnelius.

"I was trying to get you to wait," he said.

"I figured you'd have an easier time escaping your little friend if she knew we were waiting."

"'She?' Who is this 'she', Arcus?" Siobhan asked, smirking.

"Just someone Joseph used to have a crush on. She was in the sorcerer school with us. That's not important right now. What *is* important, is that we need to get out of this bar."

"We can't leave now. We're waiting for Captain Zane to come back. He said he would speak with us, but that he had a meeting to take care of on his boat, first. I think he may be willing to negotiate," argued Celeste.

"Then we'll wait for him outside. We need to leave."

"Arcus! There you are. Why don't you introduce me to your...friends," Victoria's shrill voice sounded from right behind him.

He flinched, then sighed. "Everyone, this is Victoria. She and I went to school here, together. Victoria, meet Tarnelius, Celeste and my wife, Siobhan."

Victoria smirked at Arcus, a predator's grin gracing her lips. Her eyes seeming to undress him as she stared for far too long a moment before moving on to the rest of the group. He uneasily remembered the way she use to always watch him. She would follow him around and chatter about all sorts of inane things. He had never understood why Joseph had been so enamored with Victoria. Arcus glanced at Siobhan and smiled weakly at her. He hoped she understood that Victoria wasn't a threat.

Victoria moved on to Tarnelius, who was wearing brown pants and a tan shirt, with a hunter green cloak. His hood was lowered, exposing his golden blond hair that hung down past his shoulders. His pointed ears poked through his hair. He had huge green eyes that seemed almost as if they were glowing. Victoria wrinkled her brow as if she were confused about something. She looked to Celeste, who had the same eyes. She wore a long green dress and had long jet-black hair. Victoria's eyes widened in realization. "You two are elves! I've never met any elves before."

Tarnelius nodded to her, smiling.

Siobhan stood up and looked down at Victoria, her hand extended in greeting. The paladin was wearing tan riding breeches and a blue blouse. She was tall, only a couple of inches shy of six feet, and had hazel eyes and shoulder length coppery red hair. Victoria shook her hand, wincing at the strength of her grip.

Siobhan returned to her seat. With a forced smile, she leaned toward Arcus and took his hand possessively. He squeezed her hand to reassure her and kissed her gently on the cheek. Siobhan looked up at him, her eyes conflicted. Great. She *was* jealous and worried. Arcus wished he could have kept them apart. In fact, he wished he could have kept them all out of this gods-forsaken bar.

Victoria hesitated for a moment, then grabbed a chair to join the group.

"I'm sorry, Victoria, but we were just leaving," Arcus said.

"Why? You just told me, out there, that you were coming to join them in here."

"We aren't leaving, Arcus. We are waiting for Zane to come back," said Siobhan.

Arcus sighed, resigned to his fate. He decided not to speak another word of argument, and just held his tongue. Victoria relaxed and started chattering animatedly. She seemed determined to tell Siobhan embarrassing stories about him, but Arcus couldn't care less. He didn't even focus on what they were talking about, because his mind insisted on travelling in ten directions at once. A barmaid brought them all mugs of beer.

Arcus picked up his and Siobhan's, his hands flashing green as he purified them. It had become a reflex to him, back when he often came here. The glassware was never well cleaned, and he soon learned to cast that spell, or he would regret it later. He hoped that Siobhan hadn't had much to drink before he got there.

After ten excruciatingly long minutes went by, the door opened and the unmistakable sound of someone wearing heavy armor walked in. The armored person was greeted at the door by the bartender. A moment later, the pair of them walked over to Arcus' table.

Arcus sighed. He looked up at the bartender, a resigned expression on his face. "Hi, Jack. It's been a while, hasn't it?"

"Not anywhere near long enough. You never did pay for the damages you and your delinquent friend caused here. I can't believe you were so arrogant as to think I wouldn't recognize you."

The armored guard placed his hand on Arcus' shoulder. "You are under arrest for the charge of second degree murder, as well as destruction of property and disruption of the peace."

"I think you need to take your hand off me," Arcus snarled. He gripped his staff and stood up to face the guard, who dropped his hand.

"Arcus, calm down," Siobhan said, in a warning tone.

"Will you come peacefully?"

"No, I don't think so. Look, what happened that night was a mistake, and those other guys started it. If anyone should be charged for anything, it's them."

"Did you, or did you not, kill that man?" The guard glared at him.

"I don't think I should answer that question."

"That means yes." The guard lunged for Arcus and grabbed his arm, as he prepared to restrain him.

Arcus' forearms lit on fire. The guard dropped him with a yelp, and backed up, shaking his burnt hands wildly. Arcus bolted for the door, with Siobhan right behind him.

"Arcus, stop. That is enough!" Siobhan bellowed, as soon as they got outside.

He froze, gazing up at her sadly. "I told you we needed to leave."

"You need to turn yourself in."

"You know what? I think the heat from being encased in metal most of the time might have gone to your head. Why on earth would I turn myself in? We are supposed to be leaving to head south, or have you forgotten?" Arcus frowned at the guard, who had just shoved the door open, and was hurrying toward them.

"You know what you did was wrong. But it was an accident. Truth and justice always prevails," said Siobhan.

"Not here, it doesn't. You are from a whole different world, in comparison to this place. You don't understand."

"Arcus, you need to do what is right," she urged.

He held out his hand to ward off the guard, the flames once more licking up and down his skin. "What is right would be for me to burn down this entire wretched place, and just call it a day."

"I'll take care of it. I'll make sure you are treated fairly. I'm positive I can get this whole thing smoothed over. Burning the city down is not the right course of action."

"It sure would make *me* feel better," he said with a sigh.

"Give us just a minute, guard." Siobhan stepped close to Arcus, and placed her hand on his jaw. She stared deeply into his eyes, then lowered her forehead to his. "Do this because it's right. Do this because I want you to, and it would mean a lot to me. Do this because you promised on our wedding day to be what I need you to be, and right now I need you to be a good and honest man. I swear to you, I will take care of this."

He sighed, then kissed her deeply. When they broke apart, he removed his satchel and handed it to her, along with his staff.

"I'll need to take that stuff as evidence," the guard interjected.

Arcus spoke a word of magic and flicked his hand upward in a throwing motion. A tiny, fiery bead flew up in the sky above their heads. He glared at the guard. "That's not how this works. I will go peacefully, but she takes my belongings. Believe me, nothing I carry will be evidence anyway. I don't need possessions to be dangerous."

"No, I said, I –"

Arcus snapped his fingers and a massive fireball exploded one hundred feet above their heads. People on the street screamed and pointed. "Do you want me to come peacefully, or do you want me to burn the place down?" He offered his hands to the guard.

The guard nodded once, and moved to bind Arcus' hands. Arcus gazed at Siobhan the whole time, until he was pulled away. He hoped she knew what she was doing. He would not have allowed this to happen, had it been anyone but her that asked.

"I love you, Arcus," she called.

"I love you, too," he yelled back.